THERE ARE

NO MEN

Carol Maloney Scott

THERE ARE NO MEN

Copyright 2014 © Carol Maloney Scott

http://carolmaloneyscott.com

To Jim, Nick & Daisy

For loving me in your own unique and precious ways

CHAPTER ONE

"Claire? You look just like your picture. I'm Matthew."

This evening's loser reaches for my hand and gives it a firm shake, as if we're about to conduct a business meeting. I look him up and down, and rest my gaze at the top of his head. From this moment on, he will be known as 'the old man with the hat.'

Matthew looks SO much older than his dating profile picture. I was ready to accept that he's fifty, but this is ridiculous. I tell myself that he may turn out to be nice, and what else do I have to do tonight? Clearly the worst part is the hat. My father has one of these hats, as do most of my uncles. It's the hat worn by men on 1950's TV shows. I am dating a thinner Ralph Cramden.

"Hi. Yes, you found me," I giggle nervously, mostly because this is always so awkward, and not because I'm feeling girlish or self-conscious in the presence of his manliness. Someone shoot me.

My date's profile says he's fifty years old, so obviously he posted an old picture. He's from New York, which is *usually* a plus for me. I don't do well with Southern men— apparently I'm too loud and aggressive. When I came to Virginia I was married and had no idea I would be thrust into this single woman's world, or else I might never have agreed to move.

Recently, I've joined the ranks of Internet daters. When I was unhappily married I used to say, "At least I don't have to drive all over town meeting weirdos I found on the Internet."

These days I don't have much choice. I'm a thirty-six-year-old single woman without many single girlfriends, and I work with a lot of women and married men. I guess I should be able to meet men through the old-fashioned horrors of blind dates and fix-ups, but after a couple of solo years, none of these are working for me.

I love my girlfriends and my job, but neither of them are helping me find a man, not even a decent date or two. The second date has proved itself the most elusive. It is similar to what we in the employment recruiting world call finding the "purple squirrel"—that rare set of skills perfectly matched to a position's requirements. Hard to find, but nowhere near as hard to find as a middle-aged man deserving of a second date.

The hostess steps in—I swear she rolls her eyes—and cheerfully says, "Two for dinner? Right this way!" then leads us to our table. She seats us near the restrooms, which is good in case I need a quick break from all of the stimulating conversation I'm sure is forthcoming.

There is an old couple behind us—people who are *actual* senior citizens, but probably closer in age to my date than I had hoped. They're not speaking to each other and I envy their ability to eat their early-bird specials in companionable silence.

The old man—I mean Matthew—and I are meeting at Uno's. Even better right? My town is one of the least glamorous in my metro area, and does not offer trendy hot spots or even a non-chain restaurant or bar, unless you count the scary biker bar and the Chinese takeout place. I don't—I still have some standards.

Even worse, this is my fourth first date at Uno's this month. I should try somewhere else—the hostess gives me knowing glances every time I wait in the lobby for yet another strange man. As embarrassing as this is, thank God people know about Internet dating or else she might think I was a hooker.

I can't be bothered switching things up and going to Applebee's or O'Charley's, and I am not making the effort to drive downtown or hang out late at work to meet someone in one of the hip places on the fashionable side of town. Less than an hour into these dates I'm usually hoping Uno's catches fire so I can lose the guy in the smoke and make my getaway.

Across from us there's a table full of little kids and two harried-looking parents. I don't know why people take small

2

children to restaurants. The two bigger boys are fighting over the crayons and getting reprimanded by their father, but the cute little blond girl is sitting on her mother's lap, twirling her mommy's long hair. They're coloring with crayons on the placemat and giggling. Uno's isn't all bad—I like it when I come here with my best friend Jane and her kids for pizza. We used to come on Sundays for 'kids pay what they weigh day,' while our husbands were home watching football.

Sometimes Jane tells me I'm too *picky*, or that I'm not *trying*, when I call her after every date to give her the post mortem. I have to remember that she doesn't know any better—she's married and has no clue what my life is like. She has stuck by me through a lot of bad times, but I could swear a blue streak when she tells me I'm not trying. Maybe some of the men would like to hold up their end of the deal and at least be free of any diagnosable mental illnesses.

The hostess drops the menus and runs off to seat a large group of soccer-playing middle school kids and their moms. (Silent prayer of thanks that I'm not with them). Matthew swoops in to grab my jacket, just as I'm taking it off to hang it on the hook next to our table.

"Let me take your coat. I am always a gentleman." Whenever someone tells me what they are, instead of just *being* what they are, I'm suspicious, and I don't go for the chivalry bullshit either. Maybe it's because I was raised in the North, but to me it's a silly, feeble attempt to impress a woman. Wait—this guy is supposed to be from New York.

I let him take my coat and say, "Thanks, but I thought you were from New York? Why the Southern gentleman routine?" I say this with a smile so he doesn't notice how annoyed I am already, but I'm curious if he was lying. He takes off his hat and hangs it up with his coat. He's tall and he *does* have hair, even though it looks a little weird and too perfect. However, at this point he could be a giant, with long flowing tresses like Fabio, and I wouldn't give a shit.

"Yes, I moved here twenty-five years ago and I have completely assimilated to the culture of this fine city," he replies.

Richmond *is* a good place to live. We have four seasons, lots of sunshine, good restaurants (except where I live), and lots of entertainment for all ages and interests. The culture shock takes some getting used to when coming from the North, especially when Northern transplants weren't as plentiful as they are now. There is still an element of conservative Bible Belt ideology, as well as a lingering resentment over losing the Civil War. Monument Avenue is lined with defeated Confederates' statues, and poorly-adjusted northerners refer to this street as the "Avenue of Losers."

For the most part I have gotten used to never having a good bagel and learning to like marginal pizza. There are so many people here now from the North and from all over the country, even the world, that it isn't a stereotypical Southern city anymore. Plus, there is good shoe shopping, an excellent cupcake shop, and we are only two hours from both the beach and the mountains.

Having said all of that, is he for real? Who talks like this? He isn't Thurston Howell III.

Luckily the waiter comes over to our table and asks for our drink orders. Matthew makes a big show of letting me go first.

"What would the lady like to have?" He gestures towards me as if presenting a prize cow at the county fair.

I fight the urge to roll my eyes. We are in Uno's for God's sake—what would I want? Thirty-year-old scotch? A bottle of Cristal?

"I'll just have a Coke."

"Pepsi alright?"

I sigh and say, "Yes." It irritates me to no end when servers ask that question. I know they have to ask because all sorts of whack-jobs will freak out if you bring them the wrong brand of soft drink. How can your life be so boring that you have taken the time to actually distinguish between Coke and Pepsi in the blindfolded taste test?

"I will have a sweet tea. Would you like an appetizer?" Matthew looks directly at me and I notice his nose for the first time. The hat is actually not the worst part.

"No, thanks—I just need to look at the menu for a minute. I'm not that hungry." I never eat much on these dates and I need to start suggesting shorter meetings, like

4

for coffee. But I don't drink coffee and then that gets weird, and I don't have time during the work day to meet for lunch—and I am *not* wasting weekends on weirdos. That's how I waste my weeknights.

The waiter walks away to grab our drinks from the bar while Matthew stares at me with a crazed look of forced cheer and enthusiasm. He starts telling me how he moved here twenty-five years ago with his ex-wife and kids—now grown! How his divorce was tough but he's doing great! All the while, I am looking at his nose and trying to figure out where I have seen a red nose so bulbous and full of veins and then it hits me—he looks like my Uncle Randy. Except that my uncle is seventy years old and probably not on Match.com. How do you end up with a nose like that?

"Do you eat out a lot? I love to cook at home, and I live so close to the grocery store I can shop every day. I never waste food. Last night I made a delicious salmon. Do you like fish? You can get some good fresh seafood around here..." He blabbers on and on.

Since my ex-husband, Ron, only went to the grocery store five times the whole time we were together, and several of those were during my hospital stays, Matthew gets some points for this declaration.

Ron's last trip to a store was two years ago, when I was at home recovering from surgery. My supportive and loving husband was most concerned about his embarrassment over buying Maxi Pads for me. What the hell did he believe people would think? Maybe that he was the only bleeding man in Virginia, or that he was using them to soak up oil leaks under the car or to line a bird cage? Obviously, he was buying them for his *wife*, or at least a *woman*. And why did it even matter? The bored and distracted grocery store cashier wouldn't give a crap about what he was buying, and would be focused instead on her next smoke break or why her asshole boyfriend hadn't called today.

"I don't care for salmon. Would you excuse me? I need the ladies' room." I jump up and grab my purse.

"Certainly, my dear. I will await your return." I am beginning to think he is a time traveler from the past who hasn't mastered modern speech.

I am only heading for the ladies' room because I need that anticipated break. I would be lying if I said I didn't look for a window, but of course I would never do something as ridiculous as try to climb out a window in the Uno's restroom. Maybe someplace trashier, or out of town, or not facing the main road. But not Uno's.

This man is clearly not a match for me. I summon my Internet Dating Girl strength (yes, like a super hero) and prepare myself to go back out there to face more frustration. I can get through this—I have already survived twenty-five bad first dates in the past ten months, but who's counting?

Matthew is still sitting there looking old. I experience a twinge of disappointment, as if I'd thought he might change, and become young and attractive while I was gone. I didn't say Internet Dating Girl isn't delusional at times. How do you think she copes?

I order a Caesar salad (I should be able to choke that down) and he orders a steak, well-done with mashed potatoes and vegetables. "I like my meat and potatoes." He cracks himself up again.

I do sympathize with him. He's just a person trying to find someone, and that's why I shouldn't be wasting his time, either. I just don't know how to say that without sounding mean. Instead I say, "You look a little different than you did in your picture. Was that taken recently?" I can't resist going there.

"No, that was an old picture. I don't have any pictures taken since my divorce and I can barely figure out how to upload them," he says with a laugh that is *way* too hearty.

"How long ago was that?"

"Ten years. Ten long years." He pauses and looks over at the couple with the little kids, as if he is remembering the years and paying his respects to them. The family is on their way out and I can't help but shoot the mother a look of envy, which she returns with her own look of pity. I could be imagining this, but I get angry and think about how she is going home now to bathe those little monsters and wrangle them into their flame retardant sleepwear, while her husband sits in front of the TV and watches some stupid sporting event, dropping chips on his chest and ignoring her. All she has to look forward to is a sink full of dirty dishes while *I* could still get my prince charming. Well, not tonight, but I could someday!

As they almost disappear from view I catch the little girl's eyes, and she smiles in that innocent way of young children, not knowing that one day she could be on a date with an old man with a hat. She pulls away from her mother and comes over to our table. She hands me her placemat. I open up the folded paper and see a picture of swirls and squiggles.

"This is so pretty!"

She shyly glances away and starts sucking on her thumb. She removes it with her mother's prompting. "Tell the nice lady what it is, Olivia."

"It's a pretty flower and a bunny. See." She points at her art work with a chubby finger and my heart blows up. I don't want anyone to notice the depth of my reaction as I fight the urge to squeeze this little girl. I smile and tell her it's beautiful.

"You can have it." She walks away with her mother, who is now beaming with pride. I take a deep breath and look back at Matthew, assuming he is also caught up in the emotion of this exchange. But no.

"I must say you look especially beautiful, Claire. That top is very flattering on you."

He is now leering at me in a creepy way. Was he even paying attention for the last five minutes? Crap. I never know what to wear to these things. I am often coming straight from work but I don't want to dress too businesslike, and since my office isn't stuffy I can get away with a cute lacy camisole or a tight sweater. Today I have opted for the latter in bright pink. I'm not big on top, but I have enough to squeeze together some decent cleavage, with the help of my Victoria's Secret push-up bras.

The problem is that I never know if the guy I'm meeting is going to be worthy of my sexier look, and since it's been awhile since I've gotten any action, I want to look like someone who *could* get some. I have forgotten what it's like when the man across the table is clearly not someone I want to attract. Unfortunately, I do not own a crystal ball, and now

I wish I were wearing a nun costume or a potato sack.

"Thank you. So tell me about your kids," I reply as I try to steer the conversation away from my clothing and his eyes away from my chest.

Luckily most people love to blab about their offspring, and this guy is no exception. I hear all about Matthew Jr. and how he just got married and moved to Texas, and about how his daughter (Megan, Margo?) is teaching English in Japan or some such place. I try to pick at my salad, but I have no appetite.

"Claire, you've barely touched your dinner. I guess that's how you keep that fantastic figure." More leering. If only he knew that I eat like a lumberjack in the presence of people who aren't giving me the willies. And, to be clear, the willies are NOT good!

I need to get to the ladies' room again, although I don't know what I think that's going to accomplish. This is an advanced case of the willies—if this were a heart attack it would be a Code Blue. I can't just ditch him, though. I'm trapped.

Luckily, there is no one in the bathroom. I hate when I go in looking all manic and stressed out, and there are old ladies drying their hands or groups of little girls staring at me, clutching each other. I *know* I look crazy—I don't need the validation of strangers in the ladies' room.

I need to waste a few minutes this time so I start scrolling through the messages on my phone. Oh, look—a Facebook invitation to a Pampered Chef party from a friend of a co-worker. Yay! I want to attend a Pampered Chef party about as much as I want to go to a used auto parts party where you can win a baby monkey as a door prize.

I look in the mirror and give myself a firm talking to about improving my social life and reconsidering my dating plan, but only *after* I check my e-mails later tonight for promising prospects. I fight the urge to check my account now—if there's a message from an older guy in a worse hat I won't be able to go on. I return to the table after a few deep breaths and a couple of yanks on my sweater, to pull it up higher.

"Is everything okay?" he asks.

"Yes, I'm just a bit tired. I have a huge project due at work this week and I have an early meeting. Do you mind if I get going?" I try to look apologetic.

"No, not at all." He signals for the waiter and asks him for a box. All that he has remaining on his plate is a blob of potatoes, four green beans, and some gristle. He sees me eyeing his leftovers and says, "Can't waste food—aren't you taking yours?"

Why would I want soggy lettuce and tasteless grilled chicken for later?

"No, I'll just meet you outside. I need some air."

I bolt for the door, and as soon as I make it to the sidewalk I notice that I left my jacket—and it's a nice one. I just got it at Nordstrom and it is *the* perfect spring coat that goes with absolutely everything. If I leave it, maybe I could come back for it later. The restaurant will hang on to it. I get a sudden flash of Matthew taking it and trying to return it, pretending to be worried about me, knowing damn well that I purposely ran off.

I stand on the sidewalk trying to decide what to do when a young couple—probably no more than eighteen—appears and starts kissing and holding hands. I avert my eyes, and think of Ron and me in high school. I had been a skinny, awkward little girl, and I lacked confidence, even as I was blooming into womanhood. I fell for the first guy who showed any real interest in me. I made an enormous mistake.

I was getting divorced the entire time I was married. People don't believe me when I say this. They say, "At least it must have been good in the beginning? How could the whole ten years have been bad?" They look at me as an intelligent, mature woman, and can't comprehend how I could have been such a poor decision maker in my youth.

After ten years of marriage, and several miscarriages, I was forced to have a hysterectomy at thirty-four. I mourned the abrupt and early end of my childbearing years. My hormones were wreaking havoc with my emotions. Ron was not much of a partner in life even *before* the baby drama, and that event was the final nail in the marital coffin.

I try to meet men who will have no expectation of having children, and men Matthew's age generally have grown kids.

I am also not keen on being a stepmother to a bunch of school-aged kids, or, heaven forbid, teenagers.

This girl in the Uno's parking lot has her whole life ahead of her, and will probably have lots of babies effortlessly, marrying someone she meets in college or at work, not this high school joker. Hot tears prick at the corners of my eyelids. Maybe I should start wearing waterproof mascara. While I am fighting my internal demons, Matthew appears.

"You left your coat. Let me help you with it."

I let him do it, feeling small and defeated.

"I paid the check," he says.

How do I respond? I didn't actually think he would leave without paying, so I'm not sure if he is prompting me for something more than gratitude. "Thank you."

"I had them box your salad. You may want it later. I don't believe in wasting food, especially since I'm between jobs right now, you know?"

No, I did *not* know. His profile said that he was in banking, but maybe he chose that work category by accident instead of clicking on the "retiree with hat and bulbous nose" link. *Easy* mistake. *Is* he looking for me to give him money for the dinner? I can't deal with this awkwardness any longer, but my curiosity takes over and I blurt out, "How long have you been out of work?"

"It's been about two, wait, now almost three...years."

Years. Not months—years. "My car is over there and I need to get going. Thanks so much. It was nice meeting you." This is what I am told you say after a date that you didn't like. It is polite code for "please do not ever call me again." The direct approach would be smarter in this case, but I'm too chicken. I always go with the getaway line.

Matthew looks slightly let down. The leer returns and he moves in for a hug, a kiss or something equally unpleasant. Can't men see when you aren't into them by your body language and facial expressions? I don't have a poker face—I can't lie. I hate it when I see an ugly baby and am forced to comment on its appearance, especially if it looks like a mutant baby possum. Yes, I know I am going to hell, but who cares? I am already there most of the time.

I attempt to make a dash for my car before he can complete the gesture, but he grabs my arm. I am not letting an Uncle Randy look-alike with a bulbous nose touch me. Polite is one thing but I have to draw the line somewhere.

Just as I pull away, the jerking motion rocks his head just enough to dislodge his hair from his head. What the hell? His actual *hair* is now resting on my feet, like a dead animal carcass. All of it. I jump and do a dance to get it off my favorite work pumps, as if it *was* a mutant baby possum, and look at him incredulously. He bends down to pick it up and starts to say something, but I make a run for it before his teeth fall out.

As I take a deep breath and pull out of the parking lot, he's still standing there holding his leftovers and I can't help but notice something is missing. The thing that will forever define him in future accounts of this story. Even though he has just man-handled me and assaulted me with his wig, while I am sitting at the red light I can't help myself from calling out the window, "Hey, you forgot your hat!"

CHAPTER TWO

I have a mini heart attack every time my alarm goes off. I have experimented with different types of sounds, but any that I can tolerate don't wake me up. If it's music I just incorporate the song into my dream, and if it's a pleasant noise I don't hear it and keep on sleeping. I need a blaring noise that would wake the dead.

Dixie is quiet in her crate. She sleeps all night in there without a peep as long as Mommy is right there in the big bed. She is just a little over a year old. I got her as a puppy from a breeder. I know I should have adopted a rescue dog, but I wanted a female black and tan short hair miniature dachshund puppy. Since I was lonely, childless and barren I thought it was reasonable to get exactly what I wanted.

Dixie is my first pet. When I was growing up my mother and sister were allergic, and I was so focused on wanting children that when I was married I never thought of getting a dog. When I finally decided to take the plunge, I was afraid a shelter dog would be hard to train, with potential bad habits created by a history of instability. While I feel for those poor furry babies, I don't have confidence in my abilities as a dog trainer.

It turns out I have done an excellent job of helping Dixie to adopt many of the bad behaviors I was hoping to avoid, like chewing furniture, peeing on the floor, begging for treats, pulling on walks, and pooping in my shoes—things like that. Lesson learned.

For now she is quiet, so I am enjoying a few moments in bed before I have to get up. I have a forty-five minute commute to work, and even though there is always traffic I never get stuck behind idiots as much as I do when I am headed to a date after work. Maybe I should take that as a warning—if there is a truck load of chickens going twenty-five on the highway, or a guy holding a mattress on top of the car with only his hand for support, I should go straight home. I could avoid a bad night as well as feathers stuck in my windshield wipers, or sudden death-by-mattress hurled into my face at sixty miles an hour.

Last night when I got home, I experienced an overwhelming sense of elation when I turned the corner into my cul-de-sac. My suburban cookie-cutter neighborhood no longer fits my lifestyle as it did when I was married and hoping for a family, but the house is mine now. All mine. No one can tell me what to do with it, even though it sucks being alone sometimes. The delicious anticipation of peace and freedom every night makes the long commute more bearable, even if I only have a little wiener dog to cuddle up with.

On the downside, my white four bedroom colonial needs some work. The paint is peeling on the front porch rockers and the deck needs to be stained. I don't have the money or skill to make repairs myself, and it's as if I am waiting for something to happen before I take any action. The value is sinking every day I let the weeds flourish and the driveway crack. I need a good handyman.

I walked in the house and didn't make it past the foyer before Dixie came running and performed her usual spins and jumps, and completed several laps around the house to greet me. It is always a pleasure to come home to someone who loves me that much.

I had a pile of mail to go through, but I was not in the mood to look at bills or coupons for the latest Mexican restaurant, or invitations to Bible study from the newest church asking me if I am a lost little lamb. If I want to be poisoned I can go to any number of nasty Mexican restaurants, and if I want to go to church I can just go back to the Catholic Church, where they serve up guilt as well as the Mexicans serve up heartburn.

It wasn't too late, so I decided to call Jane and regale her with the tale of my latest dating disaster. She enjoys the humor and she does try her best to give me advice or at least some sympathy.

She answered on the first ring—she knew I'd had a date and was probably eager to hear the lowdown.

"Hey, what's up? You aren't home THAT early. Was this one decent?" she optimistically started.

"He was an old man with a hat, and a nose like Jimmy Durante. Unemployed and a creeper."

"So he gave you the willies? Not good."

"No, the willies are never good. Nor is flying hair."

"What? His hair was flying? Was it windy?"

"Not at all, but that didn't stop it from coming off in one scary piece. A direct assault on my feet."

"What the hell? You're lucky his teeth didn't fall out."

"That was my thought exactly. Do you see what I deal with?"

"Maybe you should screen the e-mails better—what did this one say? I can't remember what you told me. Was it something about being romantic or looking for his soul mate? Or was it something about fishing and jazz?"

"They all say they're looking for their soul mate, and if it said anything about jazz I would have put pins in my eyes. Or fishing. Gross. It doesn't matter what he said because he was yucky and bad. And yucky."

"You said yucky twice."

"HELLO—yes I know!"

I should not yell at Jane. To be fair, she and her husband Mike have tried to set me up with some men. There was the widowed cowboy with two little kids. I found out he hated his wife and then she died, which makes being a widower even worse. Plus he wore a cowboy hat to their Christmas party last year. Hence the nickname. What is with these men with stupid hats? I am waiting for one with a pinwheel on top.

Then there was the painter. No, they didn't set me up with their painter for a date, but I needed some rooms painted in my house. After Ron left, I wanted to paint a few rooms the colors I liked, but he never allowed. Joe, the painter, came over to assess the job and said he would be in touch. He was friendly and I thought he behaved professionally on the visit. Then one night there was a message from him. I thought it would be the standard talk of his availability and pricing for the job. Instead it was a drunken rambling about my eyes looking like melted

14

chocolate, and how he couldn't stop thinking about me. I was so pissed! Now I couldn't even hire him to paint, and he has good prices and paints a damn straight line.

Jane sighed and continued, "Any new men on the horizon?"

"I haven't checked my e-mail yet, and I'm not all that anxious to dive back in. Hey, did you notice the light on in the house across the street?" I was eager to change the subject, plus I was curious.

"You mean at Susan's old house? Yeah, I was out with the kids this afternoon and I saw the car, but not the people. Mrs. O'Brien said she saw a moving van earlier. I don't know how they escaped *her* notice—she tracks *your* every move. I got to hear about how you're going to hurt yourself with those shoes you wear."

"Sometimes my feet do bleed a little, but she doesn't have to look hot when she goes out dancing. All she does is knit and spy on people, and I swear I am not ending up like that."

"When do you go out dancing?"

"I *want* to go out dancing, but it never gets that far."

"You could let us set you up again. Mike said there is a newly divorced guy at work. I think he's a psychiatrist."

She is clearly not remembering Mike's other "newly divorced friend," Pete. He came over to their house for a barbecue on Memorial Day last year. He was normal and reasonably attractive, although he had grey hair. At his age it would be unlikely that he would want any babies, so that was a good starting point for me. Unfortunately, he spent the whole afternoon talking about his ex-wife. I think I even saw a tear once or twice.

However, it didn't matter much because my behavior was no better. I drank a tad bit too much before he arrived, and was sitting on the floor in front of the refrigerator laughing hysterically for some unknown reason when he got there. They managed to get me up into a chair in the living room, but then I was screaming that my underwear was uncomfortable. This is when Jane and Mike had a meeting in the kitchen to cut me off. My next Pina Colada was a virgin, which I was too wasted to notice. Finally, after I started pulling on my bra and lying upside down in my seat, Jane announced that Mike should walk me home. Next door. They obviously thought I would pass out in the bushes on my way across the lawn.

"A psychiatrist—seriously? I'm trying to *bury* my problems, not *unearth* them. He would end up charging me to date him."

"That's a good point. So I don't know who moved in across the street, but I'll try to figure it out after I put the kids on the school bus tomorrow."

"I just hope it's someone more normal than Susan. What a whack-job she was. Remember the time she came to your house and said she was praying for you because you had never been to a real church?" I was raised Catholic and I consider myself to be a believer and a spiritual person, but Catholics do not go around handing out pamphlets asking people to come to our Church (we actually make it *hard* to join us).

"How could I forget? Mike was mowing the lawn, and I swear he mowed the same patch of grass until there was visible dirt just so he wouldn't have to come in and deal with her. Are you sure you want a husband? I'm going to hit the hay. Mike is calling me to clean up the new hairballs he found in his study. Damn cats! I'll talk to you tomorrow. Try to stay positive!"

"I will. Good night."

I hung up the phone and looked at the house across the street more closely. I have always liked that house. It's a cute Cape Cod with a bright yellow door and green shutters. All the houses in my cul-de-sac are neutral colors. This one is a cream shaded siding—nothing remarkable but the front porch wraps around the side, and it was well maintained by Susan and her husband.

I decided the new people would be more normal and sank down into my couch with a chocolate sprinkled glazed donut in hand and a hungry wiener at my feet.

"No, Dixie. Mommy can't give you this. It will make you sick. Go eat your food." I pointed to her cute lavender bowl with the paw prints all over it. She reluctantly waddled over and munched on her dry, boring dog food, which is organic

16

and healthy.

I was starving and felt perfectly justified in enjoying a fattening snack at bedtime. I have always been thin, too thin in my youth. With all the stress of the divorce and single life, I am headed back in the too skinny direction if I don't stuff myself like a big fat guy.

Before bed I checked my e-mail. I am compulsive about reading my Internet dating messages. When I first joined it was like a part-time job keeping up with all the new men. I was fresh meat on the site and I attracted a lot of attention. Almost all of it was and *still* is unwanted attention, but I console myself with the fact that at least I do get messages. Even now I get a bunch every day, with several new inquiries or continued conversations with men on the short list or the "I don't know what to say to make them stop e-mailing me" list. That one is the longest.

There was a note from Matthew—*already?*—thanking me for a good time and asking for another date. Was he present on the first one? Maybe he bumped his head trying to retrieve his hair from underneath the car.

There are a few more prospects—a sixty-year-old man (that is just too old), a big biker with a completely tattooed body, and a twenty-five-year old who said that I look hot for an older woman. Punk.

I resisted the urge to cry and then saw one with possible redeeming value. This guy is only forty (young for me lately), and he said he doesn't want kids and he's into meditation (I have tried it and need to do it more—very relaxing) and golf. The only miniature thing I like almost as much as wiener dogs is golf. I am a mini golf pro. His picture wasn't too bad, and he appeared to be in decent shape. I decided that I need to look at his profile more closely tomorrow and compose a fun and witty response.

I checked my messages one more time and saw that my mother called. It was too late to call her back. She was definitely in bed or glued to Fox News, watching a barrage of negative press about the President and yelling at the TV. As I was not in the mood for that, I made a mental note to call her tomorrow on my long drive to the office.

Dixie's whining interrupts my morning daydream, and

jolts me back to the present. Now I'm going to be late. It's amazing how I can lay in bed for an extra half an hour, reviewing the previous night's events. To say I am not a morning person is to say that Sarah Palin is not a liberal. I'm already thinking about political references because I have to call my mother.

Before I can shower, I must walk the wiener. If I do anything before I take her outside she will protest loudly. I don't blame her. If I slept in a little metal cell all night I would have a hard time waiting to pee, too. Many people let their dogs sleep with them, but I didn't want to set that precedent. I am still hoping to have a human bed partner with a different type of fur.

"Good morning, little Dixie." I crouch down in front of the crate and open the door. She stretches—what I call the "long wiener stretch," with a *huge* yawn for dramatic effect. "Come on Sweetie. Let's go outside and make a pee pee." I pick her up and carry her downstairs.

I put her harness on while dodging puppy kisses (not a big fan of dog's tongues), and head outside in my bathrobe. Every day I take her out in my powder blue terry cloth robe. I started doing this because I had no time when she was a puppy to change into anything else. I didn't want her peeing in her crate, so I ran to get her onto the grass as quickly as possible. Now I'm just lazy, and the neighbors are used to seeing me in my bathrobe and ugly old sneakers on the front lawn. Of course the bathrobe is of proper length and thickness. I have *some* dignity.

I open the back door and I'm greeted by our favorite thing—drizzle. At least it isn't a downpour. Dixie will have none of that. I would hate rain even more if my belly and chest dragged along the grass every time I had to go to the bathroom.

I carefully place Dixie on the grass and she promptly takes off. I have to hold the leash extra tight when I first put her down, as she often has spotted a squirrel or an offensive trash can she needs to bark at, and takes off, jerking the leash. She is the self-appointed guardian of the cul-de-sac and nothing escapes notice on her watch.

As soon as she makes a break for it, I notice the new

guy across the street. Jeez, people are up early, but I guess if you move into a new house there's a lot to be done. I dread the work of moving, even though I would love to live somewhere more fun and exciting, but it will be a few years before I can even consider it. I bought Ron out of this house because I was afraid of change at the time, and it was easier to stay put. With the real estate market crash depleting my equity to almost nothing, I'm stuck here for the time being.

As usual, Dixie is dragging me toward the front yard. I do *not* want to talk to the new neighbor in my bathrobe with crazy hair and no makeup, so I pull her toward the back yard. For some reason her preferred place to do her business is as close to the road as possible. I try to keep an eye out across the street while keeping myself mostly hidden from view. This guy looks quite young. They probably have tiny kids and I'll have to watch out for them on their tyke bikes when I peel out of the driveway. Clearly a Honda Civic is not a "peel out" kind of car, but I am purposeful when I'm on the move.

I should be paying attention to Dixie (I need proof that she has peed before I go in or she is likely to go behind the couch), but I'm still checking out this young guy with the sandy hair and fit body, working on boxes and taking trash out to the curb. Even though men like this are now out of my league, it can't hurt to look. Actually he is not very big and manly—maybe he's a teenaged son, but their lazy asses wouldn't be outside this early in the rain doing work.

Once again, I am losing track of time daydreaming. The cool drizzle hitting my face, and Dixie's insistent pulls towards the house, transport me back to reality. Dixie is exasperated that I am ignoring her, and rewards me with loud, shrill barking. The guy looks up and stares in our direction. Thanks to my little watch dog, he sees us right away, and his hand goes up in a wave. Dixie spots him, and decides greeting a new friend is more important than being dry and now starts to pull me towards the front of the house in pursuit of a belly rub.

In a last ditch effort to hold her back as she moves closer to her destination, I yank on her leash and raise my other hand up in a half wave so he won't think I'm rude as I attempt to fly towards the back porch, and get my bed-headed puffy-eyed self out of view.

Unfortunately, my bathrobe doesn't wrap very far around my body, and the sash isn't all that tight or easy to secure. Normally I am outside and back inside in a flash—before I am actually *flashing* anyone. Damn it! As we almost reach the front of the house and I gain control of Dixie, my robe's sash suddenly betrays me and my robe flies open to reveal—well—everything. Yes, I sleep in the nude.

I am now caught in an impossible dilemma—if I let go of the leash to adjust my robe Dixie will break free and run to the guy, and I will be forced to retrieve her and face the first man who has seen me naked in a long time. That is not happening—he's already seen enough of this pathetic show from afar.

The whole ordeal is over in a matter of seconds but seems like an eternity, as I pull Dixie back toward me and I maneuver my body around and continue my crazy wave—as if somehow my flailing hand will distract him from the rest of my body, which is now twisted in a bizarre position as I try to wrangle control of my robe. He has put his hand down by now, and even though my vision isn't great, I'm almost certain I see a big grin on his face. At least a smirk. He is cute—too bad I can't even enjoy an attractive neighbor now that talking to him will be sheer humiliation.

I finally make it to the back door, and once inside, Dixie and I work on drying off. She does the crazy dog shaky thing and I begin to compose myself and recover from my latest embarrassment.

I would love to keep my shenanigans a secret, but there is no way I can resist telling Jane about this escapade. It's my duty to entertain my friends as a reward for listening to all of my dating problems and other assorted crap. I give Dixie her treat and she retreats to her spot on the floor in the living room, where she sunbathes every morning like a movie star on vacation in South Beach.

I bet he will go inside now and tell his pretty young wife that he has encountered the neighborhood floozy. I *know* that's what my neighbors think of me. Every time I go out on a weekend, especially in warm weather when it stays light out later, I walk to my car in stilettos, wearing a sequined something or other, while the cul-de-sac families are weeding their lawns, teaching children to ride without training wheels, and looking generally sloppy and frumpy in sweat pants or shapeless dirty shorts.

Even though my bling is much more attractive than their clothing choices (which signify they have given up), the mothers are grabbing their children (and husbands) and diverting their attention, as if a porn star has just emerged all ready for a shoot.

No, on second thought he won't tell his wife—if he's smart he'll avoid being questioned or nagged when he still has 5000 boxes of toys, games and tyke bikes to unpack, and probably a swing set to assemble.

As I get in the shower I can't help smiling a little. That was actually kind of funny, and in a weird way it made me feel a bit sexy. Since he isn't someone I could ever date—I would never date a younger man, and he *is* my neighbor, undoubtedly married and with children, he is safe. Not that I am now going to go around purposely flashing the neighbor men, but I am a little less self-conscious than I normally would be, which is odd.

Unfortunately, I'll see this guy frequently and his first impression of me is less than impressive. I didn't flash a random cute guy—I flashed the new neighbor who now *owns* the house across the street. The neighborhood floozy sinks to a new low.

CHAPTER THREE

"**M**om, I know I shouldn't be driving and talking on the phone, but I'm careful. Stop worrying. You should be more worried about my spinsterhood." I'm on my way to work, trying not to speed.

"Claire Marie, you are not a spinster if you were already married and divorced. It isn't the 1800s, and your sister has never been married and we never have these conversations." She loves to bring up my sister's independent nature.

"I'm just returning your call and I figured I would tell you about my latest dating nightmare. And I have a question." I can't resist sharing these details with my mother.

"Let's hear it."

"This one I refer to as the old man with the hat."

"What? Why?"

"He had this bulbous nose that I had to look at for an hour. And his hair fell off and attacked my feet." I shudder at the memory.

"What? His *hair* fell off? No? You said he was wearing a hat."

Heavy sigh. She can never follow anything. "No, he wasn't wearing the hat the whole time, but it was one of those hats with the soft bill in the front, like a baseball cap, but they're tweed or wool and usually plaid. Do you know what I mean?" I am not explaining it well—I should have just Googled it.

"Old men *do* wear those. They wore those in the 50s. How *old* was this guy? John—Claire Marie's date wore an old man hat—like your father's hat. And his hair fell out!"

They do this all the time. If I'm on the phone with one, the other one gets to hear everything immediately. I continue, "His hair fell *off* last night. It obviously fell *out* some time ago. He's fifty, at least according to him, but I swear even Daddy is hotter."

"John, she said you're hotter than the old man with the hat," she bellows, laughing hysterically. Maybe I should work on a stand-up routine.

I bet my father is thrilled to hear this and to be referred to as hot by his daughter. I am guessing his retirement doesn't always seem like a good idea now, and he longs for time at the office.

"He said we're both nitwits. Whatever—I don't listen to him." She does.

"So what are those hats called—I can't remember?" It isn't an easy task keeping my mother focused.

"I think a Bowler...or a Pea Cap? A Panama? John what are those hats called? John? He went outside—he's no help. What did he do for a living?"

My head hurts, and now I'm stuck behind a school bus, and there are flashing lights up ahead. So much for smooth drives to work.

"Mom, his *hair fell off* in front of me—all of it in *one piece*! And you ask what he does for a living? He's been unemployed for almost three years but I don't care if he was Donald Trump. I was sitting there staring at his nose while he was talking—it was so hideous and bulbous and red and veiny—"

"Heavy drinker."

"What?"

"Your Uncle Randy's nose looks like that and he's a big drinker."

"I knew it! That's exactly who I was thinking of." It's sad that I'm excited to be right about something like this.

"Honey, you need to screen these men more carefully."

"I would like to see you try." Another clueless married woman.

"Maybe I *will* join to see what I could pick up. You hear that, John? I'm joining Match.com to check out the men! You'll have to do your own laundry from now on. He is so deaf. Claire, I know it's frustrating, but that's what happens when you get divorced."

"Believe me, I know. Maybe I should try younger men."

"They would look better, but honey we talked about this.

The last thing you need is to get involved with a man who might want children. That would break your heart."

Another sigh. "Yeah, I know."

"An older man will be established in his career and he'll take care of you. You'll see. You just need to suffer through some loonies first, but it's funny after the fact, right? And the poor man can't help it if he's bald, Claire. He was just trying to look better for his dates. Right, Honey?" she asks hopefully.

"I guess, and if I don't laugh, I'll cry."

"Are you coming for Easter?"

"Dixie and I will be there." Dixie loves Grandma!

"How is little Dixie? I can get her some of the good treats from the organic store."

"She's good. She needs some shots at the vet."

"It's a good thing she isn't a child because with this crap healthcare we're going to have, none of us will be able to go to the doctor. Did you see Fox News last night?"

"No, Mom. Remember, I was out with the old man? I'm almost at my office now so I need to go. Thanks for listening. Love you."

"Love you, too. See you soon!"

I am not near the office but I can't listen to political ranting right now. I sit in traffic, which is finally moving, and ponder my mother's comments. I do need to be more selective and not let this process get me down. I finally pull into the parking lot of my two-story suburban office building and find a spot way in the back. I'm late—it's already nine-fifteen.

Our building has a huge set of steps in the front. It was obviously a man's design because I have yet to wear a pair of shoes that can handle this climb. I feel like a mountain goat every day. It makes me want to stay in for lunch to avoid additional trips, but most days I succumb to the pain and go out to enjoy the better restaurants and shopping in this part of town.

As I walk through the office, I'm grateful I don't have to climb more stairs to the 2nd floor (there is an elevator but I'm always late or too impatient to use it when I need to go up there). I spot Rebecca at the coffee machine and motion to her to meet me in my office. I'm sure she's waiting to hear the latest scoop on my pitiful love life, and we need to get behind closed doors before someone grabs one of us ahead of the staff meeting.

She motions back, pointing to the coffee and then to me. I shake my head—no, I do not want coffee. I have worked with her for five years and she still asks me if I want coffee. I loathe coffee.

Rebecca is forty-five and single. She has never been married and doesn't seem particularly concerned about it. She's attractive and fit, but getting a bit heavier lately. I have noticed her weight go up a little every year that I've known her—she used to be a stick figure. I guess after forty your body does change, but she's probably only a size six or eight now. I envy her curves, and her wavy dark auburn hair, which she colors to hide the grey. Her eyes are slate blue, not those bright sapphire eyes where you need a dimmer switch to turn them down.

She is the human resources person, handling employee relations, benefits and payroll. The boring stuff. I am responsible for training and development, and recruiting. They split HR into these two functions about five years ago when I was hired. Rebecca used to do both, but she sucked at recruiting. She would much rather handle employee complaints about the toilet paper in the ladies' room, or how it's unfair that the smokers get more breaks. I, on the other hand, am much more adept at dealing with clueless hiring managers and teaching people the same policies and procedures multiple times. Together we make quite a team.

Rebecca is right behind me with her coffee in hand. She gently closes the door (she thinks no one notices her slipping in here if she does this), and plops herself down in my rigid purple guest chair (we don't want people getting too comfortable in here). We both have our own offices, even though most of the non-management employees sit in open area cubicles. The decision to allow us to have offices with doors was due to the "sensitive nature" of our work. What this means is that lots of people cry or freak out when they talk to HR, and no one wants to witness that. This is a huge benefit for us. We can talk about our personal lives and use "business consultation" as the reason for a closed door, since we form the HR dynamic duo.

"Your hair looks good. Did you do something different?" she begins.

"No, it's the fucking rain. It's all frizzy." I run my hands through my damp hair and shake it like Dixie would.

"Have you taken up smoking crack? Your hair has never been frizzy. It's straight, it's blonde. You look like you walked out of a shampoo commercial. And I hate you." She smiles and blows on her hot beverage.

"Whatever. What's up this morning? Besides the staff meeting at ten. Which I am, of course, looking forward to." I force a fake smile.

"We barely have enough time to talk about your date last night, rip the poor guy to shreds and get to the conference room," she says with a mischievous grin.

"It was awful. He was old and creepy and wore a stupid old man hat. He had a bulbous nose like my Uncle Randy. It's too pitiful to even discuss." I shake my head in disgust.

"That's no fun. Maybe you should screen these guys better."

"Yeah, I think so. His hair fell off, too." I add that tidbit and she bursts into a fit of hysteria.

As she is recovering and wiping her eyes, she says, "You need help."

"I've heard that one a few times lately—from my mother, Jane—"

"You never ask for help, with anything. Remember the time I caught you trying to reach under the ladies' room stall to get toilet paper from the other stall when all you had to do was ask the person on the other side of you?"

"I stretched my legs so far apart I almost ripped my underwear in half. How could you possibly have known that was me?"

"Duh, you were wearing my favorite shoes—the cute ones with the red bow on the front and the kitten heels?"

"You spend a lot of time looking down, don't you?"

"Sue me, I love shoes. So yes, I need to help you. Your mother and Jane are sweet but they're married. And old."

"Jane is younger than you."

26

"Really? Being married automatically makes her older."

"Your logic is insane but you *do* have good instincts, so yes, I want you to look at this guy that e-mailed me last night. This one is promising." Rebecca tried online dating a few times, but was even more frustrated than I am. Somehow she doesn't need it and meets men all the time. I guess this is because of her veteran single girl status—she's a *pro*.

I pull up my profile and scroll down to find the e-mail from the new guy, BuddhaGolf73.

She looks at the message below his and says, "Eww, what is wrong with that guy's face?"

"I don't know. That's another new one. And eww, you're right. Damn, I hope that's just the camera angle. Ignore him—read what this guy wrote."

Dear Bluebird77,

Hey what's up? Loved your profile—that little dog is so cute and you're not so bad yourself—wink, wink... hahahaha... I saw you mentioned you like to meditate and play mini golf (I play real golf but that's so cute—LOL). Would love to chat about our spiritual focuses and witness your mini golf pro skills firsthand. Drop me a line if you're interested.

Peace,
Daniel

"You don't meditate."

"I don't *all* the time—but I did a few times after I took that class at the community college. Remember?"

"No. Yes! The one taught by the lady who sees dead people?"

"Sharon is psychic."

"Whatever. Maybe you should ask *her* to look at these guys, or just tell you when you'll meet a good one so you can stop wasting time on this crap and come dancing with me. And by the way, what the hell does Bluebird mean?"

"It doesn't mean anything. I thought it sounded cute. So do you think I should go out with him? He's only forty, but he emphatically states that he does not want kids *and* he looks like he's in pretty good shape. I need an old man break. No?" I look at her anxiously.

"*Cute*? Why didn't you call yourself 'Little Princess' or 'Cuddle Bunny'? You should be dating twenty-five-year olds. With that body you could totally be a cougar. I can barely be a bobcat anymore." She leans back dejectedly in her chair.

I glare at her impatiently and she says, "All that New Age crap is weird, but he could be nice. At least he isn't pregnant. You're right about that."

Rebecca refers to all men with big bellies as pregnant. Apparently a lot of men in our office are with child. She claims our boss Tim is at least six months along, possibly carrying twins.

"And I need to do more meditation. It's relaxing."

"I find shaking it to be the best stress reliever. Seriously, Claire, you need to come dancing with me. You missed the St. Patrick's Day party downtown at O'Malley's Pub. That was crazy fun! There was even a younger band with a cute lead singer. They did some of that music you like."

"I saw the pictures from that event on your Facebook page. Green beer—yuck. And all those drunk people smashed into the bar. I do not go out on St. Patrick's Day. Too many amateur drunks on the road."

"Amateur drunks? As opposed to—?"

"The professional drunks. When you go out on a regular weekend night, the same people are out driving drunk every week. They have a better shot at it because they're experienced. Obviously they are still impaired and total assholes, but on New Year's Eve, St. Patrick's Day—everybody's drunk, so the roads are packed with people who don't have a fighting chance of getting home in one piece."

Rebecca wrinkles her forehead and shakes her head. "You need to get out and have real fun. You're still young—act your age. You don't have to get blasted drunk. Maybe you can dance with some cute guys for a change. If there's a slow dance you can actually let a man touch you." She blinks hard and raises her eyebrows.

I would love to go dancing. I dance in my living room all the time, fully clothed and with the blinds closed of course, just in case a neighbor peeps or Girl Scouts come along selling cookies. Rebecca dances to old music. As a child of the seventies and teen of the eighties, she's my classic rock connection. I do enjoy it—Billy Idol and Bruce Springsteen are always on my play lists, but I graduated in '95 and I listened to the Gin Blossoms, the Wallflowers, Matchbox Twenty, Sugar Ray, Green Day, and the Goo Goo Dolls. Rebecca claims that's "listening" music and her era's tunes are for "shaking it." She may have a point. We did a lot of standing around and swaying in my day. I also like some of the newer metal and hard rock, like Disturbed, Avenged Sevenfold, Three Days Grace. That stuff gets my heart rate pumping.

But what the hell, I need to branch out. "I'll go dancing. When?"

"This Saturday our favorite band, High Fidelity, is playing at Lorenzo's. They have a big dance floor and it's always packed with fun people."

"What do they play?"

"Mostly eighties but a good mix. They do a few newer songs too, to attract a wider crowd. You'll love it." She leans forward enthusiastically.

"Yeah, I like eighties music. It brings back good memories of when I was a little girl, before my miserable awkward stage started."

"Some people have a longer awkward stage, like between birth and death. Be glad you grew out of it and you're awesome now, and be careful what shoes you wear. You know how you are with that. Yay, I'm so excited you're going to go!!" She claps her hands and jumps up and down like a middle school cheerleader, only with big boobs. "Except there is one other thing."

"What now?"

"You need to join the Meetup group. It's a Meetup event."

"Can't I just go as your guest? It's a public place, right?" Rebecca is a member of a 30's/40's singles Meetup group. In theory this sounds good, but to me it sounds like all the Internet daters would be there in person, and I would be a sitting duck with nowhere to hide. How could I screen in that scenario? Plus there are a lot of younger men. It is infested with divorced joint custody dads.

"Claire, the Internet is clearly not working for you. It

wouldn't kill you to fill out the little survey and join. There is no obligation to attend anything or do anything, and you could meet more single women friends, too. It's always good to have a bigger girl posse."

"I'll look at it, but either way remind me when the band is playing."

"I'll send you an Outlook invite after the meeting." Rebecca sends Outlook invites for everything. I have been invited to "Talk about the Drunk Guy at the Christmas Party" and "Shop for Bras at Lunchtime." This whole conversation was probably an Outlook meeting. Good thing our meeting details are private. Our co-workers just assume we're busy with "important HR matters" and it is so hard to "get time on our calendars."

"Uh oh—shit, the meeting is starting. We need to get our asses over there."

"Damn it!" Rebecca jumps up and opens the door, as I grab my notebook.

We peek out into the hallway to see if the coast is clear, and I shut my door. "These fucking meetings," I mutter to Rebecca.

"Well, hello, ladies, late for the meeting too? Claire, what *language*! Proper Southern ladies don't talk that way."

I open my mouth to respond and Rebecca jumps in. "Justin, shut the fuck up."

"What a classy HR team. Claire, you're looking especially hot today. Is that Spandex?" He winks and looks me up and down.

I purse my lips and take a deep breath. "Justin, you are such an asshole. Let's all just get to the conference room before Tim starts the meeting." My cheeks are hot.

"No problem, ladies. I'll run ahead and save your seats." He walks down the hall smirking.

I stare at him and don't move for a moment.

"Claire, let's go!"

My teal wrap sweater is tight, and it has a little Lycra in it, but I do not wear spandex to work. And I will say *fuck* all I want. That is one of the things I hate about being in the South, but Justin is obviously mocking me. He isn't southern (he's a twenty-five-year old from Philadelphia—yes I have read all the employees personnel files, plus I hired that punk).

In New York, it was perfectly acceptable to say *fuck* at work. Ron's old boss used to say things like "How do youz like my fuckin' sweata?" Of course Ron *is* a UPS driver, so his Italian boss from the Bronx was not exactly a Princeton graduate, like Justin. I keep threatening him with HR, but since Rebecca and I *are* HR, he doesn't appear to be frightened. Justin is a *brilliant* IT guy, so he is pretty much untouchable, and he never goes too far. He is just annoying, like a fly buzzing around your head while you're trying to eat a delicious hamburger at a picnic.

"Claire—HELLO! Don't let Justin aggravate you. He wants you and is too immature to simply ask you out. He's like the little brat in 3rd grade who pulls your pony tail because he likes you." She grabs my arm and we break into a sprint to the conference room, which is down the hall and around the corner.

"I don't care what he wants and that's ridiculous. And if he does want me, it's just because he has an older woman fetish, and I am not having sex with someone I work with and will see every day, no matter how hot he is or how tight his abs are."

"How do you know how tight his abs are?" Rebecca pants as we reach the door.

"I punched him once." I swing open the conference room doors and Tim is in midsentence. All eyes turn to look at us and sure enough—Justin has saved a seat on either side of himself with that grin on his flawless face.

As Rebecca sits down he whispers, "Hey Becca, didn't mean to leave you out. You're looking pretty good today, too," as he peers down her shirt, chuckling to himself. She just glares at him and turns to the room, smiling at everyone. She's wearing one of those short ladies' button down shirts she favors for the office. That doesn't sound sexy, but since she's pretty big on top her cleavage is always spilling out of the too tight buttons. Going shopping at Victoria's Secret with Rebecca makes me sad.

"Hello, ladies. Nice of you to make time for us this morning. I trust you were caught up in a pressing HR matter." Tim sounds so forced when he is trying to be all proper and businesslike. He's loudly cracking his gum—not at all a Southern gentleman thing to do. Tim Rudwick is aware of his pregnancy and tries to chew gum all day instead of eat. Personally, I think a few trips to the office gym would be healthier and more effective, but Tim is a gum addict. Our vending machines must have fifty varieties to choose from, and he sends his assistant on Juicy Fruit runs the same way other bosses ask for Starbucks.

We mumble our apologies and he continues. "I was just telling the group about the sales figures in the new genre—erotica for women."

Bella Donna Press is a fairly large publishing company targeting women readers. The founder must have been a Stevie Nicks fan (see, I know my classic rock references, even from when I was a fetus). Our cookbooks haven't done well lately because most people now get their recipes from the Internet. We do produce some cute chick lit novels and our parenting section boasts a few quality titles. I have a copy of the Baby Bible at home, but I obviously won't need it now. I bought it before one of my later miscarriages. The erotica thing is not necessarily in our wheelhouse, but Tim seems optimistic.

"—and Claire McDonald Ratzenberger is going to lead this initiative."

What am I leading?

"Yes, that sounds great," I nervously reply.

"I'll get the job description to you this afternoon. It is imperative that we have editors on staff who can handle this new material."

This fantastic new material is BDSM based. Because of the overwhelming success of a certain sexually graphic trilogy, the BDSM genre has exploded. Readers don't seem to care if these books are well written or not (they are not), and our in-house editorial staff have complained about them. I can appreciate sex scenes in books that actually have a plot and believable characters, but this stuff is pure trash. Calling it erotica makes it sound as though it has some value, but it's pretty much just silly. Publishing companies are freaking out trying to churn this stuff out as quickly as possible so they can capitalize on this fad before it dies out. If someone is producing quality titles in this genre, I am not aware of it. Even though we can get anything in the catalogue for free, I will continue to cheat on Bella Donna with our competitor's offerings for my fiction fix, even though that means paying for it.

"Cecilia, please send Claire the job description this afternoon, and block off time on my calendar next week for interviewing. Frank, you'll need to do the same." I swear sometimes I think Cecilia and the rest of the admins are the ones writing the new books. Even though that is preposterous and would never happen, it makes sense based on the quality, and the front desk receptionist gets jumpy when anyone comes up behind her. I don't know how Frank, our Editor-in-Chief, doesn't see the looming problem of getting involved in a genre we know nothing about.

Cecilia makes some notes on her pad and looks bored. She is twenty-two and weighs about ninety pounds. Justin should try to date her. They could act out one of the new books, and maybe he would leave me alone. Although Justin can't be hurting for female companionship.

The meeting drags on with Linda in accounting complaining about all of the mistakes on the expense reports. Justin gives a brief tutorial on IT security issues. I update the team on our recruiting efforts. We have a few open positions in finance and new author acquisitions, in addition to the new positions Tim just announced. Rebecca reminds everyone of the performance self-appraisals that are due next month (my favorite). Tim wraps up the meeting and we head back to our offices.

"That went well." Rebecca is so poised during these meetings. I always get nervous, even when I am well-versed in the subject matter.

"Listen, I'm going to skip going out for lunch today. I need to get caught up on a few things."

"You're just dying to e-mail Daniel, aren't you?"

"Who's Daniel?"

"The Internet guy we were talking about this morning?"

"Ohhh, you mean 'meditation golf guy.' Daniel is his *actual* name. They all blend together after a while."

"Well, there's been enough of them." She rolls her eyes. "Now go and find us some editorial staff who don't mind editing dirty manuscripts." She smiles and heads towards her office.

I *am* anxious to craft my witty and fabulous message to Daniel.

Rebecca pops her head back around into my doorway and says, "Hey, when did you punch Justin? Not that he doesn't deserve it on a daily basis."

"One time when he was being a dick. I was just joking and I noticed his stomach was like a rock. That's all."

As soon as she says goodbye and closes my door, I settle in to write this e-mail. I have a good feeling about this one.

Dear Daniel,

Thanks so much for contacting me. I liked your profile, too. I would love to get together some time soon. I must warn you—I am a mini golf pro! My number is 657-8433. Why don't you take a look at your calendar and let me know when we could meet. I have a great mini golf place near my house. Have a great week!

Claire

That sucks—too boring! Not witty at all. But in the past I have been more fun and flirty and regretted it (Rebecca would die if she saw what I wrote to the old man with the hat). This cuts straight to the point—let's meet and see what happens. If he wants to get together, he will call or text. I do like the idea of an active date. I can't sit and watch someone eat or drink and make painful conversation anymore. Why didn't I think of this sooner? I am a slow learner but after a few dozen times I catch on. I sign out of my dating site and go back to my work inbox. I see Cecilia has sent me the job description. I think of Simon and Garfunkel every time I hear her name. I know even *older* musical references. This may come in handy since I am destined to end up with someone who saw them in concert the year that song was released.

34

CHAPTER FOUR

I wake up the next morning with a sense of dread. I don't know why, but then I remember. This frequently happens to me. I wake up peacefully, until reality hits me in the face like a wet noodle. Not that my life has been an endless nightmare of tragedy, but it has had its moments. I recall that I sent my phone number to Daniel, and now I am obsessing while awaiting his call. Last night I kept checking my phone every five minutes, as if it rang and somehow I didn't hear it, even though it was practically attached to my body.

I need to summon my Internet Dating Girl superhero strength to get through this. Or just find something to distract myself. I could actually do some work while at work, but that isn't interesting enough to divert my attention for long. I do get my work done, but I have never been one to pour myself into my professional pursuits. I am more of a *drift* into work kind of gal. I get there, but without as much gusto as the over achievers.

Dixie's morning potty ritual goes smoothly. It's sunny out today and I manage to stay clothed in the yard—two pluses! I haven't seen my new neighbor lately, and that's good. The more time passes the more likely he is to forget the lawn show.

I also have not seen his family. Maybe he moved first and they are coming later—that happens a lot when people take a new job. The wife stays behind with the kids to finish up the school year or to pack, while the husband leaves sooner to start his new job and get the new place ready. That's nice—maybe he's nesting for his little family of tyke bikers. I bet they *will* have a swing set.

I need to remember to ask Jane if she has met them yet but she'll be at a PTA meeting tonight, and I regret that I only call her lately when I have scoop or want some. I need to tell her about the flashing incident—she will die laughing. Scoop makes me think of ice cream. Maybe I will drag Rebecca out for some at lunchtime. It's spring-time and the ice cream stands are starting to open up.

Since it's such a nice day I decide to wear something lighter (it's so hard to dress in season transition). I hate winter and its clothes, especially turtlenecks. I once heard a comedian say that wearing a turtleneck is like being strangled by a weak midget all day. I can relate to this—I pull on the material constantly to get it away from my neck, and then it's all stretched out and the whole neck warming purpose is defeated, *and* my sweater is deformed.

I choose a peach short sleeved sweater set, a tight cream skirt that ends a few inches above the knee, and cream pointy toe pumps with scalloped cutouts on the top and sides. Pearl stud earrings complete the outfit and match the gold pearly brooch clasp on the cardigan. Another huge plus of living in the South—no one wears panty hose except in the most conservative industries. I like pantyhose almost as much as turtlenecks.

When I get to the office I am actually on time—it's only eight-fifteen! I find a parking space in the third row from the entrance, instead of my usual Outer Mongolia section. I notice that Rebecca is not in yet, nor is hot Justin. I mean Justin.

I start sifting through my fifty or so e-mails—our managers especially like to do all of their e-mailing at night when no one is around to read any of it, so you're faced with this bombardment of communication every morning. They do this because they spend their entire work days in meetings. No wonder I have no management aspirations, and I'm not jumping out of bed and *pouring* myself into work.

As I begin opening up my messages, quickly answering the easy ones and sorting the ones requiring more work, I sense eyes on me. Before I look up I know who it is.

"Good morning, Claire—you're here early." He must have pulled in right after me. The smile is electric. How is he so perky this early?

"Hi, Justin. Yes, I wanted to get a head start on some stuff...because of the new assignment I got in the meeting yesterday... remember?" Shut up, Claire.

Yes, I said it earlier—Justin is hot. He is not a "little" anything—punk, prick or asshole (although sometimes he *acts* like a bigger version of all of these). He is about six feet tall and has blond hair (darker than mine with streaks of honey) and emerald eyes. Justin could be a model. Or a Greek god, or maybe a Viking with that hair. I have been recruiting IT professionals for years, and they never look like Justin.

So even though I am *not* interested in him, a woman would have to be a blind lesbian nun to not be affected by him. It is cruel how he taunts me like this. I try to pretend that I don't like him and I think he's a silly kid when others are around, but every time I see him I get tingly from head to toe and sometimes a little light-headed. I hate when I have to give presentations in meetings when he's there. Even Rebecca doesn't know I feel this way, and I don't want her to figure it out. I try to *act* mad and indignant when he says stuff to me in front of her. She doesn't seem the least bit affected by him, but then again she is old enough to be his young mother. If she knew my true feelings she would push the issue. She is always trying to get me to go younger, but she doesn't understand my situation.

"Yes, I remember." He says this slowly as if he's talking to a cute four-year-old girl who needs to work on her finger paintings at day care today. Only with a look that would be highly inappropriate to give a child. "Have a good day, Claire. Stop by and say hi some time."

"I...will," I say to his perfect butt, which is disappearing from sight. Enough! Maybe if I didn't work with him I would indulge, but he is obviously not relationship material for me, and I can't sleep with someone I see at work every day. I still think he only flirts with me because he knows he's hot and he unnerves me. When I first interviewed him two years ago (right after I got back from my hysterectomy leave of absence), I was so flushed and sweaty I thought I needed to call Dr. Mason and ask him if the surgery was sending me into early menopause.

Justin is likely amused by my ruffled state, and probably went back to his desk to call one of his many twenty-year-old super model girlfriends. He is much nicer to me, and less inappropriate, one on one. He's a bit immature, and obviously likes the attention of saying things for shock value and embarrassing people (ME) in front of co-workers.

My reaction probably gives him more fuel, but I can't control it. Maybe I will stop by his desk later and try to act normal and professionally friendly. I need to work on breaking down this tension between us and diffusing this situation—I don't need more stress at work. To make matters worse, Daniel hasn't called yet, and I still have thirty more e-mails to answer before my eleven o'clock meeting with Frank, our Editor-in-Chief.

I arrive at Frank's office a little before eleven and he is ready for me. Frank is short, bald and skinny, and fairly new to his role. He is a former colleague of Tim's, and when the Editor-in-Chief position became available, Tim recruited him. I haven't had many professional interactions with him yet, but I'm assuming this will go smoothly. At least I hope so. This new material is such garbage and I'm sure he isn't thrilled with it either.

"Hi, Frank. How are you today? Ready to get started?" I poke my head in his office and find him cleaning his glasses.

"Yes, Claire please come in. You don't need to shut the door. I have an open door policy." He puts his glasses back on and waves me in.

I don't tell him that an open door policy means you are open to people coming to see you unannounced, not that your door is physically always open.

I walk in and Frank comes around his desk, and motions for me to sit with him at his small conference table flanked by stuffy grey chairs. His office is all grey, black and red. It works, but it's a little severe for my tastes. He asks me if I would like coffee, but I brought my iced tea, and I get tired of explaining that I don't drink coffee. "No, thanks. These are comfy chairs. The ones in my office are like slabs of cement. Good thing you have an open door policy or you would be tempted to nap."

"Hahaha...that's so funny. You're funny, Claire." It wasn't *that* funny.

"I received the job description and it seems pretty straightforward. These are standard editor positions. Is there anything specific you want me to look out for before I send you the resumes? These people *do* have to be comfortable editing some explicit material, and I am a bit concerned about that." I open up my file folder and prepare to take notes. I feel beads of sweat forming on my brow and upper lip. I am grateful for Frank's literal open door policy. I would prefer not to be in an enclosed office with a man talking about our new erotica line. At least not a man who is almost as old as my father.

"Yes Claire, I'm aware of the new material and what is driving this need. You *will* need to screen for this skill when you talk to candidates, but I don't see it as a big issue. We work in a pretty liberal industry, right?" Why is he winking?

"I do think it's going to be difficult. We need to search for people who are comfortable in that business." I lower my voice and lean forward.

"Such as…?"

I take a sip of my iced tea and say, "I don't know, Frank. Who is going to want to edit this trash? I guess there are editors with this experience. I just hate the idea of recruiting from the *porn* industry."

Frank starts choking on his coffee and some may have shot out of his nose. While he is trying to regain composure—"Frank, are you alright?"—and as I am coming to his aid, Justin walks by. He flashes his signature smirk, but when he sees Frank choking he looks more concerned. Then he starts laughing.

I ignore Justin and he walks away. He really is a dick sometimes.

Frank regains his composure and says, "Yes, I just took a sip down the wrong hole. Claire, these people need to be professional editors. So if similar books are written under the umbrella of the *porn* industry, then that's where you have to look, but this is a popular genre. It has gained more recent mainstream notoriety, but this type of story has been told since the dawn of time. You *can* find editors who have worked in this genre. These books are selling by the millions. Someone is editing them."

"I'll do my best. We probably need someone from outside of our market too, so hopefully we have some relocation budget." I can't believe I have to deal with this nonsense. It pisses me off that we are even selling this crap! And why can't Justin go fix the server or something? My face feels flushed again, and I'm resisting the urge to scream in frustration. I don't know who we're going to get. We should just hire some hookers to proofread them in between visits from their johns or drug dealers, but it's probably hard to find hookers with English degrees.

"I agree that it isn't the classics, Claire, but you saw the numbers in the meeting..." Justin walks by again and mouths "is he okay?" and starts cracking up again. I scowl at him and he makes a pouty face.

"Claire? Are you listening to me? Here, I know something that will loosen you up." He hops up and runs to the corner of his office and comes back with—holy crap—it's a whip!

"What are you going to do with that?" I turn my attention back to Frank after non-verbally chastising Justin, who is wearing a light blue button down oxford that looks amazing with his hair and eyes, with the sleeves slightly rolled up. I can see his forearms and—is it hot in here?

"Claire, relax. You're wound so tight. I am not doing *anything* with it. It's a *joke*. My wife gave it to me when I told her about the new books. She said I can use it to keep the employees in line at work, and her at home. She's hilarious. She said all of her girlfriends can't wait for the new releases." Frank puts away his weapon of torture and sits back down. He frowns when he sees his joke did not produce the desired effect.

"Claire, I would rather we produce something a little more *literary* also, but we need to make money, and the company isn't doing a great job of finding promising new authors who write quality fiction. Hopefully this is just a Band-Aid, but I know you can find us a couple of solid editors who can polish up the manuscripts to salable condition."

I hope so. If anything, I think illiterate porn stars may be writing the ones in the sub box because apparently they need a lot of basic work. "Pam Rogers in Acquisitions is working on future titles in more literary genres. We have an editorial opening over there too, and I'm working closely with Pam to get that filled."

"Great, Claire. Glad you're on top of this, even though you are clearly uncomfortable. Maybe you should talk to someone about it. We need all of our key staff members on board with the changes, and you especially, since you interface directly with potential candidates. They're just books, Claire. We aren't selling anything but fantasy and a little harmless fun." He pauses and gets up, signaling the end of the meeting. "Please just forward the resumes and we'll get the interviews set up."

I stand up, smooth my skirt and gather up my folders. "Thanks, Frank."

As I get to the door Frank is smirking and says, "You might want to try to recruit phone sex operators—they have a lot of material." Just as the words "phone sex" come out of his mouth, Justin reappears. Is he doing laps around the 2nd floor for exercise? "Phone sex?" he mouths at me and wrinkles his forehead.

"I'm sorry, I couldn't resist. Claire, you should see your face. I'm sorry—just trying to ease your tension." He is fighting back the smirk now. Jerk.

"Haha, yep. Phone sex. Hilarious, Frank. Thanks!" I close Frank's open door and turn to face a confused Justin.

"*I* get the cold shoulder and you're in there talking phone sex with good old Frank." He shakes his head and one piece of flawlessly highlighted and styled hair escapes and grazes his forehead. I resist the urge to reach out and push it back to join the others.

I grab him by the arm and pull him in the direction of his office. Justin has a big corner cubicle—no door but a nice window and a seating set up similar to Frank's. At twenty-five, Justin is the *head* of the IT department and reports directly to Tim.

"It's these stupid books we're publishing. Everyone is turning into a whack-job." I let go of his arm as he follows my march to his door.

We reach his cubicle and I plop down in his comfy guest chair. His is red. This whole floor has the same color scheme, but I like ours better on the first floor—dark purple, grey and forest green. I have never been alone with him in his office.

"Yeah, they *are* pretty stupid but I was hoping maybe you would read some and get some good ideas—I hear there's one about a steamy office romance." More smirking and his green eyes sparkle.

I sigh in exasperation. "Justin, this is getting tiresome. Would you stop it already?"

"Stop what?"

"Making fun of me."

"When do I make fun of you?" He looks so sincere.

"All the time." I fold my arms.

"Claire, I flirt with you and I tease you."

"Justin, I'm a lot older than you, and you obviously only like to shock and embarrass me. You're not interested in me, and it's cruel and unprofessional to taunt me."

He pauses and looks out the window. He has a flawless profile—what a chin. "I guess I do act like a dick sometimes. I'm sorry. I am not used to women being so difficult. I have girls following me around all the time and they're mostly airheads. I know that sounds conceited, but you're different. I don't get to meet women like you when I go out, and you do pose quite a challenge. It gets a little frustrating."

Could he be interested in me? No, it's just fun for him. Why can't I be a confident, sexually experienced super model with a uterus and a bright future? "Let's just try to be friends at work and more professional."

He looks a little hurt but he says, "I'll back off. I didn't realize it upset you so much. At least you're not punching me." He smiles broadly.

"You're going to keep reminding me of that, huh? You caught me on a bad day. That's why you keep this up. You know I won't do anything to you because you can hold that incident over my head."

"Claire, I'm teasing you again. Why don't you have a sense of humor?"

"I need to get back to work. I'll see you later, Justin," I say quietly.

As I turn to leave he slowly walks over, puts his big, warm hands on my tiny shoulders and lowers his head to my ear and whispers, "It's too bad. Our kids would be beautiful."

Hot tears immediately form in my eyes. I am speechless and my body is frozen with his hands on my shoulders. As my body stiffens, he lets go and I glance at him out of the corner of my eye, just enough for him to see my tears.

"Claire, what's wrong? What did I do now?" He looks genuinely bewildered as I mumble that I have to go and run out the door, heading down the hall to the elevator. As I leave, I hear him trying to explain about how I'm beautiful and that's why he said that, or something like that. I'm not listening. I hear his footsteps coming as I jump in and hit the "close door" button before he can catch me. The door slides shut on his dejected expression.

CHAPTER FIVE

I get off the elevator and walk swiftly to my office. Once inside, I close the door and stand for a moment up against the door and try to compose myself. Justin doesn't know. He isn't that cruel, and I can't expect the rumor mill was ever interested in my hysterectomy. It was only a life shattering event for me. For others it just meant I had surgery and was out on leave for a few weeks, and it has long been forgotten. No one told Justin after he was hired, "Hey, if you're ever looking to impregnate a co-worker, stay away from *that* one."

I relax my muscles and attempt to stretch out my neck and back, where I hold all my tension. I close my eyes, and I can still feel the sensation of Justin's hands, and it makes me shudder.

I take a few deep breaths, and sit down at my computer. I open up my Monster account to see if there are any new job applicants when I remember I still haven't heard from Daniel. Just in case, I pick up my phone—I left it on my desk when I went to meet with Frank—and I see that I do have a message from him. He wants to meet at mini golf Friday night and to have drinks afterwards. I write back telling him I would love to meet him. Now, what to wear...as I begin to ponder that dilemma, Rebecca knocks and comes right in.

"Hey, what's up? How was your morning?" She stands in the doorway and smiles.

"I met with Frank on the new editor positions. That was *interesting* to say the least. It seems everyone but me loves porn and wants to be whipped. Speaking of whipped, do you want ice cream for lunch? You love brownie sundaes and Brewster's is open now." I sit up eagerly like a little kid.

"Sure, I can eat my Lean Cuisine later—it isn't enough food to fill one tooth. You can tell me your Frank story on the way. He wants to be whipped? That naughty boy." Rebecca wags her finger in mock disapproval.

As I get up to grab my purse, I search for my file with all the info on the editor positions. Did I leave it in Frank's office? No, damn it—I left it in *Justin's* office. Great. I don't need it to do the work—everything is on my computer. I only printed it so I could refer to it in the meeting, but now Justin has a legitimate business reason to stop by. No matter what, I won't be able to avoid him forever.

Rebecca and I had a good chat about Frank and Daniel (Justin who?) in the car, and I thoroughly enjoyed my raspberry white chocolate scoop in a cup. She yelled at me for being a prude and told me how we need these books, and they're fun and all of the usual crap I'm tired of hearing.

"You're making too much of this. They are *books*! No one is going to whip you. Fantasy is fun and exciting. I keep telling you to loosen up. Sometimes I think your libido is so tightly shut it will take a socket wrench to pry it open." She licked her spoon suggestively just to piss me off.

"He brought out a *whip*! Isn't that sexual harassment? I was *not* comfortable with that!" I slammed down my red plastic spoon to emphasize my discomfort.

Rebecca just sighed and rested her head in her hands. "Claire, he was just joking. He didn't know you were really offended, because most *normal adults* in our industry wouldn't be. If he cracks you with it, let me know." She rolled her eyes and resumed stuffing her face with brownie and chocolate sauce. "Maybe you should get a job at the Bible factory—". She ducked in time to miss getting nailed with the red spoon.

The rest of the workday was uneventful, thank God! I found a few good candidates to send to Frank (they will have to pay relocation for most of them), I had a good meeting with Pam about the acquisitions position, and Justin was nowhere to be found (but I was *not* looking). I bet he took the rest of the day off, probably to run a marathon and have sex with a porn star. He has probably forgotten all about the hormonal lunatic crying in his office.

Speaking of sex, I need some soon. With a man. Preferably one who is age appropriate and will not humiliate me, ruin my career or even worse—make me fall in love with him and subsequently dump me for a young baby making machine with no cellulite. It would be nice if he doesn't bring any weapons to bed, either. Who knew this would even be a consideration?

My lack of sexual experience is clouding my judgment and making everything more daunting than it actually is. I may need to just pick a guy and do it. Get it over with and remove the mystique. Maybe Daniel will be a good prospect.

At home now with Dixie, I settle in to read a good book (*not* a Bella Donna Press selection), but then decide to call Jane.

"I saw you were home. I was waiting for you to settle in. Are you in the bubble bath yet?"

"No, that will be later. I do need the heat—my neck and shoulders are killing me. I *must* make a massage appointment with Julie. I've had a crazy couple of days." I put down my book and sink back into the sofa with my feet up on the coffee table.

"I bet. I've been dying to hear, but I had the PTA meeting the other night and then last night Shannon had Girl Scouts. And for once I have some info for you too. But let's hear yours first."

I pause for a moment to decide where to start. "Let's see...I have a date tomorrow night with a new guy."

"I'm impressed. I thought you might take a break to recover from the old hat man."

"No, I jump back in pretty quickly. There's always another one. Men are like buses—there's one every fifteen minutes. Unfortunately, they are always headed in the same direction. Maybe I should consider waiting at different stops. The Internet *is* getting old, but it is an endless supply."

"Hmm...I guess that's a good attitude. So who's the new guy?"

"His name is Daniel. Plays golf and meditates. He's into a lot of the New Age spiritual stuff. Not pregnant and he's only forty." Dixie jumps up on the couch with her squeaky toy. She's like a toddler when I'm on the phone.

"You're almost robbing the cradle now. What does he do for a living?"

"You sound like my mother, but I actually don't remember. I'll have to look at that before I meet him. I am *so* looking forward to this date. We are going mini golfing since I am a pro. He said that sounds cute. Oh, and what else? Let's see—the other morning I flashed the new neighbor. Have you seen him yet?" Dixie gets fidgety and jumps off the couch.

"You did *what*? You are *so* crazy. How the hell did that happen?"

"I was walking Dixie in the rain and she made a run for him, and in the process of trying to regain control of the wiener, I lost control of my bathrobe sash."

I grin at the memory.

"So he just saw your nightgown for a second. That's no biggie."

"Umm, no. There was no nightgown." There is no way to avoid sharing this part.

"WHAT? Do you think he saw anything? What did you do?"

"I ran for the backyard and turned around as quickly as I could. I waved though, so he wouldn't think I was rude."

"A strip show in the cul-de-sac is one thing, but we certainly don't want him to doubt your *manners*." Jane can't stop laughing.

"It was pretty humiliating at the time, but now it's kind of funny. I haven't run into him, and maybe he didn't see much. He was at the end of his driveway, but I was fairly far back in my yard. He's just another one of those young neighborhood fathers—he doesn't count as an actual man. So *have* you seen him? I don't know where his family is—probably not here yet."

Jane is silent.

"Are you there? Did a cat throw up?"

"No, I'm here."

"What's the matter? Did you meet him and he said something? Or *no*—you met his wife at the bus stop and she said something?" My worst fear.

"He doesn't have a wife."

"What? Is he a single dad?"

"Nope. Just a young single guy buying a house in a cul-de-sac full of families and a floozy."

"That's crazy. Why would a good looking, young guy

want to live here? Maybe he's a sex offender or on the lam?" I pause a moment. "I got it—he's in the witness protection program!"

"I don't know about witness protection—and people don't usually admit to that right off the bat. It kind of defeats the purpose. I didn't consider the sex offender thing. I will check the website. Wait. I need to write that down. Hold on. JOEY, CAN YOU BRING MOMMY A PENCIL?"

"Never mind that right now. So you think he's just a normal guy who wants to live in a boring suburban neighborhood for no good reason?"

"I didn't talk to him. Mike saw him outside when the kids were playing and introduced himself. He said he's a writer, so he works from home. I don't know what he writes. Men never get any details, but yet Mike knows he's from the DC area and he's a Redskins fan. Like who gives a shit about that?"

"At least he didn't mention my incident. I guess it's silly for me to expect that a guy like that would even notice me."

"I have not seen you naked, and I don't want to, but I would imagine men of all ages with a pulse and a beating heart would enjoy it. But either way, I have an idea."

Jane's ideas can be scary. She has way too much time on her hands as a stay-at-home mom with kids in school all day. "What now?"

"I thought it would be *nice*, since he *is* all alone, to bring him some kind of food to welcome him to the neighborhood and—"

"Are you crazy? He saw me naked and I'm supposed to bring him pie and welcome him to the neighborhood?"

People actually do this in the south. My parents moved to Virginia a few years ago and a neighbor lady rang the doorbell with a pie in hand while I was helping them unpack. It took my mother about five rings to answer since she is used to hiding from the Jehovah's Witnesses (they were active in New York). My father was in the background making fun of the way the neighbor said "pie" in her thick southern accent, affecting a woman's high pitched drawl. "Haa y'all, Ahh made you some paa for your paahole," which is obviously *not* what she said. My father is impossible! I laughed for hours and my mother wanted to kill him, as she tried to keep the woman out of earshot.

"Claire, we are not going to bring pie. We don't even know how to *make* pie. We could bring a fruit basket or maybe a healthy treat basket with hummus or something."

"Hummus? Why would we want to do this?" I can't wrap my head around this idea.

"You said it yourself. He's cute, and now we know he's single."

"Jane, he looks like a teenager, and he's obviously a weirdo since he's living here. And bunnies are cute but I don't go out of my way to make up a carrot and grass basket when a new one hops onto my lawn."

"You *know* you're interested. And it can't hurt to be friendly. It's always good to have another man around. You always say you need help with things around the house, you have no brothers or male friends, and Mike is useless so I can't even offer him…"

Heavy sigh. "Fine, but I am NOT interested in him. Maybe it would be good to break the ice, though. Someday I *may* need help getting mulch or lifting a heavy box." I am so easily manipulated.

"I knew you would come around. So let's do it Saturday afternoon—around lunch time? Not too early because young people like to sleep late."

"Even though I said he *looks* like a teenager, he is an actual adult—he did buy a house. I'm sure he wakes up before noon." On second thought he could be a heavy partier. "Fine. Noon it is."

"Yay! I'll get all the stuff when I go grocery shopping Saturday morning."

"I will be in bed. That's all the teamwork I can offer. I am hoping my Friday night won't end too early." Fingers crossed for my date with Daniel.

"Fair enough. I'll let you take your bubble bath now. Have fun tomorrow night and don't stress too much."

What have I gotten myself into? Jane means well, and I guess it will be good to welcome him to the neighborhood and act like nothing ever happened. I am undoubtedly making *way* too much of this. He will probably call his mother and tell her about the nice neighbor ladies, and she will be happy her son is living here instead of some city apartment with bums on the corner and *real* floozies.

I am curious as to why he wants such a big house. It even has a large basement. When Susan lived there it was like Lord of the Flies with all the kids descending upon that enormous room.

With all this focus on his youth I have overlooked what could be an important fact—he's a writer, but I don't know what he writes, thanks to Mike's less than stellar sleuthing. It could be reviews for Car & Driver magazine, or Cute Young Guy's Quarterly, or Highlights, but as an employee at an unstable publishing firm I owe it to myself to find out. Even if he isn't a literary fiction writer he may have some leads on promising new authors, and it can't hurt to ask.

I just realized why he probably wants the basement—keg parties.

CHAPTER SIX

Friday night is here, and I am trying on the numerous outfit combinations that Rebecca and I discussed. I want to look nice, but I'm going to be playing mini golf *and* the weather is volatile in March. I settled on a pair of black Capri leggings with an aqua baby doll top—one of the bra tops from Victoria's Secret. Clever invention, but I still wear a bra with them. They don't have enough padding and I need to work my cleavage trick tonight. I touched up my makeup, slipped into a pair of comfy black ballet flats and I was all set. After looking in the mirror I realized I was probably too dressed up for the sports park, but screw it. I added long dangly silver earrings, so they would sparkle when I shook my head under the lights.

Of course now that I'm in the car I realize that it's cold and dark, and I will freeze. I do have a jacket with me, but I will try to play without it. Also as I am a mini golf pro, I must not beat him. I need to work on dumbing down my game, but he plays *real* golf and should have no problem winning. I want him to win to stroke his male ego, but I also want to do well enough to show off my skills as a woman who can excel at fun activities. It's a delicate balance.

I arrive at the sports park a few minutes early and check my hair and makeup again. Satisfied as I'm going to get, I get out of the car and walk to the check-in area where you pay, and get your clubs and balls. My eyes dart around trying to spot my date. I'm busying myself reading the promotional signs about kids' birthday parties and multi-visit passes when I see him.

"Hi. You must be Claire. I'm Daniel. It's so nice to meet you." He takes my hand in his and looks into my eyes. His are brown, the color of dark chocolate, and several shades deeper than mine. They're soulful, like Dixie's eyes, and even more expressive.

I pause a second before responding. "Hi, I'm Claire. Nice to meet you, too. Did you find this place okay?" Since he's standing here, that's obvious.

"Yes, it was easy. Sorry I'm a few minutes late. I had an emergency at work."

"No problem." I still don't remember what he does for a living, and I forgot to check his profile again. I will just play along. "Was everything okay with the work emergency?"

"Yeah, but cockroaches are stubborn little bastards. Shall we go hit some mini golf balls?" He gestures towards the check-in counter.

I stare at him and stammer. "Great." Cockroaches? What the hell work emergency involves cockroaches? Uh, oh. That's right—his profile said he works in the *service industry*. Men often put that when they clean septic tanks or kill bugs. He's a pest control guy, or whatever they call them. However, he *is* cute, not pregnant and pleasant enough.

We get our gear and Daniel pays for the game. I am always awkward in this situation, but he steps up after a slight pause and puts down his credit card.

"Claire, are you going to be warm enough without a jacket and that little shirt?" He assesses my wardrobe with concern.

"I'll be okay." Once I get my game into action I will warm up. Hopefully.

We get started at the first hole, after laughing at the "practice" hole—we don't need practice. Daniel certainly looks like a golfer with his proper grip and stance. I even enjoy watching him. He's wearing jeans and a polo shirt— just casual enough, but not sloppy. We were thinking alike when we got ready, and *he* even had to rush to change out of his bug uniform. Wait, I wonder if he showered after the cockroach murdering episode. If I decide to touch him later I don't want bug poison on me. Maybe he wears some kind of hazmat suit.

We both sail through the first couple of holes effortlessly. It's only around the third hole that things start to go downhill.

All of a sudden Daniel can't play golf anymore. He hits it too soft, too hard, into the next green, in the bushes, and several times "in the drink" (this is what I always say when it goes in the water).

Daniel laughs with me, but after fishing the ball out several times, he is clearly getting frustrated. I am only able to suck so much, and therefore I am beating the pants off him (not literally—at this point he is still wearing pants—there are children around).

"Goddammit!"

Now the group of dads with the Boy Scout troop is looking over at us with concern and a bit of negative judgment.

"I don't know what my problem is. I golf all the time at Windy Hill—a *real* golf course. This shit is impossible." He throws down his club.

I'm noting that he is not all that "Zen" for a guy who practices meditation, but maybe he's just nervous. He is losing at mini golf to a woman.

"It's just silly mini golf. I suck at all sports, but I like this one because I can do it a little bit. Do you want to stop playing? I'm freezing." I *am* freezing—that part is not a lie for the benefit of Daniel's ego.

"I hate to disappoint you, but if you want, we could head over to a bar or something and get a drink and chat a bit." He gathers our clubs and balls, and is clearly ready to go.

"There's a little place up the street." There is a bar that recently opened called the Wild Rose Café. It looks decent, probably not too scary. They serve food too, and I'm starving.

"I'm following you." He waits for me to get moving and stays close behind.

I'm glad he doesn't ask to drive in the same car. I am always leery of that with strangers, but he seems like a sweet guy, and things will improve once we have a few drinks.

We arrive at the bar and find a booth in the back. The waitress comes over and takes our drink orders. This is the truly awkward part. I don't want to say I'm hungry because maybe I was supposed to eat before the date. It wasn't clear if we were eating or not. I don't want him to think I expect him to buy my dinner, but then if I pay for my own dinner will that make him look bad? He already looks bad enough after completely blowing it on a mini golf course that little Boy Scouts were destroying. If I order food then will he do the same? Will I get stuck paying for his food? I decide to just drink and worry about eating later.

Three or four drinks later I realize this is a bad idea. He is completely sober since all he ordered was club soda. I need to be more observant. My alcohol tolerance is low, and I haven't eaten since noon. Daniel is looking at me and smiling.

"You doin' okay there, little lady?"

"Yeah, but I think I'm getting drunk. Haha...oh no, I have to drive!"

"Don't worry. I'll get you home safely. Maybe you need some bread." He begins to look around for the waitress.

If I were sober I would be angry. I need real food, but in this state bread is better than nothing.

"I love golfing. I go at least once a week to Windy Hill— I'm a regular there. Lots of those guys are the big hot shots—lawyers, doctors, you know the type. But I hold my own. The meditation keeps me so grounded. Gets the Chi flowing." He looks pleased with himself.

Daniel is talking fast, and I'm only getting bits and pieces. The conversation is getting weirder, but I am too intoxicated to focus. Normally this is where I would ask him about kids, but the topics have steered so far away from that line of questioning, I let it go.

"And I keep the root chakra in line and that helps me, you know, sexually too...tantric sex...Sting does it. Mind blowing..."

I force a smile and nod. He looks cute with his hair messed up from the wind. March is so windy! It's dark and thick, and he actually looks a lot younger than forty. Suddenly I'm ready to go home.

I interrupt him. "Daniel, we should go."

"Check?" He motions to the waitress.

I guess he has no problem paying for alcohol, which is good since my purse is in my car. He helps me out to the parking lot, and I can barely stand up. I am also noticing that sometimes there are two of Daniel and everything else.

Shit—work tomorrow is going to be fun. Wait, it's Friday. Yay! Suddenly I get renewed energy and make a dash for the car, and some warmth. However, my feet and my brain are not working well together, and I trip and fall forward onto the gravel driveway.

"Babe, are you okay?" He comes over to help me up and his arms are so warm that I just melt into them. "You are freezing cold. Let's get your purse out of your car and get you home. Do you live far?" He sounds so logical and competent.

Miraculously I am able to tell him where I live. I decide that I'm going to invite him in. Why not? He's such a gentleman for paying for my mini golf and drinks, and now driving me home.

We pull into my driveway and he walks me to the door. Before I have a chance to say a word, he starts kissing me hard on the mouth. Screw it. "Do you want to come in?" He takes my key and we are in with the door shut before I get the words all the way out.

Dixie is flipping out, not only because she is excited that Mommy is home, but she brought a new playmate.

"I need to take her out first." I am slurring my words, but try to annunciate. He doesn't seem to mind, and grins at me and says, "Take your time, Babe." I can't remember at what point he stopped calling me Claire and started calling me "Babe." It may have been by my third drink or so. My stomach churns.

I take Dixie out and she quickly does her business. I glance across the street, and see the porch is lit. At the rate I'm going tonight I doubt I will join Jane in bringing food over to the new neighbor tomorrow.

I walk back into the house and go to the kitchen to give Dixie her treat. As I round the corner I catch a glimpse of Daniel sprawled out on the couch. Is there music playing? What happened to the lights? What the hell is he wearing? Or not wearing? I wish the double vision would merge into one image already.

Dixie runs off with her treat and I move into the living room. Daniel is drinking wine. Where did he get that? I see the corkscrew on the coffee table, and the open bottle, but what is even more bizarre is his change of clothes.

"I had some silk boxers in the car so I thought I would get more comfortable. You don't mind, do you?" He pats the space on the couch beside him.

My brain is so fuzzy, and there are conflicting thoughts in my head. Drunk Claire still thinks he's cute and Sober Claire is trying to scream that this is all wrong. Unfortunately, I don't listen to her. She sounds pesky, like a mosquito. I eventually tell her to shut up, even though I have never known a man to bring silk boxers on a date. Or keep them in his car, like jumper cables or a spare tire. I guess if he gets stuck on the side of the road at least he can get comfortable.

"I opened some wine. Would you like some?" He must have brought that, too.

"No, I should probably eat something." I put my hands on my stomach.

"Why don't you just sit a minute? You look so tired, and you must still be cold."

In a moment, I am on the couch and he is all over me. It's not entirely unpleasant, and isn't this what I wanted? I need to get this out of the way and end all of this frustration. Daniel is the first cute guy I have been out with in a long time, and so what if he isn't relationship material? I am a modern woman and all the better that it's casual. I watched Sex and the City. This will help prepare me for my next real prospect.

Now he has his shirt off and my reality has shifted. With clothes on, he is in decent shape. He isn't pregnant, like some of the men at work, but he has the body of a hairless cat or a ten-year-old boy. He has absolutely no hair on his body. I am suddenly repulsed and want him off of me.

His hands have multiplied and he now has lots of them, like an octopus, and they are attached to long gangly arms—isn't there a super hero or a comic book villain like that? Rubber Band Man? My nose rubs against his neck and I almost gag. Do I smell a hint of bug spray in his hair?

"Claire, you're so tense. You need to breathe, Babe. Keep your body relaxed and your mind clear of the mundane, so your inner goddess can be fully present."

"What are you talking about?" I pull away and try to

extricate myself from his many arms, but I actually lose my balance and pull us off the couch onto the floor. A wave of nausea comes over me.

"You need to open up all your chakras and let the pleasure in. Come on, breathe with me and awaken your senses." He starts taking off the boxers and I start to say something—but then I see what he's wearing underneath is even worse than if he wasn't wearing anything.

"Do you have any aromatherapy oil? Let's create a sacred space for our orgasm to unfold." He's now standing with his legs apart, wearing a BLACK LEATHER THONG! His whole body is shaking and he looks like he's having a seizure. I do not want to explain this to the volunteer ambulance crew.

My inebriation is clearing up now as I stare at Daniel, in shock. I clearly missed some important details in our earlier conversation if he thinks I am on board with—whatever this is. While I'm wishing I could make him disappear, Dixie runs into the room, growling and on a mission. Whatever he's doing must be freaking her out, too.

He manages to dodge her and falls over. Laughing, he says, "I don't think your little doggie should be here for our...sensual experience. Come sit on my lap." He reaches for me and I roll away. I jump up to my feet and stumble as I try to straighten out my clothes. This is when I notice my shirt is off—damn it! While looking around for my top, I start to gag.

"Uh oh, Babe—get to the bathroom quick—no throwing up in here. Bad vibes."

As he continues to dodge a snapping, barking wiener dog, I run to the powder room and throw up everything in my system, and what feels like several internal organs. I stay in the bathroom a few minutes, hoping he'll leave. Dixie is quiet and that's a bit alarming.

"Claire?" He sounds a bit worried now.

"Just a minute." The first words I have uttered in a while come out weak and hoarse.

I swing open the bathroom door and Daniel says, "Oh, you don't look so good."

"Really? I don't look so good?" I catch a glimpse of my

mascara stained face in the hall mirror as I am poking him in the chest with my long red lacquered finger nail. I suddenly remember Dixie. "WHERE IS MY DOG?"

"I put her outside—she was biting me!"

"WHAT? You can't do that! Wiener dogs can't go outside off leash." I open the front door and I thank God she's sitting there waiting for me. So much for assuming she would run away if left outside unattended. She probably wants to get back inside and have round two with Daniel. I let her back in, and go into the living room to find his clothes and car keys. I throw them at him as I pick Dixie up and put her in the bathroom with the door closed, to keep her under control until I get rid of this fool.

"Get out of my house!"

He instinctively puts his hands up to protect his face since I'm pointing at him with my enormous talon. "I thought you were into it. I even blew mini golf to let you win, and I bought you all those drinks. You seemed so eager when I was telling you about tantric sex at the bar! I thought we shared a connection, Claire."

"You asshole! I don't know what you're talking about. I could have beaten you with my eyes closed, and what kind of a whack-job keeps *alternate underwear* in his car!"

"You're crazy. We were having a good time. You shouldn't drink and take off your shirt if you're going to behave like this. You are most definitely not in touch with your spirituality."

As I stand there in my bra (thank God I don't take the bra top concept literally), I push him towards the door and swing it open. "Get out! And if you ever come back here, I will call the police, you bug killing freak!"

As he runs down my front steps in a thong, holding his clothes, his keys, and amazingly enough—the bottle of wine—I look up and see my neighbor across the street standing on his porch staring straight at me. Shit.

CHAPTER SEVEN

"Jane, I am not going over there. You are insane! The flashing episode was bad enough but at least that was an innocent dog walking mishap. Now he has seen me standing in my doorway, in my *bra*, throwing an almost *naked* man out of my house and calling him a bug killing freak!"

"I agree it's not ideal, but you're overreacting. Maybe he didn't hear anything. It was far away and dark out. He may not have put the whole thing together."

"No, he heard and saw everything. Now it is *possible* he was concerned for my well-being and thought there was a domestic disturbance going down, but even if that is the case, that's the *best case scenario*. And to top it all off I feel like total shit."

I woke up about seven this morning and it felt like little men with hammers were pounding the inside of my head. They have not quit working despite drinking a gallon of water and taking four aspirin. It's like they're in the union and they get double time on Saturday. I need to medicate *before* I go to bed. Clearly I have a lot to learn—I will add this to my ever growing list, right after don't bring home strange men and pay for my own fucking food if I'm hungry.

"Claire, I have bought about five pounds of healthy snack foods to bring this man and we are bringing it over there! I can't do this alone. I am a married woman and it will be inappropriate."

"And bringing me will legitimize the whole operation. I couldn't agree more."

"Pleaaaase? We'll just drop the stuff off and go home. It's sunny—you can wear sunglasses without it looking odd. Just please get up and get ready. You'll be glad you did this."

"Alright! I'll go. Give me half an hour to make myself presentable."

"Yay! I will take you to get your car after. I'm assuming it's still at the bar?"

"Shit, yes. I forgot all about that."

"I'm sure it's still there. Meet me outside in thirty minutes. I will even give you forty. Put on lipstick. You aren't *that* hung-over. Now get going!"

Jane's insistence that I meet this guy is so absurd. She's trying to help, but meeting a guy who is a) too young, b) my neighbor, and c) has seen me in various stages of undress not *once* but *twice*, is not going to positively influence my dating life.

I'll pull myself together and go to Lorenzo's tonight to see that band, and focus more on dancing and socializing than drinking. And I'll eat a big meal before I go, in case I decide to drink again—but just a little. When I mix alcohol with an empty stomach I get as sick as an unsupervised four-year-old who finishes off all the booze left in the plastic cups at a family barbecue.

Forty-five minutes later I emerge from my house into the brightest sunlight I have ever seen. It's like I am staring directly into the eye of the sun (if there *is* such a thing as the eye of the sun—I am not good with astronomy).

Jane spots me and starts laughing.

I stick my tongue out at her as I descend the porch steps and meet her in the cul-de-sac. She's carrying a big basket of food. "Shut up...sunglasses aren't even enough for this. I need the goggles OSHA requires for people who work with lasers."

I reach Jane in time to see her rolling her eyes, which don't appear to have any problem adjusting to this blazing illumination.

"Seriously, do you feel any better?" she asks.

"A little bit, but I need to eat something. Let's ring the bell and get this over with, before he sees us standing here having a meeting in the street, like a couple of freaks."

We walk up his porch steps and I ring the bell, since Jane is laden down with heavy organic fruit and nuts.

I still maintain that this is a stupid idea. Can't Mike stop her from doing these things? Or actually, why couldn't *he* come with her? I glance over at her house and see him in his pajama bottoms and no shirt. His hair is sticking up all over the place and he's putting a ladder up to the side of the house. I point towards him. "What the hell is he doing?"

"He's going to try to clean the gutters. I hope he doesn't fall off that ladder. He is so bad at these man chores—"

The door suddenly opens. Before us stands the famous new neighbor. He is even cuter up close, with sandy hair and bright blue eyes (thank God I'm wearing sunglasses—the intensity would knock me over), and a little bit of stubble on an otherwise baby face. He is not that tall, probably only about 5'8", and even up close he has the slim build of a teenager. I am wondering if he is hairless too, but I can see a little bit of fur sticking out of the top of his olive green Henley shirt, which is unbuttoned and loosely revealing a good amount of skin. Grey sweat pants complete his Saturday lounging outfit.

"Hi, ladies," he says pleasantly and leans against the doorframe. Maybe I'm paranoid, but I already see the beginning of an amused grin forming in the corners of his mouth, which is perfect, with full lips and rows of straight white teeth.

Jane takes charge. "Hi there, we're your neighbors. I'm Jane. I live over there." She points to her house and the goofball hanging onto the side of it. "You met my husband, Mike, and this is Claire. She lives across the street with the little wiener dog."

I'm waiting for her to shut up long enough to get a word in, but our new friend beats me to it. "Brandon." He reaches out and shakes Jane's hand first, then mine. His hands are slightly rough, and I shudder at the jolt of masculine energy.

Jane is still standing there smiling while struggling to hold on to the basket, which she finally hands over to Brandon. "Welcome to the neighborhood! We know bachelors don't like to cook or shop." Why is she giggling like a thirteen-year-old girl meeting the new high school varsity football player?

He takes the basket from her and puts it on the floor in the foyer behind him. "Thanks so much, ladies. Everyone has been so friendly, and yes I did have a good chat with Mike while your little ones were playing the other day. I also met a lady up the street—Mrs. O'Brien?"

As if he doesn't already have enough negative information on me, now he was talking to that nosy old bag. They probably discussed how I'm bringing down the property values. He looks at me and I feel the heat rising on my face. Maybe it's just the alcohol poisoning, or the combination of dehydration and starvation.

"Mike told me...he said you were a writer? That's so interesting. Claire works at the publishing—"

Jane is interrupted by a loud crash and subsequent scream. We turn to see Mike sprawled out in the yard with the ladder on top of him.

"MIKE!" Jane runs to his aid while Brandon and I just stare.

"Should we call someone? 911?" he asks.

"No, he's always doing things like this. He needs to hire people to do man jobs!"

Jane yells out, "He's okay! He didn't fall far!" Mike gets up and waves, as he leans forward with his hands on his knees and his head between his legs.

"What was he doing?" Brandon and I wave back to acknowledge that we will call off the ambulance and rescue helicopter.

"Cleaning the gutters. God love him, but he is such a bad handyman. But who am I to talk? My gutters haven't been cleaned in years—there's a little tree growing out of my roof." I point to the spot on my house.

Brandon doesn't seem sure if he should laugh or not. "So...thanks again, for the food. That was nice." He runs his hand through his hair while the other one rests casually in his pocket. I am trying not to stare, but I'm wearing sunglasses so he can't see my eyes. "Jane was saying something about you working in publishing?"

"Yes, I work at Bella Donna Press. We specialize in mostly women's titles in various genres, but of course women can read whatever they want, so I hate that label. I'm in HR though, so I don't have much say about what we put out there. What type of writing do you do?" Stop rambling.

"Literary fiction. I have several self-published novels that have done okay on Amazon. I am still looking for a publisher, though." He smiles expectantly.

"We are looking for some new talent, and I stress the *talent*. I'm embarrassed to say we are publishing some pretty awful stuff lately to stay in the black. If you're interested, I could read some of your work, and submit it to our acquisitions editor for review."

"That would be awesome. Thanks. Did you want to come in and talk about it?" He gestures towards his house beyond the entryway.

"No, thanks. I'm not feeling so well. Why don't you grab your phone and I can give you my contact info at work?"

Brandon looks disappointed but recovers quickly. While he's in the house looking for his phone, I experience another wave of nausea. I *really* need to eat something soon.

He comes back out with his phone, I find mine, and we exchange information. He agrees to send me a manuscript later today, and I promise to read it and pass it on.

"Hey, Claire?" Uh oh. He stops me as I am turning to leave.

I turn back around and take off my sunglasses. "Yes?"

"Never mind...none of my business. Thanks for the food basket, and for this." He holds his phone up as a symbol of my willingness to help his writing career.

"It's my pleasure. I can't wait to read your work." I awkwardly lower my head and make my way down the steps. "Have a good rest of the weekend."

"You too. Stay safe!" He waves the same way he did when he saw me in the yard.

I make it to my house and collapse on the couch. Dixie jumps, runs and spins, like she always does. Stay safe? He wanted to ask me about what happened last night. I wanted to tell him it was nothing, and there is no need to worry about me or the state of the neighborhood, but it's too much to explain and it's mortifying. I don't have any desire to bond with Brandon, or make a bigger fool of myself. I have Justin at work to fill my "young guy crush" humiliation quota. Brandon seems nice enough and he *may* be a good writer. I'll read his manuscript tomorrow, but first I need to eat, take a nap and call Rebecca. I need a night out of pure fun without worrying about men.

Rebecca was "super excited" (her words) that I decided to come out tonight and see the band. I did not join the Meetup group first because it's absurd to do that in order to go to an event at a public place. I figured this would be a good way to scope out the people who go to these things, and get out and do some dancing. I can shake it, too! I told her about my date and as always she assured me that there are normal men in the "real" world, and I need to get out of cyberspace and interact with people.

I was told not to wear high heels because my feet will bleed, but I ordered the hottest shoes last week and the UPS man brought them yesterday. They are four-inch black suede sandals with a two-inch platform. The strap wraps around my ankle and there are two bands of fabric across the front—one is covered with silver glitter and the other with purple. I am wearing them with tight jeans with bling on the pockets, and a lavender cold shoulder top (the style with the shoulder cutouts). It's a short-sleeved bra top from Victoria's Secret (I went crazy shopping online a few weeks ago—just click and pay!). This time I am doing something totally *zany* and not wearing a bra (there is no way to hide the straps with this style). My eyes are extra made up—lined in black with my sparkly purple eye shadow palette from MAC, and my lips are shiny eggplant.

I am feeling much better than I did this morning. I ate soup and some bread, and took a few more aspirin, and I have been loading up on water. I have cut back in the past hour or so because I have a forty-minute drive to this place and I may pee my pants. When I drink the recommended amount of water, I might as well spend my whole day in the bathroom.

Jane also took me back to the bar to get my car. Thank God it was still there and in one piece. I was worried Daniel may have vandalized it after he left my house, but I suppose I sufficiently scared him with my police threats to deter any further incidents.

I *am* slightly wobbly in the shoes, but I've been practicing walking all over the house. I am shocked because I can normally *jog* in heels. Maybe not jog, but certainly *walk*, even briskly. I have always prided myself on the durability of my feet. When I was in college I worked in a shoe store, and I stood on my feet for hours in spike heels and never had a problem. Ironically, I was forced to listen to women telling me about their bunions and flat arches—all day every day. I don't know where these women come from. I was taught that shoes need to look good and match your outfit. Comfort is for men, toddlers learning to walk and the disabled. Therefore it's a bit disconcerting that I am not entirely stable in these fabulous shoes.

A quick trip to the mailbox would be a good idea to see how hard it will be to walk in the parking lot. I feel the urge to grab on to things as I make my way to the front door. Lately I have been lazy and opting for more comfortable shoes, but tonight I want to feel young and sexy. No one needs to know I'm infertile and pre-menopausal. I hold onto the front porch railing as I make my way to the driveway, since stairs pose their own challenges. I am so tall! I must be 5'10" in these shoes. No shrimpy men are going to bother me tonight. Oww—damn it! I almost twisted my ankle on the last step. Hopefully there won't be any at Lorenzo's.

The driveway is sloped but I am handling it like a pro— look Mom no hands! These shoes have *some* ankle support. They're almost like stiletto hiking boots. Who is that talking a few houses up the street? I squint to see—the sun is going down and my eyesight is not perfect. I can finally make out my neighbor, Joe. He and his wife, Sarah, have four kids ranging in age from two to ten. It makes me tired just thinking about it, but the little girl is adorable. She comes over to my yard sometimes when Dixie is out, dressed in her snow boots and her sister's ballet tutu, pointing and asking to pet my "doogie." Then Sarah sends one of the other kids over to collect her and yells out an apology. She must think I don't want to be bothered by kids since I don't have any, but who can resist the bouncy curls and sweet chestnut eyes? She reminds me of Jackie when she was little, always chatting up the neighbors until my mother called her home.

Joe is talking to Brandon. For a young stud in suburbia, he's certainly making the rounds. I can't imagine what he has in common with any of these men. They're probably talking about lawn mowers, mulch and other things he is unaware of as a new homeowner.

Mesmerized by my thoughts, I don't notice Jane's cat, Butterball, running over to rub himself against my leg, and I'm startled by the contact just enough to lose my balance on these precarious shoes. The same ankle twists and I start to go down, but have the good sense to grab onto the mailbox for support. Except the mailbox isn't stable, since it came loose from the base last year and I never fixed it. So I am hanging on for a split second in safety before it begins pulling me towards the ground. I almost have a chance to right myself but the other shoe has given way now too, and...I'm sprawled out in the yard. Clutching the mailbox to my chest.

Luckily the grass isn't wet, since the sun today could have dried the protected wetlands. What I dread more than anything is being spotted, and the neighbor men running to my rescue. If I am going to fall off my shoes, hugging my mailbox, onto my *own* lawn, I would like to do it in private, thank you very much!

I dare to sit up and peek over at the guys, and unbelievably they are still yapping away and have not even noticed me. I am guessing Joe is trying to keep an eye on his brood while Brandon's back is to me. They appear to be engrossed in all the home repair talk—plus it's baseball season! Men are oblivious to everything when they're talking about sports and hardware. Hopefully none of the kids will take a header off a bike or bash skulls on the trampoline.

CHAPTER EIGHT

There were no bars in strip malls in New York—at least not that I remember in northern Westchester County. They also don't sell fried chicken at gas stations, as they do here. However, when I make these comparisons I am also reminded that moving here increased our standard of living by a *huge* margin. The quirky differences of life in the South are easy to accept when you consider that you can afford a nice home for the same price as a posh trash can or fancy lean-to in New York.

Lorenzo's is in a grocery store shopping center. My ankle still hurts a bit, but luckily there is ample parking and I whip into a close space and emerge from my car. The band has already started and it sounds like there is a large group assembled on the patio. Lorenzo's is an Italian restaurant, with a semi-enclosed patio area and dance floor. I'm self-conscious now that I'm walking in alone, and I wish I had met Rebecca at her condo and ridden here with her.

I pay my cover charge and scan the room. A bunch of people are dancing and the band is playing a Tom Petty song. I weave through the crowd and make my way to the bar. I shout my drink order to the bartender and hand over my credit card to start a tab. As soon as I get my Bahama Mama, someone pokes me in the side.

"Hey, you made it! Yay!" Rebecca is already a little toasted.

"It looks like a good crowd."

We start the rounds of introductions. It's so loud that I barely catch any names. Maybe when the band takes a break it will be easier to have a conversation. I suddenly feel awkward at this height and wish I had worn something that would let me blend in with the masses.

"Are you going to be okay in those shoes?" Rebecca is yelling so I can hear her over the Billy Squier cover. I was about three years old when this song came out.

"So are we going to dance?"

Before I get this sentence all the way out, the band starts playing "Rebel Yell," and Rebecca drags me out onto the jam-packed dance floor. This is her favorite song so I am obligated to join her. There must be seventy-five people smashed into this little space, so that we have to dance without moving our arms too much, unless we want to give someone a black eye or knock their teeth out. I'm glad there are a lot of people around me. They're forming a human force field that may protect me if I start to wobble or go down in these shoes.

"Hot shoes!" The woman next to me shouts her approval, and points out my footwear to her girlfriends. It is *hot* in here. Whew...uh oh...here comes some weird guy dancing over my way. He seems to view my presence on the dance floor as an open invitation to touch me, as if we are at an orgy instead of an eighties cover band show. Didn't his mother teach him that grabbing random women in the waist area is unacceptable?

I wiggle away from him and move over to the other side of Rebecca, where the shoe admirers are dancing in a group. This is much safer. I let the music infuse me with good memories of being in first grade and hearing this song on the radio. I had no clue what it was about—it sounded like a little girl wanted to stay up past her bedtime and dance with this nice man with the spiky hair. At six that was the only thing I could imagine wanting more of at midnight, except ice cream or another drink of water.

The song is over, but not before I'm grabbed again—this time by a gyrating guy who is unsteady on his feet, even though *his* shoes are flat. I maneuver away and find the closest chair.

"This is fun, right?" A breathless Rebecca follows me to the table.

"Yes, Rebecca. It's great!"

She flings herself into the chair next to me and wipes her forehead with a napkin. Her long, thick hair has grown two sizes from the heat and humidity, so that her look matches the era of the music. She's wearing a short denim mini skirt and a tank top, but comfortable looking shoes.

"So how many of these guys have you dated?" I glance around the room at the array of single middle-aged men.

"Too many. That guy over there (she points to a fairly cute guy holding a beer). Tom, the one going outside to smoke, that guy you were dancing with—"

"You mean the groper?"

"No...yeah...I don't know. Was he groping you? Define groping?"

"He grabbed my waist!"

"Men usually touch you when you're dancing. Unless they grab your ass or more it doesn't count as groping."

"Being on a dance floor should not be an open invitation to be molested."

"Claire, you need to loosen up. Have another drink and just let the music take you away..." Rebecca pulls herself to standing and starts rapidly shaking back and forth to the music. If she isn't careful she is going to need a hip replacement in a few years.

"Hi, Becca! This must be your little friend from work?" A tiny woman has approached the table and is leaning in to shake my hand. It's odd that she would refer to me as "little" because she looks like she needs a booster seat to drive home. "Hi, I'm Sherry!"

"Hi, Sherry. I'm Claire." I shake her doll-sized hand.

Sherry quickly sits down, with bird-like movements. She looks like a kindergartener sitting at the big people's table. "Rebecca told me her friend from work was coming. You look so pretty. I saw you dancing. You're so tall, but so skinny—I hate you—but of course those shoes are huge! I would fall right on my face in those. So are you having fun?"

I proceed to talk with Sherry (actually she is doing most of the talking) about the Meetup group and her divorce—it has been four years and she has two elementary school-aged kids. She is friendly but it is so loud in here, and I'm having a tough time hearing her. In the meantime, Rebecca has brought me at least two more drinks, which I have barely touched. I must interrupt Sherry for a moment, so I can order something to eat. Surely she will have to stop for a breath at some point. A waitress walks by occasionally, but she is serving the one hundred plus people in attendance by herself.

"—and I will not date a man who is not at least six feet tall. And he has to earn at least six figures and I prefer they not have kids at home. If they have to pay child support that cuts into the money they can spend on me. Do you have any kids, Claire?"

When I hear women talk like this I can understand why men can be assholes. *She* has kids at home, I'm betting that her job as a social worker does *not* pay six figures, and why does she need a man who is *that* tall? I am not even six feet tall in these *enormous* heels, and Sherry is like a dwarf compared to me. I may be taller than her on my knees. Does she need a man she can climb?

"Sherry, I'm so hungry and I have to pee. I need to order some food and find the ladies' room."

"Sure, honey. It's right through those doors on the left. The waitress will come back. What do you want if I see her?" She points towards the menu.

I ask Sherry to order me the burger sliders and wander off in search of the ladies' room. My feet hurt a lot now, and it's difficult not to limp. It was nice of her to offer to order my food, but I forgot that meeting new women friends for my "girl posse" is going to involve hearing about divorces, exes and custody battles. Suddenly I'm wishing I had stayed home. I don't want to tell a whole bunch of people why I was married for ten years and I don't have any children. It's also impossible to meet people and have a decent conversation in this environment. I decide that I'll eat my food, check on Rebecca's level of inebriation, and head out.

On the way back to the patio I'm stopped by a guy who looks thrilled to see me.

"Hey, I saw you on the dance floor. Nice moves...I'm Andy, a friend of Rebecca's. You work with her right?" He is still moving to the music in the most awkward white guy way.

I shake Andy's hand and then I remember he is groper number one, and one of the men Rebecca dated. Before I can do more than tell him my name I'm back out on the dance floor. This time the band is playing "867-5309 Jenny" by Tommy Tutone, and Andy's hands are on my waist. I give

THERE ARE NO MEN

in and decide that maybe Rebecca's right. This isn't so bad. After all last night I was groped in my own house and had to tuck and roll to escape rubber tentacles. At least we're in public and I won't let Andy walk me to my car. I learn my lessons slowly, but I have a couple of them down. Don't bring home strange men, especially when blasted drunk. Check! But I still haven't eaten, and that's how I ended up blasted drunk. That was on the new rule list, too. Food before alcohol. But I haven't had much to drink tonight, and my little burgers are probably already waiting for me on the table. I am perfectly sober.

High Fidelity is not a bad band at all, and Andy isn't a bad dancer. The song is coming to an end, and Andy grabs my hand and pulls me into a twirl. My weak ankle wobbles and the velocity of the spin flings me out of Andy's grasp and across the dance floor. If I were wearing normal shoes (like a responsible adult who eats proper meals would wear), I would be able to regain control of my body and stop it from hurling directly towards the band.

The song stops and Andy makes a lunge for me, but it's too late to prevent me from crashing into the guitar player, bouncing off the keyboard, and landing at the feet of the drummer. The sound of the cymbals crashing is the last thing I hear before it all goes silent.

CHAPTER NINE

It's hard to believe that I feel worse than I did the previous morning, but I do. Much worse.

"Claire, don't you have any coffee in this house?" Rebecca is apparently rifling through my kitchen cabinets and making far more racket than is necessary.

I wish I could yell but I can't find my voice. How did I get home? I was talking to Sherry about her dating woes, and then Andy asked me to dance. Uh oh…shit.

"I remember, you don't drink coffee, and you only used to own a coffee maker for when Ron's psycho mom came to visit. Right?" Rebecca pops her head in my bedroom door. "Ooh, you don't look so good."

Wasn't she blasted drunk last night? How does she not get sick? She is almost ten years older than me. "My head is killing me. I remember what happened now. Is anyone going to sue me? Did I go to the hospital? Where's my car?"

"You did make quite a scene. The guitar player said he was happy you don't weigh much more than a mouse or he would have internal injuries. Haha…"

Suddenly I burst into tears.

"Claire honey, I'm sorry. Don't cry. You need to stop wearing shoes you can't stand up in. You could really hurt yourself."

Now I'm bawling.

"Okay, okay…" Rebecca wrings her hands and frowns. She comes over and pats my hand, and reaches for the tissue box on the nightstand. Dixie comes running into the room and tries to jump up on the bed. All I see is her little head appearing and disappearing, over and over, as she frantically tries to propel herself up on her short little legs. I reach down and pick up her wiggly little body. She is too excited to see me to settle down.

"Hi, Sweetie. Mommy missed you, too." I let her give me

kisses because at this point I need any comfort I can get.

"Claire—seriously—you need to make better choices."

I am not crazy about receiving a lecture from someone who was already slurring her speech at nine o'clock last night, but she's right—I've been out of control lately.

"You were the one who told me to relax and have another drink so I would enjoy the men feeling me up on the dance floor. Thank God I didn't get drunk on top of sustaining a brain injury."

She sighs and says, "At least it's Sunday. You can rest all day and I'll check on you later. You will probably be a little sore—your head and your shoulder took a beating. There were a couple of nurses there last night, and a volunteer EMT. They checked you out and thought you were okay to go home and sleep it off. But if your head hurts too much we should go to the ER."

"Thanks, Rebecca. I'm sorry I humiliated you in front of your friends."

"You didn't. Maybe next time you can come to an event that is quieter and more casual. Get to meet a few more people. That place was a madhouse. I left you some soup if you're up to eating, and I told Jane to check on you later."

"When did you see her?"

"I took Dixie out this morning and she was taking her son to a soccer game. I also saw a cute young guy across the street. Who's that? He looks familiar."

"That's my new neighbor (why is he always outside?). He's a nice guy. A writer. He was supposed to send me his book to read." Oww. Just trying to sit up in bed hurts every muscle in my body. I feel like an old woman who just survived three rounds with a kangaroo.

"Maybe it'll be Pulitzer Prize winning material, and you can pass it on to Pam. I have to go now. The cats are starving and I'm not exactly the poster girl of wellness either. The drinks are too strong at that place. I hardly ever drink like that."

"Where the hell is my car?"

"In the driveway. Andy was already giving Sherry a ride home—they both live closer to this side of town and they carpool a lot. The three of us drove the three cars, and they drove home in Andy's car, so I could stay with you and we could avoid the trip of shame to Lorenzo's to retrieve your car this morning. I didn't think you would be up for that." She smiles and pets Dixie, who has now settled down to sleep on me.

"I need to send them a fruit basket or flowers or something. That was so nice of them. Wait, are they dating?"

"Are you kidding? He isn't tall enough for her. I gotta run, Sweetie."

Rebecca leans in to give me a hug and Dixie sneaks in a lick. She wipes the dog slobber off her face.

"Thanks, Rebecca. See you at work tomorrow."

"Feel better, Kiddo. Hey, maybe I should have told the cute guy to check on you later. Hmm...on second thought maybe you should let the color return to your face before you talk to him again."

"Good bye, Rebecca!"

The last thing I plan on doing today is talking to Brandon, but I would like to see if he sent his manuscript. Maybe I can find a new author and have some success at work, since I'm not excelling at my personal life. I reach for my phone and remember I only gave him my work number and e-mail. As I ponder where my Blackberry could be I start to doze off and fall into a deep sleep.

I wake up hours later to the sound of lawnmowers—yes, plural. One of the worst things about living in a suburban neighborhood is the weekend symphony of roaring motors. It sounds like the monster truck show is doing a special performance in the cul-de-sac, except no one jumps over their sheds with the lawnmowers or names them things like "Gravedigger."

I roll over and sit up. Dixie is awake now and I let her down off the bed. My little napping partner is going to need to go outside. I look like hell but I gather my hair up into a sloppy ponytail and pull on a pair of shorts and a t-shirt.

I look around to see if the coast is clear—I don't want to see anyone right now, especially Brandon. I still haven't looked to see if he sent his writing, and I don't want him to see me looking like crap in the middle of the afternoon. I'm sure he heard me coming in late again, and this time with

THERE ARE NO MEN

multiple people.

I don't see anyone other than the men who are mowing, so I head out to the backyard with Dixie. The sun is once again intense, and my pale skin burns under its warmth. It's an amazing sensation and I decide I should shower and come back out—sitting in bed makes everything worse. Some fresh air is in order to get things back on track. Or at least *on* track. I can't go back to where I haven't been yet.

Dixie does her business quickly and we head back inside. I notice the paint is peeling and chipped around the back door. I absolutely must get a handyman to work on some of these home repairs. I remember the mailbox and decide that I can certainly handle hammering a nail or two to secure the mailbox to the base. Not that I plan on using it to break any more embarrassing falls, but it's a good idea to take care of these things. Responsible people who are *on track* have sturdy mailboxes.

Ever since Ron moved out everything has broken in the house, inside and out. Maybe not *everything*, but I have had more than my share of incidents. With all the bad luck, I began to think that my house was built on an ancient burial ground, and somehow my divorce triggered the wrath of the departed souls. After I shower I'm going to fix the damn mailbox. At least it's a start.

I feel better after showering and eating some of the soup Rebecca left for me (I have no idea where it came from because I don't go grocery shopping). I found my Blackberry and checked my business e-mail account. Brandon did send me a manuscript to read. I'm going to get to that tonight. I take Dixie out with me and attach the leash to the tie-out stake in the yard. I bought one of those so she can be outside with me when I'm doing yard work. Since that doesn't happen often this is the first time I've used it. I hammered it into the ground when we had all that rain, so it should be pretty deep and secure. She will love being able to run around the yard a little and sleep in the sun.

I grab my hammer. I found it under my gardening gloves, so that shows how much it gets used, with all the gardening I do. I know I have some nails, too. Yuck, there are so many cobwebs in my garage. When Ron lived here you could perform surgery in the garage, and now I practically need a hazmat suit just to find the few remaining household maintenance items. Now that reminds me of Daniel. Double yuck. I manage to locate a few nails that should work, and head out to do the job.

Now that I'm looking at the mailbox and the base I'm confused. How can I nail the base to the mailbox when the mailbox is metal? I can't drive a nail through metal. How did Ron do this? Why does everything have to be so damn hard? How do women live alone and not have these problems?

I see Brandon walking across the street out of the corner of my eye. Crap.

"Hey, Claire, do you need some help with that?" His big shiny blue eyes are boring holes through me.

"I just want to get the mailbox to stay on the base. It came loose and I don't know how to fix it. You don't need to worry about it—I'll figure it out."

"I don't mind helping you out at all." He looks at the hammer and nails in my hand. "But I think you're missing a few screws."

"That's not nice! I had a bad weekend!" I blurt this out before I remember I don't want Brandon knowing my business. "Why are you laughing?"

"Claire..." He can't stop laughing. "I'm sorry, I didn't mean that *you* have screws loose, like in your head. The mailbox gets secured to the post *with* screws. They came with the mailbox. If it's loose, the screws probably came out and you need new ones. You can't hammer a nail into it."

His smile is making this so much more embarrassing. This man must think I am the biggest idiot in the world. I want to tell him that before he came along my clothes never came off in my yard and I didn't get drunk and bring home strange men. I also graduated from Smith College (that's a good school—all girls—Ron insisted!) with a 3.2 GPA in English Literature, and I have only had sex with one man in my whole life. So there!

Just as I am about to respond Brandon kneels down to receive a little wiener dog into his arms. How did she get free? Another strike against me. Now he can add "irresponsible dog owner" to my list of shortcomings.

"Aww...she's absolutely adorable. My sister has two of these. They're the funniest little dogs." Dixie is doing her Cirque du Soleil moves while Brandon tries to pet her. She has pulled the tie-out stake out of the ground, and has dragged it across the street, along with the leash. She's a strong little thing.

"I can't believe that little whack-job broke free. That thing must not be secure." I know he's thinking—who's the whack-job here?

"I can take a look at it for you. It's hard to get these things screwed into the ground tight enough. I could do this and the mailbox screws. It's the least I can do since you are going to read the manuscript I sent you, right?" He holds onto Dixie tightly while she licks his hands. He must have had something to eat recently.

"Great, you can do all of my screwing." My heart immediately flutters and my cheeks burn upon realizing what I just said.

Brandon is smirking. Why do men always smirk when a woman is squirming?

"That's pretty funny. Seriously, I have to go to Lowe's later. I will pick up the mailbox screws for you, and I'll get Dixie's tie-out stake in the ground safely. You don't want this little cutie getting away." He removes the stake from her leash, and she runs to me.

Dixie is in heaven with all the attention, and her tail is moving like a windshield wiper in a monsoon. "Thanks. I appreciate it. As you can see, I'm clueless with this stuff. And yes, I will read your book. I'm looking forward to it."

"Great. Why don't you take her inside and get some rest? And Claire—everyone gets drunk once in a while or does something silly."

"Silly? I don't know what you're referring to. I don't do silly things." I manage a smile. Am I flirting with Brandon?

"No never...hey, do you ever walk Dixie? Like on the road? In clothes?" He can barely contain his glee over this reference to my unfortunate incident.

"You're just mad it was raining and you couldn't see well." I pick Dixie up and put her on my hip, like a baby.

"Yep, you got me pegged, Claire." Brandon chuckles and nods his head. "But seriously, let me know some time if you want a dog walking partner. The weather is getting nice and I kind of like the walking trail in the neighborhood. Now go inside and read my book. I intend to be a millionaire author and time's a wastin'."

I smile and turn away. I look back as I carry Dixie to the door, and wave to Brandon. He's still standing there by the mailbox, awkwardly holding the tie-out stake. As we retreat to our separate corners, I try to pretend that both of us don't look just a little bit sad.

CHAPTER TEN

I hear a light tap on my office door. I listen more intently. There it is again.

"Come in!"

The door opens a crack and Justin appears in the doorway, holding a folder.

"Hey, Claire. Did you have a good weekend? Uh, you left this in my office last week, and I figured you might need it." He waves the folder like a white flag.

I sit up straighter, as if better posture will erase the memory of his touch and those whispered words. "Hi, Justin. You didn't have to bring that by, but thanks." I am dodging the weekend question.

He tentatively enters the office and hands me the folder. He looks like a cross between a little boy who is afraid of the headmistress at the orphanage and a puppy who wants a belly rub. I'm hoping he'll turn around and go, but he pulls my guest chair a bit further back from my desk and slowly lowers himself into it.

"We also need to talk about that training you're going to host for me."

At least he's keeping it professional.

"Right. The IT Security rollout. When did you want to do that?"

"I sent you an e-mail with the dates and the calendar invites. I just need you to book the rooms for the sessions." He pauses and looks right into my eyes, and I'm aware of the empty space where my hope used to reside. "Claire...?"

"I'll take a look at the e-mail and..." The tears start before I can finish my thought. I am not sobbing, the tears are just rolling down my face, like rain water on a window pane.

"Claire, I don't understand why you're so upset with me. I was a dick to you all the time and embarrassed you, and now when I say I'm sorry and try to be nice, I'm making you cry. I was only trying to tell you you're beautiful." Justin looks so painfully young. When he's talking about software and malicious spyware he looks like a grown man, but when his emotions soften his finely chiseled face, I can see the adorable little boy he once was. He's right—he will have beautiful children.

I take a deep breath to fuel my response. "Justin, it's not your fault. I'm sorry for acting so foolish. It's just not something I want to talk about. You didn't do anything wrong and I'm flattered that you would have any interest in me. But—it's complicated." I reach for a tissue to wipe my face and look away, as if I am fascinated by the guys pruning the bushes across the parking lot.

Justin sighs and says, "If you ever want to talk about it, let me know. I am really not *that* much of a dick. My mother taught me *something*."

The word "mother" starts the tears again and I quickly wipe them away. "I'll get that training set up for you. Please send me a copy of the presentation notes, if you have them."

He rises from his seat and turns to leave.

"And Justin?"

"Yeah."

"You're not a dick."

I smile at him and he slowly lets a grin creep up at the edges of his mouth, and relaxes his shoulders, as if I have given him permission to let things return to normal.

"I could say something obnoxious but I'll let that one go."

I yell, "Out," playfully as he closes the door.

I need to stop letting my emotions show at work. This exchange has only made my neck hurt worse. After all I did fall twice this weekend, and once hard enough to knock myself out cold. I wish I could call Justin back in and let him give me a full body massage right here on my desk, but I need to leave that poor guy alone. I reach for my cell phone and dial my massage therapist's number.

Julie's receptionist kindly informs me that she has a cancelation tonight. I readily accept and she takes down my information. I hang up with a more optimistic attitude. An appointment with Julie in the same week is a blessing, so same *day* availability is a freakin' miracle.

I open up Outlook and my calendar pops up. Even though I will not forget I have this appointment, my superb organizational skills dictate that I must record it. Unlike Rebecca, I only record actual business and personal appointments. She has invited me to "Remind me to Show You My Cruise Brochures—You're Going!" No, I'm not, I say out loud to no one. I am afraid of water, I can't swim, and the idea of being on a huge boat in the middle of the *ocean* is not even something I will consider. I get nervous at the car wash and repeatedly check to make sure the windows are closed.

I enter my appointment and then I notice the thing that I wish I had forgotten. I have my yearly exam with my gynecologist today. Awesome. So now I can get felt up by two professionals today, Julie and Dr. Mason. One is definitely more pleasurable than the other, and I guess paid, clinical touching is all I'm going to get right now. At least I won't cry, fall down, or end up with a hangover today.

Dr. Mason is the rock star of gynecologists in Richmond. Not only is he a superb physician and a highly skilled surgeon, his bedside manner is off the charts (he is also fairly young and attractive, as far as doctors go). He was genuinely compassionate when I had my hysterectomy, and during every one of my miscarriage ordeals. I wish I could say the same for my husband. Mrs. Mason is a lucky woman. Because of his extreme popularity, he's a busy man. Similar to Julie, if I miss this appointment I won't get another one for a month.

An hour later, I take the elevator up to the 2nd floor of the hospital, where all the doctor's offices are located. Dr. Mason is a partner in a large practice—they must have twelve or more doctors, and an unbelievable array of nurses and support staff. I am ushered into the office, checked in and sitting in the comfortable, yet stark, waiting room in a matter of minutes. Although I love Dr. Mason, I hate his waiting room. It's reminds me of bad things. I wish I could wait in my car and be taken in through a back entrance, like a celebrity or someone with a highly infectious disease.

I should be getting over this by now, but seeing

pregnant women makes me physically ill. I can avoid them out in the world, but in here their maternity smacks me in the face like ice pellets in a Nor'easter. Why are these women able to give their husbands children? Fulfill their destiny? And all sorts of women who have zero education, money or the ability to care for a child have no problem getting pregnant. There are tons of fantastic couples on long waiting lists to adopt the babies of these super breeders, who often keep the children and do an abysmal job at parenting. I wish the stork brought babies.

I pick up a People magazine (my one indulgence at the doctor's office and hairdresser's), and start flipping through the pages to take my mind off my problems. Of course this is the celebrity baby issue—pages and pages of babies and gorgeous women with baby bumps. The worst is the couples—the radiant little mothers with the proud fathers. Thankfully, I am interrupted.

"Hey, Claire?" A woman I instantly recognize sits down next to me.

"Hi, Roberta. How are you?" We exchange awkward hugs in our waiting room chairs. Roberta is the wife of Ron's best friend, Jeff. They met playing softball years ago, and Roberta and I used to watch them play game after game, cheering our boys on. It was a fun time, before I tried to get pregnant, and she was always nice to me. I haven't seen them since the divorce.

"I'm doing great. Both of the boys are in high school now. Jeff is pretty busy at the car dealership—people are finally starting to buy again, thank goodness. And I'm getting my dog sitting business off the ground."

"I have a dog now. A little wiener dog. Give me your card—I'll keep you in mind."

Roberta rifles through her purse and comes up with a card with the cartoon drawings of several breeds of dogs, and of course one looks like Dixie. Wiener dogs are so popular. "Here you go, thanks. So what's new with you? Have you met anybody new?" My favorite question again.

"I've met lots of men, but let's just say they have all fallen short of the mark so far." I smile as I always do when married people ask this question. Plus I don't want anything negative getting back to Ron.

"Have you talked to Ron lately? I guess you wouldn't. I keep forgetting that when you have no children there is nothing to keep you in touch with an ex."

I wince at this and she notices. "I'm sorry, Honey. I forgot." She pats my hand and quickly shifts gears. "Ron has this new girlfriend. Not so new—it's been like six months or so. I swear she's a mail order bride."

"What? Why would you think that?" I look at her like she's on drugs.

"She's Russian for starters. She doesn't seem to work anywhere. She isn't forthcoming about her background and she says they met online." She does the air quotation marks so I will understand how rare and unusual it is to meet someone this way. Roberta has obviously seen the movie "Lars and the Real Girl," where the main character orders a blow up doll online and pretends she's his new girlfriend from Russia.

"I see. But you have met her and she's a real person?" I do want to rule out Ron having a new mental illness.

"Well yes…," she says slowly. "She's a real person, but not like you and me."

I wish they would call my name now. I don't want to talk about Ron, and this woman is so sheltered. I don't care if she's married, has she been living under a rock? People still come to this country from *other* places, and *millions* of people are meeting "online." She probably can't even use her e-mail. Good thing dog walking doesn't require any skills.

"As long as he's happy." I force a smile.

"Yes, you're right. Of course. I just think our Ronnie could do better."

"Claire Ratzenberger?" Mercifully the nurse assistant is calling me.

"That's me, gotta go. It was nice talking to you, Roberta. Say hi to Jeff."

As I gather my things to go, she says, "You kept Ron's name?" I pretend I don't hear her and disappear into the exam room area.

The young assistant asks me the usual questions, takes my blood pressure, and records my weight. Even though it's been two years, she's still asking the date of my last period. My age is probably throwing her—most of their post-hysterectomy patients are much older. I don't blame her. I just wish they would highlight this fact on my chart so I can avoid this question every year.

She ushers me into the exam room, which is below zero, as always. She apologizes for the arctic chill, and points out the little space heater they have provided. They never get the temperature right in these rooms. It's warmer outside. They could set up tents in the parking lot and it would be more comfortable, since women sit naked in these rooms in paper robes. They aren't going to be hanging any meat or preserving dead bodies in here, so they could turn up the heat. My mother would say it has something to do with Obamacare.

I do my obligatory undressing, put the robe on and drape the white paper over my legs, as if the sight of my legs is going to be so inappropriate for the doctor to see, when in a few minutes he will have his whole hand inside of me.

I wish I hadn't run into Roberta. Why do people assume I want to hear about Ron? I guess seeing me is awkward and she doesn't know what to talk about. She never called me after we split up, but I get it. He got custody of those friends, and she shouldn't feel guilty. I can't help but wonder about his new woman. Maybe he did try to find someone who would be more compliant under his regime. The only way he ordered a mail order bride is if they were free. She must do something to make money. The last thing Ron would want is a dependent.

A knock at the door derails my thought train. "Come in!" This is the 2nd time I have said this today, and a little piece of me wishes it was Justin at the door.

"Hi, Claire. Here for the annual fun and games?" He says this every time. Dr. Mason shakes my hand and sits down in his chair, and whips out his computer.

I smile and say, "Yep, I really have no choice."

"So let's see—your weight is down. How is your appetite?"

"I guess I haven't been eating a whole lot."

He peers at me over the top of his reading glasses. "A

84

healthy diet is important. I also received your lab work and your cholesterol is high."

He goes on to explain all the different numbers, and basically they amount to the fact that I am a heart attack waiting to happen, even though I am roughly the size of a large sparrow.

"Thin people can have high cholesterol, too. Your blood pressure is good, though. Claire, you need to take better care of yourself. Are you exercising?"

"No, not really. I know I should." I hate being shamed by my doctor.

"You need to find some activities that you like doing— that's the key. I'm assuming there have been no further issues resulting from the hysterectomy? My guess is that you're not missing that uterus."

If any other doctor said something like that it would be creepy, but Dr. Mason is so funny. However, he has obviously momentarily forgotten my situation—most of his hysterectomy patients are much older and happy to kiss their uteruses goodbye.

"No, in some ways I'm glad to be rid of it. It is nice not to have my period anymore."

He reads my mind, or at least my face. "Claire—I am so sorry. My standard hysterectomy joke is probably not appropriate in this case. I must be getting senile."

"It's okay."

"No. It's not. It was unprofessional and I'm sorry. How are you doing with everything? Are you recovering emotionally?"

"I'm getting better. Staying busy."

He can obviously tell I don't want to talk about this. "Based on your blood work it doesn't look like you have any menopausal signs, and since I left your ovaries you should have a number of years before that happens."

"So I won't be turning into a man any time soon?"

Dr. Mason laughs, and we steer the conversation towards lighter subjects, as his nurse Melanie comes in. That indicates it is time for the exam to begin. Dr. Mason proceeds to go through the "fun and games," which I barely notice as he and Melanie chatter away about all sorts of topics.

"Claire, have there been any new sexual partners? If so, I will check for STDs."

"Uh, no, that won't be necessary." I wish I could explain how elusive that has become, and I swear Melanie is giving me a sympathetic look.

He asks about my bruised shoulder (my hair covers my bruised head) and I tell him I had a bad fall, but it looks worse than it is. He looks worried, and tells me to have it checked out if the pain lingers.

"All finished. Melanie has some information for you on diet and exercise to combat the cholesterol problem. I would rather tackle it that way before we put you on medication. You're young and healthy, and you've just been letting yourself fall into some bad habits. Let's get you back on track."

I thank him and he's off to the next patient.

Melanie is sticking around. She usually leaves too, and I meet her out front to get any information or prescriptions.

"Claire, I have the perfect guy for you."

I am a bit blindsided by this unexpected announcement.

"Uh, really? That's great." I am trying to pretend that it isn't weird to get a hook up from your gynecologist's nurse while sitting virtually naked on the examining table.

"Yes, a doctor I used to work for. Dr. Mason knows him too. Super nice guy. Never married, in his early forties. You two would hit it off!"

"Why would a doctor need dating help?" And why do people assume that any two single people would "hit it off?"

"It's hard for doctors. They often only meet nurses and patients with their busy schedules. It's unethical to date patients," I would also say the same for nurses acting as pimps, "and a lot of the nurses are old, fat married ladies like me." She chuckles at her little joke.

"I guess you can give him my number. It's on the chart." I only agree to get Melanie out of here so I can get dressed and back to work. I can always ignore the call.

"I'll do that. I hope you like him. Now get dressed and I'll drop off your paperwork at the front desk. Bye, Honey."

She's out the door and so am I in the next five minutes.

As I am riding down in the elevator, I realize she didn't even tell me his name.

CHAPTER ELEVEN

Back at work and fully clothed, I begin to work on Justin's training project. I send him a pleasant e-mail about the logistics and I forward the Outlook invitation to all employees. Justin replies with an equally cordial thank you and attaches the slides for the presentation. My stress level is reduced now that I have that situation under control. We are both pretending we never had any inappropriate emotional conversations in the office.

I do find myself daydreaming a bit about his firm hands and that crestfallen look in his eyes, when Rebecca comes barreling in my office.

"So how did it go at the doctor's? All your organs still in the right places?" I made the mistake of telling her that Dr. Mason said he has post-hysterectomy patients who are afraid their ovaries are floating aimlessly around their bodies once they are not attached to the uterus, as if they could get stuck under an armpit. She enjoyed that story.

"Yes, everything is in place. Thank you for your concern. So what's been going on here?" I don't want to tell her about my cholesterol—she will yell at me.

"Not much. I saw Justin. He looks like someone killed his puppy. One of his super models must have rejected him."

"I didn't notice. I am desperately trying to find editor candidates."

"Yeah, I don't envy you that one. I was involved in a dispute all morning over Paul's display of a crucifix in his cubicle. Apparently people are complaining that it's offensive."

"We are producing porn and now people are mad about Jesus. I say with all the filth we have around here, it probably wouldn't hurt to have the Lord watching over us to balance things out."

"Speaking of which, are you going to your parents' for

Easter?"

"Yeah, are you sure you don't want to come? My mother will make a big ham and my father will have tons of wine selection."

"Absolutely. I use holidays like this to catch up on my reading and napping, and Saturday night I have a date with a guy I met at the St. Patrick's Day thing. He is only forty-two so that makes me something cougarish—maybe a Lynx or an Ocelot."

"Absolutely, one of those. You'll have to tell me all about it. Oops, I'm going to be late for my massage."

"Okay, but we still need to talk about that cruise!"

I shoo her out, promising we'll talk about it tomorrow, and lock up my office. I hope she has better luck with her date than I've been having lately. I'm planning a low key weekend with a night in on Friday for a movie marathon ("My Cousin Vinny," "Love & Other Drugs," and my all-time favorite, "Jerry Maguire"), Saturday night dinner with Jane and Mike, and a nice Easter dinner with my parents.

I'm in a great mood as I stroll into Julie's office, ready to let her expert fingers release my tension. Her receptionist is gone for the day, so I sit down and wait for her to come out to the waiting room. I'm enjoying the soothing nature sounds—birds, water flowing, and the candle scent. Is that lilac or lavender?

"Hi, Claire. I'm so glad I had a session available for you." Julie is tall—probably almost six feet, and has huge hands. I would be a useless massage therapist. I am only powerful enough to massage small mammals (Dixie would give me two paws up). Julie also speaks softly—barely above a whisper. I wonder if she's this way at home, or if she turns back into a normal person and yells at her kids to clean their rooms.

"Me, too. My neck is incredibly tense, and I had a bad fall this weekend."

"You hold all your stress in your neck and shoulder area. Are you sure you didn't sprain anything? You need to practice relaxation techniques on a regular basis. Have you done any meditation lately?"

This reminds me of Daniel, and I would prefer to get that

image out of my head before I go into my massage trance.

"No, I'm just a little bruised on my shoulder and head. And I haven't been meditating. I've been busy with a lot of work stress." That's sort of true.

"Why don't you get undressed and under the sheet now. Take your time and I'll come back soon."

Julie tiptoes out of the room. I get undressed and focus on serene thoughts. Work is going smoothly. Justin is going to let things be. Never mind, images of Justin increase my heart rate. Let's see, Dixie is sweet and I have a nice family. Hopefully Brandon's book will be good. I didn't start to read it yet (I fell asleep early on Sunday after my tumultuous weekend), and that is causing some anxiety so I let it go. I get under the sheets and lay face up with my head in the neck cradle. I barely hear Julie's knock at the door. "Come in." I don't yell it out this time. In this environment everything is turned down a few decibels.

Julie asks if I am warm enough, and begins working her magic, as I drift off again, listening to the soft flute music and breathing in the faint scent of jasmine and vanilla. As Julie's fingers press into my weary muscles, Justin and Brandon both drift into my dreamy consciousness. Justin is the taller and more masculine of the two. He has a strong jaw and his hair is more golden. Plus he has eyes the exact the color of emeralds or lush green grass after a rainy season.

Mmm...I feel Julie's hands and I momentarily forget where I am, and begin to slowly imagine substituting her touch for Justin's.

Just as I am settling into that warm sensation I see Brandon's face with the stubble on his chin, his lazy grin and his boyish hips. Mmm...did I even look at his hips? His hair is sandier, and he is smaller than Justin in height and stature, but with brilliant eyes the color of the ocean viewed from the sky or perfectly ripened blueberries. His hands were firm and a little rough, and there was that little bit of chest hair peeking out of his shirt. Ahhh...

Just as Justin's hands begin to fade into Brandon's my spell is interrupted by a loud motorized noise outside. I jump and Julie immediately tries to steady me on the table.

"I'm so sorry, Claire. That was a loud truck. I never get

noise like that in this room. Try to relax and put your head back down. It's time to turn over."

I silently obey and nod. That scared the crap out of me and my heart is pounding. Is the startling noise responsible for my rapid heartbeat? Or the two young men competing for attention in my fantasy?

CHAPTER TWELVE

Monday night I went home feeling much better physically, but even more confused. There's nothing wrong with a good fantasy that involves hot young men touching me, but why those men? It could be plain old sexual frustration, but my mind doesn't usually wander to thoughts like this, and it wasn't purely sexual, or sexual at all. It was more comforting, which is weird. And why both of them? It's so silly because not only are Brandon and Justin too young and wildly inappropriate for me (a neighbor and a co-worker), they are not even my type.

It's hard to believe I have a type since I have veered so far away from any one type by dating old men and whack-jobs, but I do. Or I did. Ron was my type, at least physically. When I met him, I was too young to know any better, and I was lured by his strength and masculinity. He was broad, tall and dark. Blond men have always seemed youthful to me—almost childlike. They aren't masculine enough. I don't want a guy who is prettier than me. Light eyes are all wrong, too. I have always preferred soulful brown eyes.

Now, of course Justin is pretty big and Brandon has that hair peeking out of his shirt, and logically they are grown men. Losing my ability to have children has skewed my whole world. I don't know who is in my dating pool, and I'm drowning in all of them. Older men often have grown children, but I'm never attracted to them and we have nothing in common. Many younger middle-aged men are more attractive to me but they usually have kids at home, and I don't want to be a stepmother. Everyone hates their stepmothers. Ron wanted to throw his father's wife down the stairs. Younger men will want children, maybe even if they already have them. If they do have them it will seem like a million years until the kids are grown, and they don't have daily contact with their exes about custody, visitation and money anymore. It isn't that I would be angry that they had less to spend on me—it's just that all of this causes tremendous conflict.

Some days I think I might be better off joining a convent. I could get away from my men *and* work troubles. But I don't like church, I swear too much, and I have improper fantasy thoughts about young men while being massaged by a woman, *and* to top it off—I'm divorced. Bad nun material.

It's lunchtime on Tuesday, and I go home to bring Dixie to the vet. She's due for a couple of shots, and I gave her sedatives before I left for work. Yes, Dixie suffers from extreme "veterinary phobia." It's ridiculous that this is an actual disorder, as if any dog loves to go to the vet and get stabbed with needles and have things stuck up their butts. After a few unfortunate incidents I was told she had to be sedated before they would treat her. I don't see how they can't control a nine-pound dog, but it does make it easier and less stressful for her to be woozy when she goes in.

I come in and pick her up and she looks so cute and sleepy. I take her outside first, and she walks around the yard like a little drunk on a Friday night (just like Mommy!), but finally waters the lawn. As I get her seat in the car, I see Brandon walking my way. It must be nice not having a real job and being home at lunch time every day.

"Hey, Claire. What's up?" He has that stubble on his face again. Doesn't he own a razor?

"Hi, Brandon. I'm taking Dixie to the vet. For some shots."

"Aww, look at her in there." Brandon bends down to look in the car at Dixie in her car seat. "She looks so tired." I am staring at his chin and it takes me a moment to respond.

"I have to drug her. She is scared to death of the vet."

"That's funny. Does she bite him?" He laughs at the suggestion of little Dixie being fierce.

"Let's just say she's not happy there and she shows her displeasure. She's a little angel when she's all sleepy like this." I smile back and continue to stare like an idiot. He should never shave.

"I can see you're on your way out. I just wanted to ask if you'd like to come to my party. It's kind of a birthday/get to know the new neighbors party." He smiles. His parents must have spent a fortune on his teeth. I can't decide if his teeth or eyes are brighter.

"It's your birthday?" What an intelligent question, Claire.

"Yep, the big 2-8! At least I'm not thirty yet." He blushes and looks down momentarily because he obviously realizes that I am in the unfortunate over thirty group. "I'm inviting the neighbors, a bunch of friends, and the people in the band."

What band? "That sounds good."

"So here's an invite I printed up. I also wanted to send out messages about the party. Can I add you to the e-mail list? I only have your work e-mail." He hands me the invitation and grabs his phone in anticipation of the information.

I give him my personal e-mail and phone number, and he stores them in his phone.

"And can I have Jane and Mike's too? I haven't been able to connect with them."

I'm deflated. I know he wasn't asking for my personal contact information for any reason other than the party, but it makes me a little sad. But Brandon is way too young for me, and now he may be in a band? He probably has groupies, especially with that amazing facial hair. To him I'm just the quirky neighbor lady with the cute dog. I give him Jane's contact information and stuff the invitation in my purse.

"I really hope you can come. It should be a lot of fun." Brandon's hands are in his pockets and he looks down at the ground, playing with a stick with his foot.

"We'll all make it, thanks. I need to get going. See ya later."

I climb in the car and close the door. He leans down by the car window. Before he says anything I add, "I've started reading your book. It's good. I'll send you some feedback soon, I promise." I smile and back down the driveway. Out of the rearview mirror I see Brandon watching my car until it's out of view.

Of course—he wants to know if I read his book. I keep forgetting that I have that power over him. I could pass his manuscript along to important people who can help his career. That's his interest in me. Duh. Claire, get your head on straight!

Later on, Dixie is home sleeping off her traumatic afternoon, and I'm back in the office. I sit down and open up Brandon's book. I have not started reading it—I lied. I hope it is good or I'll feel pretty silly.

I e-mailed Tim and Frank, and scheduled a meeting with them to explain my strategy for the editor positions. Tim is still on vacation—in Las Vegas. Nothing says holy week pilgrimage like a jaunt to Sin City! He is either not Catholic or didn't grow up with a mother like mine. The guilt was laid on extra thick the week leading up to Easter. "Claire, you're going out partying when Jesus was nailed to the cross?" How do you argue with that?

I have some quiet time so this is a good opportunity to delve into this story and see if Brandon has anything to offer. He did look cute today with his birthday party invitations in his hand, like a little boy. About fifty pages in, I hear a quick tap on my door and Rebecca is in my office.

"Hey, what's going on? I'm so bored. Any new gossip around here?" Her eyes are huge with anticipation.

I tell her how stressed out I am over filling these editor positions.

"It isn't just because of your own discomfort with these books?" She shifts in her seat and leans forward.

"What? No." She's staring at me and I cave. "Okay, yes! I hate these books and I don't want to talk about sex with Frank and Tim. This was never in my job description!"

"Claire, we are not the moral police. You need to stop being such a prude. These books fill a need and a desire in society—*mainstream* society, Claire. My *mother* reads them. Not everyone comes from a sheltered, conservative background. Yes, they are not high level literary works, but they sell. There is a place for every genre in the publishing world."

My lips are pursed and my glare tells her that I am not going to respond to her speech.

"I have no choice but to deal with this, but I don't have to like it." I pause and continue, "I am also going to find out who works at our competitors and maybe steal an editor away from them. We need to generate more candidates."

"That's a good idea, but just remember you can't let your own sexual frustration and fears skew your professional judgment."

"Thank you for the lecture, but it isn't my *sex life* causing the problems." I roll my eyes and sigh. "Between you and me, I hope I can find a woman for this job." I regret those words as soon as they leave my lips.

"That's because you're afraid of talking to men about sex? Wait, where's my socket wrench? You're looking a little constricted again." She tilts her head and folds her arms across her chest.

"Don't hold back, Rebecca. Just tell me what you really think!" She can be so infuriating. "It *is* true—I am not a sexually experienced woman and this whole thing is *freaking me out*. It's bad enough I'm dealing with this crap in my personal life—I had a strange man in a leather thong in my living room! Is it too much to ask for work to be boring and sex free?" I rub my temples and roll my neck muscles to ease the tension. "So yes, I guess I need a socket wrench!"

"I'm sorry, I didn't mean to be so harsh. I just hate to see you struggle so much. You're making a big deal out of nothing. Maybe once you demystify sex with other men you will see that you are overreacting on both fronts." She looks at me hopefully.

"Maybe so, but I am more comfortable with a woman in this role. I know admitting that puts me in violation of HR policy, even though brandishing a whip at your co-worker is apparently acceptable."

"So dramatic!" Rebecca puts one hand on her heart and the other across her forehead, like a modern day Scarlett O'Hara.

I stick my tongue out at her and sigh. "Maybe if I can get Pam to pick up Brandon's book we can have something more enticing—in a *professional* way—to dangle in front of the new editor, after she finishes with the smut."

"Who's Brandon?"

"My neighbor. Remember? He gave me his manuscript to read? I started reading it just now. I'm not too far in but it's well written. Odd topic though."

"He looked familiar. I've seen him someplace before.

What's the book about?" Rebecca looks around my desk and adds, "Where are all your treats? No donuts? Cookies?"

"I can't eat that stuff anymore. The doctor says I'm a ticking time bomb. But never mind that. The book is about adoption."

"Like adopting *children*? Is it fiction?"

"Yes. It's about a family who adopts a baby but the birth mother wants an open adoption. I guess that's common now. Isn't that scary? Can you imagine adopting a baby and you have to let the mother see the child? And then sometimes they come back and sue to reclaim custody. I've seen that in the news."

"Is that what his book is about?"

"I don't know yet, but it will be a difficult read for me if that happens."

"Yeah, I can see why." She pauses and looks at me tentatively.

"What?"

"Claire, have you ever thought about adoption?" She blurts this out and looks away slightly.

"No, and I don't even want to talk about it. There are so many ways that can go wrong. I couldn't even get up the guts to adopt a *dog*. And besides, I would have to be married, and for a certain number of years." I start aimlessly moving papers around on my desk. "Let's talk about something else."

"How was your massage?" She folds her hands in her lap and forces a cheerful expression.

My mind wanders back to my fantasy. Hmm... "It was good. Yep, Julie has the magic touch."

"Good. I need to get back to work. I have about a hundred self-evaluations to read, but I don't have yours yet." She folds her arms and tightens her lips, but with a whimsical grin.

"Damn it, that's another thing I need to do. I'll get it done by Friday."

"I'll cut you some slack as a fellow single gal. Have fun tonight!"

"Tonight?" What did I forget now?

"Didn't you tell me you were having dinner with Audra

and Rachel downtown?"

"Crap, yes! Thank you. I need to check my e-mail and see where I'm supposed to meet them."

"Claire, you need more than a massage. You need a vacation. I could show you those cruise brochures." Rebecca smiles optimistically. I feel sorry that I don't want to go with her, but I would have to take a whole bottle of Dixie's sedatives every day if I went on a cruise ship in the middle of the ocean. I wonder where Rebecca has seen Brandon.

CHAPTER THIRTEEN

I'm meeting Audra and Rachel at Cous Cous, which is downtown by the river, on a cobblestone street. On the weekend nights they feature dancing girls and the bartenders perform flaming tricks. The music is thumping and the crowd is barely legal, but during the week they offer abundant Mediterranean food and a unique atmosphere, with jewel toned draperies and linens, and dark wood furnishings.

They're already there when I arrive, enjoying a glass of wine and sitting on the deck. It is unseasonably warm, and I give silent thanks that it isn't raining.

"Hi, ladies! It is so good to see you both!"

We proceed to give hugs and kisses all around. "You look great!" "Love that skirt!" "Did you change your hair color?" "Isn't it a beautiful day?" Back and forth we exchange pleasantries and do the dance of compliments that women perform with their girlfriends.

Audra and Rachel were roommates years ago, when Audra first came over from England. I worked with Rachel when I was newly married. She's a stay at home mom now and Audra is a physics professor at the university.

"So, Claire, how have you been? Any new men on the horizon?" I try not to visibly cringe at Rachel's question. I tell myself that she has to sleep with her husband every night, and while there is nothing wrong with him, she is likely jealous of my thrilling single girl escapades.

I entertain them with the stories of my recent dating debacles—the old man with the hat, the bug killing freak. I even tell them about our new line of books, and how difficult it is to fill the editor's job. I share the Meetup experience and how Rebecca and her friends had to drive me home, but I leave out Brandon and Justin. Matthew's hair falling off kills them. That one is a real crowd pleaser.

They are both laughing hysterically. Audra slaps her leg and throws back her head. "Claire, you kill me. So many 'whack-jobs', as you like to say. I can't even bother trying to date. I never see any men I like. Of course you're a lot younger than me so your prospects are better."

I choke on my water. Did she not hear about the furry thing on my feet?

"Are you alright?" Rachel is such a mother. In a good way. She is my age and has two little children. The boy, William, is four. And I can't remember how old Anna is— maybe almost a year.

"I'm fine. So how are the kids? George? Little Anna must be getting big."

"She's nineteen-months-old now. She's starting to talk, and she and William are so cute together. You should come visit some time. Let me show you their latest picture." She starts scrolling through her phone and stops when she looks up at me. She forces a smile and she squeezes my hand.

I pull it away and fumble with my napkin. So much time has elapsed. I meant to visit when Anna was born, but it was so soon after my hysterectomy I couldn't bring myself to do it. I kept saying I need to get over there, but I put it off.

"I'm sorry, Rachel. I would love to see the kids. Is George still working from home?"

"Yes, but at least he travels a lot. I adore the man, but it drives me crazy having him under foot sometimes."

Why do I feel like I am the only woman who wants a man around? And why does that not improve my odds?

After a delicious meal and easy conversation, we say our goodbyes with promises to get together again soon, even though it will probably be months before we coordinate our schedules and take the initiative.

In my car, I check my phone for messages. Justin called, right after five. "Hey, Claire. I was hoping to catch you before you left the office. I was going to head downtown and wanted to see if you could meet me for a drink at O'Malley's, since I'm not a dick now. Haha…call me."

O'Malley's is two buildings away from Cous Cous, and I am parked in the lot across the street. Maybe he didn't come since I never called him. Who am I kidding? Justin doesn't have a problem finding a drinking companion. My rejection isn't going to send him home from work to a beer and Domino's delivery.

It's already eight o'clock. He must assume I'm snubbing him. I slink down in my seat in case I'm spotted, even though it's dark. I will just send a friendly text and drive home. I will probably have to see him at the office tomorrow, but it's a perfectly reasonable excuse that I had other plans. He just assumes I'm free at the last minute because I'm old and not as attractive as his stable of hot chicks.

"Hi, Justin. Sorry I missed you—had a fun dinner downtown with my girlfriends. Didn't get your message until I was on the road."

No, I don't have to explain when I got the message. I am not obligated to respond to him right away.

"Justin—sorry I missed your call. I was out with some friends and I'm just getting in."

What if he saw my car? He's probably parked in this lot too, if he did come down here. I suck at lying.

"Hey, Justin—just heard your message. You probably already had that drink. I was..."

Oh hell—"Justin—let's just fuck. I know you have a thing for older women, so come on, let's do it."

Before I get to delete that one (obviously I am not sending that—duh!), the knock on my window startles me, and I jump and hit my head on the windshield.

"Oww!" I rub my head and cringe (it's barely healed from my floor diving stunt at Lorenzo's). I turn and hope that it's Audra or Rachel returning a lipstick I left on the table.

"Hey, Justin. What are you doing here?" I try to act pleasantly surprised.

"Did you get my message? Were you wanting to meet up?" He gestures towards O'Malley's. Crap. Now he thinks I didn't call him back, but I decided to show up and hide in my car.

"I did just get it, and I was actually here having dinner with some friends over there." I point to Cous Cous, as if I have forgotten the name.

He looks a bit disappointed. "So, did you want to have a drink?"

"I've had enough wine and I need to get home. I have a new manuscript I'm reading for work, and I took Dixie to the vet today and I need to check on her." I am explaining too much, but my mouth keeps running on like an old fashioned wind up doll with a broken pull cord.

"I just thought it might be fun to hang out outside of work. I'm going to have a beer then. I'm sure some of my buddies are here. See you at the office." He turns to walk away.

"Justin?"

"Yeah?"

"Maybe another time?"

"Sure, Claire." He walks away looking as though he is not expecting another time. I could have just gotten out of the car and gone in there. What is one drink going to hurt? Oww, speaking of hurt. I need to get home and put some ice on my head before it looks like Quasimodo's. Maybe the ice will cool down my thoughts, too.

On the highway my phone beeps with a text. I normally don't text and drive, but I'm curious and won't be home for at least twenty minutes with the bridge construction delays. Good, we're stopped. Uh oh, it's from Justin.

"Claire, is this a joke? Because if it is, it isn't funny."

What is he talking about? I didn't send him a text. I gasp and my heart starts racing. No...!

I frantically scroll back through my sent messages and the last one I composed to Justin went through. This is a nightmare! I must have hit send by accident when I hit my head. I should have known I was tempting fate writing text messages for my own amusement. Can't I just think funny things like normal people? Now what am I going to do?

Traffic is moving again so I can't respond. Now the phone is ringing. He must have realized that I can't text because I'm driving.

I look down and it's only Jane.

"I'm in big trouble."

"What's the matter? I was just calling to see if you're still coming over Saturday night."

"Jane, I did a stupid thing. A bad thing."

"Worse than flashing the neighbor or hurling yourself

into a band?"

I explain the events of the evening, and my costly mistake.

"He'll know you're not serious, right?"

"If I wasn't serious, it would be a sick joke, and that is even worse. Now he probably thinks I'm mocking him or that I think he's a dick again. I'm going to throw up." That big, delicious meal isn't settling so well.

"Calm down. Just explain it was a mistake. You were just being silly. Apologize. What else can you do?"

"I have to get a new job. By tomorrow."

Jane continues to attempt to console me, but to no avail.

"Are you going to call him?"

"I don't want to, but I guess I have to. This is such a mess. I need to get out of town. Too bad I haven't witnessed a mob hit—I could join the witness protection program."

"Right, like Brandon?"

"Don't remind me. He's another one I don't want to deal with."

"What did he do?"

"Nothing. I'm going to throw up and then call Justin. Or maybe throw up before and after."

"Good luck. See ya Saturday."

I'm sweating, my heart is racing, and my stomach is doing flip flops. I feel worse than after doing the Jillian Michaels video, but with none of the slimming and toning benefits. I take a deep breath and dial Justin's number.

It rings many times, and just as I am thankful for being lucky enough to get his voice mail, he answers. "Claire?"

"Hi, Justin. Listen…about that text—"

"Hold on, Claire," he shouts. "I need to walk outside. I can't hear a thing in here." I hear the bar noise as he heads outside. Try not to make this worse, Claire!

"I'm outside. You were saying?" His tone is annoyed and flat.

"Justin, I am so sorry about that text. I got your message and I was trying to figure out what to say, so I wrote a bunch of different messages and kept erasing them. That one was just a little joke to myself. I didn't intend to send it, but then you startled me and—"

"Stop. You clearly don't want to see me outside of work or even at work, and you obviously still think I'm a dick with one thing on my mind. And you were hiding in your car!"

"That's not true. I—"

"You think I don't know what you and Rebecca gossip about with your heads together all over the office? 'There's Justin, the good looking young asshole'."

"Well, a lot of guys—"

"I'm not a lot of guys! You barely know me, and I said I was sorry for all the times I acted like a jerk. But I do NOT have an older woman fetish, and you aren't even old!"

"I wasn't hiding. I just didn't want you to know I was there."

"That's very different, Claire. Seriously?"

"I'm sorry, Justin, but I'm not used to this type of attention from someone like you."

"Fuck! You are so frustrating!" He pauses and I hear him breathe deeply. "Claire, I like you. I am attracted to you, and you're not old. I'd like to get to know you and have some fun. Is that so terrible?" He sounds defeated.

"No, Justin. It's not." I sigh. "I think I may be the dick now."

He's silent for a moment. "Listen, I'm going to go back inside now. Watch that accidental texting. Who knows what you could get yourself wrapped up in." The smile has crept back into his voice, and I can imagine the green eyes shining like jewels in the night on O'Malley's sidewalk.

"Good night, Justin. I really am sorry, and I'll see you at work."

I let out my breath. Whew…now all the stress in my neck that Julie loosened up is back. I wish I could keep a massage therapist on retainer. Maybe I could go out with Justin for fun. I never have any fun. I survive the rest of the ride home without doing any more stupid things, and as I turn into my cul-de-sac I giggle to myself. I'm the dick now.

CHAPTER FOURTEEN

The office is quiet on Good Friday, and Justin is making himself scarce, but maybe he's busy wrapping up the IT audit (or he's still mad at me). Lots of employees take this day off to travel for Easter weekend, do stuff with their kids, or go to church. I am hoping to have an uneventful day in the office followed by a quiet night at home. My mother warned us about Good Friday partying, and since I didn't give up anything for Lent, *and* I have eaten meat on more than half the Fridays (by accident!), I have some penance to do. Plus, I have committed five or six of the seven deadly sins just this month. Yep, still going to hell.

Tim calls from Las Vegas to check in on our editor positions. Clearly, he is having a great time and is not the least bit remorseful about the suffering of our Lord. My mother would be appalled.

"Claire, I got your e-mails. I slipped out of the casino to call you. So how is it going with the editor position?"

I tell Tim more about my phone interviews and I go on to explain my new strategy, which I will put into action on Monday. He says he has accepted the meeting invitation, and he and Frank look forward to my updates when he gets back.

"That sounds like a proactive approach, Claire. Good work. Also, between you and me, the company desperately needs the sales from the new line."

"Yes, of course. I know the sales are important."

"No, I mean if they don't do well in the next quarter we will be facing massive layoffs."

Are things that bad? I go to all the meetings and see all the numbers. Have I been so pre-occupied with my personal life that I've been ignoring a much bigger problem? I see flashes of me living at my parent's house, far from my friends, in a houseful of WW2 history books and Fox News

24/7.

"I didn't realize our situation was so dire. I'll increase my efforts on this project. Also, I have a manuscript from a potential new author." Boy, I hope Brandon's book is still good past page one hundred.

"Really? Any good?"

"Yes, so far. I'm going to pass it on to Pam once I'm done and I've made some notes."

"That's terrific. Heaven knows, acquisitions isn't coming up with a damn thing. I am not crazy about this new line either, but we have to stay in step with the times. Modern women don't get excited over cookbooks anymore, and excitement sells. If we don't do something to salvage our bottom line, we'll be selling comic books. Also have the vending machine people refilled the gum?"

I want to tell him that he is the main consumer of the gum, so there's no inventory problem. Instead I reply, "I'll check with Cecilia."

We say our goodbyes and I start pacing around the office. They will let me go in the first round. I'm late all the time, distracted, and training and recruiting are the last things a company needs in a downturn. Rebecca has the essential HR functions covered. Why couldn't I be the one who is good at settling employee conflicts like a playground monitor or a boxing referee?

I need to be careful about sharing my opinions with other staff. Even my best friend in the office thinks I'm a prude from the dark ages and I am sabotaging the new work, but that's not true. Is it?

I sit down and rub my temples. My neck hurts again. I wish I could massage my own back. The only productive thing I can do now is read Brandon's manuscript. I need to get through it this weekend so I can intelligently report on it by Monday.

Four o'clock rolls around and there is no one in the office. I look out at the parking lot and there are about five cars left, so it's safe to leave for the weekend. I start to shut down my computer when I notice a message from Brandon.

To: Claire McDonald Ratzenberger
From: Brandon Harmon

Re: Book Manuscript

Hi, Claire. Hope you're enjoying the story! Is Dixie all better from her traumatic experience? I haven't seen you around lately—I hope you have a Happy Easter! You should stop by some time if you're around this weekend.

Take care,

Brandon

What the hell does that mean? Stop by? As in walk to his door and ring the bell? Does he want more snack baskets? I decide not to respond, as my texting/e-mailing skills leave something to be desired. I have made an idiot out of myself enough with men lately.

At home on Good Friday evening, I am bored and lonesome. I had pasta for dinner (no meat Mom!). I was going to do my movie marathon tonight, but finishing Brandon's book was more pressing than watching movies I have seen a hundred times. It is quite well written. The story line resonates emotionally. I would never adopt—it's too scary. I need to talk to him about this plot. I wonder why he wrote it.

I pace around the house and pick up Dixie. She is so soft and warm. It's soothing having a little companion. I kiss her tiny head, lay her back down on her blanket and peer out the window.

It's dark and still. Joe and Sarah have company—there are a bunch of cars lining the street in front of their house. Jane is probably working on Easter baskets. Brandon is probably out, but I do see lights on in his upstairs window. I wonder if that's his bedroom. Maybe his mother made him stay home on Good Friday, too. It is still early. I could go over there, but what would I say?

Saturday is spent cleaning the house (it's about time!), shopping for Easter gifts (baskets for Jane's kids, chocolate bunnies for Jackie, a pretty spring floral arrangement for my mother, and wine for my father), and napping (it's raining so no lawn mowers). I'm looking forward to spending a quiet evening at Jane and Mike's house. I have not responded to Brandon's e-mail. I am pretending I left the office before I saw it. I should have done the same with Justin's voice mail the other night.

At seven o'clock I walk across the yard with a bottle of wine and Easter baskets for the kids, Shannon, six, and Joey, eight. Jane is making her famous lasagna and I can already taste it. I knock on the door and see at least two dogs trying to greet me, and three cats milling around, but no people. After a minute Shannon comes to the door.

"Hi, Sweetie, how are you?" Seeing her cute round face and blond curly hair always makes me smile.

"Good." Shannon says this in a sing-song way and shyly gives me a hug. I kneel down to her level to see her toy.

"Which Barbie is that?"

"She's Barbie Fashionista. Isn't she pretty?" Shannon pets the doll's hair and thrusts her forward for my inspection.

"She is gorgeous, just like you." I reach out to tickle her and she runs away. "Mommy, Claire's here!"

Barbie actually looks like a hooker in her hot pink mini dress and stiletto glitter boots, but Shannon's future wardrobe choices are for Jane to deal with. I guess slutty Barbies are more realistic than bride Barbies, and my all-time favorite disappointment machine—Cinderella Barbie!

"I'm in the kitchen!" Jane is frantically running around setting the table and checking on the lasagna.

"Hey, it smells great in here." I give Jane a hug and set the wine on the counter. I spy a delicious looking chocolate cake. I am tempted to ask to have dessert first, but that won't fly in a house with kids, and I don't even want to think about Dr. Mason's warnings.

"Hi, can you put this bread on the table?" Jane's face is flushed.

"Claire bear, how's it goin'?" Mike swoops in for a hug and kisses my cheek. "You haven't been here in ages." He spots the wine on the counter and starts opening it.

"Life has been hectic." I open up the cabinet with the wine glasses and take a few out.

"I know, Babe, Jane has told me a few things." He winks and looks at Jane. She glares back with a look that says, "Not in front of the kids." What has she told him?

I give Jane a look that says, "Really, do you have to tell him everything?" But I get it. When I was married and someone asked me not to tell anyone something, I still told

Ron. They would have to specifically tell me not to tell him.

"Kids, why don't you go upstairs and play. Dinner will be a little while." They run off and the adults sit down in the family room. Mike hands both of us a glass of wine.

"So Claire, the new neighbor is cute, right?" Mike is like a gossipy old woman.

"Yes, he's cute. Lots of people are cute. Lots of dogs are cute, like little Sammy here." I pick up their Pekingese and sit him on my lap. "But Sammy isn't for me and neither is Brandon!"

Jane shoots Mike a nervous look and her eyes dart around the room.

I soften my stance. "I'm sorry, Mike. Honestly, I'm just sexually frustrated. I don't mean to take it out on you." I sit back in my chair and start petting Sammy.

"Jane's not. We've been having sex constantly. Right, Honey?" He looks at her with a devilish grin.

I give Jane a quizzical look.

"We're going to my parent's house in Rochester next week to visit, and we can't have sex there." She blinks hard and tightens her lips. "So we're storing it up."

"I wish I would have known about storing it up. I might still have some in my attic. I hate to ask this, but why can't you have sex in your parents' house? You are over twenty-one and married."

"For one it's too small—" Jane begins.

"Too damn cold. You can't take your clothes off." Mike looks dead serious, but I know him better.

"How do you shower?"

"Painfully. Everyone is sick all the time because the whole town is freezing cold all year round. When we lived there we were sick at least four out of seven days every week." Mike exaggerates a bit.

"Even in April? Never mind, the weather in upstate New York is torture. Ron's sister lived in Syracuse, and one time she called me here on Mother's Day. It was snowing there and we were at the pool." The memory gives me a mock shiver.

"So Claire, you seriously can't find a man to have sex with?"

"Mike!!" Jane looks like she wants to kill him.

"I'm sure I *could*, but I'm debating whether I should try to get into a relationship or just find a guy and get it over with." I stare into my wine glass as if it may contain the answer.

"But why?" Jane is confused in the way long term married women always are when the topic of sex comes up.

"To remove the mystique."

"Yeah, there's a lot of mystique, Jane." Mike is going to get punched in a minute.

She gives him another warning look. "What do you mean?"

"I have only been with Ron. Remember I met him in high—"

"Only one guy, Jane." Mike suffers from attention deficit disorder. Or at least annoying husband disorder.

"Are you a parrot?" She folds her arms and glares at him.

"Don't you already have one of those?" I thought I saw a bird when I walked in. They would have chickens and goats if it wasn't for the zoning laws in the county.

"Yes, but apparently, we have two. Isn't there something you could be doing? Paperwork? Letting the dogs out? Flossing your teeth?" She waves her hand in multiple directions.

"You had sex with other men before Mike (he nods his head in agreement and does not appear to be going anywhere until this conversation ends), and Rebecca must have had a hundred men by now, and I am sure my sister is even in the double digits—"

"Yep, you're all sluts, Jane." The pillow hits Mike right in the face. I knew she wasn't kidding when she asked him to find an activity other than teasing the poor single girl.

"Seriously, why do you want a man?" Jane moves towards him with her hands in strangling position and Mike throws his up in surrender. They are both smirking and he gets up and starts rounding up the dogs.

"Everybody, Mommy is cranky. Let's go outside." Several furry creatures run to the door (*their* dogs obey voice commands *and* can go out off-leash) and follow Mike out the front door, which he leaves wide open. I don't say anything, but I was taught to close doors at all times or you will let in "every bug in the neighborhood."

"Let me help you finish setting the table. So what's new with the kids? Shannon told me she got a gecko?" I saw her outside the other day and she came running over to tell me about her new pet. I had to hide my look of disgust. The one on the TV insurance commercials is cute, but I would not want any actual crawly things in my house. That gives me the willies more than the old man with the hat.

"Yeah, she loves that thing. It's adorable. I let it crawl on me while I watch TV."

Jane should have been a zookeeper.

The table is set. Jane yells "Guys, what does everybody want to drink?"

I'm counting the place settings and getting confused. I am not good at math, but I do know there are five people in this house. So unless one of the dogs has been invited to dinner there is a mystery guest. They're probably trying to set me up with someone again. I hope it isn't the newly divorced guy Mike works with at the hospital—the psychiatrist. If it is I am going to kill Jane. I was looking forward to a man-free weekend and a peaceful dinner. I want to stuff myself with lasagna and chocolate cake without feeling like I'm on another Internet date.

"Hey, is anyone here?"

No. She didn't. Holy crap. She did.

Jane is flustered and comes running to the door. "Yes, we're here. Did you see Mike in the yard? How are you? Claire's here. Surprise!" Jane smiles weakly and looks apologetic.

I shoot her an exasperated look. "Hi, Brandon. Let me take those flowers." I need to do something useful, and he has brought a beautiful Easter floral arrangement.

"Those are so nice. Thank you." Jane gives him a big hug.

He follows me into the kitchen and we hug awkwardly. It's not even a hug. It's more like a weird exchange of arms touching without any destination or purpose. I quickly retreat and busy myself with the salad.

Mike comes back inside with the dog pack, and they

disperse back to their various beds and hiding places. I'm grateful for Mike's presence now, and I hope his nonsense creates a lot of diversion.

"Brandon, my man. Glad you could come. Let me get you some wine." Mike shakes Brandon's hand and slaps him on the back.

Jane and I go back to busying ourselves in the kitchen while Mike escorts Brandon to the dining room and calls the kids down. "Let's go, guys, your mother's got the grub on the table."

In the kitchen I am speechless. I am not going to yell at Jane. She means well and Brandon may be lonely. I could be a little nicer. At least there's chocolate cake.

"What does everyone want to drink? No one ever answers me! Joey, come down here! Shannon, tell your brother to stop playing his game, dinner is ready." Jane is irritated and I don't want to add to it, so I take my wine and head to the table.

"Claire, I have something for you." Shannon is so cute, I immediately smile. She draws pictures for me and makes me silly little things out of toys in her room. One time she gave me a tiny stuffed mouse riding in a matchbox car.

"What do you have, Sweetie?" I bend down and Shannon opens her hand, and before I can even scream in protest a creepy crawly creature has jumped onto my leg, and is making its way up my body. I am horrified, and Shannon and Joey are on the floor screeching in fits of giggles.

"Ahhhhhhhh, get this thing off me. Ahhhhhhhhhhhhhhhhhhhhhhhhhhh!" Running around the house in circles is not going to help because this creature can hold on tight, and I know staying still and removing it would be the better choice. However, I have lost all sense of reason and he's a quick mover.

By now, Mike, Jane and Brandon have obviously come in search of me to find out what's wrong. The two laughing hooligans are enough to help Jane figure it out. "Shannon, did you put Simon on Claire? Claire, stop running, stay still and I'll get him off!"

Now he has moved up my stomach onto my chest. Holy

shit! It's in my shirt! "Ahhh!!!" Simon needs to go, and I don't care if I have to throw him against the wall. He is heading for my bra, and I run away from everyone towards the formal living room and rip off my shirt. I'm doing this on the fly, and I smack right into Brandon, who is running the circular downstairs floor plan like a NASCAR driver in the opposite direction. He grabs me by the arms, pushes me back, and grabs the little freak before he's in my cleavage.

The gecko wriggles out of his hand and hits the floor. It scurries away and now everyone is chasing it down before it ends up in the jaws of a curious dog or cat. I'm left in the living room alone with Brandon, and my face is burning with mortification and perspiration.

He bursts into hysterical fits of laughter. "I'm sorry, but that was hilarious. Now that it's over."

I just glare at him while standing there in my pink lace push up bra (at least I didn't wear my ratty white one). I look at him and his sweet, handsome face (unfortunately he shaved for dinner), I hear the family in the background reuniting their renegade pet with its mischievous owner, and all I can do is silently weep.

"Claire, I'm sorry. Don't cry. I don't particularly like creepy things, either. My cousin had a snake when we were kids—"

"Brandon?"

"Yeah?" He looks worried about what's going to come next.

"Can you find my shirt?" I look down at my feet and fold my arms across my chest.

He glances around the floor, but it isn't in here. Before he walks out into the hall to see if he can find it, he lifts my chin and looks into my eyes. I'm afraid he's going to kiss me, yet I wish he would kiss me (even at night, in Jane's living room, in the front of the house, with the blinds open and the lights on, in my bra). He slowly wipes the tears from each of my eyes, and pulls me into a real hug. "Claire, it's okay. We need to go eat the lasagna before it gets cold."

He takes my hand and leads me out of the room in search of my shirt. As we round the corner Jane is coming towards me with it in hand. "Claire, I am so sorry. I can't believe she did that. I sent her to her room, but now *she's* crying. And the food is getting cold."

I take the shirt and pull it over my head, and run my hands over my messy hair. Brandon is standing there as if he isn't sure what to do next. I motion up the stairs and say, "I don't want that poor little thing to cry. I'll go up and talk to her. We'll be down in a minute."

"Thanks." She gives me a pouty look and says "Brandon, let's eat."

"Coming, Mom." He flashes her a smile and as she turns away he leans down and whispers in my ear, "Nice bra by the way. Is that Victoria's Secret? If so, her secret's out." He laughs again as I punch him in the arm.

"Go get your dinner." I push him towards the dining room. On the stairs I peek down and catch his sparkling blue eyes (maybe I'm wrong about the color). Why is he looking? And catching me looking? I return his smile and turn away to deal with this poor little girl who thinks her friend Claire is mad at her.

We have a peaceful dinner. The food is awesome and the conversation is fun, but safe. Mike and Jane are avoiding any further matchmaking tactics after tonight's episode of "Claire Makes a Fool of Herself." I should call the reality show people and make some money out of this.

We finish up with the delicious chocolate cake. Mike says he's tired and takes the dogs out for their final run of the night. I remember Dixie and my drive to my parents' house tomorrow, so I begin to say my goodbyes. Brandon jumps up and helps clean off the table and put stuff away in the kitchen.

"You guys don't need to do all of that. I've got it from here." Jane leads us out the door. In all the craziness I forgot that I had Easter baskets for the kids. I hid them by the door when I came in, and meant to give them out at dinner. We take a few extra minutes to take care of that, and Shannon and Joey give me hugs, and Shannon says she's sorry again. I accept her sweet apology, and they both trot off with their new treats and treasures.

Mike has brought the dogs in and the house is shut up for the night. Brandon and I are alone on the front porch.

"That went well." Brandon looks at me hopefully for a sign that I am over my embarrassment. His eyes are shining in the moonlight like a lighthouse across the foggy sea.

"Yeah, fantastic. At least this time I wasn't drunk, improperly dressed or making any bad choices. Well, I was improperly dressed, but it was all Simon's fault." I laugh but then remember Brandon has been a witness to many of my mishaps. "I promise I'll behave better at your party and keep all my clothes on the whole time." I cross my heart.

"Don't bother coming then." He pokes my arm. "Hey listen, I got you a little something too, for Easter. It's at home. I was going to bring it over tomorrow before I left for my parents' house. I didn't know I would see you tonight."

"You didn't have to do that. I got your e-mail. I guess that's why you wanted me to stop over?" Oops. I forgot to pretend I didn't see the e-mail. I suck at deception. If I was an abducted spy I would talk if they just pinched me or looked at me sternly.

I am helping him with his book. I keep losing that perspective. That is why he's being so nice to me. Although the shirtless hug and tear wiping is more gratitude than is necessary.

"I wanted to do it. I'm going to run to my house and get it. I'll meet you at your house?" He looks as eager as an excited kindergarten boy who has made a macaroni necklace for his mommy.

"Thanks." I stand on Jane's porch and watch him run across the cul-de-sac. I turn around and see eyes peeking out of the blinds. Seriously? When I was married was I this nosy? Probably.

The culprit spots me and quickly retreats. I text Jane. "Thanks for the lovely dinner and surprise guest (I mean Brandon, not Simon). I will fill you in on any details you weren't able to collect on your spy mission."

She won't respond right away. I find that married people don't care as much about their phones. All the people she wants to be with are in the same house with her.

I sigh wistfully and walk across the lawn. I am going to sit on my porch because the last thing I need is to invite him in. It's awkward waiting here in the dark, and Dixie is going to be flipping out since she will hear me. I will just risk it and clean up the pee later.

Brandon darts back across the cul-de-sac with a gift in hand. "Here you go. I hope you like it." He hands me a pink gift bag with bunnies all over it.

"That's adorable." It's a figurine of a wiener dog dressed as a bunny. It's perfect.

"Do you like it? I ordered it from a website I found that carries wiener dog stuff. I know Dixie's your baby." He sits down in my other porch rocker and leans forward, wringing his hands.

If he only knew how *much* she's my baby. My only chance for a baby. "I love it, Brandon. Thank you so much."

We just sit for a moment in silence. "It's a nice night, isn't it? It really cleared up. I bet it will be sunny tomorrow." He looks like he has more to say.

"It's beautiful. It won't rain on the little girls' Easter dresses." I pause and say, "Brandon, I need to go. I have to get up—"

"I know. Me, too." He jumps up. "You have to drive to Charlottesville, and I have to fight the 95 traffic to see my crazy family. Have a happy Easter, Claire."

I step back. My heart is beating fast. "Good night. Thanks again. Happy Easter. I hope you have a great day with your family."

He's standing on the porch steps as I walk inside. Dixie greets me with the usual shenanigans. I grab her leash and wrestle the wiggle worm into her harness, and head for the back door.

Before I do, I glance out the front door windowpane and see Brandon still looking over at my house, now from his front porch. I wait a moment for him to go inside, and take the little wiener bunny out of my purse. I show it to Dixie, and place it on my mantle.

CHAPTER FIFTEEN

Jane called this morning, and I assured her I was not mad at her and Mike, or Shannon and Simon. I didn't tell her about what transpired in the living room with Brandon, or any of the recent Justin escapades. I'm telling myself she doesn't need to know everything and my secrecy doesn't mean any more than that. Justin sent me a "Happy Easter" text and said he has a gift for me, too. I have never gotten so many Easter gifts.

I pack up Dixie and the gifts, and get a reasonably early start to my parents' house. It only takes about an hour and a half, but the ride is so dull, like trying to stay awake during a lecture on employment law. I am zipping along I-64 with the radio blasting and singing my heart out to tunes from my generation—"*Hey Jealousy...*" —Goddammit! Yes, I am taking the Lord's name in vain on Easter Sunday. Behind me on this sunny open road is a cop!

Whew, he passed me by. I am now noticing that there are a lot of cops out today. I can see why—Easter is such a *wild* drinking holiday. Idiots. Would they rather I fall asleep at the wheel and kill everyone on the road? That is clearly a possibility if I don't get this drive over with soon, and at fifty-five it's hard to steer, like Sammy Hagar said. Thanks to Rebecca for another early MTV reference.

I finally pull into the driveway, let Dixie do her business on the lawn, and ring the bell. My father answers the door. "Hello, Claire Marie, and little Dixie." I let her loose and she runs off to find Grandma, her second favorite person.

"Happy Easter, Honey." My father gives me a big hug. He is dressed in his Sunday retired man uniform of khaki pants and a plaid dress shirt. I'm sure they went to church this morning.

"Can I help you bring anything in?" I am weighed down with my bags and the flowers.

"Thanks, you can take this bag and—"

"John, are you standing there with the door wide open!?" My mother's voice can be heard all the way over at the guard house in their gated community.

"Your mother's in her usual frenzy," my father whispers and gives me a wink.

"You'll have every bug in the neighborhood in here." She arrives at the door in her apron with a spatula in her hand. I don't often see my mother without a kitchen themed wardrobe or accessory. Dixie is at her heels and jumping on her legs.

"Sorry, Mom, it's my fault." I come inside and close the door to secure the perimeter and keep the insect intruders at bay. We hug and exchange Easter greetings, and I assure my mother I did not "go out partying" on Good Friday. We move to the kitchen where I deposit all of my stuff on the desk, and get Dixie set up with food and water in her bowl (not that she will touch a bit of her food with Grandma's cooking ready to drop on the floor at any moment).

We exchange the Easter presents. They perform their ritual of appreciation for my thoughtfulness, and I'm presented with my Easter basket, complete with a Godiva chocolate bunny, assorted cosmetics and bubble bath. My poor mother needs grandchildren. Her lack is even more evident when she gives Dixie her presents. Many human children don't get the equivalent of Dixie's chew toys, organic treats and squeaky balls.

"Do you like that, little Dixie?" My mother is holding her up by her front paws and "dancing" with her. It breaks my heart to see my mother enjoying her only substitute for a grandchild, no matter how sweet the alternative. Of course I am not her only child. She still has my sister and it isn't my fault she hasn't reproduced yet. Speaking of which, where is Jackie?

"Mom, where's Jackie? Is she coming?" I accept the glass my father has poured for me, fresh from his cavernous basement wine cellar.

"No, Honey, she's feeding the homeless today." My mother gives Dixie some treats and goes back to checking on her dinner. The ham smells delicious and she is working on mashing up a load of potatoes.

Jackie volunteers her time. A lot. I don't know where she got this proclivity, but it isn't from these two. My parents do not volunteer. It isn't that they are uncaring—they are just not the proactive, get "involved" type. When we were children my mother taught religious education at our church for a few years (no doubt all of those kids now get nervous when asked out on Good Friday, too). But my father was always busy with work and my mother never had the activist mentality.

"So, Claire Marie have you heard any more from the old man with the hat? Haha..." This phrase will live on in family folklore for years to come, earning its place in our permanent history.

"No, Mom. I actually wrote back to him the first time, thanked him and told him I was seeing someone else." I click my fingernails on the base of my wine glass and shift in my seat. These hard kitchen chairs are so uncomfortable, yet this is where we always gather in their 5000 square foot house.

"So you lied or you are seeing someone else?" My mother's hands are ensconced in thick potholders, and she looks like a clown as she gestures with her hands.

"No, I'm not. Not really. I didn't know what to say and I didn't want to make him feel worse if I—"

"Claire, leave her alone." My father stops reading his Money magazine long enough to chastise my mother. He calls her Claire because I am named after her. We are both Claire Marie, hence the reason my father always includes my middle name when addressing me—to avoid confusion. My sister's name is Jaclyn Marie. My mother was a big Charlie's Angels fan. I said she could have named me Kate or Farrah, but for some reason that would have been preposterous according to her logic—"I was a fan, not a fanatic." Jackie didn't get her own middle name either—my mom is a creative one.

"John, I'm not judging. I am just trying to understand." She speaks slowly and looks at him like he is a senile old man, instead of a recently retired successful businessman.

She shakes her head and turns back to me, "So are you

119

dating anyone?" She opens up the top oven and pulls out a ham big enough to feed twenty people. Dixie's tongue is hanging out as she follows Grandma to the carving station for the inevitable pieces that will hit the floor.

"Claire!" My father is getting irritated.

"There are a couple of guys actually." I pause and consider whether or not I should mention my young potential suitors, as my mother would call them. "They are a bit young, though." I glance down at the table and twist my hair like I did when I was thirteen.

"*How* young?" My mother turns around with the big meat cleaver in her hand. She always looks menacing when holding cutlery.

"In their twenties. But late twenties!" I wince in expectation of her response.

My mother's eyes are popping and she puts the knife down. "Claire Marie, you can't be serious?"

My father sighs and puts down his reading material. "I'm going to show our daughter the work we recently did on the pool area. You'll love it, Honey—you can come here in the summer. Maybe you can bring one of your new friends." He gets up and glares at my mother.

She returns the look and addresses me again with a more sympathetic gaze. "Honey, I'm just trying to protect you, and remind you that younger men are not good for you. You can't—"

"I know. I can't give them what they want!" Now I'm on the verge of tears and I almost knock my wine over trying to figure out what to do with my hands.

"Why do you keep saying this crap about younger men? I am younger than you!" My father looks like he wants to eat his ham in peace, or he wishes he had boys and could be watching sports while dinner is being silently prepared.

"Only by a few years, and I was young then and I—" She stops herself and turns back towards the ham.

"You had all your body parts. Yep. That's why I'm here today enjoying this lovely visit." I didn't mean to let this get out of hand.

"That's enough. Claire Marie, you're coming outside with me. Dixie can stay here and beg for scraps. I'll be out in a minute. I need to find my shoes."

He is going to tell my mother to knock it off, and I dutifully follow his paternal order and go outside on the deck. On my way I can hear them arguing in hushed voices, and my mother sounds like she's crying. This is turning into a fiasco. I wish Jackie was here.

"Well now, here's your wine. I poured some more. You'll need it to get through dinner. And there's paa for your paahole." My father imitates the lady who welcomed them to the neighborhood. I manage to crack a smile. We sit down at the little bistro table and my father explains the work they've had done on the landscaping and the fencing around the pool. It's a pretty space, and takes up a good bit of the backyard. My father has worked hard, and my mother raised us well. She's just afraid I'll get hurt. I will never know that maternal instinct.

We sit outside for a few more minutes making small talk and my father finally says, "You know your mother loves you and she does mean well. She's just a nitwit about it sometimes."

"I know, Dad. Thanks." I give my father a hug and we head back inside. "She's probably flipping out now because all of the food isn't ready at exactly the same time, and we aren't coming in to eat fast enough." We share a laugh over my mother's affectionate neurosis and sit down to a lovely Easter dinner.

"So, Claire Marie," my mother begins. She looks at my father as if she is steeling herself against being chastised again for venturing into another danger zone of questioning. "How is work going, Honey?" She looks at my father and grimaces, as if to say "see, I can talk about safe subjects too, Mister Peacekeeper."

"Actually the company isn't doing so great." They both stop eating and look alarmed.

"I'm not in danger of losing my job." Not yet. "It's just that sales are down in some of our key markets, and we're looking for new authors and genres to boost our profits and stay current with modern readers." This is a much better topic. At least work is an area of moderate competence for me.

"All anyone wants to read today is filth. I was in the bookstore and everywhere they have displays of these novels with names like "Burn" and "Desire". Now I realize there is a market for everything, but those damn smutty books that came out last Christmas opened up the floodgates. I, for one, would never read such crap. I only read the classics. Well, and history and biography, of course. But seriously, who wants to waste their time on all that filth?"

The speech comes to an end and I am in turn, speechless.

"Did you even take a breath?" My father marvels at my mother's ability to churn out a record breaking number of words before needing to inhale. "I don't see why you're afraid to swim. You could stay underwater as long as a fish."

"Zip it, John. You're too busy stuffing your face to make conversation."

He doesn't make a peep and gets up to open another bottle of wine.

"You're right, Mom. That stuff is poor quality, but we need to do something to make money." She didn't know my company was publishing in that genre. Damn it, Claire! Sometimes I wish I would get laryngitis.

"Seriously? Bella Donna Press has stooped to that level? I used to get all my cookbooks from them. Such a shame." She shakes her head and butters another roll. My mother scoffs at the low carb craze.

In an effort to make my mother proud and improve this discussion, I begin to tell her about Brandon and his book, and my quest for a promising new author.

"Is this one of the young men you met?" She peers at me over the top of her reading glasses, which she has not taken off since she read the directions on the Pillsbury dinner roll package.

"Yes, Mom. He's my new neighbor, and he's very talented. And cute." I should have left that part out after the earlier drama.

My mother lets out the heaviest sigh imaginable. "Honey, cute is overrated. And you have cute right here," she says while feeding Dixie another piece of ham. She hasn't left my mother's side since we sat down. She is going to transform from a hotdog into a sausage before our eyes.

"Mom, the point is, he's a good writer and his work could help us. I'm trying to be part of the solution." I silently plead with my father for back-up.

"Yes, that's great. It's better than being part of the problem. Very proactive of you, Honey." He pats my hand and looks at my mother. I would love to be a fly on the wall after I leave here today. On second thought—no. One of the perks of being an adult is retreating to your own home when your parents argue.

My father and I attempt to change the subject to other areas, like Jackie and what's going on with her. I tell them I plan on asking Jackie if I can visit her for a weekend.

"She would *love* that. You should call her tonight." My mother is serving her pie with the golden crust and the juicy apple filling.

After dessert I help my mother clean the kitchen and make my excuses to leave. I'm tired and I would like to have some time to unwind before tomorrow's work day begins. And I must finish the notes on Brandon's book. I whisper a special thanks to my father on the way out, and assure him I'm not mad at my mother. She hands me a big bag of leftovers, which immediately attracts the attention of Dixie's long snout. She stops sniffing long enough to lick everyone goodbye and we're off.

I get in the car and remember the swarm of cops that were out earlier, hoping they nabbed some wild Easter egg hunters and ham eating revelers. Now I need to be extra careful driving home. It's dark out and I must fight to stay awake. The window is cracked and the radio is blasting to keep me alert (worse than getting a ticket would be falling asleep and dying). With the additional noise, I am oblivious to the phone buzzing in my purse, like a swarm of angry bees.

CHAPTER SIXTEEN

"Is it too short notice? I know you're busy between showing houses and your volunteer work." I hold up one finger and silently mouth the words "give me one minute" to an eager looking Justin, who has been pacing in front of my door the whole time I've been talking to my sister. Frank was wrong with the open door idea—I need a *closed* door policy.

"Don't be silly. You haven't even seen my new place, and of course I can make time for you. If I have to show a house you can busy yourself until I'm done, and you could come with me if I have a volunteer event. I think the homeless shelter thing is the following weekend, though." Jackie sounds upbeat and on top of things.

I'm still trying to craft a suitable response now that I've heard the words "homeless shelter."

"It's too bad. There are some cute guys at the homeless shelter," she continues.

"Now you think I should try to date homeless men?!" Justin walked by again. There is something wrong with him. I am at least old enough to be his maiden aunt. Maybe I should show him my driver's license to see if that helps reality set in.

"Of course not! There's this crazy concept—people *other than me* volunteer at the homeless shelter. There is actually a whole huge group of people in the world who help others. You should look it up and read about it. It's sweeping the nation—more popular than wedge heels this season." Now she has moved into her sarcastic tone, but I suppose I deserve it.

"You don't have to get all self-righteous. Maybe a man who volunteers his time would be better than assholes who get you drunk and try to attack you in your living room, or Internet liars with pictures from the eighties."

Jackie sighs softly and I can picture her sitting cross-legged on the floor like a little girl, and shaking her head full of black curls. "You still may be missing the point, but let's make this a girly weekend of indulgences. You need to treat yourself better. Mom said you were a nervous wreck at their house."

"Really? Did she tell you all the crap she was asking me? Thank God for Dad's intervention." I pause and take a deep breath, letting the air fill my lungs and help me find my words. "I've just had a...hard time lately. I need to get away. This will be a fun weekend."

"It'll be fun for me, too. Now go make a reservation at the pet resort for the little ankle biter and start packing your girliest gear. Take off Friday so we can make it a three day extravaganza." Her enthusiasm is catching—I can see why people buy houses from her.

"I'm on it! I'll text you when I'm on my way. Have a good week."

Somehow Jackie grew up in our family and escaped being neurotic. I guess it's because she has more of my father's personality. My mother drives me nuts because I'm too much like her. I just don't have a child to nag so the circle of life is broken. I bet that's what a therapist would tell me.

I'm going to have to let Justin in if I plan on getting anything accomplished today. I do not understand his persistence, but it has to be the challenge. At this point if I was a snaggle-toothed hag, he would court me to the altar just to win. Maybe there is something to this playing hard to get thing, except I'm not playing. He called four times on my way home from Charlottesville last night, and Brandon called twice. I didn't hear a single buzz thanks to my blaring music. When I got home I didn't feel like calling either of them back. When I see their names on my caller ID I don't see "Brandon" or "Justin." I see blinking words in big letters, shouting warnings like "Disappointment" and "Heartbreak."

"Hi, Claire. Are you off the phone? Sorry to keep stopping by, but I wanted to give you this before my big meeting this afternoon. I'll be tied up most of the day." Justin places a pastel gift bag with Easter eggs all over it on my desk. There's lots of multi-colored tissue paper sticking out at odd angles, but it's a sweet presentation, and he looks genuinely pleased with himself.

"Thank you, Justin. You really didn't have to do this. It's only Easter and..." I stop myself before I say something mean like, "and we're not even dating." Instead I finish with, "...it is very nice of you." Good recovery.

He's standing in front of my desk staring at me, so I begin to sift through the paper to see what's in the bag. I fish out a big Lindt chocolate bunny and a pair of pink bunny slipper socks. "These are so cute, Justin. Thank you. Chocolate is my favorite."

"There's something else in there." He sits down in my guest chair in anticipation of the next gift unveiling. Crap. Now I'm worried.

I reach back in the bag and pull out a small box. This looks like jewelry. It better not be jewelry. I unwrap the box and sigh before lifting the lid. A perfect sterling silver bracelet with little dangling wiener dogs.

"They had one with bunnies but when I saw this one I thought it would be much more fitting for you." He is still waiting for me to say something. "You do have a wiener dog, right? Daisy?"

"Dixie," I quietly respond as I keep my head down, still staring at this gift and not knowing how to receive it.

Justin jumps up and moves forward, reaching for the bracelet. "Here, let me put it on you. I had them make it smaller because I noticed how tiny your wrists are." He gets down on one knee to get close enough to see what he's doing, and clasps the bracelet around my left wrist. I hope no one else walks by my office and sees this scene. The morning sun is streaming in through my office window, and as I shake my wrist little happy puppies are dancing and sparkling against my skin.

"Justin, this is such a thoughtful gift." My eyes are filling with tears and I wish his meeting was starting now so he would have to go.

Instead he gets up and walks to my door and softly closes it. He comes back to me and pulls a chair up next to mine. "Claire, please just come out and have a drink with me. We don't even have to call it a date. It'll be fun." I notice the contrast between his youthful features and his furrowed brow and troubled expression. I see more man than boy now, realizing that sometimes we see only what we want to see.

Justin has patience—I will give him that, and maybe maturity beyond his years. I don't remember the last time I had actual *fun* with a man. Actually I do, but it wasn't a date. I wonder if Brandon and Justin have the same source for wiener dog swag.

"Okay, I'll have a drink with you." I wipe my eyes and sit up straighter. "Anyone who goes to this much trouble deserves a night out with Fun Claire. I'm going to see if I can find her. She may have been stuffed under the bed a couple of years ago. I'll dust her off and dress her up." I smile warmly and squeeze Justin's hand.

"Wonderful. It would be awfully good to make it through a conversation without making you cry, too. I need to work on that."

"Justin, you don't make me cry. I make me cry." I release his hand and look into his confused eyes.

"Maybe someday you'll explain that, but for now—when can we have this fun night out? Friday?" He looks hopeful so I hate to tell him about my plans.

I wince and say, "I'm visiting my sister this weekend. I'm taking off Friday—driving up there either Thursday night or Friday morning. Can we go when I get back? I have to go to a work conference tomorrow night—I still need to find an editor—"

He puts his finger to my lips to silence me. Thousands of electric currents course through my body. Breathe, Claire.

"I have to meet a software supplier on Wednesday night. This will give me more time to plan something special next week." He gets up to leave.

"Hey, I thought you said a drink? I agreed to a drink." I fold my arms and pretend to look indignant.

"A drink is like a code word for 'expertly planned date of Justin's choosing.' So sorry, you walked right into it and now you're stuck. You accepted the bribes." He smirks and points to the foot high pile of exploded tissue paper on my desk.

"I see how it is. There's a secret language *and* a plot!" I fake my exasperation at this discovery of his manipulative tactics.

"Hey, I don't want to *completely* stop being a dick. That was your original attraction, right?" The bunny slipper sock misses his big grin by an inch and bounces off the door.

He looks down at the pink bunny with the big embroidered eyes and says, "This is going to be quite a time, little bunny. Keep Claire warm until I can." He is out the door before the second bunny beans him in the head.

I e-mail Rebecca to see if she's free for lunch. She quickly responds and wants to hear about what just went on in my office. I hope she's the only one who noticed how long Justin was in here, and I'm thankful that flying bunny slipper socks don't make much noise on contact.

I spend much of the rest of the morning preparing for my meeting tomorrow. I'm attending a publishing networking event in the hopes of snaring an editor to save our asses. I received a list of attendees from the coordinator and I am looking them up on LinkedIn to narrow down my list of targets. I found a few good prospects and practice my company sales spiel.

I had a long lunch with Rebecca. I told her a condensed version of the Justin visit, leaving out the tears. She almost ripped my arm off to get a good look at the bracelet. It isn't an expensive gift, but it was only Easter and our relationship does not warrant gifts. Clearly, he was making a statement and Rebecca was hearing it loud and clear.

"He is *so* hot for you." She shoves another forkful of pasta in her mouth, and rips off a big hunk of bread.

I pick at my salad. "Rebecca, it isn't like that." I have no intention of explaining to her what it's actually like.

"Whatever. Men don't buy women jewelry unless they're in hot pursuit." She winks as if I don't know what she's referring to by using the word "hot."

I steer the conversation away from Justin and back to work, but that only brings us down the Brandon trail.

"So are you done with his book?"

"Yes, I'm going to send it to Pam with my notes before I leave for Jackie's. I looked up his other books, the ones he self-published on Amazon. They're about rock stars and life on the road. Nothing about families or adoption or anything remotely like this story."

"You'll have to do something crazy and just ask him why he wrote it." She glares at me with a smug look.

"Of course I'll ask him. He doesn't make me nervous. I just like to be prepared, like a boy scout."

"That makes so much sense. Boy scouts are often pretending they aren't interested in cute young neighbor men. There's a badge they earn for that." I cringe at Rebecca's twisted humor and ask for the check.

I continue to dodge any questions or topics related to men on the way back to the office. Up until now Rebecca and I have talked about every detail of my dating life. However, I now realize that's because I didn't have one, just a ridiculous string of encounters that never had a chance of going anywhere. Going on a date with Justin isn't exactly a move in the right direction either, but slowly the cobwebs in my head are clearing. The ones in my heart are triggering all the tears.

CHAPTER SEVENTEEN

"**Y**es, this editor candidate is highly professional and she completely understands the requirements of the job." I'm on the phone with Tim explaining my conquest of Gina Rossetti. She was one of the editors I targeted to meet on Tuesday, and it just so happens she is looking for a new opportunity. She's on board with the work we need her to do, and appreciates the realities of the economy and Bella Donna's mission. She's also committed to building new business and finding new authors. She was smart and savvy, and could be the injection of life we need to stay afloat and grow the business. Plus she kept making S&M jokes, just like Frank. What is wrong with these people?

"Good work, Claire. I'll be back from the conference on Friday. I know you're out then and I'll need a day to catch up. Let's bring her in early next week. If she's as good as you say she is we'll get her on board as soon as possible." Tim's voice is beaming with pride and joy. I promise to arrange the meeting and we hang up.

I promised myself (and Rebecca) I would join the Meetup group and attend more events, and line up fun weekend plans. Jumping into any potential dating pool is like venturing into shark infested waters, but I don't want to stay in the kiddie pool with the plastic fish, either.

I open up the site and fill out the profile form to formally join. Rebecca is right—there is no commitment and nothing to be afraid of. I see there is an event at the Charter House. I know that place. It's on a big lake (sharks are *highly* unlikely), and they have a sprawling outdoor deck. I sign up for happy hour next Friday and notice that several people I recognize from Lorenzo's are going, including Sherry and Andy. Hopefully they have forgotten about my unfortunate stage diving incident. However, I think that term refers to diving *off* the stage into the *crowd*, *not* the band. I vow to make better footwear and alcohol choices, and RSVP "yes" with a self-satisfied flourish.

Brandon's book is the last thing on my agenda. I open up my e-mail to send Pam the manuscript and the MS Word document containing my notes, and I pause. Why am I so reluctant to ask Brandon about his book? He gave it to me to read. My mind wanders to Jane's living room, and his arms wrapped around me, his thumb drying my tears.

To: Brandon Harmon
From: Claire McDonald Ratzenberger
Re: Book
Hi Brandon,

I have finished your story and I'm sending it off to Pam Rogers, our Acquisitions Editor. It was well written and deeply moving. I liked the humor as well—the little family dog was a nice touch and the grandmother was a quirky character. Of course the little boy was precious.

I looked up your other work and saw that the genre was quite different. Just curious—why this topic? Adoption is a pretty specific and personal type of story. People usually can't write about things if they haven't touched their lives. Do you know someone who is adopted?

Fantastic job! I am hopeful that Pam will schedule a meeting with you soon. Thanks again for the chocolate and I love my little wiener bunny!

Have a good weekend,
Claire

There. That's a perfectly normal, pleasant e-mail. He probably won't get it right away. I am sorry I never called him back. I don't like to call men back unless I know why they're calling. Oh, I have a message already.

To: Claire McDonald Ratzenberger
From: Brandon Harmon
Re: Book
Claire,
I am adopted.
Brandon

That's it. He must be mad at me for not calling him back. He was so compassionate at Jane's and I blew him off. I act like he's pursuing me and I have to put up huge barriers to protect myself from his advances. I must look like such a self-absorbed asshole. I decide to call him.

"Hello, Claire." He doesn't sound thrilled to hear from me.

"Hi, Brandon. I figured I would just call since e-mailing is so impersonal." I'm talking too loud and fast.

"Thanks for passing the book along." His tone is flat.

"You're welcome. But you could really be the one doing us a favor—"

"Claire, are you just going to keep babbling or are you going to tell me what you're really calling about?"

My heart stings from the slap of those words. "I'm sorry, I just—"

"You just what? Don't want to talk to me but you're hoping my book will save your job?"

"That's uncalled for! I'm helping you, too!" They heard that down in the cafeteria, even with my door closed.

Brandon sighs. "You're right. You are helping me and I'm grateful. I just can't figure you out. I've never met a woman like you. We had a nice night at Jane and Mike's, and then as soon as we were alone outside you got all weird. Then I tried to call you on Sunday but you never called back. So I give up. I guess you just want a professional relationship, and to be cordial neighbors."

"No, that's not what I want." Even as I say these words I know what the next question will be—and I can't answer it.

"Then what *do* you want, Claire?"

I whisper, "I don't know. Or I do know but I don't think I can have it, and it's almost the same thing. There's a lot you don't know."

"It's pretty easy to find me to tell me."

"I don't want to talk about me. Why don't you tell me more about being adopted," I say hopefully.

"Not today. You're going to have to meet me halfway if you want to hear my story."

"I'm going to my sister's for the weekend. I'm leaving tonight." The tears are flowing again.

"Have a great time. Maybe when you come back, you can come tell me what you want or why you don't think you can have it, or whatever you just said. Then I'll tell you the tale of little orphan Brandon. Bye, Claire."

"Brandon, wait...bye," I say to a dead phone line.

I wipe my face and turn off my computer. I need to go to the ladies' room before I leave the office—my bladder isn't much bigger than Dixie's. I walk in and see Cecilia at the sink. She's dressed in a short black skirt and a tight red sweater. Her raven hair is short and spiky. I am always struck by this. She would be prettier with a softer, longer hairstyle. I guess I'm awkwardly staring at her too long and she turns around.

"Hello, Claire. Something wrong?" Her tone is not friendly.

"I'm sorry, I didn't mean to stare. I was just looking at your hair. It's so spiky."

Cecilia finishes rinsing off her hands and grabs a few paper towels. "So, I hear Justin has been pursuing you pretty heavily." Her dark eyes are narrowed.

This catches me off guard. "I don't know if I would say *that*. Why *do* you say that?" I fold my arms and face her stare.

"Come on, Claire, it's a small office. Everyone sees it. You know he's only twenty-five, right? And what are you, like forty?" She smirks at the implied folly of my situation.

"No, I am not forty and yes, I am aware of how old he is. What business is this of yours?"

Cecilia must have a thing for Justin. There isn't a woman here or anywhere who doesn't. The ladies in the cafeteria probably get flustered when serving his tuna sandwich.

"I don't *care*, it just makes you look ridiculous. You should know he's not serious. He dated Amanda and dumped *her* pretty quick, and she's like half your age."

I would like to slap her. "Cecilia, this is none of your concern, and if you're jealous because you're interested in Justin you should just say so."

She walks towards the door and reaches for the handle. "Claire, I would not waste my time with Justin if I were you." She turns to leave and pokes her head back in. "And don't think everyone isn't aware that you're slandering the company and talking shit about the new books. It's called being open-minded, Claire. Sex sells—you're such a prude."

I open my mouth to reply but she's gone. She has some nerve! I wonder if Tim sees her bad attitude. She must be jealous. I don't interact with Cecilia often, but she doesn't look happy most of the time. She is just as prickly as her hair. *Did* she have a thing with Justin and she's mad at him, and now me by association? I bet Rebecca knows.

"She's always been a bitch, Claire. You just don't notice." Am I this clueless that Rebecca has known this all along and I never gave it a thought?

"So did she ever date Justin?"

We're in Rebecca's office, which looks like a bomb blew up and shot out paper, tissues, dirty cups, extra shoes, and what looks like a *blanket* in the corner?

"What are you looking at? My legs get cold in here sometimes. No, I don't think they ever dated, but Justin is obviously on the radar for any single girl in the office. He did date Amanda. Cecilia and Amanda were good friends before that, and now they don't speak to each other."

"I have a date with him next Thursday and I will be damned if I let that little pixie witch stop me." I'm not sure if I'm madder over the Justin comments or the crap about those idiot books. What the hell does *she* know about quality fiction? I'm pacing the floor in front of Rebecca's desk, looking down so I don't trip on any more bedding she may have stashed around.

"Don't worry about her. Just go and have fun at your sister's. All this bullshit will be here when you get back." She grins as I turn to leave.

"Thanks, something to look forward to."

She sticks her tongue out playfully as I close her door behind me.

I manage to miraculously make it out of the office without running into anyone, and reach the safety of my car.

As I pull into my cul-de-sac I nervously glance at the house across the street. I go inside and finish packing, and scoop up the least complicated thing in my life—little Dixie. When we get to the pet resort she will practically leap out of my arms to get to the ladies, and play time with the other little doggies. I put her in the car along with all my mismatched luggage.

I don't travel light—I must have my own pillow. Jackie has those weird pillows that are made of some kind of molded foam. The last time I tried to sleep on one of those I almost got whiplash from smacking my head against it, trying to put a proper dent in it. It's like laying your head on a big charcoal briquette. My pillow is from the nineties. That could be an exaggeration, but it is of the soft and mushy variety, with a well-worn crater for my head.

I would bring Dixie to Jackie's, but she's allergic (my mother supposedly was too, but seems to have been cured). Because of this unfortunate affliction she didn't have much exposure to dogs as a child, and that makes her fear them. When I first got Dixie as a three pound puppy she was jumpy around her. This irrational fear goes way back. When she was little I always told her to stay calm when a dog approached and let them smell her. She said she knew why they wanted to smell her legs—"dogs think your legs are chicken." Dixie happily goes to the pet resort so Aunt Jackie doesn't have to worry about her nibbling on her thigh meat in the middle of the night.

As I lock the front door and make one last sweep to ensure I have everything, I steal a peek at Brandon's house. I don't see any sign of him. His car isn't there, but it could be in the garage. I wish I could tell him I'm sorry again, but what's the point? He's right about me, and I was right about getting close to someone who I have to see all the time. Between Brandon and Justin I have no peace anywhere.

"Dixie, isn't this why they say dogs don't shit where they sleep? Or something like that?" She looks at me with her confused, shiny brown eyes.

No matter how the saying goes, at home and at work—I am in deep shit.

CHAPTER EIGHTEEN

I pull into the gated complex and punch in the code Jackie gave me. I hear the intercom static crackling and my sister's voice.

"Hey, I'm so excited you made it. I have pizza. Come on up! Oh, and park anywhere."

Jaclyn Marie McDonald lives in McLean, VA, across from Tyson's Corner, which is a huge conglomeration of retail space. It's like the god of shopping opened his mouth and spit out every imaginable store, restaurant or service in creation. You could eat food from a remote Southeast Asian nation while getting your pet hedgehog groomed, and pick up a fifty dollar lotion dispenser in the shape of a banana. Of course I plan on taking full advantage of this indulgent mecca of commerce. After all, it's girls' weekend. We're not going to smoke cigars or play poker.

I park and grab my bags, and head up the stairs to apartment 2A. The door flies open as I raise my hand to knock. Jackie reaches up on her tippy toes to hug me. I am wearing high heeled boots and Jackie is short. She is just barely five feet tall, making her my little sister in more than one way. Her curly black hair is framing her perfect face, and her dark blue eyes are wide and animated. Our very opposite looks always attracted stares when we were little, but I look like our mother and Jackie is 100% dad.

She's wearing pajamas with Hello Kitty on them, so I would say we are in for the night. Since I have had a long day and it's almost nine o'clock, I am fine with that plan.

"Come in, I'm so glad you're here. What can I take from you? Let's put your bags in the guest room. Do you want some wine?" She is like an excited little girl on Christmas morning.

"Sure, wine would be great. I need to get out of these boots." I plop down on her big fluffy white couch and consider asking for white, instead of red, wine. I pry my boots off and my feet sigh with the relief of liberation.

Jackie is a smart and educated thirty-two-year old. It turns out she wasn't just cute when she was little. There was a secret brain in that silly head. I used to drop her off at her kindergarten classroom every day the year I was in 4th grade. She had a little clear book bag with butterflies on it (mine had ladybugs). She would wave to me and I would think that it was a waste to send such a little airhead to school. Boy, was I wrong. She completed a master's degree in school psychology at a prestigious university in Pennsylvania, only to learn in her internship that she doesn't like kids. Or their parents. Especially their parents. She decided to go into real estate while helping a friend on an interior decorating project (yes, she's creative too), where she met the realtor who was listing the house. She has been a natural and has been a top salesperson in her office for the past three years. I haven't seen her new apartment yet, but she still has her eye out for the perfect condo in DC.

Jackie's in the kitchen pouring the wine, which I see is red. I need to watch my motor skills. "Why would you wear shoes like that to visit me? Honestly, why torture yourself when no one is even going to see you?" She hands me a half-filled glass, which I gingerly rest on the glass coffee table after taking a sip.

"I have a thing with shoes and not learning lessons, and you never know who you could meet. What if I got a flat tire and a cute guy stopped to help me?"

"You're right. If you were wearing frumpier, more practical footwear there is no way he would be interested. *Hello*—only gay men care about your shoes! It's a cruel reality. I guess we are going shoe shopping tomorrow, right?" She tucks her legs under her body and sinks into the equally stuffy powder blue side chair.

"Yes, absolutely. I will defer to your knowledge of the rat maze over there, though. Last time it seemed like we walked for ten miles and then couldn't find the car."

"I'm a pro now. I will draw a battle plan with a map and attack points. Food stops. Bathrooms. The works. It will be like we're invading a small nation, but we have to pay for the stuff we take instead of conquering and pillaging." Jackie giggles at her own joke.

I smile and say, "Hey, where's that pizza you said you had. I'm starving!" I jump up and almost knock over the wine. I pick up my glass, slowly move to the kitchen and sit down at the table.

Jackie preheats the oven and gets out the plates and napkins. "So I hate to ask, but what's happening on the men front?"

I take a deep breath and I begin to tell her about my recent escapades, from the old man with the hat to the bug killing freak. I tell her about Meetup and my decision to take a break from Internet dating. I chronicle the Brandon and Justin debacles, and unlike Rebecca and Jane, Jackie gets the unedited versions. Of course I am crying again.

Jackie jumps up to get the tissues. "Let's go back in the living room and sit down. I don't know why everyone in our family sits in the kitchen." She starts moving pizza and wine back to the coffee table.

We head back to the sofa and suddenly I am so uncomfortable in my jeans. I go in the bedroom and change into my pajamas, which of course feature dancing wiener dogs (I do wear pajamas when visiting people). The irony in the difference between my mood and that of my sleepwear is not lost on Jackie.

"Those are hilarious. See, now this is really like a slumber party. Maybe we should stop talking about boys and do the séance part. I wonder if girls still do that. Remember when you had to lift someone with two fingers?" I smile at the childhood memories and her attempt to bring me back to a happier time.

"Jackie, I don't know what I'm doing." I bite my lip and blow my nose.

"You need to stop focusing on finding a man, and you clearly overanalyze everything—"

"You don't understand what it's like for me. If you meet a guy you could give him a child one day. It may not matter at first, but it will become important if it gets serious, and by then it could be a disaster of disappointment and loss all over again for me." I sink deeper into the couch, wishing it would swallow me up.

"I'm sorry you can't have a baby, but there are different ways to be a mother, or even *like* a mother. You have such tunnel vision on this issue. You're torturing yourself." Jackie leans forward in her chair and looks at me pleadingly.

"I just don't feel like a real woman."

"Men seem to think you are."

"They don't know the truth."

"Maybe that would be a good start."

"What?"

"Tell them the truth and let them decide for themselves if it's a deal breaker. You can't decide what someone wants before you even ask them. And don't tell me they could always change their minds and men can have children forever and—"

"But that's all true!"

"Yes, but anyone can change their mind about anything, anytime. Claire, there are no guarantees in life."

Jackie looks at me, forlorn, waiting for my response. The wine is making me ever sleepier, and the couch is sucking the consciousness out of me while the pizza is getting cold.

"I don't mean to be harsh, but what you're doing is clearly making you unhappy. You're young and beautiful. You have a good job, and family and friends who love you, even the little ankle biter. You are free to date one guy or ten guys, and you have much more to offer than babies." Jackie takes a bite of her pizza and motions for me to do the same.

I sit up a little and run my fingers through my hair, which is now greasy and sticky from the morning's hairstyling ritual. "I'll think about it. You're right, and I'm sorry I'm throwing a wet blanket on our carefree girls' weekend. You must want to knock me out. I'm such a whining sap and you help people who are homeless, for God's sake. I am running around saying 'look at me, I can't find a boyfriend' and 'I have a date with a hot twenty-five-year old—poor me.' You should punch me in the head." I roll my eyes at my own stupidity and dig into my slice.

Jackie is cracking up. "I have a lot of patience for whining and unreasonable complaints. Do you know how annoying people are when they are buying a house? They can currently live in a moldy hoarder's den, but they will negotiate 5K lower if the new house has a dated light fixture in the foyer or they don't like the way the toilets flush."

"Yeah, I would *not* do well with those people. I need to go to bed now." I get up and stretch like Dixie, from my tense neck down to my sore, boot weary toes.

"Our first agenda item tomorrow is a spa visit. I wasn't sure what you would want to do. I'm getting a massage." She looks super excited about her choice.

The mention of a massage reminds me of my Brandon/Justin fantasy, and I am wondering what activities will ever keep my mind off men. "I had one pretty recently. I'll get my nails done instead. I need to unveil my toes soon— it's sandal season."

We say good night and I settle in the warm, cozy guest bedroom. The queen sleigh bed has a down comforter, which is too warm for this time of year. Luckily, Jackie layers her beds with blankets of every texture and weight. I pull up a lighter quilt, littered with tiny pastel tulips, and nestle in for a long, and hopefully dreamless, sleep.

Saturday is sunny and the mall is calling my name— "Claire, come buy pretty things and rack up more credit card debt." That isn't an entirely positive message, but at least it has nothing to do with men. I jump out of bed and find Jackie already dressed and making breakfast. She was always an early riser, up at six watching cartoons while I slept in.

"Good morning!" I am starting out the day on a positive note.

"Did you sleep well? That bed is pretty comfortable. Do you want pancakes?" She has a spatula in her hand and is wearing a long embroidered peasant skirt and an off the shoulder sweater. Her hair is pulled back in a silk ribbon. Jackie was born in the wrong decade or on the wrong continent. She must hate wearing suits to show houses.

"Yeah, but I'm going to take a shower first. Is that okay?"

"Of course. We still have a little time. Our appointment is at eleven."

I leave her cutting up strawberries and head for the

guest bathroom. I shower, and dress in jeans and a lightweight wine colored sweater set. Passing over the several pairs of heels I brought, I opt for ballet flats. This is the only thing Jackie and I have in common with our outfits today.

The spa is posh and indulgent, the kind where they give you elaborate aromatherapy hand massages before they polish your nails. My feet have been soaked, scrubbed, rubbed, buffed and shined. They are all ready for flip flops and hot sandals.

We settle on a trendy Asian fusion place for lunch, which to me is just fancy Chinese food (I'm like a country bumpkin in the wealthy suburbs). Jackie is even more Zen-like now that she has had her hot stone massage.

"That was phenomenal. I should do that once a week. Your nails look pretty." She grabs my hand to examine the perfect manicure. The deep garnet lacquer matches my sweater.

The waitress brings our water and gives us another minute with the menu, which is a bit confusing. Not as Chinese-y as I anticipated.

"So I have another idea. Don't get mad—this is about men but a completely different approach." I cringe and anticipate Jackie's wrath.

She puts down her menu and sips her water, sighing audibly. "What now? You're going to hang out at NASA and try to meet astronauts?"

"Close. I'm thinking I should go to bars wearing New York sports jerseys."

"And this is to meet men from New York, I am presuming?" She is slowing her speech as if she is talking to a toddler or a crazy person with a weapon.

"Don't you think that's a good idea? Like right now—it's baseball season. So we could buy Yankees shirts. Or one of us buys a Yankees shirt and the other Mets, just to cover all the bases. Haha, that's a baseball pun." I slap my leg to congratulate myself on my wit.

Jackie looks as though she wishes she had some houses to show today. "What if you meet a guy who likes you, except he's a Red Sox fan? Now he doesn't like you, even though you are only a fake Yankees/Mets fan? Didn't we decide last night that honesty was the best policy?" She folds her arms and shakes her head, her bangle earrings smacking the sides of her face.

"I watched baseball with Ron *and* Daddy, and I know some things. I am trying to meet men from New York, *not* Boston!" I pause and glare at my smirking sister. "Okay, I guess *New England men* could be normal, too. Damn it. I never thought about repelling other men with New York fan apparel! I give up." I start eating the crunchy noodles on the table. Where the hell is the waitress?

"I *wish* you would give up, at least for a little while. Why don't you try to meet men at the dog park? Don't you ever take Dixie?" The waitress returns and we pause to order.

"Thank you. Yes, with fried rice." I turn away from the waitress and answer Jackie's question. "Are you kidding? I can't meet men at the dog park. I have to take Dixie to the *little* dog area, unless I want her to be a hot dog snack for a Rottweiler. Single men do not have little dogs. Gay men. Couples. Women. That's it."

Jackie sighs and changes the subject to our battle plan of attacking as many shops as we can before nightfall.

Hours later my feet can't take another step. Fortunately we *do* know where the car is, but if we didn't I would have to sit down and pay someone else to find it and bring it to us. Ballet flats are flat, but not cushioned. My feet feel like they have been bludgeoned to death and for some reason Jackie is still tip toeing around like a dancer, and she has to walk twice as fast to keep up with me with her little stump legs. It's almost like walking Dixie.

I am weighed down from all my packages, but it was a productive day. I bought three pairs of sandals (only one super high), two bras at Victoria's Secret, costume jewelry, and some clothes for both work and going out.

"How could you possibly buy shoes and bras without trying them on?"

I have tried to explain this to her, but Jackie fails to comprehend my logic. "I told you—I have worn the same size shoes since I was twelve years old. I only buy bras at Victoria's Secret, and I know my size. It's not that complicated."

We pull into Jackie's apartment complex and haul our loot up the stairs. She returns a call from our mother and tells her all about my purchases and how I don't try anything on. After she gets off the phone she tells me that my mother said, "She also dates men in their twenties."

"Yeah, she wasn't too happy to hear any of that, and she got the very censored version." I hold up my new rhinestone earrings to see if they sparkle in the lamp light.

"She just worries about you. It doesn't matter what Mom says, but you really should try on shoes before you buy them." Jackie clears off a space on the couch and squeezes herself in between the bags. I am sitting on the floor admiring my purchases, and making a big mess.

"Why doesn't she worry about you? Actually—why don't you ever seem to care that you're single? Don't you want to meet someone?" I look at Jackie tentatively, realizing how selfish I am in monopolizing all our time talking about my problems.

"I would like to meet someone, but I don't let it run my life. Or *ruin* my life, which is often the case. Claire, you spent your whole life with Ron, and you're used to having someone. It's natural to want to replace what you've lost." She moves all the packages to one side of the room so the couch and chairs are free. She pats the couch, prompting me to sit.

I get up and sit in the corner of the couch, surrounded by pillows. I lay my head down. "It's a hard habit to break, and then when I add the whole child thing into the equation it makes me crazy."

"You have to stop viewing men as potential fathers. You did that with Ron. Wasn't that one of his complaints? I know he's an asshole, but he had a point."

"He was so unsympathetic with all the miscarriages. I just wanted to be a mother."

"But he didn't want to be seen as nothing but sperm and a paycheck. Would you want a man to look at you as nothing but a uterus and a home cooked meal?"

"No, of course not, and if they do I am sorely lacking on both fronts. But I get what you're saying. Men probably aren't judging me the same way I have been judging them." I rub my eye sockets and remember I haven't taken my makeup off yet. I look at my hands, now full of black smudges.

"The days of men assessing women as breeders are pretty much over. Back then we *both* would have been spinsters because our hip width would have been deemed unsatisfactory to produce enough young to work the land and survive the plague." She jumps up and runs to the kitchen. "Now let's have the best thing I bought all day—the black and white cookies."

"Oh, did you separate them yet?" When we were little, our father would bring home black and white cookies from a bakery in the Bronx. The little white box with the red string was a source of great excitement for Jackie and me. We both loved the cookies, but she liked the chocolate side and I preferred the vanilla. We always split them and gave each other our favorite halves. That way each sister got exactly what she wanted.

"Let's make a toast with our cookies," Jackie proclaims. "To both of us getting what we want, in cookies and life." We tap our treats and gobble them down.

"Claire?"

"Yeah?"

"Just ask men what they want. If you can't give it, or don't want to, simply move on. There's a perfectly formed all-vanilla cookie out there with your name on it. You just have to nibble a little to find it." Jackie smiles at her clever analogy.

"You're not a bad therapist, but don't quit your day job." I roll up the wax paper from the cookie and toss it at her across the table.

That night as I settle into the guest bed, I think about nibbling. I toss and turn until dawn.

CHAPTER NINETEEN

"Are you ready to have a fun and crazy night?" Justin's eyes are animated and shiny, like green sea glass.

"Yep!" I return his enthusiasm and big smile.

Today is J-Date Day. Justin Date Day, not Jewish Date, like the dating website. You have to be Jewish to join that, which is unfortunate because in my experience Jewish men treat their wives very well. Or at least the ones I have known.

Justin informed me yesterday that I should bring a change of casual clothes to work today, since we're leaving from the office. I must have looked disappointed, as if I wanted to be wined and dined, and he had an evening of McDonald's and bowling planned. He looked quite pleased with himself, so I can only assume he has something interesting up his sleeve. That reminds me of his bare arms when his sleeves are rolled up. Ahh...

The day passed by uneventfully and I am ready to go. My bag is packed and my heart is pounding. This is absurd, but somehow a drink has turned into something that involves luggage.

Justin arrives in my office promptly at five o'clock and picks up my bag. He offers his hand to lead me away from my desk, which is my last line of defense between me and disappointment, disguised as a delicious, sexy young man.

Needless to say I'm a little keyed up. There is a gloomy, mean little fairy on one shoulder telling me I should not be doing this and this has no potential whatsoever. The other shoulder features a happy, positive little fairy who's encouraging me to have fun and live adventurously. Their constant banter is making me dizzy. I did, however, pull Fun Claire out from under the bed and shook the dust off her.

"Let's take my car and I'll drive you back to yours later. Is that okay?" He gestures towards his cute little sports car. He better not plan on taking the top down because the last thing I need is for my hair to look like someone went at it with an egg beater.

"Don't worry, I'll leave the top up. I wouldn't want to mess up your perfect sleek tresses." He touches the ends of my hair and electrical currents travel to my scalp.

"You read my mind." I hope that's not true, and jump in the passenger seat before he can open the door for me. He puts my bag in the trunk, which can't be bigger than a shoebox, but somehow he appears without my bag, and I presume he has one back there, too.

"So my curiosity is at an all-time high. Can you reveal the big secret outing yet?" I wedge my purse on the floor in the miniscule space where my legs are supposed to go. Justin is a tall guy, but somehow he fits perfectly behind the wheel.

We pull into the parking lot of a nearby casual pizza place. "I know this looks lame, but I want to eat someplace quick so we have more time for the fun part." He looks at me expectantly.

"I love this place. The pizza's great." I'm secretly relieved he isn't taking me to some fancy restaurant downtown where I might spill red wine on the white tablecloth, and it's so quiet everyone can hear your conversation.

We follow the "please seat yourself" directive and find a booth towards the back, away from the large tables of families and happy hour co-workers. The waitress promptly comes by to take our drink orders. Justin orders a beer, but I'm sticking with Coke. I absolutely must not get drunk tonight for a myriad of reasons. I get an encouraging pat on the shoulder from the good fairy.

We settle into an easy conversation about the office and work. I tell him about Gina, and my hope that she can help the company get back in the black (now I will be humming AC/DC all night—great). I also bring up Brandon's book, and my efforts to find new material.

"So who's this Brandon guy? Sounds a little geeky." Justin sits up taller in the booth and takes a swig of beer.

"He's actually my new neighbor. I found out he's a writer and has a manuscript to sell. Lucky coincidence, right?" I put another slice of pizza on my plate and don't point out that Brandon is the lead singer in a hard rock band and Justin works in IT. But my guess is neither one has ever been called a geek.

"Yeah, I guess so. Is he married?" Justin attempts to look vaguely disinterested in his own question, glancing around the room.

"No, he's not married. He's young." I say this as if married is the exact opposite of young.

"Then there's no worry there. You don't date younger guys." He laughs as he dodges the straw wrapper I just threw at him.

At times I have forgotten how young Justin is because he's so skilled in his field and has a position of responsibility. If he wasn't a boy wonder Princeton grad he would probably be playing video games and riding roller coasters.

We finish up our pizza and Justin pays the check, while I head to the ladies' room to change into navy capri cargo pants and a short sleeved t-shirt. I was told to be comfortable, so I slip on my Sketchers sandals, which show off my impeccably manicured toes.

"You look cute." He takes my hand and leads me back to the car. He's changed into khaki shorts and a Phillies t-shirt while I was gone.

This time he opens the car door and waits for me to get in to close it. This gentlemanly gesture doesn't annoy me as it so often does. I guess when it's performed by a hot young guy from Philadelphia it's more appealing than when I am with a "Southern gentleman."

"Hey, I don't want to kill our light mood, but can I ask you about something weird that happened at work the other day?" I wince a bit.

"We have a little bit of a ride. Tell me all about it." He turns the radio down and looks like he's all ears. This could be a benefit of a younger man—he hasn't been beaten down by years of nagging women, so he doesn't dread having "a talk."

"I had a weird conversation in the ladies' room with Cecilia," I begin tentatively.

"What happened?" He's either worried that this pertains

to him or he is about to hear a story about an embarrassing female problem.

"She was quite nasty and berated me for my displeasure over our new line of books..." I pause and he glances over at me anxiously, "...and she said I was a fool to go out with you."

Justin grimaces and says, "She is such a manipulator. She did the same thing when I tried to date someone else in the office. She's just jealous because I wasn't interested in her."

"Was it Amanda? The other woman you dated?"

"Yeah, we went out a few times, but it was no big deal. Honestly, she's a sweet girl and pretty, but there isn't much upstairs. I know that sounds harsh, but seriously she is like a little girl. That's what you don't understand about the age thing—intelligence and maturity matter as much as looks." He looks over at me to gauge my reaction.

I don't say anything and look out the window.

"What? Did Cecilia say something about your age?"

I sigh and say, "Yes, she said you're much too young for me and I am making a fool of myself and everyone knows it."

Justin shakes his head. "She's such a bitch. I am telling you she's playing on your fears because she's vindictive. She treated Amanda horribly after we dated, and all because I didn't fall for her tricks."

"What tricks?" I ask apprehensively.

"She did crazy things. I don't even want to tell you. Let's just say Cecilia is persistent and pretty open with her sexuality. That's not a bad thing, but it is when you've said no numerous times, especially in the office. She's a freak, Claire. Ignore her. I'm sorry she rattled you." He pauses in reflection. "The part I don't get is how she knows any of this. I certainly didn't tell her we were going on a date or that I had any interest in you. I haven't told anyone. Unless..." I can see the wheels turning in that beautiful blond head.

"I was wondering the same thing. How *could* she know? I told Rebecca but she doesn't talk to Cecilia."

"Have you *e-mailed* anyone about this? Shit, you and I have e-mailed a bit. And probably you and Rebecca, too?" He raises his eyebrows to draw out my confession. Even

148

men Justin's age know that women talk about men.

"Yes, a little bit. What are you getting at? She can't see our e-mails." I am confused and technologically challenged.

"But I can. I just need to figure out how our CEO's admin could possibly have access to the e-mail server." Justin looks like a man on a mission. "But no matter," he says, switching gears back to the present. "Let's forget about her and focus on tonight, but thanks for telling me, Claire. I like it that you wanted me to know." He smiles, and I melt like chewed gum under a park bench in the sun.

I settle back and reply, "Hold on—what do you mean you can see our e-mails?"

"I'm the IT Director—obviously I can get on the e-mail server and read the files. There is no expectation of privacy on the network, Claire. Weren't you at the IT Security training?" He smiles playfully. "But don't worry. I don't have time to do much spying."

Shit.

I have been so engrossed in our conversation I haven't noticed where we're headed. Where the hell are we going? I don't even recognize any of this. As we meander along a country road I see the sign—Hanover Spring Carnival. Holy crap.

Since I live in the country suburb of East Bumblefuck Nowhere you would think these delightful amusements would be available in my area. Fortunately, this is not the case, and I have managed to avoid these activities, especially since I don't have children, and Dixie is not into rides.

Unfortunately, neither am I. The same motion sickness that is causing my avoidance of Rebecca's cruise conversation wreaks equal havoc on amusement park rides. My stomach does more flips and flops than the most modern rollercoaster, and by the looks of the Hanover Spring Carnival we are headed for a trip down memory lane as opposed to the cutting edge of technology. These break-down and set-up carnivals are notorious for old, poorly maintained rides, and workers. When Jackie and I were little we begged to go to these, and my over- protective mother only took us once or twice. Now of course I can see why—

that toothless guy selling tickets is probably not a skilled mechanic.

I don't want to hurt Justin's feelings (he's looking at me for signs of approval), but I doubt I'm going to go on a ride without throwing up, and I'm unprepared without my motion sickness pills.

Maybe I can avoid the bad rides and hide my panic. He is a little boy after all, even though he is the hotshot IT Director.

While I'm fighting my internal struggle, Justin says, "So what do you think? Fun, right? I wanted to do something different. Plus my father taught me that girls will be scared on rides and grab you a lot. That's how he met my mother."

He is so painfully sweet, and there's that "mother" word again. I need to address this so he doesn't think I am a crazy woman who randomly cries. I doubt he has made any connections between references to motherhood and my emotional state. However right now any tearing up will be a result of my impending doom on these flying death traps.

"Claire, what's wrong? Was this a bad idea?"

He does have patience and will make some girl a kind husband someday. "No, I was just remembering all the times I went to these carnivals as a kid," I lie, but nostalgia can be an excuse for moist eyes.

Justin looks elated now. "I used to ride the roller coasters with my brothers for hours, until we could barely stand up and had to be dragged to the car."

Great.

"So what do you want to do first?"

I avoid the question, and steer him to the ticket line. While Justin buys the tickets, I glance around frantically trying to plot a course that will avoid the worst rides, like the roller coasters and the Ferris wheel. Oh no—the swirling teacups. I may need to sabotage that ride—sorry, little kids with strong stomachs!

We walk into the main area and I begin to drag Justin to all the non-sick activities, like the fun house (even the mirrors make me a little queasy) and some silly thing with a bearded lady. I pretend that I want a huge pink stuffed bunny, telling him it reminds me of the cute slipper socks.

Justin takes the bait, repeatedly playing a silly shooting game to win the prize. I feel badly that he is wasting money, and I reward him by letting him kiss me in the Tunnel of Love (not that this is a huge sacrifice on my part).

As I carry around my pink bunny (what the hell I am going to do with this when I get it home?), I feel guilty about using my feminine wiles to distract Justin from his favorite rides. Maybe I should tell him about the motion sickness and suggest that he ride something alone, but that will be no fun for him. I spot a little kiddie rollercoaster, and as I am considering whether or not I can survive it without puking on the person in front of me, Justin says, "Hey, do you want to ride this little roller coaster? I am sensing you may be afraid of the big ones. Don't feel bad—most people are more apprehensive on rides as they get older." That word is not out of his mouth a second before I can see that he realizes his mistake.

I don't say a word and he quickly jumps in, "I didn't mean it like that. I'm not as adventurous as I used to be, either. Really. Claire?" He pulls up my chin, which has been pulled downward with the shame of my advanced age.

"Let's go on the ride." I avoid the issue and grab his hand to lead him to the short line. I look around at the little kids waiting and assume that it can't be that horrible. For God's sake, there's a stroller parked over there! If someone who isn't old enough to walk can handle this ride, I can make it through with my dignity and stomach contents intact.

It turns out that was a bit presumptuous and overly optimistic. I sit in front of Justin and he wraps his arms around me. This is nice and I can see why his father taught his sons to take their women to amusement parks. My moment of comfort is interrupted by the jerky spasms of the archaic ride starting up. I look over at the hunched over, bored teen ride operator and begin saying the Rosary. I wish I paid more attention in church and hope that I won't be smitten for forgetting how many Hail Marys there are before the Glory Be.

"Ahhhhhhh..." I'm already screaming in terror. Luckily I'm in front of Justin, so I have not blown out his eardrums.

He holds on tightly and I can tell he's enjoying this. To

the casual observer (or maybe any observer) I look like a lunatic. The ride makes a few rolling twists and turns, with the steepest being a few feet. As I said there are preschoolers on this ride, attended by their elementary aged siblings, and I am the only one screaming and carrying on. The laughter of little children fills the air, which I hope to keep vomit free.

On the last turn, I feel like I'm going to be sick and I wish I hadn't eaten that last slice of pizza. I bargain with God now—"please don't let me puke and I promise I won't sleep with Justin or any other men until I am lawfully wed. And I will stop drinking and swearing." As I finish my prayer, the ride comes to an equally jerky halt. I'm recovering from my whiplash as the ride operator announces that we may disembark from the ride (actually he says "everybody off" in a tone that makes me feel we are keeping him awake against his will).

"Wasn't that fun?" Justin spins me around and his smile turns to a look of concern. "What's wrong? You look pale."

"Justin, I'm sorry. I get sick on rides. I have motion sickness and if I don't take medicine for it I feel awful." I wish I wasn't forced to share this information.

"I had no idea. Why didn't you tell me? You must be miserable. Do you want to go? We can do something else, it's still early."

We *could* do something else—something I will regret tomorrow, but I can't let my mind go there. "I should have said something, but I'm better now. You spent money on tickets and you even won this awesome bunny for me. I can't let you leave here without riding at least one ride you really love. Name one ride and I'll go on it with you."

"Are you sure?"

"Yes, I swear, and the bunny agrees." I shake the bunny's head in solidarity.

"How about the Ferris wheel? It *is* high, but it doesn't move very fast and the views are cool up there." He looks at me hopefully. "I will hold onto you the whole time."

I ponder this logic, as if holding on to me is going to protect me if we are dropped a hundred feet to the pavement. I will just close my eyes and go back to saying my shoddy version of the Rosary. "Let's do it."

It's not too bad when we first get on, although the swaying of the car is making me dizzy and I feel completely out of control. Now the nausea is kicking in as they move us backwards up the line in succession, filling each car with more brave or deranged souls. I can see this is going to take hours, or so it seems. It stops at each car to let more people on. This time I don't even want to look at the guy in charge, and I'm glad Justin is sitting beside me, and not in a position to hear my heart beating like it's going to combust.

When we get to the top and they're filling the car that is straight down below us, my heart is racing double time. I have never gotten this level of cardiovascular workout in a sedentary position—not even sex, nor my workout video, can rival the sweating and pulse rate caused by this activity. You can burn a lot of calories at a scary carnival!

Justin is holding my hand and I am squeezing it so hard he's going to be branded. He kisses my cheek and I forget to be mad at him again—this is my own fault. What am I trying to prove? By now the anticipation is killing me and I hate the swaying of the car.

As I begin taking deep breaths, all of the cars are full and they start the wheel. As it rises I leave my stomach behind and focus on my fear of heights. I can see all the farmlands and the parking lot and houses that are getting smaller and smaller. We're so high up! Don't throw up, don't throw up! I have abandoned formal prayer for this mantra. I close my eyes and suppress a scream.

By the third trip around the wheel I'm becoming slightly more used to it. Having a settled stomach and a normal heart rate are overrated. I loosen my grip on Justin's poor hand as I put my other arm up in the air, focusing on the wind in my face. It is now dark and colder, and I lean in closer to Justin's warmth (his father is a genius).

By the time the ride comes to a screeching halt (they need to work on their starts and stops), I'm woozy but simultaneously invigorated.

"You liked it, right? I could tell you were scared at first"—he shows me the claw marks in his hand and I cringe apologetically—"but after we got going you liked it."

I catch my breath and pull him to a bench to recover. "You're right. At first I was freaking out, but it got better." I shiver and wish I had brought a sweater.

"You're freezing. Want to go back to the car?" He motions towards the parking lot.

His smile reminds me that being alone with him in the car is going to be dangerous, and I reply, "Do you think they have hot chocolate? And I want a funnel cake."

The funnel cake always seems like a good idea until I start eating it and remember it is a poor quality donut that has been fried to a crisp, and loaded with powdered sugar that I end up wearing. Tonight is no exception. I'm feeling greasy and covered in white dust in a matter of minutes. The hot chocolate is warming my insides (which have taken a beating), but I still need a sweater and the warmth of the car. "This was fun, Justin. And thoughtful. Thank you."

"Finally, I'm rid of my dick reputation!" He laughs as I throw my funnel cake wrapper at him. "I guess I should be glad you don't throw heavier objects at me. I guess that may come in time."

In time. There can't be any "in time" with Justin. I avert his eyes and continue sipping my hot chocolate.

He misses my pause and its meaning. "I'm going to check out the e-mail server issue tomorrow and see if I can figure out what's going on with Cecilia. Maybe she's screwing one of my staff." He studies my expression and says, "What, she could be?"

"Definitely. I just don't understand the whole e-mail server thing."

"Maybe the bunny can help." He takes the bunny and places it on his lap, moving it side to side as he says in his bunny impersonation, "You see, Claire, the e-mail server is where all the messages are housed and Justin is smart and knows how to spy on everyone..."

He can't keep a straight face when he first sees my glaring eyes, followed by my suppressed smile. We both laugh as we clean up the table, and begin walking to the car. He puts his arm around me and the heat feels good on my icy skin.

We drive home in relative companionable silence. I am

lost in thought. At one point Justin places his hand on my leg and I let it rest there a few minutes, keeping my hands folded in my lap. Eventually he pulls it back to adjust the heat and doesn't return it.

CHAPTER TWENTY

"I guess I should be glad you didn't stalk us in the parking lot last night." I barely turn the key to my office door and Rebecca is right behind me.

"I *did* need milk, and I *do* pass the office on my way to the convenience store, but I refrained." She looks pleased with herself.

I put my purse under my desk and start signing on to my computer. "I am *so* impressed," I say while rolling my eyes.

Rebecca sits in my guest chair and leans forward, wide eyed and jumping up and down in short bursts. "Soooooo?"

I sigh audibly and plop down in my seat, rubbing my temples. "I just keep digging a deeper hole."

"Did you have fun? Did he kiss you? Are you going to see him again? Where did he take you—"

"Stop it! Yes, I had fun. He took me to a carnival, the spring one in Hanover. Yes, he kissed me and before you ask—it was amazing. And no, I am not going to see him again, except here in the office, which makes everything a big mess." I'm breathless and weary from reliving the night's events.

"I don't understand you." Rebecca crosses her arms in her all too common defiant pose. "You have a good time with a hot young guy, who is obviously into you, and you won't see him again? Can't you just date him until you meet the right man? I know that sounds shitty, but don't you deserve a little fun?"

"*He* deserves more. He won a *giant pink bunny* for me, for God's sake! I think he wants more, but he's also too young and inexperienced to realize what more entails, and I am not ending up like Demi Moore! Am I am making any sense?"

"I get it, sort of. But does a bunny seal the deal on everlasting love and commitment? If he had won something more domestic for you, like cutlery or china, then maybe you would have a point." Rebecca is trying to lighten the mood, but she shrinks back in her seat under my unamused glare. "I'm sorry, I know this is serious. How did you end the night?"

"I was quiet on the way home and he had to feel the distance growing as we got back to the office. Then I got the hell out of his car as quickly as I could with the typical excuse of being tired and having a long drive to get home, work the next day, blah blah, blah. He looked a little hurt, and I know he's confused—"

"Then why don't you just tell him the truth?"

It's hard to argue with this point. "I will tell him that I'm too old for him and I can't have children. He's going to say he doesn't care about that, and I am going to have to make him understand that he will one day, and that will leave me old and grey and alone. Or something cheery like that." I frown and drop my shoulders.

"It's probably implying too much seriousness on his part to even bring it up, but I would tell him that you don't want to get hurt, so you can't let it go any further. He doesn't have to understand. But damn, I wish I wasn't old enough to be his mother, because I wouldn't mind consoling him." She smiles playfully.

I let the mood shift, faking a smile and moving on to safer topics. We chat a bit about work and our weekend plans. "Did you see I signed up to go to the Charter House Meetup tomorrow?"

"Yep, there are some new people going, too. You should check it out ahead of time and see if there are any men you want to meet."

"Good idea. I'll look right now." I pull up the Meetup site and sign in, scrolling to tomorrow's event. There are already thirty people signed up! I guess this is a popular venue and the weather is supposed to be beautiful. "Come over here and look at the guest list. Wait, I have a message in my inbox." Members can e-mail each other through the site, and someone has contacted me.

"Who is it from? Sometimes men will check out the women beforehand, kind of like what we're doing, and send a note of introduction. It's usually weirdos, though."

"The last thing I need is more weirdos. Can't there be one normal, age appropriate man in the whole city?" As I send this question out into the cosmos I open up the message and begin to read. I may have my answer.

"If you don't tell me who it's from I am going to implode with curiosity!" She is jumping up and down again, a little girl in a nosy middle-aged woman's body.

"I'll read it! Settle down, you're acting like Dixie waiting for a piece of meat." I begin reading. I had forgotten all about this.

Hello Claire,

I hope it isn't too forward of me to send you a note, but when I recognized your name on the Meetup site, I thought this was a perfect opportunity. I'm Nathan Kleinman, the doctor Melanie told you about. She told me that she asked if I could call you some time during your appointment with Dr. Mason. I was quite embarrassed (probably not the most ethical fix up), and I have been struggling with whether or not I should call.

Since we will both be at this event tomorrow night, I wanted to introduce myself and hope to meet you in person. Based on your profile it looks like we have some things in common (other than knowing your gynecologist).

Best Regards,
Nathan

"Hmm, formal but with a playful side? That's not a bad picture—he looks like a Jewish Alec Baldwin, before he gained weight." Rebecca is nodding her approval and I can almost see the wheels spinning inside her head like a windmill in a tornado.

"Yeah, he is attractive in a smart doctor kind of way. Is he Jewish? How do you know that for sure? My Catholic mother will love that." I laugh a little.

"Your parents would be upset about that? Are they that religious?"

"No, I'm being *serious*. My mother was the one who taught me Jewish men are good to their wives. And he's a *doctor*, so he could be a pagan wizard or a Jehovah's Witness and she would still be jumping for joy. Maybe not the latter, if he rang her doorbell during her favorite show." I am bordering on giddy as I continue to scroll through Nathan's answers to the Meetup profile questions.

"He's from New York, too. That was a safe bet since he's Jewish, right?" Rebecca, like many people, assume all Jewish people are from New York.

"I'm surprised they let him out, and how is he surviving without good bagels?" I respond with yet another eye roll.

Rebecca narrows her eyes in mock anger and says, "Whatever. So let's see—he's from Manhattan, but grew up in Brooklyn. I bet he has a humble rags to riches story. How romantic." Rebecca is swooning now.

"I just care that he's attractive, looks a little older than me, and seems nice. Melanie wouldn't have told me about him if he was a jerk," I say hopefully.

"I agree. I'm excited for tomorrow now." She claps her hands and smiles broadly. "You must pick out the perfect outfit, and for the love of God don't drink too much or wear shoes that cause you to fall on your ass."

She runs for the door as I look for something on my desk to throw at her, and I remember Justin's comments about me throwing heavier things in time. I probably need to stop throwing things at people. Never mind falling on my ass. That could *bite* me in the ass one day. "Yes, staying upright is vital to my social success. I need to make sure he doesn't meet Sherry or Andy, and for that matter you need to make yourself scarce, too. I'll be nervous enough."

"I promise I'll behave." She crosses her heart and claps her hands again. "I am so excited!"

"Let's try to do some work now." I look down at my keyboard and something dawns on me. "Crap, I just remembered Saturday."

"What's Saturday?"

"Brandon's party. I haven't talked to him since last week, when we had a semi-argument. I wonder if I'm even still invited." My mood deflates as I replay our last conversation.

"He didn't *say* you were uninvited, right? If Jane and her husband are going you should show up with them. Gauge his reaction and attitude, and if he's become a dick, go home. Better yet, maybe you'll have a date with Nathan and you can skip the whole thing." Rebecca is on her way to the door.

"I'll just stop by to save face as a neighbor and let's face it—he will probably sign a contract with us, so I don't want to completely alienate him. Pam is *going* to like his book. I wish I could keep all of the areas of my life separate." I let a frustrated sigh escape my lips.

"That's all about to change with the good doctor," Rebecca replies and quickly closes the door, as if expecting something heavier than the usual paper to fly in her direction.

My mind wanders to plotting my outfit, and I can't wait to get home and try on all my possible clothing combinations. As long as I don't drink I can wear whatever shoes I want, and there won't be any dancing, so I'm in no danger of falling on my ass. Besides, last time I fell on my head.

I chuckle at my own escapades, and all the ways I need to protect my ass.

CHAPTER TWENTY-ONE

"All I can say is they better be looking for someone who has murdered *multiple* people! A *single* murder does not warrant this level of inconvenience." I'm driving to the Charter House straight from work, and I'm sitting in what looks like miles of traffic because the cops appear to be stopping every car.

"Calm down—don't get yourself all worked up. Tell me what you're wearing." Rebecca volunteered to get there early and help the organizer reserve some tables on the patio, and therefore left work early enough to miss this bullshit festival I am currently experiencing.

I take a deep breath to soothe my jangled nerves and respond, "I am wearing that off the shoulder top with the blue and green swirls. You remember—I bought it when we did our spring shopping spree at the mall last month? And capri jeans—the ones with the holes and rips in them, and blue sandals that match the top." I strain my neck to see what's happening up ahead, and it looks like traffic is starting to inch along again.

"Aha, and how high are those sandals?" She asks in an accusatory tone.

"What? I was looking at the cops. They're not that high." I am totally lying. They are five inch platform wedges, but they have a stable base. Plus they match my top perfectly.

"We'll see about that. I'll reserve an area for you to prop yourself up so you stay in one spot. Let everyone come to you. You'll be tall enough to see from a mile away."

She never stops taunting me, but I'm glad I provide her with a world of mirth. "Very funny—I'm getting closer to the cops now. Hopefully I don't resemble any wanted fugitives and I'll be there shortly. Any sign of Nathan?" I ask optimistically.

"I haven't seen him but I bet doctors don't get to leave

work as early as we do. He'll be here. Just try to relax and think happy thoughts, and I'll see you and your stilts soon."

I say goodbye and continue my crawl towards the officers and their important agenda. I shouldn't be so nervous about Nathan. I don't even know him.

It's finally my turn and I pull up to the cop, who is young but quite serious looking.

"Good evening, Ma'am. Can I see your license, please?" He peers at me with that cop look that always scares me.

I fumble around in my purse and find my wallet, handing him my license with a big, fake smile. "Here you go, Officer."

He takes it and studies it intently. I want to ask what he's looking for, but I'm afraid to incur his wrath. He hands it back to me after what seems like an eternity and sets his gaze on Dixie's car carrier, which I haven't bothered to remove since I took her to the vet.

"Do you have a baby in there, Ma'am?" He is dead serious.

I pause before responding with any one of the smart mouth thoughts running through my head. I know police officers deal with the general population and all its loonies, but do I look like someone who would put a baby in a dog carrier?

I stifle a grin and say, "No, Officer, of course not. That's a *dog* carrier."

"Is there a dog in there now?" Is he kidding? He's not smiling. What the hell difference does it make if there's a dog in the dog carrier? Is there a wanted poodle on the loose?

"No, she's at home. The restaurant I'm going to doesn't allow pets." Be careful, Claire! "Is there something specific you are looking for today? I know it's probably not my business to ask, but I'm a little confused." I'm rambling and the cop is staring at me like I'm an idiot, even though he is clearly the mayor of Idiotville. However, they let him have a gun.

He is still not saying anything, and just when I fear he is going to slap the cuffs on me for snarky remarks he replies, "No, Ma'am. Just a routine check. Good night." And he waves me on. I have no idea what any of that was about. I wish I had a hovercraft so I could avoid driving on roads

162

altogether, but with my luck I would crash into birds or get accosted by an air traffic controller.

Shaking off the weirdness of that awkward waste of time, I pull into the Charter House parking lot and astonishingly it's still light out. I am told the sunset on the lake is beautiful from the deck. If I can find a parking spot, *and* walk in these shoes, I'll get there before I miss it. Suddenly my footwear confidence is waning. I see a cobblestone path that looks like it leads to the deck.

I find a reasonably close spot, but I will still need to navigate the ancient walking path. Why does anyone think it's quaint and charming to have roads made of any non-paved surface? In the past they didn't have pavement because it wasn't *invented* yet.

I brace myself and pray that I won't start out the evening on the ground. It is rough going—luckily there are some trees to grab onto. A couple is walking towards me now and I stand still and pretend to be looking at something fascinating on my phone, so they don't witness my struggle and offer to call for assistance. Once they are out of sight I try to move as quickly as my compromised balance will allow, and hope my ankles hold up.

I miraculously make it to the deck, still standing. I pause for a moment and take in the view. The lake is beautiful and the sun is beginning to go down over the water in a brilliant array of reds, oranges and pinks. How nice it would be to have someone special to share it with. My peaceful day dreaming is interrupted by my name coming from a loud and shrill source.

"Claire! Look, Andy, it's Claire from Lorenzo's. Rebecca's friend." Sherry must think Andy is going deaf, senile or both.

Andy nods his head in recognition, and they both head in my direction, as I slowly make my way to the main deck area. There are two tiers, the top one containing a large bar and numerous high top tables. The lower deck is close to the water and features dining tables. There are tons of people here and I am actually grateful that I've been noticed by friendly faces.

"Hi, guys. This place is great. It's nice to see you both

again." I am genuinely cheerful now that I have finally arrived and my exasperating trip here is over.

They both greet me with a warm welcome, including big hugs. Apparently this group is heavily into hugging. Rebecca had forewarned me.

"Don't you look so pretty, and so tall again! Rebecca is over at the bar talking to some new guy." My eyes quickly dart in that direction to see if she's talking to *my* new guy. I immediately see that the shorter blond man she's with looks absolutely nothing like *my* man. I silently chastise myself for laying claim to someone I haven't met, and thinking, even for a nano-second, that Rebecca would make a move on a guy I'm dying to meet.

I turn back to Sherry, who is waiting for me to speak. "Thanks Sherry, you look nice, too. Have you guys been here before?"

"The group comes here a couple of Fridays a month in warm weather. We're so glad you're here. Sherry and I were just having a laugh about Lorenzo's. When you fell I just about died. I didn't know what the hell to do. It wasn't funny at the time, but now it's hilarious, don't you think? I mean you crashed into the most popular cover band in Richmond!" Andy is bent over in peals of laughter now.

Sherry is giggling nervously because she appears smart enough to know I may not find it funny that I was not only humiliated, but suffered a concussion. Well, practically. "Hey Andy, why don't you be a gentleman and grab me and Claire a couple of drinks. Is white wine okay, Claire? I find it so refreshing in the warmer weather."

Sherry is clearly from Iceland because it is not that warm out, and I am starting to regret my summery attire. She must hail from a frozen land of tiny fairies, as her forehead is moist with perspiration. I look down at her and reply, "That would be lovely."

"Put it on my tab, Andy," she says to him as he disappears into the crowd, looking a little sheepish since his joke didn't go over well.

Sherry turns back to me with a concerned look and touches my arm. "I am so sorry for that knucklehead. Men—I swear. Are you okay now? That was a bad fall."

"I'm fine, really. He didn't mean any harm and someday I'll find it funny, too." I smile and we stand in silence for a moment as I begin to scour the area for Nathan.

"Are you looking for someone special?" I am not going to tell Sherry anything. These groups are gossip mills, which is another Rebecca tip.

"No, I'm just taking it all in." I smile as Andy returns with our wine and apologizes.

"Think nothing of it. I will do all I can to avoid another tumble tonight. Thanks for the drink!" We clink glasses and eventually meander away from each other. Everyone is here to meet someone and mingling is key.

I try to locate Rebecca but I'm intercepted by a woman with short, mousy brown hair wearing khaki pants and a button down shirt. I imagine she came straight from a conservative office because she looks like she's wearing men's clothes. She isn't entirely unattractive, and I have an overwhelming desire to take her to the Urban Decay section at Ulta and spruce up that plain face.

"Hi, are you new? I'm new." She extends her hand and I can see she's nervous.

I take her hand and introduce myself. "Yes, this is only my second event. I'm Claire."

She smiles and shakes my hand a second longer than is comfortable, as if she forgot what she's supposed to do next. "Silly me, I'm Chris. Nice to meet you. This is my first event."

"There are lots of people here and no loud music, so it should be easy to circulate. My first event was dancing to a loud band," I say as I jokingly cover my ears.

Since Chris doesn't know me, she misses my humor. Or maybe she misses humor in general. "I would hate that. It's loud enough here."

I just now notice that there's a band on the far side of the upper deck. Thank God they aren't playing jazz, but it's some kind of *reggae*? Like island music. I hope no one asks me to dance. How do people dance to reggae? It's not a salsa...I remember Chris is standing there and reply, "I did like it but my night ended abruptly."

"How so?"

Chris is boring holes through me with her unadorned brown eyes. This poor woman needs to work on her social skills, but I give her credit for coming out.

I remember the rumor mill and decide to change the subject. "So are you divorced, Chris?" I'm still scanning the deck for Rebecca, Nathan or anyone else I know. As my eyes move back towards the dining area, I do spot someone. My ex-husband. Ron and the Russian blow-up doll are enjoying a cozy waterfront meal. Great. Hopefully, I can avoid them. I slowly steer Chris to the bar out of their line of sight, pointing to my empty glass as she begins her long speech about her divorce. I did ask for it.

I nod and add a stray word here or there, but she seems to need to talk and I can be a good listener. I have all but given up hope of finding anyone I want to see when Rebecca comes up from behind Chris, and makes a face as if to ask who I'm talking to. I can't respond in sign language, or any other language, while the woman is right in front of me yapping away.

"Hey, Claire. Excuse me—hi, I'm Rebecca, Claire's friend." She moves in between us and shakes Chris' hand.

Chris looks flustered. "Rebecca, this is Chris. She's new to the group."

"Hi, Rebecca. It's a little overwhelming here, but Claire has been very friendly."

"Awesome! I see you don't have a nametag on. Diane, the organizer, is over there giving them out. She is really good at introducing new people around, too. She knows everyone!"

Rebecca is a master at this, and I stand back and marvel at her charm. Chris has no idea she is being dismissed, but Rebecca is right. She needs to be sociable for God's sake, and I need to find my Dr. Charming.

"I'll do that. Thank you both." Chris rushes over to the table where Diane is holding court. As she walks away I make a mental note to schedule a lunch date with Chris. She needs help. Is she even wearing any makeup?

"Now where the hell have you been?" Rebecca glances down at my shoes and widens her eyes.

"I don't even want to hear it. This is only my second

drink and these shoes are positively unwavering. Now where is Nathan? Some other woman has probably snatched him up," I say in a worried tone.

"I checked with Diane and he hasn't claimed his nametag, but neither have you, and I threw mine in the first trash can I saw. Have you eaten?" She gives me a suspicious look.

"Are you my mother? No, I haven't eaten. It took me forever to get here and then there was that whole bullshit with the cops, and I haven't been able to escape people who want to talk. However it is a social event, not a free buffet." I look triumphant after my little speech.

She sighs and says, "I just don't want to have to nurse you back to health tonight and drive your crazy little ass home. What if I hook up with a hot guy? Let's get you some food."

I reluctantly let Rebecca lead me to the bar and amazingly we find two empty stools. Rebecca puts my drink down on the bar and asks for menus. "I'm sorry, but you need to be watched."

"I really didn't want to sit on this side of the bar. Ron and his girlfriend are over there eating dinner. But I guess my back is to them and it's so crowded here. They'll never see me."

"Hey, Claire." Oh come on!

Exasperated, I turn around. "Hi, Ron. How are you?" I give him a hug that makes my pathetic hug with Brandon at Jane's resemble a lover's embrace. This time I'm only touching his air space.

The blow-up doll clears her throat and I extend my hand. "Hi, I'm Claire and you must be..."

"Natasha." She gives me a weak handshake and a shy look.

Rebecca is now introducing herself—friendly as always.

Natasha. She's Russian and her name is Natasha? What a cliché! I recall what Roberta said, and suppress a laugh. If she was a Russian blow-up doll that's what he'd name her—I guarantee that's the only Russian name he knows.

"What are you guys doing here?" I regret this question

instantly because I will now be forced to reply to the same inquiry.

"Just having dinner. Beautiful sunset here. You girls just having one of those girls' nights out Claire likes so much?"

I feel the sarcasm in his comment. Yes, I do like to go out without the man in my life once in a while. Is that a crime? Clearly this woman must be more submissive and clingy.

Luckily, even though his question is obnoxious, he gives me an out so I don't feel compelled to admit I have joined a single's group. "Yep, it's a GNO tonight."

We are all nodding and smiling, and no one is coming up with any topics of conversation. Natasha breaks the silence.

"It is good to meet you, Claire. I have heard much about you." She has a strong accent. I fight the urge to ask her where she's from or what brought her here. I would rather not prolong this exchange.

"I bet you have, and it's a pleasure meeting you, too." I shoot Ron my biggest smile and I hope he is too dumb or intoxicated to notice that I wish the ground would open up and swallow him. What a mess it would be if Nathan appeared right now!

Natasha appears to sense my discomfort, as well as the general weirdness in the air, and says, "We have to get home. Nice to meet you too, Rebecca. Have a good evening."

I avoid Ron's purposeful eye contact as he turns away, even though I feel the heat of his stare trying to connect with me.

"That was odd," Rebecca comments quietly.

"I ran into an old mutual friend of ours when I was at Dr. Mason's, and she said she thinks Natasha is a mail order bride."

"What?" Rebecca practically spits her drink. "That is ridiculous."

I agree, and we proceed to order some appetizers. I'm forced to be content with sipping warm wine because Rebecca won't let me order any more alcohol until my belly is appropriately lined with food.

A few more Meetup members have joined us, and we form a little social circle around the bar. Rebecca gets up to go to the ladies' room and I know she won't come back for a while. She ordered all of that food just for me, and now has her eye on another guy.

Rebecca is gone, I want another damn drink and there is still no sign of Nathan. This is looking like another disappointing night, but I intend to make the best of it with the good company right here.

"Claire, you look sad." Chris has returned to this side of the bar.

"There was this guy I was hoping to meet here tonight, but he hasn't shown up." I pick up one of my stuffed mushrooms and take a small bite, and make a face—the food is already cold.

"That's a bad sign. I mean him not showing up. But you're so pretty—you'll definitely meet someone." Chris is as innocent as a little lamb who hasn't been to the slaughter yet.

I smile and go back to my food. There is the usual clamor of conversation and laughter around me. Brandon's party tomorrow is going to be yet *another* disappointment. I should have called him to smooth things over.

Suddenly, in the din of voices I hear a hearty, super loud laugh. This guy is forcing it big time. No one here is that funny. Can't people just be themselves? My curiosity gets the better of me, and I abandon my cold food to see who this buffoon is on the other end of that annoying voice. Then I stop and stare. It's him. *Nathan* has a booming voice and jolly laugh. Dr. Nathan. He's here after all.

"Hey, Nathan," I hear some guy say, "She's over here. That girl Claire—the blond one— she's back." He points to me like he's found buried treasure, and I shrink a little as all eyes in the group turn my way.

CHAPTER TWENTY-TWO

He makes his way through the crowd of wide eyed gawkers with surprising ease. "Claire? I've been searching all over for you! I'm so glad I found you."

Nathan takes my hand and helps me off the bar stool, looking at me as if appraising a diamond. I navigate the short drop from the stool to the ground without twisting my ankle, and immediately notice that he's still taller than me. His dark hair is sleeked back and he's wearing black slacks and a striped button down shirt, with the cuffs slightly rolled up. He does resemble a younger Alec Baldwin, only slimmer and more expensive looking.

"Yes, I'm Claire. I was looking for you, too. I think half the people in Richmond are here tonight," I nervously reply.

"I know, it's crazier than the downtown ER on a Friday night, except no one is bleeding." He laughs at his medical joke. "Let's see if we can find a quiet corner somewhere to get better acquainted, shall we?" He takes care of ordering a fresh drink for me, as well as paying my bar tab. I protest but he ignores me. For once maybe I should just let a man take care of me and enjoy myself.

Miraculously, we find a corner table towards the back edge of the patio. It doesn't have a great view of the water and that's probably why it's empty. However, I don't think either one of us is interested in the lake any longer. As we set our drinks down, Nathan pulls out the chair and I work on climbing up on the seat gracefully.

"So this was a great coincidence that we both joined this group around the same time. I was hesitant to call you. Melanie means well, but as a doctor I do need to be careful of my professional reputation when dating."

I stop staring into his deep brown eyes long enough to say, "It was weird for me too when she told me about you. I was getting dressed at the time, after all." I laugh and blush a little. I can hear Rebecca's voice in my head telling me to loosen up. "I had honestly forgotten all about that exchange and assumed you weren't going to call, or maybe she had decided against giving you my number after all."

"Thank goodness she did, and I saw your name and made the connection. So tell me a little about yourself. I'm dying to get to know the real Claire."

He has a dazzling smile.

I shift in my seat and begin to tell him the usual information—occupation, family background, I'm from New York, etc. I am starting to bore myself with my story and I'm leaving out all the personal parts, such as my divorce and hysterectomy. I suddenly panic—maybe Dr. Mason or Melanie told him, but that would be super unprofessional and decide against it.

"You're from New York, too? What a coincidence. I was born and raised in Brooklyn and started practicing medicine in Manhattan. I came down here to escape the high cost of operating a business in the city, just like most of the transplants here, I would imagine."

I already knew this from his profile, but I am still elated to meet a man from New York. He has only been here five years and his accent comforts me like a warm blanket as the alcohol warms my insides. However, a glance at my empty glass brings me back to the present moment, and I shiver at the sudden drop in temperature.

"It's getting chilly out here. Claire, please take my jacket." I notice that he's been carrying a sport coat around. Normally, I would want to appear to be an independent woman and tough it out, but I don't hesitate to accept Nathan's offer. He places the coat delicately around my shoulders, and gently gathers my hair from under the collar and lets it fall across my back. The touch is soft—barely a whisper, but it warms me more than the finely lined tweed fabric.

"Now, isn't that better? So, you're an Irish girl. The Irish and Jews go way back in New York in the old neighborhoods. Did you read Angela's Ashes?" He leans forward in anticipation.

"Yes, I did. My mother insisted. The Jewish family

helped the Irish family when one of the children was sick? Something like that, right? I guess the Jews were a lot more prosperous."

"They were, but still discriminated against, so they had to live in the lesser neighborhoods. We should both be proud of how far our people have come."

I have never been around a man who speaks like this, and it's appealing and refreshing. We continue to discuss our backgrounds, and a few times he grazes my leg with his under the table. He also keeps my wine glass full, returning to the bar several times. The crowd is starting to thin out, and it's easier to attract the bartenders. Plus, Nathan doesn't have a problem commanding attention.

I am feeling a bit woozy, but determined not to replay any of my recent negative behavior patterns. The alcohol has fueled my courage to veer down the path I dread most— I ask if he has ever been married or has any children.

"I haven't had time. Medical school, internship and residency took up all of my youth, I'm afraid. I just turned forty last year and now I'm finally at a place in my life where I'm ready to settle down. I know some people manage to do it all, but I don't see how."

I try to conceal my disappointment. "So you are still hoping to have a family?" I'm cutting right to the heart of the matter this time.

Nathan looks uncomfortable. "No, actually I would prefer not to have children at this point. My sister has two girls and I see them occasionally, and that's enough for me. Besides, child rearing is for younger people, and think of the fun we could have with all that freedom!" He catches himself when I raise my eyebrows. "I mean 'we' as in anyone our age, not as in you and me. Since we just met. But I must say Claire, you are the most beautiful and intelligent woman I have met in a long time." He pauses and takes my hand, which is freezing cold. "Your hands are like ice—do you want to move inside?"

I had been holding my breath waiting for him to say he doesn't want kids, but he may assume I do, and that my biological clock is ticking. Of course, he would be thinking that about a single childless woman my age.

I agree to move inside, and we head into the warm and bright indoor bar area. We grab a couple of stools, and the closer proximity of the seats only increases the intimacy of this conversation. As my eyes start to adjust to the light, after sitting on the dark patio, I ask, "So I guess you aren't a pediatrician?"

We share a laugh at his lack of desire to be around kids, but I'm already feeling vulnerable and afraid of rejection. I am being hasty hoping he could be the one, and I am tipsy again, only this time on more expensive wine.

"No, I couldn't listen to babies crying all day. I'm a cardiologist." He asks if I'm hungry and I tell him I'm famished. "You need to eat to soak up some of that wine; you're just a little thing."

I order the apple pie with vanilla ice cream, and proceed to eat it all by myself. I offer to share, but Nathan politely refuses. "I like a woman with a healthy appetite." He smiles and touches my leg again. Leaning in he returns to the previous discussion. "Claire, I know you don't have any children. Melanie did tell me that much about you. Is that a wish of yours? To be a mother?"

This question always brings forth tears and this time is no exception. As I try to hold back the water works, I decide to go ahead and tell him the truth. This emotional response is going to be misinterpreted if I don't. I will scare him away with thoughts of baby carriages and expensive college tuitions screwing up his retirement years.

"I can't have children." I pause and take a deep breath. "I had several miscarriages in my early thirties, and was forced to have a hysterectomy." I put down my spoon and wipe my mouth, even though I know it's clean.

Nathan's face softens into a genuine frown. "I am so sorry, Claire. I know that must be awful for a young woman with hopes of being a mother, and your beautiful figure and freedom are small consolation for that loss. But I do hope you are able to see the positive side of what life has dealt you." He takes my hand and holds my gaze. I break eye contact first.

Normally this type of comment would make me angry, and for a second I feel resentful—assuming that he is secretly relieved. But then isn't this what I have always wanted? An age appropriate, mature, successful man who doesn't want children and accepts me as I am?

"Thank you, Nathan. I was devastated at the time, and it was the final nail in the coffin of my marriage, but I have found ways to be happy. I have an adorable little dog—she's the daughter I'll never have." I manage a sad smile to soften the mood.

"What a nice way to redirect your maternal instincts. What kind of dog?"

It's probably my tendency to jump to the worst possible conclusions in a single bound, but I am getting a vibe that Nathan isn't too keen on dogs. "She's a mini dachshund." He looks puzzled so I add, "You know, a wiener dog."

He finally shows signs of recognition and replies, "Yes, they look like little hot dogs." He reflects further and says, "They can be snippy, right? I knew someone who had one once and she was an ankle biter."

"Not at all—she's a sweetie. She loves everyone."

Nathan sits back and pauses, sipping his drink before replying. "Of course, how silly of me. You couldn't raise a snippy dog."

I smile and stare into my empty glass.

"And besides, if I can have you Claire, I'll take the dog." He winks and notices my glass. "Would you like another glass of wine? How about an after-dinner cordial?"

I don't need any more alcohol, and I'm already panicking about how I'm going to get home. I don't live around the corner, and I am not repeating the incident with Daniel, even though Nathan is clearly not in his category.

"No thanks, I would prefer some water. I need to sober up to drive home."

"I will get you some right away, and have no worries about getting home." He squeezes my hand and saunters off to the bar.

Crap. I hope he isn't expecting me to go to his house to sober up, or planning on driving me home. Why do I keep putting myself in these uncomfortable positions?

Nathan returns to our table with a glass of water and a couple of pills. "Just what the doctor ordered." I must have looked nervously at the pills so he adds, "I promise they're just aspirin." He smiles and glances at his watch. "It is getting late, and I do apologize, but I have an early tee time tomorrow. Have you ever played golf, Claire? I'm afraid I indulge in the stereotypical doctor hobby." Again he displays his dazzling white smile, and I make a mental note to buy some teeth whitener tomorrow.

"No, but I'm a mini-golf pro. I know that sounds silly."

I'm hoping he's going to suggest that we play some time, but instead he says, "No, that's cute. I play regularly at Windy Hill. It's a good stress reliever. My job can be pretty intense, as I'm sure you can imagine."

That sounds familiar. I think Daniel said he plays golf there? I hope they don't know each other.

"We should get going then. I'm alright to drive now." Rising from my seat I am about to announce a trip to the ladies' room when Nathan interjects. "You will not be driving anywhere." I open my mouth to protest and he continues, "I have called a cab service and they should be outside for you any moment."

"Thanks, but I live almost thirty minutes away from here. That's going to cost a fortune."

"Claire, don't even think of it. I have already paid the driver with my credit card over the phone, tip included."

He walks away before I can say anything else. I decide to accept his generous offer and be quiet. After all I am not going to be valued if I devalue myself, and it's rare to meet a real gentleman these days. I go to the ladies' room and meet him back at the table.

"Are you ready?" He offers his arm and I accept the gesture. His arm feels strong and warm, and I relax into him.

"Thanks for everything, Nathan. It is so nice to finally meet you." I stop myself before I add "and I hope to see you again." Over eager, neurotic Claire is not going to blow this for me.

"You're welcome. I hope you have a great weekend. Do you have any plans?"

For a second I want to say no, but I do have that damn party at Brandon's tomorrow night. If he wasn't my neighbor, and if I wasn't involved professionally with him, I would blow it off. That whole situation is such a mess.

I am probably frowning and I have hesitated too long. "Yes, I'm going to a party tomorrow night. A birthday party. For a neighbor. He's a friend." Why would I tell him my friend is a "he?" I hope the cab comes soon so I can't say any more stupid things. I glance outside in order to avoid eye contact.

He looks outside as well and says, "Here's your coach, Cinderella."

I smile and we walk outside, still arm in arm. "Sleep well, Claire."

I stand there a moment too long and feel like an idiot. After spending hours together in intimate conversation I can't believe he isn't going to kiss me goodnight. I wait as long as I can and walk towards the cab. He jumps forward and I once again anticipate a kiss, but he opens the door and makes a sweeping gesture for me to get inside. I smile weakly and climb in.

The door begins to close and abruptly opens again. "Oh, and Claire?"

I start to reply as he leans into the car and takes my face in his hands and gives me the slowest, sweetest kiss imaginable. I do not care at all about the cab driver, and I'm assuming Nathan has tipped him sufficiently to give us enough time to do whatever we want before getting on the road.

As my mind wanders to what that could be, Nathan abruptly stands and says, "Good night, Claire." He closes the door and steps to the sidewalk.

"Good night." The driver interrupts my trance with verification of my address. As we begin to pull away I see Nathan on the sidewalk waving frantically. "Can you stop, please?" I ask the driver. "I must have forgotten something."

Nathan opens the door again and pokes his head in. "I almost forgot the most important thing—when will I see you again?" He cracks up laughing. Why is this funny? "Did you honestly think I was going to let you leave without making plans to see you again? You silly girl."

Actually I *did*, and so did the driver apparently, if his eye rolling and sighs are any indication. "You *did* walk away, but yes, we can make plans," I say playfully so he doesn't know I was worried.

"Wonderful. How about Sunday afternoon? We could do brunch somewhere downtown?" He winks and flashes the white teeth again.

"That sounds nice."

"I'll call you." He stands up and closes the door, waving as the car finally pulls away.

"That one's a charmer," the cab driver says as he smiles and shakes his head.

"He surely is." I look out the window and lean back in my seat. "He surely is," I whisper to no one but myself.

CHAPTER TWENTY-THREE

Sleeping in feels good and Dixie cooperates this morning. When she was a puppy she woke me up every day around five, and I was scared that would continue, but she has adapted to her mommy's lazy schedule. I enjoy the only perk of being alone and childless.

Today, I'm meeting Rebecca for lunch. I shower and dress in comfortable black cargo capris and my short sleeved eggplant sweater. Mid-April is coming in warm, but tonight it may get chilly. I will probably change for Brandon's party. Brandon. Shit, it's also his birthday. I didn't get a present or a card. Men are impossible to buy gifts for, especially ones you barely know, who are also mad at you.

I arrive at Rebecca's condo in the west end at noon. She lives in a newer area near the big, upscale mall. All of the apartments are built above fancy shops and restaurants, but the condos are separate buildings.

I am leaving my car at her house and she's going to drive to lunch, and then the mall. She pops out the door before I get a chance to ring the bell.

"Hey, do you need to use the bathroom before we go?" She is holding several shopping bags, which means she needs to return purchases at the mall. Rebecca is an impulse shopper.

"No, I'm okay. Where did you want to do lunch?" We walk to her car and deposit her bags in the trunk, discussing our food options.

"Italian? So, how was your night? I saw you *deeply* engrossed in conversation with the doctor, so I left without saying goodbye. I couldn't bear to interrupt." Rebecca fiddles with the rearview mirror and roots around for her sunglasses.

"I'm almost afraid to tell you about him for fear of jinxing it." I go on to regale her with the tale of our dreamy evening—Nathan's consideration of my needs, his complete attention when I spoke, the heart melting eye contact, the not-so-accidental brushes of our legs, and the dreamy kiss. I leave out the cute way he came back to the car to ask me out again. I thought that would just be gloating.

Rebecca wrinkles her nose, now cradling her rhinestone encrusted sunglasses.

"What, you don't think he sounds amazing?"

"He sounds nice, but I don't know. You seem captivated too quickly. This guy is smart and quite a few notches in experience above Ron, Justin and all the other eligible men you've been meeting lately. That's a good thing in many ways, but a guy like that could be a smooth operator." When I don't respond right way she adds, "I just don't want you to set yourself up for disappointment."

The car jerks forward as Rebecca notices that we have come to a stop sign. Normally, I would tease her about her bad driving, and her opinions that stop signs are "a suggestion," but I'm too annoyed.

"I know where you're going with this, but he is not an arrogant jerk. He's an important man—a cardiologist, and he grew up in Brooklyn, so he's an assertive type, but he was a perfect gentleman. Justin didn't put me in a cab after our date. And last night wasn't even a date."

"Justin also didn't get you drunk. The point is that he sounds sure of himself and you are like an innocent little kitten. Just take it slow, that's all I'm saying. When are you seeing him again?" She maneuvers the car into a parking spot close to our favorite Italian restaurant.

"Sunday. For brunch." I should have kept that to myself. What if he doesn't call to make plans?

"Why not tonight? Oh, I remember. Have you talked to Brandon since your argument?" The hostess tells us we can sit anywhere and we choose a booth away from the other diners, as always.

I sigh deeply and reply, "No. There's been too much going on and I'm a big chicken. I'm going to arrive with Jane and Mike, if I can, to soften the blow. I probably won't stay long."

We order our lunches and I steer the conversation away from my dating life, and ask Rebecca questions about work and her personal life. That plan isn't too successful as she turns the discussion full circle back to me.

"So Nathan has no kids? How old is he? Forty, you said? Did he pass your test on that front?" Rebecca butters a roll and wipes the crumbs off the table.

"Yes, he's forty." I glance around the room before continuing. "I did something I never do. I told him about my hysterectomy."

"That's great, Claire. You must have felt comfortable with him. Maybe I'm wrong." She pauses, and knowing Rebecca, she's likely pondering how she could possibly be wrong. Continuing, she says, "You should continue to date other people, even if you like him. If you put all your eggs in one basket you might accidently sit on it and crush them all at once."

"I love your clichés, but they're never quite the way I remember them."

Rebecca smiles and stabs the salad the waitress just dropped off with gusto. "Just trying to inject some sensible wisdom around here."

I roll my eyes and say, "I can't date multiple men. I am a one man woman. The juggling is impossible. To your point, too many individual eggs in the air will result in egg yolk on my shoes when they all hit the ground at once." I move my hands in a juggling motion to illustrate my point.

"You're not very coordinated, that's true." I almost throw my napkin at her, but stop myself since I have decided to change that behavior pattern when people annoy me. She continues, "So you're not going to see Justin again? And what about Brandon?"

"I don't think so. Justin is hanging around like a puppy, but he's obviously confused. If I don't see him again he'll be released to more sensible dating choices. I'm just some silly challenge for him, and I still think he has a cougar fetish. And Brandon and I are not dating, nor will we be dating. He gets angry way too easily. I don't need any brooding, overly sensitive artist types. No, Nathan is what I need." I pause to take a sip of water. "But I will offer another cliché—when it rains it pours. I always complain that there are no men, but lately there have been too many."

Rebecca laughs and breaks into a too loud version of the song "It's Raining Men," attracting the curiosity of the other patrons. Happy the mood has lightened, I dig into my pasta and thoughts of Nathan's lips.

Later in the afternoon, after a couple of hours at the mall, Rebecca drives me back to her place and my car. I say goodbye and jump in, headed for home and a night of stress. At least that's what I'm afraid of.

In the hopes of alleviating my concerns, I call Jane to discuss our plans.

"Are you guys going tonight? Please say yes," I ask hopefully.

"Yeah, we're going. Britney is coming over to babysit. You're going right?"

"Yes, but I want to walk over there with you and Mike. I can't face Brandon alone." I regret phrasing it that way immediately.

"Why, did something bad happen?"

I explain what happened the last time Brandon and I communicated, and how he was frustrated with me.

"You think you blew it with him?"

"No Jane, I am not interested in him, despite your matchmaking efforts. I just want to get along because we're neighbors, and I'm working on getting him a book deal with my company. Did you get him a gift?"

"Mike picked up something—some kind of alcohol. How about you?"

"I got him a sweater. That feels like a stupid choice now." I debated in the store for an hour, going back and forth to the men's department in Macy's. Rebecca was no help as she ran from store to store, returning all her hasty purchases from last weekend.

"It is a more personal gift. I wouldn't get a sweater for a man I wasn't interested in. What color is it? Does it match his eyes?" I hear the mirth in her voice.

"You are *not* helping me at all. I should stay home and pretend to be sick. Or hung over—*that* he would believe."

"Claire, I know you don't want to hear it, but he really likes you. Don't you see how he looks at you? He wouldn't be around all the time if he didn't—"

"Stop it! Why does everyone keep telling me who I should or shouldn't date?"

"You *do* ask me and I suspect you do the same with a few other friends. I am not trying to be bossy or interfering. I just see something I think you're avoiding."

"I met a much better man last night, so all these young *boys* are off my radar and no longer my problem." I tell her about Nathan and our fantastic night.

"A doctor, huh? I'm sure you know what you're doing, but just be careful." Since when did doctors become dangerous to date?

Exasperated, I steer the conversation back to the party logistics and we decide to meet at their house at eight. I go upstairs to agonize over what top to wear with my jeans. Actually, I need to decide which jeans to wear too, and I need to wrap the gift. The sweater is a dark cobalt blue and it will match his eyes. What's wrong with getting someone a nice present? That doesn't mean anything—it just shows that I was raised to be polite and thoughtful.

No one knows what they're talking about. Nathan is a good man, and I deserve that. Speaking of Nathan, he hasn't called yet. I have been busy, but I would be lying if I said I haven't been checking my phone all day, as if I have selective deafness and might have missed the call, with the volume on the highest setting.

I look out my bedroom window as I start to gather possible clothing choices and lay them on my bed. Brandon is pulling into the driveway and gets out of his truck with a big, tattooed guy. They are weighted down with alcohol and snacks. Just as I start to turn away to my task at hand, I freeze as I see him staring at my house. He pauses for a long moment before his friend comes out to get another load of bags, and they disappear inside the house.

CHAPTER TWENTY-FOUR

Standing on Jane's front porch I gaze up at the clear, starry sky. As I wait for Mike and Jane to emerge, I grasp my meticulously wrapped stupid blue sweater. I have decided that nothing screams boring old lady or maiden aunt like giving a man a *sweater*. At least I didn't knit it.

The door flies open and I'm almost knocked over by running dogs, followed by Mike. "Hey sweetie, I need to take the dogs out before we go. I want to check my e-mail again, and I thought of a couple more things to tell the sitter, so you girls should go ahead without me. I'll be along soon." He gives me a quick hug and peck on the cheek, and heads to the back yard to supervise his furry brood.

"We'll see you later. Is Jane coming?" He's already out of sight and earshot. I peek inside the foyer. "Hello!" They do a terrible job of answering the door. The Jehovah's Witnesses have zero chance here.

"Hey, you look cute." Jane finally appears, assessing my outfit, and leans back into the house to yell some final orders to the kids. She closes the door with a sigh of relief. "It is *not* easy to get out of my house." She has the wrapped bottle of alcohol and I feel a twinge of embarrassment over my stupid sweater again.

"Does this look okay?" I am wearing tight skinny jeans with black peep toe sandals with a *reasonable* heel, and a long sleeve t-shirt with a New York City scene print. I'm going for sexy casual to counteract the old lady gift.

"You look gorgeous, but tell me why that matters?" She smirks and starts down her porch steps.

Following behind, I fight the urge to push her. "Jane, I like to look good no matter where I'm going." I'm surprised she hasn't asked if Nathan has called yet, which he hasn't. I check my phone instinctively and there is nothing but the time displayed.

Now that we're walking towards the house I notice how many cars and people there are milling around our little street. Inviting the neighbors was a genius strategy to avoid complaints and visits from the police. Although I doubt Mrs. O'Brien is here.

We smile at a few people in the driveway and make our way up the front steps. He has recently bought rocking chairs and a little table to decorate the porch. How domestic. As the door opens I wish I could sit out here for a while before I face this crowd of people.

"Hello, ladies. Welcome." Brandon's eyes are even more blue than usual. They will match the sweater perfectly. He smiles at both of us, and his eyes linger on me a moment longer. "Where's Mike, Jane?"

"He's coming. He's multitasking, and if I waited for him I would never go anywhere." She laughs as Brandon ushers us into the house.

Jane spots our other neighbor, Laura, and excuses herself to talk to her. She has likely remembered something about baseball practice or dance class, or some other activity their kids do together. I'm left standing there with Brandon, holding my stupid sweater.

"So how have you been, Claire?" His voice is low and he leans in a little closer.

"Good. Busy. I think Pam is going to love your book."

He sighs and runs his fingers through his hair. "Listen, Claire, I'm sorry about that last conversation we had. You don't owe me anything, and if you want keep things professional—"

"There's no need to apologize, please. You've been sweet and I should have gotten back to you sooner." I spot a picture on the hall table of two little children playing. Assessing the time frame based on their clothing, I would guess it's Brandon and his sister. She has curly blond hair, and she's laughing and halfway upside down, hanging on to Brandon's arm. Once again I am fighting off the water works as I glance around into the kitchen, where there are tons of guests milling around.

"Let's just call it a truce and have fun tonight. There's a lot of people you should meet." As he says this a thin girl with lots of bright red hair comes bopping over.

"Hey, is this Claire? I was in the basement. Those guys have a killer sound Brandon, but shit, it's hot in here." She's a bit breathless from her jog up the stairs, and fans herself with her shirt, revealing a perfectly flat tummy with a belly button ring.

"Yes, this is Claire. Claire, this is Bianca. She's a band groupie." Bianca punches him in the side as he quickly moves to protect himself, although she doesn't look like she packs much of a wallop.

"Claire, I have heard *so* much about you." She takes my hand and pulls me forward, trying to get a closer look. Luckily, I have blinked back the tears and am sporting a fake smile. "You *are* very pretty." She glances at Brandon knowingly and he returns her look with mock disdain.

"Thank you. So are you." Was that a stupid thing to say? I have got to get rid of this sweater and get a drink. I avoid Brandon's eyes.

"Come with me and let's get you a drink." She read my mind and starts to lead me away. "You brought a *gift*? That's so sweet." She peeks at Brandon over her shoulder.

"Yes, I would love a drink. Can I put this somewhere?" I hold the box out willing someone to take it.

"I'll take it," Brandon grabs the box and looks sheepish. "Thanks. I'll put it upstairs for now." I give him a puzzled look. Didn't other people bring gifts? It's a *birthday* party.

He hesitates and then shoos us off. "You girls go mingle." He starts up the stairs and turns back, "And Claire, don't listen to anything she says."

Bianca makes a playful fist again, but Brandon ducks and runs.

"He's so cute, isn't he?" She takes my arm and leads me into the kitchen. Jane is lost in animated conversation with two of the neighbor women, Laura and Sarah. I take in the decor and I am again confused. Why would a young single guy want a country farmhouse kitchen set? Even my style is edgier than this.

"So how do you know Brandon?" I find a glass and sort through the wine selections. I'm surprised they have wine here, but I bet the neighbors brought it. No one else here looks like they would drink wine. It's a divided crowd. We have the neighborhood young parents on one side, and an assortment of much rougher looking young people on the other. The big tattooed guy from last night is coming up the stairs and into the kitchen. He looks familiar now that I see him up close.

Bianca opens a cooler, pulls out a hard cider and twists off the cap. "I know him from the band. I used to date the drummer. Hey, why don't you try one of these? They're delicious, just like apples and you won't get a headache, no matter how many you drink. Wine absolutely kicks my ass." She hands me a bottle and I put the wine glass back.

"Thanks, I've never had one of these. I drink wine all the time, but you're right. I always get a headache. Of course that could be due to occasional over consumption." I laugh and we toast bottles.

"N-o-o-o-o, you don't look like an over consumer of alcohol." She opens her mouth in exaggerated surprise and joins me in laughter. "Seriously, you don't. But I'd love to see that."

"What's so funny, you two? Are you corrupting this beautiful young lady, Bianca?" Big tattoo guy has joined the conversation. I instantly straighten up and assess his look. He is huge! And not "fat" huge, he's "muscular" huge, and tall! His head is shaved and he is wearing a white t-shirt with some band logo on it, and a denim jacket with the sleeves ripped off. He has lots of chains hanging from various places and now I also notice a nose ring. He taps the kitchen chair leg with his black biker boots (also full of chains) and waits for Bianca's response. I'm waiting my turn to ask about this band connection? I could be just naive enough to be living across the street from a famous rocker hiding out in suburbia, and not even know it.

"Claire, this charming guy is my ex—Max."

"Is this the drummer? From the band?" They are both looking at me expectantly before they respond, waiting for me to finish my dangling thought. "What band are we talking about?"

"You know, *the band*? Brandon's band. Chain." She notes my surprised expression and continues. "You didn't know Brandon had a band? That's why he bought this house. It was impossible to practice in his city apartment and none of the other guys have big places, either."

"Yeah, I live in a dump." Max and Bianca break out into fits of hilarity. "She hated coming over. I don't even have a lock on the bathroom and the whole place is basically one room."

Bianca smiles at the memory and adds, "Yeah, he isn't much into home improvement."

"Hey, I have other priorities. Did you see my new bike out there, little Miss Opinionated? Claire, do you like motorcycles?" He winks at me.

It's clear that Bianca and Max have a good friendship now—all of these barbs are traded in jest. "So let me get this straight. Brandon has a band and you all practice here, and you play shows out in public?"

"That's pretty much what bands do, Honey." He laughs again. "Brandon's got his hands full with you."

"What? Oh no, Brandon and I aren't together. We're just friends, and I'm helping him with his book." I look around to see if Brandon could be overhearing this conversation.

"You're the publisher chick! Awesome. Smart *and* hot. What a combination!" He takes another swig of his enormous beer. He must sense my discomfort and says, "I'm just messin' with ya. You actually look familiar, but I'm guessing you don't frequent any of my usual hangouts." He smiles broadly and I have to say—he has sparkling teeth.

It just hit me. He's the tattooed guy that e-mailed me on the online dating site. This town is way too small. Hopefully his beer-clouded brain won't make the connection.

"Just ignore him." She gives Max an exasperated look. "The band does some covers— nineties to the present, and they're working on some original stuff. Hard rock, alternative rock, some metal. They're awesome, even though they let this asshole stay in the band." She punches Max in his massive bicep, and in comparison her hand looks like it belongs to a toddler. Talk about a man you can climb.

"So the band is called Chain?" As I say this I make the connection to the many chains on Max. "What does Brandon do in the band?"

"I can't believe he hasn't told you all of this, as close as you two are?" Bianca and Max grin at each other and she continues. "Brandon is the lead singer and he plays the guitar."

I drink my hard cider, which is delicious. "So where do they play?"

"They play at all the usual bars in the area. Rocky's, The Shark Tank, sometimes O'Malley's—"

"Did they happen to play at O'Malley's on St. Patrick's Day?" Rebecca said the band had a cute young lead singer and they played music I like.

"Yes, we most certainly *did* tear up O'Malley's that night. Bianca wouldn't remember, though. She was too wasted."

"I do so remember. I met a hot guy that night and he kept buying me green beer. I remember every detail of that night. Claire, this guy was unbelievable. What he could do with his tongue and—"

"Can you guys point me to the powder room?"

They exchange a look and Max responds. "My dear, the *powder room* is in the foyer." Max bows and points while pronouncing foyer—"foyay"—to mock my formality in calling it the "powder room." I guess I should have asked for the toilet.

"Thanks, Max." I put my empty bottle in the recycling bin with the others, and walk to the foyer.

"Claire, come back when you're done. I want to show you the basement and the band set up." Bianca yells after me.

I turn back and smile. The powder room is also decorated meticulously, with pretty finger towels and a deep rose color on the walls. Brandon has a pink bathroom, but he's the lead singer in a metal band called Chain. I wash my hands with the lavender scented soap, swing open the door, and narrowly avoid hitting our host.

"Hey, are you having fun?" Brandon has a beer in his hand and gestures towards the kitchen. "I saw you deep in conversation with Bianca and Max. He's a character but he's a good guy, and if you ever need any heating or air conditioning work done, he's your man."

"That's good to know. They're both nice." I glance again

at the pictures on the hall table.

"That's me and my sister at our old house in Arlington. I'm about six or seven there, and she's only maybe three."

I pause. I want to ask if she's adopted too, and all sorts of other questions about his life, but I just say, "Cute. So I heard about the band."

"I keep meaning to tell you about it, but we always seem to get interrupted." As if on cue, the doorbell rings.

We both smile and I point to the door as he apologizes. "Sorry, more guests. Why don't you check out the downstairs with Bianca and I'll catch up with you later."

I mumble something and head back to the kitchen. Bianca grabs two more hard ciders and we head to the basement. Max is off in loud conversation with some other guys who look like they may be in the band. He has one of them in a headlock and he's messing up his hair.

Finally my phone starts vibrating in my pocket. This must be Nathan! I don't get to answer before Bianca starts talking again. She proceeds to introduce me to a bunch of other people. Jane is down here now and she's excited over the band, too. "I told Mike we need to get a babysitter and go see them some time."

"Where is he?"

"He was here and then he left again to make a phone call. Someone from one of his side businesses."

Jane is a trusting wife. If I were her, I would wonder who he's talking to all the time.

"So did Nathan call yet? About your date tomorrow?" She looks anxious now that she's introduced this potentially touchy subject at a party.

"My phone just rang, but I haven't had a chance to look at it yet. Someone left a message." The second buzz after a minute or so confirmed that it wasn't a hang up call. "I should go listen to it."

I walk back up to the kitchen, but it's crazy in there, too. I glance at the stairs. Why not? It's the only quiet place in the house, and I can grab Brandon's gift off the bed while I'm up there. I would like to give it to him before I leave. Not in front of people, but I can keep it near the door. No one will notice.

I had been in this house a couple of times when crazy

Susan lived here, but I don't remember if I have been upstairs. It looks like the usual layout. Did he say he was putting the gift in his bedroom? I think that one at the end of the hall is the master suite. Or would he put jackets and stuff like that in a guest room? I tiptoe down the other end of the hall, even though there isn't a soul up here. As I get to what I think could be the guest room door, I hear voices. My heart starts beating fast—I don't want to get caught snooping. I'm not, but it looks that way.

My inner dialogue is interrupted by a moaning sound. I jump and brush against the door just enough to see that it isn't closed all the way. I peek in and all I see is a pile of coats, and there's the present on the floor. I must have imagined the noise. Does he have a cat? I begin to tiptoe into the room to grab the package, when all of a sudden a naked woman sits up and starts screaming—I hope in pleasure. I jump back behind the door and peek again. I see hands tied to the bed with—what is that? Ties? Scarves? What the hell is going on? This is not a typical suburban cul-de-sac party.

I glance around the corner again and duck out. My heart is pounding now and I realize I dropped my damn phone. I get down on the ground and stick my hand back in, fumbling around for the phone on the ground. It couldn't have gone too far—it doesn't have legs. I grab it just in time to hear—

"Claire?"

I jump up and smack my head on the door, which somehow slams it shut. There's not a peep of recognition from the busy occupants inside. "Brandon, hi. I was just coming up here to check my messages. It's so loud downstairs and this was the only quiet place, but I think I'll go out on the porch—"

More screaming and moaning from behind the door. I rub my battered skull—this is becoming a perpetual injury.

He looks at my head, but points to the bedroom—"Is there someone in there?"

"I don't know. Maybe it's the cat?"

"I don't have a cat."

"Bianca said you guys were getting ready to play Guitar Hero. Are you going to sing?" I start towards the stairs, followed by a bewildered Brandon. He looks back at the bedroom again, but shrugs his shoulders and follows me down the stairs.

Once we get to the kitchen, we are pulled aside by Bianca and her friends. They were looking for Brandon to get the game of Guitar Hero started. Bianca looks at both of us as if she's wondering why we were both missing at the same time. She smiles and squeezes my arm.

I have zero familiarity with Guitar Hero, but I follow the crowd back down to the basement. They're all into it, taking turns playing the drums, bass and guitar on the pretend instruments. I'm enjoying it, and watching the scrolling notes on the TV screen is mesmerizing. Brandon does some singing, and even though this isn't the best quality set up to showcase his voice, he's good.

The music is getting loud and the crowd is starting to thin a bit. Most of the neighbors are going home. They are a "come early and leave early" crowd, anxious to relieve their babysitters and get some sleep before their little ones wake up tomorrow, wanting cartoons and pancakes.

As Jane and some of the other neighbors come over to say good night, I remember Nathan's call. Plus I need to escape before someone asks me to sing. I do not sing in front of anyone. Ever.

I say good night to everyone and duck out to the front porch to listen to my message from the dreamy Dr. Kleinman.

CHAPTER TWENTY-FIVE

I replay the voice mail about five or six times. Nathan wants me to meet him downtown for brunch at eleven. I am a bit surprised that he doesn't want to come pick me up, but he *does* live downtown so why would he drive all this way? He also called pretty late—maybe he's on another date? It's foolish and naive for me to assume he isn't dating other women. I think Bianca is wrong about the hard cider—my head *is* starting to hurt. Oh that's right, I banged it on the bedroom door.

"Hey, it's getting cold out here. You missed everyone singing happy birthday. It was epic." He smiles and then looks concerned when I don't smile back.

"I didn't know you were doing that. I'm sorry, and you didn't open your present." I stand up and Brandon motions for me to sit back down.

"Don't worry about it. Everyone is so drunk they could barely get the words out." He smiles again. "Do you need anything? Did you have a good time?" He quickly adds, "Not that I'm saying it's time to go."

"I'm fine, but it probably is time to go." People have been filing past me, but I've been in my own little world. I wonder which couple was "tied up" in the guest room.

"You don't have to go. Why don't you stay and we can talk a bit after everyone leaves? I was going to do a little cleaning up tonight and then leave the rest for the morning. I'm beat. I think Bianca and a couple of the other girls are in there doing some now."

I should go home and get some proper rest so I don't have bags under my eyes at brunch, but I don't feel like being alone yet. "I should help Bianca and the others. I'm so lazy." I manage a grin and walk past Brandon into the house. I am freezing and it feels good to absorb some warmth. I feel Brandon's body heat close behind me and I jump. I have stopped walking and I'm gazing at the pictures on the hall table again. I want to hear his story, but that is just professional curiosity—I like the book and the adoption thing is interesting. That's all. I have a date with Nathan and he doesn't want children. Uncomplicated, charming Dr. Nathan.

Brandon pauses and gives me time to look, but feeling his presence snaps me out of my trance, and we continue to the kitchen. Bianca and her friends are finishing up the worst of it.

"I'm sorry I got distracted and didn't help you guys," I offer.

"No worries. We've got it under control. We've done this a time or two. Brandon's parties are legendary. This one was a little tamer with the neighbors here and all." She looks at me and adds, "But not you. You're not a mommy like all the others here tonight, right?"

My eyes dart around the room. "So is there anything I can do?" I am looking for a task to divert the conversation.

Max comes upstairs and starts teasing Bianca and the other girls again. He sees me and says, "I knew you had to be here. You wouldn't go home without saying goodbye and I didn't think Brandon was going to let you go so easily." He smiles at Brandon.

"Are you sober enough to drive, big guy? Or do you need to crash here tonight?"

Bianca jumps in. "I'll drive him home. We don't want to get in the way. Right, Max?" She gives him a look of warning. If I didn't know their situation, I would swear they were married. Too bad he can't get a better apartment, she's good for him.

We all say good night, and Brandon and I are left standing in the kitchen. He leans on the counter and says, "So did you want to go back downstairs and hang out?"

"I really like the front porch." I quickly respond.

"I just thought you were cold. I know, you go out and I'll bring you something in a minute."

He pushes me out the front door, and emerges a few minutes later with a mug of hot chocolate and an afghan.

"Here, I hope you don't mind this microwaved, and my mother sent this for my birthday. She likes to knit, but seriously I don't use stuff like this. It's good for a cold little chick."

I peer at him and he continues. "I don't mean that you're cold, like emotionally. I mean in the temperature sense." He breaks my gaze and looks up at the sky. "Look at how many stars are out tonight?" Brandon sits back in the other rocker and pulls a sweater over his head. It's just like the one I got him, only green. I should remind him to open my gift, but I want to talk about other things, and it's getting late.

"Thanks for inviting me tonight. It was fun. I like your friends." I pull the afghan tighter around my shoulders and take a baby sip of the boiling hot chocolate. I don't want to have to kiss Nathan tomorrow with a burned tongue.

"I hope they weren't too much."

"No, they're nice people. It gave me a much better idea of who you are. I mean as a writer." I look up at the sky and say, "Yes, the stars are beautiful."

Brandon begins to give me the lecture on astronomy that most men seem to enjoy delivering. I don't know the Big Dipper from a wood chipper. Cassio who? We talk about the band and he tells me that they have been playing together since he was in college, but have only gotten more serious in the past few years. The conversation fades into companionable silence after a while. We are running out of small talk, dancing around the bigger issues on our minds. And maybe in our hearts, too.

"So you want to know about little orphan Brandon?" Finally.

"Yes, I'd like to know what happened. So the book is fictionalized reality?"

"My birth mother was sixteen when I was born. She came from a good family, but her parents were adamant that she should not raise a child. She dreamed of being a singer—apparently she was an amazing talent. They didn't want her to give up her dreams for a baby."

"That's where you got your voice. Did you always know you were adopted?" I lean forward and put the hot chocolate on the table.

"Yeah, my parents wanted me to know the truth. They had been married about ten years, couldn't have kids.

Typical story. My mom had some problems. They adopted me, and then my sister a few years later, both as infants. They met my birth mother, but they didn't have much contact with her, and that's all they knew about her situation. My sister's birth mother wasn't quite as well off as mine, and Colleen had some early developmental problems. But she's great now. She's a museum curator in DC."

I want to know why his mother couldn't have children, but that seems like prying. "Have you found your birth mother?"

He leans forward, looking into his mug of hot chocolate, avoiding eye contact. "No. I would like to, but all adopted kids will tell you that it's not easy, emotionally or logistically. I know her name and where she lived back then, but that's all. That's why my book is about open adoption. I think that's what people should strive to do—for the child's sake." He looks up and waits for my response. "What? You think that's bad?"

"I just, well...I could never adopt a baby and let the birth mother in its life. I would be too afraid. What if she had wanted you back? Your parents would have been devastated."

"That's true, but that sort of thing hardly ever happens. I want to raise awareness for this issue with my book."

I take another gulp of hot chocolate and swallow hard.

"Claire, I need to ask you something. How come you didn't have any children? You were married a while, right? You seem to really like kids. I see you with some of the neighbor kids, like that little Emma who wears the dance costume all the time. I saw her showing you her new shoes and giggling with you the other day. You seem close with Jane's kids, especially Shannon, the gecko wielding menace." I smile at that memory and I feel my cheeks getting red. When I don't respond right away, he adds, "I'm sorry, I know that's a personal question."

I sigh heavily and take a deep breath. There's no reason not to tell him. I've told Nathan and he's the one I'm dating. Brandon is just a friend, and he'll understand if his mother went through it. "I had several miscarriages in my early thirties and I was forced to have a hysterectomy. Then I got divorced."

"I'm sorry, Claire. Something similar happened to my mom, and it almost ruined my parents' marriage. Did your husband leave because of that?"

"No, I wanted the divorce, and he graciously agreed to move out." I shake my head and continue. "He handled the whole situation poorly. He told me to get over my loss and it was no big deal—"not everyone has kids, Claire." He just didn't want it like I did. But that's over now."

"There are other ways. You could adopt. You're still young."

A sad laugh escapes my mouth.

"What? You *are* young. My parents were in their early forties when they adopted me and Colleen. What's stopping you?"

"For one I don't have a husband, and most men want their own children or they already have them." I think of Nathan. "Or they don't want them, and that is the best case scenario for me. I met a new guy last night. Finally an age appropriate man who is not a father, and doesn't want to be one."

"I'm confused. I thought you wanted to be a mother?"

"I did, Brandon. Desperately. But now this is for the best. I have Dixie and my career. My friends. Hopefully I will end up married again to someone who can accept my limitations."

Brandon stares at me for a moment longer than is comfortable and sits back in his chair. "I'm happy for you. I hope it works out."

"Thanks. I really should be going. I have a brunch date tomorrow and I need to get some rest." I stand up and pull off the afghan. "I had a great time, Brandon. Thanks, and happy birthday."

Brandon rises and takes the afghan from me. "Brunch, huh? Sounds fun. I won't keep you, then." He runs his fingers through his hair and sighs. As I turn to walk down the steps, he says, "Hey, Claire?"

I turn and face sad eyes and a downtrodden expression. He looks like a little boy holding the afghan to his chest. "You don't have limitations."

My heart jumps and I respond quietly. "Thanks. Good night, Brandon."

When I reach the safety of my house I think of the sweater wrapped up in the box in the guest room. I could have said "Hey, let's go open your present," but after everything I told him tonight, Brandon and his bedroom are permanently off limits.

CHAPTER TWENTY-SIX

I wake up feeling much more level headed, and excited about my date with Nathan. We're meeting at the Stardust Café. It isn't quite as pretty as it sounds, but it's located in an area of the city with lots of old row houses with lovely accents, such as wrought iron front porch railings and window boxes with bright flowers. The tree lined sidewalks are a favorite with joggers and dog walkers, and the neighborhood feels alive with people running into friends on the street corners with their steaming freshly brewed lattes in hand.

Nathan lives in this neighborhood and I'm surprised he didn't suggest meeting at his house first. Men often take advantage of that opportunity so the woman has to return to his place for her car. On second thought, Nathan is too good for those cheap ploys.

Last night is becoming a distant memory as I circle the block looking for an easy spot to pull into. Even though my car is small, I suck at parallel parking! Actually that isn't even accurate—you need to be able to *do* something, at least a little bit, to suck at it. To say I suck at parallel parking is like saying I suck at speaking Chinese.

I sigh as I circle the block for the second time. Once again I left Brandon with some awkward unfinished business. Why does this keep happening? It was a perfectly pleasant party, and I had to get all stressed out over a picture and a few comments. I should have gone home when everyone else did, but my curiosity was too persistent. If I hadn't been so nosy I could have avoided the whole uncomfortable conversation.

I finally locate a spot where I can park my car by just pulling in. Maybe the people on this block are all at church. This must be the holy block. I glance in the mirror one last time to see if my eyeliner is even and my lipstick is still perfect. I am hoping it gets ruined today, but for now I want it to be flawless. I tried on three different shades, trying to find one that complements the color green I'm wearing. I opted for a shade in the peach family. Bright and flirty, but not too over the top. This little bright emerald dress is lycra, with an empire waist, so I don't have to suck in my stomach if I eat too much at brunch. It has a swirly black and white pattern on the flouncy skirt.

Satisfied as I am going to be with my appearance, I step out onto the sidewalk, and look down at my sensible shoes. Black peep toe sandals with white piping. Two inch wedge. Summery, yet not beachwear.

I scan the area to see if Nathan is here and watching me, but this isn't an Internet date, and therefore I don't need to be overly concerned about my "spot them before they spot me" rule. I can also guarantee Nathan will not be wearing a stupid hat and his hair will stay firmly rooted to his scalp.

I enter the restaurant and again begin looking for him when I feel a presence behind me, breathing down my neck.

"Hey." I nearly jump out of skin until I realize the guy standing behind me with his hands resting gently on my hips is Nathan.

I turn around abruptly and in mock anger say, "That's a good way to get my heart rate up. Trying to drum up business?"

He leans down and whispers in my ear, "I don't think a little thing like you has anything to worry about on the heart attack front, but I certainly intend to continue to raise your heart rate every chance I get."

His plan is working so far because I feel like I am going to throw up my heart. Nathan is intense, but I like it!

The hostess leads us through the crowded dining room, past the bountiful display of food. They do a brunch buffet, as well as a full menu. The food is awesome, but looking at it now is not rousing my appetite. I should have eaten something, like a banana, to settle my stomach so I wouldn't feel so yucky. We arrive at a cheerful table by the window. As Nathan pulls out my chair, I notice him slip the hostess something while I'm sitting down. Did he tip her for this fantastic table?

"I hope you like sitting by the window. I love to watch the activity in this neighborhood." Nathan snaps his cloth napkin open and drapes it across his lap. He is wearing navy twill pants and a striped polo shirt. I bet this is a golf outfit. His dark hair is combed back and looks sleek, like Dixie's fur after a bath. I smile at my comparison and Nathan smiles in return, taking this as a sign of my approval of our seating arrangement. Before I can tell him it's perfect, he continues. "I love living in this neighborhood. Have you ever considered living in the city, Claire?"

"I would like to, but my home's value has sunk and I owe a lot on it. It'll be difficult to sell." I rest my hands in my lap and scan the room for the waitress. I need a drink—my mouth is like cotton.

"I wouldn't worry. If things work out for us, I will take care of selling your house. Would you like the buffet or the menu today? I can't wait to dig into those sausages, and did you see how fluffy those pancakes look?"

I'm afraid he's going to scrutinize my lack of eating. I can't believe I thought I would need this dress to hide my stomach—I haven't eaten anything since a few chips at the party last night, and I have no desire for a fluffy pancake. Wait, what did he say? He wants to buy my house? Sell my house? Say something, Claire. "Yes, the food looks great. I'm not that hungry, though. Not much of a morning eater."

"Hi, folks. I'm Janice, and I'll be taking care of you today. Can I start you off with something to drink?"

God bless Janice. "Yes, can I have some water please?"

"You're not going to have a drink? Bring two Bloody Mary's." I open my mouth to protest and he continues, "I will drink both if you don't want yours. You may change your mind, though. They're so good here." He flashes me an irresistible smile.

Janice walks away and I think I see her roll her eyes. I hope Nathan didn't notice that.

I look back and catch him staring at me. "So how was your party last night? Birthday party, right? Did you play pin the tail on the donkey?" He cracks himself up.

I know he's joking, but I feel mildly protective of

Brandon. "No, it was a lot of fun. Brandon, my neighbor, is in a band so there were a lot of cool people there." I sound like I'm in high school.

Amused, Nathan responds, "Cool people? What kind of band?" He takes his Bloody Mary from Janice and takes a sip. She places mine in front of me and I thank her, even though I have to intention of touching it. Even if I felt well, that would not be my alcoholic beverage of choice at brunch. Tomato juice—yuck!

I regret bringing this up. "Rock, some metal—"

"*Metal*? How old is this guy?" Nathan's face is contorted in displeasure.

I knew I shouldn't have said anything as soon as I started to respond. Nathan is a real adult and he would never understand Brandon's music. The thought of him in the same room with Bianca and Max makes me squirm in my chair. "He's in his late twenties." I add, "Some of that music is really good."

"You're so sweet to be supportive of your friend, but I doubt Bradley has appreciation of good music, like classical or jazz." He motions for the waitress—she should have taken our order by now.

I don't bother correcting him—the name mix up is an easy mistake. Janice returns and records Nathan's order. I am digesting the mention of the word "jazz" when I am interrupted by Nathan's voice, "Sweetie, what would you like? I'm having the buffet."

"The buffet sounds great. Thank you, Janice." I absentmindedly hand her my menu as sounds of jazz invade my brain—that incessant repetitive "doodle deedle" noise—I don't even know what instrument makes that sound.

"Do you like jazz, Claire?" He raises his glass and I notice his watch, which is huge, expensive and diamond encrusted.

"I can appreciate the value of all music." There, that was a safe response.

"I'm so glad! There is a wonderful little wine bar I want to take you to. Great food, too. You'll love it—the jazz trio that plays there on Saturday nights is amazing."

"Why don't we go get our food? Those fluffy pancakes

are calling your name." My voice sounds suddenly too cheerful.

"Yes, let's go. That's so sweet of you."

We get our food and I can see Nathan is hungry. His plate is piled high with sausages *and* bacon (double heart attack meats), and he has at least three or four blueberry pancakes, *and* a mound of scrambled eggs.

"I don't know about you, but I'm going back for seconds."

Where does he put all of this food? I do my share of eating (when not with a man), so maybe he just has a fast metabolism like me.

"I would have offered to meet you at my house this morning. I just live around the corner, but it's being redecorated and there are ladders and work *things* everywhere." He gestures around the room to illustrate his description of disarray.

"Meeting you here was a great idea. So what kind of decorating are you doing?"

The conversation switches to a less stressful topic—I can talk about paint swatches and accent pillows as well as the next girl. It sounds like Nathan has an eye for color. The curtains in Brandon's kitchen *totally* did not match his countertop.

"I'm glad you think you'll like the color scheme. I agonized over it, you know? Trying to figure out what a woman would be happy with. There is nothing I want more than to share my life with a good woman, Claire." He leans in closer across the table, almost getting maple syrup on his shirt, and says, "I think you could be that woman."

I am stunned for a moment, but then a warm smile spreads across my face. Yes, I have just met him, but you just know when you meet the right man. We do have to get to know one another, and I have to relax, but yes, this feels right.

"I don't know what to say Nathan, I'm flattered—"

"You don't need to say a word. It's so hard to meet a good woman, and in my profession especially, it is vital to have a quality lady by my side."

I can be a good doctor's wife. Maybe I could even do

some of the volunteering I have been meaning to do—be more like my sister. Yes, this could be great. Maybe at the hospital.

"Do you have any tattoos, Claire?" He butters another croissant—doesn't he *know* about cholesterol?

Flustered by the question, I reply, "No, I don't. Why do you ask? I would probably get a little one somewhere, like on my ankle—"

"Oh God, no!" He says this loudly and then looks around to see if any of our fellow diners noticed. He looks relieved and wipes his brow with his napkin. "No, I'm just glad to hear that you don't have any. That way you can be buried in a Jewish cemetery."

He studies my puzzled look and adds, "Jews don't believe in body modification. It's desecration of God's holy temple."

"I did *not* know that." I do like the idea of a serious relationship, but how have we jumped from paint colors to burial in one fell swoop?

I steer the conversation away from my final resting place and back to something more normal, like his work. Nathan tells me some stories about patients and his decision to become a doctor.

"I do earn a great deal of money, but it's all about saving lives, Claire." He takes my hand under the table and rests it on his leg. He removes his hand, and after a moment I swipe mine back.

"I'm sure it's rewarding work." I manage to eat a bite of now cold pancake. "Hey, I was thinking—maybe you could teach me to play golf. Since you're so into it." I blink hard and grin.

"That is such a *lovely* idea, Claire. I can't believe I didn't think of it, since you're so good at *mini* golf." Where is he going? His chair is right next to mine now and his lips are all over my neck. I immediately feel eyes on us—the room is filled with families and senior citizens.

I extricate myself from his embrace. I love the way it feels, but the sudden public display of affection has caught me off guard. Maybe golf talk is an aphrodisiac for him. That makes me giggle.

Nathan thinks I'm giggling at the neck nuzzling. "Ticklish, are you?" He motions towards my sides with his fingers poised in tickle monster mode, and I jump up in time to avoid a scene. "I'm sorry, I need the ladies' room."

"I'll be right here when you get back, Sweetie." I turn to walk towards the restrooms, and halfway there I look back over my shoulder, and yes—Nathan is watching me the whole way.

He's flirtatious, so why is he keeping me from his house? How bad can it be? He's currently sleeping there, isn't he? I hope he's not married. No, Melanie would have known that. These doubts are probably my lack of experience talking. I have read all the relationship books, but none of them seem to help when I'm with a man. Maybe he just wants to avoid temptation out of respect for me.

I wash my hands and take a peek in the mirror. My lipstick is all worn off, but all the better for the goodbye kisses I am anticipating. He acted like this at the Charter House, too. This man is full of surprises.

Back at the table it looks like Nathan is settling up with bill with Janice. I hope he gave her a good tip, she's so busy today.

We walk out to the sidewalk and he asks which way my car is parked. He takes my hand, and when we get to my car he takes my keys and opens the car door, climbing inside and starting the engine. He pops out and slips my purse off my shoulder, gently tossing it in the passenger side seat. Then he quickly grabs me and locks me in a full blown kiss, complete with hands moving so quickly I couldn't catch them if I wanted to, which I don't. Except when they reach my ass, since I spot the shocked look of the old couple in their Sunday finest headed towards the Stardust. I don't want to ruin their appetites for their after church pancake breakfast with our sexual display in broad daylight. If it were late at night, or in a neighborhood full of bars and clubs, it would be different.

I wiggle out of his embrace and whisper in his ear. "Nathan, you're an incredible kisser, but people are staring. Maybe this isn't the best place for this—"

"Let them stare, Claire." He holds both of my hands and

steps back to arm's length, looking me over. Smiling from ear to ear he says, "Yes, I think this is going to work for us. I have a good feeling."

He closes the gap between us again and gives me a feather light kiss on the lips. "Have a wonderful day. I will be thinking of this." He points back and forth between us and starts walking in the other direction.

"Bye, Nathan. Thanks for brunch!" I call out to his disappearing frame. He raises a hand in acknowledgment but doesn't turn around.

CHAPTER TWENTY-SEVEN

"Hey, have you heard from Justin?" Rebecca starts off Monday morning with a bang.

"No, I haven't actually. But we just went out on Thursday, and I wasn't exactly a bundle of fun at the end of the night. Why?"

"I just saw him in the elevator. He looks sad." She comes in my office and closes the door.

"I know I'm going to have to deal with him, now that I've met Nathan, but I haven't figured out what to say yet. It's awkward. We've only been on one date, but it feels like I owe him an explanation."

"Well, duh? Obviously you do. The poor guy is so confused. He probably keeps looking at his pretty face in the mirror wondering where he went wrong." She smirks and then puts up her hands in self-defense. "I'm sorry. I know this is serious. So how was your weekend? I can't believe you didn't call me to tell me about the party and your date. You did have a date, right?" She raises one eyebrow.

"Yes, I did. Yesterday. Brunch at Stardust. The whole weekend was such a blur of activity I didn't get a chance to call anybody. I haven't talked to my mother since Easter, or Jackie since my visit. And I knew you'd be here front and center first thing today to get the story."

"I should have been a reporter. So-o-o-o?" She assumes her usual position in my guest chair.

"I don't even know where to start." I tell her all about the party—the people I met, the band, the conversation with Brandon at the end of the night. I leave out some details, like crying over his picture in the foyer, and the awkwardness I felt when telling him about Nathan.

"I like this Brandon. So you think he was the one at O'Malley's? That kid has a set of pipes on him! That music isn't my cup of tea, but that place was rocking."

He is a kid. A handsome blond kid who likes good music, and has a smile that would melt the polar ice caps. *I'm happy for you. I hope it works out.*

"At least you guys talked and he's not mad. So tell me about Nathan."

You don't have limitations. "What did you say? My date? It was nice. We met at Stardust and—"

"Wait a minute. Stardust Café? Doesn't he live near there? Why didn't you meet at his house?" Rebecca picks through the candy bowl on my desk. Yes, I have started buying candy again.

"He does, but he didn't ask me, and I thought it was best. I didn't want to be tempted to go back to his place. Besides I think it shows what a respectful gentleman he is, and he's having his place decorated."

"Hmm…I guess." She chooses and unwraps a peanut butter cup. "Decorated, huh? That's odd. So was it a good date? What did you talk about?"

I tell her about the jazz and what he said about Brandon's band—but leave out the Jewish cemetery/tattoo exchange. If she thinks decorating is weird, I can only imagine her reaction to that subject.

"Jazz? You hate jazz! Claire, honestly if I didn't know better I would say you were into this guy for his money and status. But I know it's his lack of interest in reproduction. You're going to listen to jazz? That's a big sacrifice for you. I would adopt triplets from Mars before I would hook up with a jazz lover." She pops the chocolate in her mouth. That should shut her up for a moment. "You know…" she continues with a mouth full of chocolate, "…I don't like Brandon's band's music so much either. What are they called?"

"Chain."

"Right, Chain. Silly name, but they *were* talented and people loved them. I was drunk enough to have fun and not even care about the music. I'm just saying Nathan sounds like he may be a little stuffy. Does he like the ballet, too?"

Thank God I didn't tell her he likes classical music. *Did he mention the ballet?*

"Rebecca, he's a more cultured person. He probably

worked hard to become that way after growing up in Brooklyn."

"I guess that could be the case, but you need to have things in common, other than physical attraction and a desire to be childless." She stops herself and says, "I know that isn't your *desire*—well you know what I mean. I shouldn't give you such a hard time. I'm just looking out for you. Sometimes you don't think when it comes to men." She pushes the candy bowl away to remove temptation. "Don't tell Dr. Heart about your high cholesterol. He may put you on a diet. Lord knows I need one." She holds her stomach.

"I didn't tell him, and why would you think that?"

"Just seems like he could be controlling. I'm sorry. It's probably just my own paranoia talking because of all my own bad experiences. So did he kiss you? Any action to report?"

I tell her about the kiss by the car and the nuzzling at the table. "He's confident, but that doesn't mean he's controlling."

"Did he order for you?"

"Of course not!" She doesn't have to know about the Bloody Mary.

"You know, if he wasn't obviously into you sexually, I would say he was gay."

"What the hell are you talking about?"

"Think about it. He's dramatic, he knows how to decorate, likes wimpy music—if he said anything about show tunes I would have to call in a pro to figure this out."

"Who?"

"My neighbor, Jeffrey."

"He's gay?"

"Yes, you know that. Don't you remember the *Halloween* party last year?"

I do now. I have never seen such outlandish costumes. I thought all of the guests were women until they spoke or I shook their hands. "Yes, I do. What a waste of a night *that* was— there wasn't one eligible man in the place, and I wore fishnets." I pause and continue. "Nathan is absolutely not gay. He's just more refined than the usual slobs we go out with."

"You're probably right. After all you were the one

swapping spit with him—you should know. I'm happy for you if you're happy. Just try to take it slow. When are you seeing him again?"

"I don't know. He didn't say."

"He was so into you with that kiss and then he doesn't—
"

Rebecca stops in mid-sentence and we both stare at my phone vibrating on the desk. "Maybe that's him."

I pick up the phone and see that I have a text message.

"It's him. He wants to see me tomorrow night."

"Maybe you can try to introduce him to some better music." She stands up and tosses all her candy wrappers in my trash can. "Can you do lunch today?"

"No, I need to run some errands. My head is in the clouds lately and I don't even have any laundry detergent. I need clean underwear if I'm going to keep going on dates." I smile and respond to Nathan's message—yes, I would love to see him tomorrow night. Things are heating up. Gay, my ass.

I would not admit this to a living soul, but I'm going to McDonald's for lunch. I just don't have time for a proper meal out, and there is nothing in my refrigerator but some Angry Orchards (I did have time to pick those up—they were so good at the party), expired yogurt and maybe a stray shriveled grape or two.

People are such liars about eating fast food. Everyone at work claims they would never eat at the convenient McDonald's on the corner, as if I'm suggesting that they should eat bugs off the sidewalk or snack on the contents of the dumpster out back. I barely passed my math classes, but I don't see how it is possible that *no one* goes to McDonald's. There is a McDonald's within a mile radius of everywhere, and they have sold *billions*. I find it funny that many of my co-workers have no problem selling porn, but they're embarrassed to own up to chowing down on an occasional Big Mac.

I just hope eating too much of it isn't going to land me in the ER, as I try to forget about my cholesterol. I smile as I think of Nathan. If I had a medical emergency, he would be right there holding my hand and saying things like "stat" and "code blue," giving me drugs with names I can't pronounce and telling me how brave I am. As I'm sitting in my car eating fries, I'm startled by a knock on the window. I sigh and roll it down.

"Hey, Claire. I saw your car and—I see you're eating. Is this a bad time? I just wanted to talk for a minute."

Ron is wearing his UPS uniform and now I see his truck parked on the other side of the lot. I'm going to start wearing a disguise when I go out alone.

I can't help but sigh again. "Get in." I open the passenger side door and Ron tries to wedge his huge body into my little car.

"Damn, these Japanese cars really don't have any room. But I guess you never did need much room, right Claire?"

I hope he gets to the point quickly.

He takes my silence as an invitation to continue. "It was weird seeing you out the other night, but then I can't believe it's never happened. I bet you're out all the time. How's life been treating you? You look a little tired."

I am seething already. He always said I looked tired, when what he really meant is that I look like crap. "I've been busy, which is why I am choking this down for lunch." I motion to my wrappers and bucket of Coke.

"Don't get testy. I just wanted to tell you a little more about Natasha."

"Is that really necessary? I wish you all the best with her. She seemed nice." I crumble up all my wrappers and napkins, shove them into the bag, and toss them in the backseat for now.

"She said nice things about you, too. Here's the thing. She's pregnant." I feel all of the color drain out of my face. "I wanted you to find out from me and not some random person."

I tell him how I met Rhonda in the doctor's office and she told me all about Natasha. I can't resist telling him that she thinks she's a mail order bride.

"Are you shittin' me? What a nut. I swear I can't believe Jeff is still married to her. She must weigh three hundred pounds by now." He shakes his head in disgust.

My weight, or should I say *lack* of weight, was one of Ron's favorite things about me. I wince at his comment as I try to ignore his expanding girth filling up the entire circumference of the passenger seat. "Congratulations." I look away and pretend I'm interested in the people walking into McDonald's. Of course, as if on cue, a woman holding an adorable baby in an insanely cute hat gets out of her car.

"Claire, I'm sorry about what happened with us—"

"Ron, please don't do this again. It's over. Let it go."

He sits back in the seat and stares ahead. "I know I didn't handle things well. I just felt like having a baby was all you cared about. My therapist says you probably never really wanted me, and we're better off apart."

"You have a *therapist*?" I tried countless times to get him to come to counseling with me after the pregnancy losses and the hysterectomy.

"You don't know everything about me, Claire. But you're right, it's in the past, and I'm sure you're meeting lots of nice guys now. Ones who are better for you than I ever was."

I tell him about Nathan.

"Wow, a doctor! Your parents will be excited about that. I hope it works out for you. And hey, you could always adopt." Ron turns back to me with a weak smile.

My stomach lurches and I respond, "I really need to get going, Ron. Good luck with the baby, and tell Natasha I said congratulations."

"I'm going, Claire. Take care of yourself." I turn away before he gets any ideas about hugs or pecks on the cheek. I also don't want him to see my eyes.

He gets out of the car and heads back to his truck. I almost take out a couple of old ladies backing up, and floor it out of the parking lot. In Target, I can barely remember what I came to buy, and when I pass the baby section I can no longer hold in my tears. I run to the ladies' room, picturing Ron holding his baby with a smiling Natasha.

Later in the afternoon I'm sorting through e-mails, and I can't concentrate. Ron is right—I didn't love him enough. I was young and afraid, and I wanted my life to be settled. So I settled. Maybe I was punished for that, but if Ron and I were still together we wouldn't be happy, even if I had all the babies I wanted. It just wasn't meant to be. Maybe I should call him and apologize, but I won't. No matter what, he's still an asshole.

Nathan e-mailed me—he's working at the hospital closer to my house tomorrow and he will come by and pick me up. Hmm, that's different. I write my response and tell him I'm looking forward to seeing him. Then I erase that and tell him to have a nice day. Then I remember he could be working with dying patients, so that isn't appropriate. I settle on a simple agreement of the proposed plan.

Speaking of the opposite sex, there is also an e-mail from Brandon. He thanked me for the sweater and for helping clean up after the party. I'm glad he opened the sweater when I wasn't around. I didn't have to see his reaction to my lame gift.

A knock on my open door startles me and I look up. "Hi, Justin."

"Hey, Claire. How's it going? You busy?" Justin barrels in with papers in hand.

"I have a minute. What's up?"

"I've been doing some digging trying to find some dirt on Cecilia and...nothing. Of course none of the guys in my department will admit to anything." He smiles and continues. "But I did see some messages *you've* been receiving. Who's Nathan and Brandon?" He's smirking, but I feel my cheeks get hot. I have absolutely *no* privacy anywhere!

"Why are you snooping in *my* e-mails?" I fold my arms across my chest.

"I'm teasing you, Claire. I didn't even read them, and I know Brandon is the guy with the manuscript. Remember it came up at the last staff meeting when Pam was talking about his book?"

"I think you're back to being a dick again."

He snaps his fingers. "Damn, and just when I exonerated myself with the funnel cake and pink bunny." He pauses and looks more serious. "But seriously, I guess you are dating this Nathan guy?"

"I thought you said you didn't read the e-mails." I peer at him accusingly.

"I *glanced* at them, and I could see they weren't internal

communication." I love when he decides to get all professional.

"Yes. I met him on Friday. It's nothing serious. Yet. But yes, we're dating." I wish he would drop this.

"I was going to ask you if you wanted to see Shinedown with me next week, but if you're dating someone, maybe I'll ask someone else."

He's a tricky bastard. He knows I'll want to go to that show, and Nathan won't go with me. I quickly blurt out, "I can go. It'll be fun. That is if you still want to take me?"

He stands and gives me his best Justin smile. "I would *love* to take you, Claire. I'll e-mail you the specifics, but nothing too personal. You can't assume privacy on the company network."

He ducks and runs before I locate something to throw at him. What just happened? I should not have agreed to that, but I really *do* want to see Shinedown. A few years back, when I was still married, "I Dare You" was my ringtone on my cell phone. Ron made fun of it, but that's because he never graduated from listening to Nirvana and Pearl Jam. I always hated grunge—flannel shirts are so ugly.

I roll my shoulders to release some of the tension. I owe Justin an explanation. After the show I will tell him the truth about why I can't date him. He'll understand. The world needs Justin's seed. Or at least the movie studios and modeling agencies do.

CHAPTER TWENTY-EIGHT

Tuesday at work I feel sick all day. I know it could very well be nerves, but the glands in my neck are swollen. When I was a child that is the first thing my mother checked in order to diagnose our illnesses. If they were swollen or even the least bit tender, we were off to the doctor for a strep test. I hate to say it but Dr. Mom was usually correct, and we came home with our bubble gum flavored antibiotics, put on our Wonder Woman pajamas, and watched cartoons for days, until our necks went back to normal size. Even though I want to ignore this telltale sign, I keep feeling my neck all day like a mental patient, hoping each time it will feel normal, instead of lumpy. And I *don't* have a low grade fever—it's just hot in this office.

I've been around so many people in the past few days—who knows what I could have caught, but knowing me I am tormenting myself for no good reason. Except this is my first *real prospect* since my divorce, which is pathetic since that was more than two years ago. A lot is riding on this night.

The real reason I am so anxious is this could be the night we have sex. I know that I *do* have some control over this. It isn't like sex is just going to come upon me like a herd of wildebeests in the jungle, but if he initiates it I will go for it. Nathan is a good man who treats me well. We could have a future.

He's coming to my house to pick me up, but of course he's working at St. Vincent's today, so it's just convenient. He probably won't even come inside. I don't recall him saying where we're going, so I don't know how to dress.

I pick my head up off my desk and gather my things to head home. I hope I wasn't sleeping—is that drool? I want to get home well before Nathan's arrival to freshen up, i.e. shower, exfoliate and change into a perfectly coordinated outfit.

I get home in plenty of time, attend to Dixie, and prepare myself for a fantastic night. Just as I'm studying my neck in the long mirror in the upstairs hall, the doorbell rings. Dixie begins the language of her people—sharp, shrill, LOUD barking accompanied by the usual Cirque du Soleil acrobatics.

I run down the stairs and open the door with a flourish and big smile pasted on my face. I don't feel flushed at all! Nathan is looking all around my porch and yard with a look of disgust. Maybe that's too strong. Distaste? Concern? I hate when new people come to my house—I see my neglected home through their eyes, and feel small and ashamed. I quickly greet him and usher him inside where things look better.

He leans down to kiss me. "Hello Sweetie, did you know you have a little tree growing out of—"

I kiss him again, only longer and deeper. Yes, I know about the little tree. It's hard to find a good gutter cleaning service and besides, where will the birds live?

Our embrace is broken up by Dixie, who will be recognized. She's spinning and jumping on Nathan's leg. Does he not know what she wants? Now she's trying to look extra cute, rolling over to expose her belly.

"Claire, what is the dog doing? Is this a trick? Like playing dead?" Is he serious? He's not smiling.

"No silly, she wants you to rub her belly."

"O-o-o-oh. Her belly." Dixie and I both stare at Nathan as he bends down and touches Dixie's belly with two fingers. "There's a good girl." She swiftly flips over and runs into the family room, returning with her ball.

"Nathan, have you ever had a dog?" I pry the ball out of Dixie's mouth and throw it into the kitchen, where she slides across the tile floor and almost smashes her head into the island, as she takes a sharp turn into the dining room.

"No, my mother thought having animals in the house was filthy." He clears this throat. "But she is clearly a cute little animal." He pauses a moment and continues. "So do you have any wine? I had a rough day at the office."

Nathan is wearing jeans and a t-shirt, which is the most casual I have seen him, by far. I guess he must have changed at the hospital. I feel silly now in my cute sweater dress, tights and booties. I casually slip my shoes off to indicate I am comfortable with staying in for a while.

I locate the best bottle of wine I have—an Australian Shiraz my father gave me the last time my parents came to visit. I uncork it when I see he has no energy to come into the kitchen and take over. I guess he did have a hard day. I need to be mindful of his profession—he is saving lives! All I do all day is answer e-mails and make Power Point presentations.

When I bring the wine back in the family room, I see that Dixie has jumped on Nathan's lap and she's trying to kiss him. "Dixie, get down. I'm sorry, I don't let her lick my face, but she tries with everyone else. She's a loose woman." I laugh at my little joke, but Nathan is still wiping dog slobber off his lips and doesn't seem amused.

He gets up and goes to the powder room, where I hear the water running. Is he washing his mouth out? This is a bit extreme but he isn't used to dogs.

"I know Dixie takes some getting used to, but once she gets to know you, she'll be better behaved."

Nathan is standing in the kitchen, apparently looking for his wine. He waves his hand and says, "It's fine, I'll just keep checking for infection for a few days." He laughs at my grief stricken expression. "Claire, I'm kidding. It's just a little dog saliva. Now tell me about your day."

We sit on the couch and drink wine for what seems like a long time. My throat is getting worse, and it hurts to swallow. Nathan suggests ordering in because he's so tired. I went in the kitchen to look for take-out menus, but by the time I return he has already found a Chinese restaurant in the area on his phone, and placed an order to be delivered.

"Sweetie, I hope you don't mind me ordering. All Chinese food tastes the same, right?" He pats the spot on the couch next to him. Daniel did that, too. But he also brought alternate underwear and made my flesh crawl. I shake my head to dislodge these thoughts and snuggle up to Nathan. Is it hot in here or do I have a fever? Maybe it's this sweater dress and tights. It's too late in the season for this outfit, even though it's short sleeved.

"So you had a rough day today?" He hasn't volunteered any information, and I'm concerned.

"I'd rather not talk about it, Sweetie. It's a stressful life. So many people are so ill. I get tired of watching people die, especially when some of it is due to their own poor lifestyle choices." He stretches his neck and shoulders. I would offer to give him a massage, except my hands are so tiny it would be like getting a rub down from a gerbil. Plus a wave of nausea is coming over me.

The doorbell rings, and the food has arrived. Maybe I will feel better if I eat something, but history has not proven this cliché to be true. Nathan runs to the door to pay the driver, and I drag away a barking Dixie and set the table.

"Nathan, I'm interested in volunteering at St. Vincent's. "I put a small spoonful of pork fried rice on my plate. It looks greasy.

Nathan is piling his plate with rice, chicken and broccoli, and shrimp lo mein. The smell is making me want to heave. "Really, Claire? What would you do? You know that hospitals are full of germs and they can be so depressing. Would you pass me the egg rolls, Sweetie?" He smiles and holds out his hand.

I hand him the bag and reply, "I just think it would be nice to do something for people. I could work with children or maybe rock the babies in the NICU." This may be healing for me, but until now I haven't had the courage to take this kind of step. Or even say it out loud. I bite my lip and peer at Nathan for a sign of approval, or at least understanding.

"Sweetie, can you put the dog in another room? Or in her box?" Nathan is pushing Dixie off his leg as she begs for food.

"You mean her crate? No, that's upstairs. She only sleeps in there."

"Can't you put her up there now?"

"No, she'll know it isn't bedtime and she'll cry."

Nathan smirks and says, "Sweetie, she can't cry. She's a dog. She can bark, but you can close the door." He sighs. "It's just that she's staring at me the whole time I'm eating, and it's a bit uncomfortable."

"I don't even notice that anymore. She knows she can't

have Chinese food."

"Aha. She must be smart then. Can't you give her some of her own food?" He points to her empty dog bowl in the corner.

"She won't eat that while we're eating. Just try to ignore her." I put a forkful of rice in my mouth and feel like spitting it out.

Nathan looks exasperated. "I think she may need to go for some dog training. They have classes, you know?"

Obviously, I know. When I got Dixie, Jane warned me that men don't like little dogs. Not that I am regretting my decision to get Dixie. She is the light of my life and my baby, but I need to find a way to make her more endearing to Nathan. She will grow on him. "So what do you think about the volunteering? Do you know who I would contact?"

Nathan wipes his mouth and takes a drink of wine. "If you really think that's something you want to do. Do you think that would be good for you—I mean working with babies? I'm only thinking of your emotional well-being, Claire." When I don't respond right away he says, "But of course I can help you with that. I know the volunteer coordinator at St. Vincent's. I'll ask her to call you." He pats my leg and I smile in return. I am glad he's done eating so we can sit on the couch again. My head is foggy and my face is on fire.

On the couch we resume kissing. His hand is slowly moving up my leg and my bra is becoming deliciously uncomfortable. While other parts of my body are responding quite nicely to Nathan's advances, my stomach is not cooperating. I feel like a bartender poured all the ingredients of a mixed drink into my belly, and is shaking it up to pour into a tall frosty glass. Except in this case I am going to pour it into Nathan's mouth if I don't extricate myself from his ardent embrace.

Gagging, I pull back and cover my mouth.

"What's wrong, Sweetie? Are you not feeling well? You do feel warm. I thought I was responsible for that, but now I seem to be making you gag." He laughs nervously.

For a doctor, he isn't adept at noticing symptoms. If I went to see my mother I wouldn't make it past the foyer without her diagnosing a major illness, just by looking at me. If she *touched* me then she would have a full diagnosis and treatment plan within minutes. But to be fair—Nathan has never taken care of a sick child, and I am not having a heart attack.

I jump up during his speech and run to the bathroom. How many more of my dates are going to involve throwing up? Of course I made it through a ride on a *Ferris wheel* with Justin. However, I am *clearly* sick now, but it's still so embarrassing.

I barely make it to the toilet before I throw up everything in my system. Throwing up is not pleasant under any circumstances, but heaving up recently eaten Chinese food is truly one of life's great misfortunes. Especially when a good looking, wonderful man is in your house and you were just about to move to the next level of intimacy. Fuck!

"Claire, let me in. I'm a doctor." Nathan is tapping on the bathroom door. I know he's a doctor! That's even more reason for him to go home. Now he's going to see me as a patient. Another sick person. We're not far enough along in our attraction for that.

"Claire, open this door." I hear some commotion and Nathan's voice is now farther away, although he sounds angry. "Come back here with that, you little beast!" Uh oh. Dixie.

In order to restore some order to the situation, I open the bathroom door. Who knows what Dixie has made off with? She can be like a child who misbehaves when her parents are arguing, feeding off the chaos.

I steady myself against the doorframe and survey the damage in the foyer. Nathan's coat is on the floor and the contents of his wallet have spilled out on the floor. Where is Dixie? Wait, is that a condom? I don't have time to find out as Dixie and Nathan whiz by me into my office. Miraculously Dixie is running at top speed with Nathan's shoe in her mouth. He must wear at least a size ten—the shoe is almost as long as Dixie. That girl has a strong jaw. As I am admiring Dixie's strength and speed, Nathan is screaming. "Claire, would you please help me get this crazy dog of yours? She has my shoe!" As he runs past me and Dixie has already completed another lap, I can't help but laugh that my dog with the three inch legs is faster than a grown man.

I take a step and the room starts spinning. I definitely have a fever, but I need to gain control of Dixie before I can share the extent of my illness. I am wobbly, even in my bare feet, and the tights are slippery on the wood floor. I lean forward to lunge for Dixie as she runs by again, and I manage to grab her. She yelps and just as I start pulling on the shoe to extricate it from her death grip, I feel another wave of nausea. Just as I pull the shoe free and lay down on the carpet up comes more Chinese food, only this time it hits Nathan's shoe and a wiggly wiener dog. Nathan turns the corner in time to witness Dixie licking vomit out of his expensive Italian loafer. I think there is some in my hair and on my inexpensive Target carpet.

Nathan's face is red, contorted with panic and frustration. He is winded, but manages to say, "Look at my shoe! Look at you! Look at your rug!" I know this is a bad scene, but for a man who went to medical school, is a little bit of vomit really that distressing? I guess it is when it is all over a woman you were about to have sex with, and the shoe you need to wear home, if you ever hope to get out of this mess.

I manage to sit up and I feel the tears coming. "I am so sorry, Nathan. I'm really sick. I didn't feel well all day, but then I was looking forward to our date and I didn't want to cancel and have you think I wasn't interested, but I started feeling feverish and then the Chinese food..." I am sobbing too loudly to continue.

"Oh, Sweetie. This is awful. Let's get you cleaned up." He helps me to my feet but glances at Dixie and his shoe with a look of disgust. She looks like she is smiling while covered in vomit. Her tail is wagging and she follows us to the bathroom.

"I need to clean Dixie and the carpet." I catch a glimpse of myself in the mirror and cover my face with my hands. I lean over the sink and continue sobbing. My makeup is horrifying.

"I'll take care of everything out here. You just get yourself together, and I'll meet you on the couch. Can you manage that?"

I shake my head and he turns back to survey the carnage in the foyer. I can't imagine how he is going to do anything about it. He doesn't know where the carpet cleaner is. Dixie is going to run away if he tries to grab her, and God forbid he tries to wash her—his fingers may suffer a career ending injury.

I hear more commotion, but I need to put myself back together before I worry about anything else. I hold onto the sink and take a good look at my face. I wash out my mouth as best I can (no toothbrush or paste down here), and scrub my hands. My eyeliner is a mess—all I can do is rub off the smudges with a piece of toilet paper. My vomit encrusted hair is another story. I need to go upstairs and take a shower. I take a peek out the doorway and the coast appears to be clear. I head for the stairs and make my way to my bathroom. I turn on the shower, and quickly undress and jump in. I lean up against the wall of the shower stall another wave of sickness hits me. My throat feels like it's on fire, as if I'm swallowing glass.

I quickly rinse out my hair, dry my body and get redressed, careful to check my clothes for any signs of bodily fluids. I skip the tights—they're ripped now, and towel dry my hair a little more. As I flip my head back up and almost pass out, I hear more yelling, only now it sounds like it's coming from outside.

I pull back the bedroom curtains and open the blinds to unveil Nathan attempting to spray Dixie and his shoe with a hose at the same time. At least the shoe will stand still, although I doubt Italian leather is going to respond well to being saturated. While washing his shoe out makes no sense, what he's doing with Dixie is ludicrous. It is so obvious that she hates water, and she must be so scared. I know Nathan isn't familiar with dog care, but seriously? Now I have to run out to rescue my baby with wet hair and a fever.

I throw a sweater around my shoulders and head out to the back deck. On the way I notice Nathan's phone vibrating all over my kitchen counter. I hope his patient from today hasn't taken a turn for the worse. I reach the deck and yell around towards the side of the house. "Nathan, stop! She hates water, and she wasn't even that dirty. I could just sponge clean her in the house. Please come in!"

I am not happy that my little girl has been traumatized, but I have to turn my head so he doesn't see me laughing. He looks like a wild man with his hair all sticking up, wet spots all over him, and a yelping dog all tangled in her leash. At least he was smart enough to put her on the leash— otherwise she would be in the next county by now.

He turns off the water, and drags a wet, sad Dixie to the deck. He lets go of her leash and she runs to me. She's shaking. I am biting my tongue because I don't want to make this night any worse than it is. Nathan follows behind and bolts for the bathroom, I presume to try to dry off.

"Nathan, are you okay? Do you need a towel?" I wait outside the closed door for some recognition.

He slowly opens the door. One hand holds a drenched hand towel, and the other is rubbing his temples. "Claire, that dog needs serious obedience training." He pushes past me into the kitchen, looking around aimlessly. He grabs his phone and almost puts it in his pocket, but obviously thinks better of it since his pants are also drenched.

"Wiener dogs don't like getting wet. They're afraid—"

Nathan puts up his hand and hangs his head, while his other elbow rests on the counter. "Let's not argue. There is plenty of time for us to work out all the kinks. You're not feeling well and I've had a stressful day. I called in your prescription and someone is going to deliver it as a personal favor to me. Along with something for your fever. You definitely have an infection." He grabs my shoulders, glancing at my wet hair with a puzzled look, and then guides me back to the family room couch. "Lay down here with this blanket, and just rest." He picks the blanket up with two fingers—probably paranoid of dog hair.

"You're right, Nathan. This is a terrible night. Nothing is going right. I'm so sorry about your shoes and—"

"My shoes will be fine. I just need to dry them off a bit. I'll do that and then be on my way. We'll get together on the weekend when you're feeling better."

I sit back and exhale the long breath I have been

holding for what seems like the last hour. "Uh, oh."

"What now?" Nathan has the paper towels and is walking towards his discarded shoe.

"Where's Dixie?" I know wherever she is she's still shaking like a madwoman and rubbing herself all over the carpet, and I can't blame her for doing it far away from Nathan. We have a lot of work to do on their relationship. "Dixie, come to Mommy." She comes running back in the room and hops up on the couch, just as I hear Nathan's latest outburst.

"Jesus Christ! There's dog shit in my other shoe!" I am really hoping he found that out by sight and not because he put his foot in it. He comes barreling back into the family room. I can see he is making a Herculean effort to control his temper, but the veins in his neck are throbbing. I don't want my heart doctor to have a heart attack.

"Dixie, damn it!" She knows she's in trouble now. She hops off me and runs into the office, presumably under the blanket on her little doggie couch to hide. "Nathan, I will pay for your shoes. I wish we could hit rewind and start this night over." The tears are flowing again.

He is now hopping on one foot and swiping at the other one with the damp paper towel. He throws the paper towels in the trash can in disgust and carefully picks up his shoes, holding them with the tips of his fingers. He walks over to the couch, and plants a kiss on my forehead. "Feel better, Sweetie."

I open my mouth to respond but all that squeaks out is a barely audible, "Bye."

I hear the front door close and I gently raise myself up, kicking off the blanket. I turn out the light in the foyer and sneak up to the front door. Dixie's head is poking out of her blanket in the office—we're both trying to remain incognito.

I squint to see if Nathan has left yet. His car lights aren't on. Now I see him. What is he doing? Is he picking up the lid of my trash can and dropping in his *shoes*? He pauses for a second, looks up at the sky, and tiptoes barefoot to his car. He glances at the house for a second and I jump back up against the wall. I don't want him to see me spying or defying doctor's orders to rest.

I grab some tissues from the bathroom, dry my eyes, blow my nose and snuggle under the blanket. Dixie runs back to me and hops up, burrowing under the covers. It will take some effort to turn this around, but I'm so tired and feverish that I can't hold onto these thoughts. Dixie's steady breathing is soothing me, and I'm drifting. Just before I fall into a deep sleep I ask myself—why did he bring a condom to have sex with a woman with no uterus?

CHAPTER TWENTY-NINE

I woke up an hour later to my doorbell ringing, and the guy delivering my medicine. I don't know why he owed Nathan a favor, but maybe when you're an important doctor the pharmacies cater to your every whim. Hopefully, I'll get to stick around and enjoy more of this VIP treatment. After this night I'm not so sure. I don't know if I am more upset about being sick or possibly blowing it with the first good man I have met in…well…ever. Nathan sent me a text to see if I was doing any better, and issued a few more doctor's orders.

Once my fever came down it dawned on me that he brought the condom as a precaution against STDs. I find it odd he would think I have any—I've been honest about my sexual history, but I guess a doctor would be ultra-responsible about something like that. He wasn't sharp with his canine knowledge, but he is a cardiologist, not a veterinarian. And like a dummy I haven't even thought about STDs, condoms or any of that.

I was sick most of the week, but felt progressively better towards the weekend. I was out of work, but I don't think I was missed. Justin texted me a few times, and we had a little bit of witty flirting back and forth. I need to think long and hard about my plan to go to the concert with him. What am I doing?

I decide to wait until my return to work next week to worry about it. I am using the Scarlet O'Hara approach to problem solving—I will think about it tomorrow.

It's Saturday and I'm finally better. I still feel a bit weak, but my throat is healed and my fever is gone. I am definitely not contagious any more. Luckily, Nathan has a super human immune system developed from clocking numerous hours in disease infested hospitals (his words), so he has avoided this illness.

We have another date tonight and I am not going to let this one become a disaster. I am wearing sensible shoes, I am eating before I go, and I am meeting him downtown, so there will be no more run-ins with Dixie. I need to keep him away from her until he is smitten with me enough to deal with her bullshit. I adore her but she isn't helping.

Speaking of my little whack-job, it's a nice day and I am taking her for a walk around the neighborhood. Brandon said he would like to go for walks, but hopefully he isn't home or is still in bed after a night of debauchery with the band and its groupies.

I grab Dixie and begin the usual process of wrangling her into her leash and harness. The warmth of the sun hits my face as I walk down the front porch steps. I take a deep breath and I'm soothed by the fresh air. I should exercise more often. I am going to do this every day when I get home from work. And stop eating so much crap and cut out all the alcohol and...

"Hi, Claire."

Brandon is standing on my walk way, at the base of the stairs, wearing shorts and a t-shirt. He is wide awake and his twinkling eyes match the blue sky.

"Hey, Brandon." I'm holding onto Dixie as she strains the leash; she's anxious to get this rare walk underway.

"I heard you were sick. Are you feeling better?" How would he know I was sick? As if he read my mind, he responded, "I e-mailed you at work and got your out of office message. I was going to come over but I figured your new boyfriend was probably taking care of you, especially being a doctor."

"Yeah, I'm a lot better. Thanks. I went out last night with my girlfriends." Brandon keeps staring so I feel compelled to explain myself. "Nathan was busy. He had an emergency at the hospital." I look down and pretend Dixie trying to eat a worm on the driveway is the most fascinating thing ever. I haven't seen Nathan since our disastrous evening.

"I'm glad you're feeling better. A night out with the girls is always fun, right?" He does that thing he does again—running his fingers through his hair. This makes me want to go back inside and lock the door until it's time for my date with Nathan. "Bianca and the other girls really liked you. They were hoping you would come out and see the band some time."

"They were nice. Hey, I don't mean to cut you off but as you can see this little girl wants to get moving on this walk before her lazy mommy changes her mind."

Brandon bends down to pet Dixie and she jumps up and licks his nose. "Aww, I think Dixie would like me to come on the walk. What does Mommy think?"

I take in his sparkling smile and say, "Let's go." A simple walk around the neighborhood can't hurt.

We start walking, largely in silence. Dixie is sniffing every ten feet and I pull on her leash a bit, to redirect her. We come up on a storm drain and she stops walking and digs in her heels.

"Dixie, are you still doing this? You can walk past the storm drain. Mommy's got you." I turn to Brandon. "I know I sound like an idiot when I talk to her, but she's afraid. I thought she was over this, but apparently not."

"No, I think it's cute how you treat her like your baby. I wonder why she's afraid."

"I guess it's my fault. When she was a puppy and super curious, she would try to stick her head in there and one time she chased some kind of creature that disappeared in there. That scared me, you know? I probably yelled at her and reprimanded her harshly enough that now she's afraid to even walk past storm drains."

"It is probably a healthy fear. What if she broke free again like she did that one day? You don't want her exploring the storm drains."

Brandon motions to me to hand him the leash. I hesitate for a second and surrender it. He walks over to Dixie and gently picks her up, talking to her quietly. He carries her past the storm drain and safely deposits her back on the ground, where she resumes her mad dash to the walking trail.

My eyes get misty. "Thanks, but you don't have to hold the leash. I can take it back."

"I like walking her. If you don't mind?"

The rest of the walk is relaxing and we complete the full loop around the neighborhood trail, which is one and a half miles. Not a long walk for us, but Dixie's legs are pretty short, so for her it's a good work out. Still I am sweating, and I wish I had brought water.

We get back to my house and talk about Brandon's book and his desire to work with Bella Donna. I assure him it looks promising and he should hear from Pam soon.

"Thanks for letting me tag along on your walk. It felt good to get out." Brandon lingers at the bottom of my porch stairs.

"It was fun. Thanks for being so sweet to Dixie." I pick her up and squeeze her.

"So, are you doing anything tonight?"

"Yeah, I have a date with Nathan. Why, is something going on?'

"The band is playing. I thought you might like to come out and see us, but maybe next time. You could bring Nathan. See ya later, Claire."

"Bye, Brandon." I was too embarrassed to tell him I am meeting Nathan at a wine bar to hear jazz. That even sounds snobby and boring to me. It will take time to introduce Nathan to some of my interests. After our last date, this isn't the time to push any of that. For now, it's wine and jazz, but for my sake hopefully not too much of either one. That condom is still in Nathan's wallet. At least I hope it is, because if it isn't I have more problems.

I take a break from worrying to run some errands before our date. After an afternoon of grocery shopping, waiting in line at the post office, and a trip to the pet store for Dixie's treats, I head back home to get ready to go out.

Since our lovely walk this morning, the weather has turned to shit. Now it's pouring rain. Wonderful. People in this town drive like the world is coming to an end when it rains. It's like the apocalypse or the rapture. What's the difference? Catholics rarely read the Bible, so I don't know for sure. I think one of those things is good and the other is bad? Either way if it's the rapture, a lot of cars in my town will be unmanned, as many bumper stickers warn.

I finally pull into my driveway, and hit the garage door opener, so I can stay dry and avoid nosy neighbors. I haven't been to this wine bar, but Rebecca told me it's pretty upscale. Actually, she said it's full of uptight assholes. Apparently, the Meetup group went there once, and the prices were so high and the atmosphere so stuffy that they staged a mass exodus to a sports bar around the corner. This is not surprising to me—they are a loud bunch and the wine bar people probably breathed a sigh of relief when the middle-aged party crowd vanished.

The usual "what to wear" predicament begins. I settle on a black matte jersey dress with reasonable black heels and my real pearls. I look like a proper grown up, not like the mob of tattooed and pierced crazies who are probably going to be at Brandon's show tonight. Still, I would like to check out the band. Maybe we can swing by after dinner and jazz.

I arrive on time and surprisingly find a close parking spot on the street that I can navigate. Good start. I walk through the revolving doors into the wine bar, scan the room a moment, and spot Nathan at the bar. He turns to me and smiles—he's smoking a cigar?

"Hello, Sweetie! Come join me. Our table is almost ready. You look lovely, and the color has returned to those beautiful cheeks." Nathan kisses me and wraps me up in his big arms.

I divert my face from the cigar smoke and return his embrace. "Thank you. I feel much better. That's new?" I point to the smelly cancer stick.

"Yes, I do enjoy a good Cuban cigar. Just once in a while. I know it isn't good for me, but there are worse things, right?"

I suppose there are, like crack or crystal meth, or even regular cigarettes, but I am not a fan of anything that produces a burning ember and is not warming me or cooking my food. Or setting a romantic mood. Three strikes and the Cuban is out.

"Would you like some wine, Claire?" Nathan gestures to the wine list.

The jazz trio has started playing and I instantly feel like jamming forks in my eyes. Maybe I can slit my wrists with that butter knife. "Yes, I would like red—"

"This one is perfect for you." He points to the most expensive Cabernet on the menu and signals the bartender.

I would have preferred a Shiraz, but I am not the one paying twelve dollars for a glass of wine, so I smile gratefully.

I am even more grateful for the hostess, who has arrived to show us to our table, which is thankfully far away from the jazz trio. As Nathan pulls out my chair and I sit down, I feel my phone vibrate in my little black beaded evening purse. I normally ignore my phone when I'm out, but I decide to check it quickly. I can tell it's a text by the number of buzzing sounds.

"Hey, Claire. We're playing at O'Malley's tonight, if you and your man want to stop by later. Music starts at nine."

"Is there something wrong, Sweetie?"

My expression must be giving away my angst. "No, not at all." We start to look at our menus and I approach the subject. "So did you have anything you wanted to do later?" Shit, I didn't mean for that to sound suggestive. At least I didn't ask if he has any condoms in his wallet.

Nathan looks amused and his eyes widen. "Why yes, I can think of a few things. What did you have in mind?"

"I was thinking maybe we could go see my friend's band?" Nathan looks puzzled. "You know the one I told you about? The birthday party?"

"Yes, the neighbor friend. What kind of music do they play again?" He swirls his wine in the glass and inspects the sides.

I take a sip of wine and pause. "Rock." His smile immediately fades. "Hard rock. Some metal. I think I told you this. They do some stuff from the nineties, like the Gin Blossoms and the Goo Goo Dolls, but they also do more modern heavier stuff, like Linkin Park, Avenged Sevenfold, Disturbed. Brandon is a versatile singer." He even did Slipknot at his house last week, but I am not going to share *that*. Not that it would mean anything to Nathan. He would think that was a method of tying rope that you learn in the Navy.

"I do remember this now. I must confess I don't know any of those bands. Disturbed? That does sound disturbing. Haha...All of that is just noise to me, Claire."

"Oh." I look down at my napkin, folded neatly in my lap. I need to be more mature. Nathan is right. If I want to be in a relationship with a real man I need to abandon some of these youthful ideas, but Nathan is only a few years older than me. How could he not know music from the *nineties*? He couldn't possibly have been listening to jazz *then*.

"When I was young I listened to some of that stuff, and in my neighborhood there was a lot of rap and hip hop, too. But my mother taught us to listen to classical music. And jazz. Sweet jazz and blues."

Thank you, Mrs. Kleinman.

He closes his eyes in a dreamy way, straining to hear the jazz trio play what sounds like the same exact song they were playing when they started. I have a sneaking suspicion there are no jazz *songs*. It's just one song and it lasts for four hours at a time. "Deedle deedle, doo, doo."

"I don't need to see them tonight. This is nice. It's a lovely place."

"I'm so glad you think so. I wanted tonight to be special after the unfortunate incidents earlier in the week." He takes my hand under the table.

I almost begin apologizing again, but I would rather move on to more positive topics.

"So have you had a chance to ask your contact at the hospital about volunteering?"

Nathan looks up from his menu. "What did you say, Sweetie? No, not yet. Look at this seafood special they have? And it's for two! All of that seafood we have to eat with our hands. How decadent, don't you think?"

I don't know that I want to take a bath in butter sauce, but he seems excited about it, so I smile and nod. I'm not even hungry—I had a Lean Cuisine at home a couple of hours ago. And I thought Jews don't eat seafood, but I am not asking because I don't want to hear any more about my final resting place.

"I make a dish just like this, so I know it will be superb."

He cooks? Was that one of Rebecca's clues to look for? It doesn't matter. Obviously, he is not gay. Lots of men cook. He just enjoys good food and wine. He isn't a "keg and Doritos" guy. I wish I could return Brandon's text.

"When will you see the person at the hospital? Can you e-mail her?"

"Yes, Honey, but let's not talk about all of that. Let's just enjoy tonight and talk about us." He squeezes my hand.

"Good evening, my name is Jason and I'll be your server. I see you have wine. Would you like another glass? Perhaps a bottle?" Jason's timing sucks.

Nathan orders a bottle of the Cabernet and the seafood dish. I excuse myself while he's talking to Jason about the fantastic jazz trio.

Once safely inside the ladies' room, I whip out my phone and send Brandon a text.

"Thanks for the invitation. I don't think we'll get there, but maybe I'll stop by if it's not too late."

That was stupid. Now he is going to wonder if I plan on cutting my date short or if I am already sneaking around on Nathan. And how do I plan to do this? I *am* driving myself but we may go back to Nathan's house after dinner. I should just leave my phone at home when I go on dates so I can't get myself into any more trouble.

Just as I pop the phone back in my bag, it buzzes.

"Sounds great, Claire—hope to see you there. I just told Bianca and Max. She said to look for her when you get here."

I glance at my reflection in the mirror, fluff my hair and march back to the table.

I put down my purse and look up at Nathan.

"More wine?" He picks up the bottle and refills my glass.

"Yes, thanks. So how's the home remodeling coming along?" I carefully butter a small piece of bread.

"It's still a complete mess. I'm afraid we won't be able to go there tonight. I want everything to be perfect for you." Again he goes for my hand under the table. "Claire, I know we have only known each other a short time, but I feel a connection with you. You have such a way about you. You're so ladylike and demure, yet you have a feisty side. I see it. I think we have a future together." He raises his wine glass in a toast. I clink his glass with mine out of ritualized habit.

"I'm so glad you feel the same way," he continues. He read a lot into a silent, returned toast, but I do think he is husband material. Did I say that out loud? No? Good. Whew.

"My parents will love you. What do you think about

going to Miami in the fall?"

"Is that where they live? That would be nice." This is what I have always wanted. So why am I thinking of O'Malley's and heavy metal lyrics?

"Yes, and I can see a church wedding if you really want one, but where there's priest there has to be rabbi. Interfaith weddings are popular these days."

Is he getting a little ahead of himself? I haven't even been to his house yet. We haven't done any more than kiss. "Nathan, I can't get married in the Catholic Church again. I'm divorced and the only way I could—"

"That's even better. Makes it easier. And you have absolutely no tattoos right? I know I asked before, but I just want to be clear. With your musical interests I wasn't sure." He smiles just as Jason brings our food.

It is a *huge* plate of every seafood imaginable, but the shrimp are glistening in a sauce and need to be peeled. The clams and mussels are waiting for the little fork to pry them out and dip them in the butter. At least I don't have to suck them out with my tongue.

As we eat our food, I mull over Nathan's comments. He is still chatting away about our future, but I would like to have a bit more present first.

"I just thought of something wonderful! You could host the next Kleinman family Passover Seder with me. It was amazing at my parents' house this year, but I would love to have the family to my house. The renovations will be done and it will be stunning. It gives you plenty of time to study the dishes to prepare and learn the prayers in Hebrew."

Hebrew? I don't even know anything in Latin except Adeste Fideles, which is "O Come All Ye Faithful." I need to interject before this train flies off the tracks tonight. "Nathan, I'm not trying to slow things down, and I think everything you're saying is great, but I haven't even been to your house yet and—"

"You're so right, Sweetie. We will get to that as soon as we can. But you're right—there's no rush. It's not like your biological clock is ticking."

There it is! Derailment.

"And I *am* sorry for coming on so strong at your house. I

should have noticed you were sick. I am a doctor, after all."

"That isn't really what I meant—"

"I know. I need to be more mindful of your needs and pace. I shouldn't have come to your house so soon."

The meal comes to an end about an hour later, and I still can't figure out what happened. Did I say he was rushing me by coming to my house? I didn't mean he was rushing me sexually—I was referring to the pace regarding marriage and the future. Was I not clear?

After a passionate, but short, kiss at my car, Nathan says good night and saunters off to his car, which is parked a couple of blocks down, he says.

I sit in my car and ponder this night, staring into space. It's only nine-thirty. The band will only be a few songs into their first set, if they even started on time. I am dressed much too conservatively and I am soaked in butter sauce, but I reapply my lipstick and turn the car towards O'Malley's.

I can't stop thinking of what he said. *It's not like your biological clock is ticking.*

Nathan may be a doctor, but he's still a man. I am beginning to think no man will ever understand my feelings about my hysterectomy. Maybe it's time to let it go.

In a matter of minutes I arrive and circle the block for a parking space. The only available spots seem to be in the pay lot across the street. It's only five bucks, so what the hell. This is the lot where I had my run-in with Justin. I shudder when I think of the concert and our plans this week. I need to tie up all these loose ends and concentrate on Nathan. Getting to know him better. Justin does deserve an explanation, and Brandon is just a friend. Coming to his show is merely exhibiting friendly behavior. Of course I didn't tell Nathan I was going, but that's simply because I am not doing anything wrong and he doesn't like this music.

There are a ton of people smoking on the sidewalk. I look down at my outfit after I pay and park, and I am frozen in my seat. I feel like an idiot going in there like this. Everyone is going to ask where I had dinner and I don't want them to think I'm a snob, or that Nathan is one. They will ask why he didn't come. There are no good answers to these questions—at least not truthful ones. These people are nice enough, but they aren't going to be a part of my new life with Nathan. There's no point in forming relationships that I won't be able to maintain.

I send Brandon another text. "Hey, I'm not going to be able to make it after all. Sorry! See you on Dixie's next walk."

Perfect. Friendly. Not flirty. No unnecessary explanations that are none of his business. I bet they're having fun in there, though. I sigh and back the car out of my spot—they got a dollar a minute from me tonight. I find my IPod in the glove compartment and scroll through for a song to help me feel better. I begin the drive home listening to "Down with the Sickness." I do feel "disturbed," but not because of the song.

CHAPTER THIRTY

"Are you really going to see Shinedown with Justin?" Cecilia peers at me with a cup of steaming hot coffee in her hand. I instinctively step back, fearing for a split second that she's going to throw it at me. I have never thought of the complimentary coffee in the break room as a company provided weapon. Until now.

"How do you know that? Did he tell you?" I know he didn't. Or maybe he's playing me?

She shakes her head and not a single strand moves. She must use Crazy Glue to get those spikes to stick up like that. She flashes an evil grin and replies, "You're so naïve, thinking you have a boy toy. You probably don't even know what to do with him." She drops her coffee stirrer in the trash can and walks out, looking over her shoulder once last time, mocking me with her smirk.

What the hell is going on? I can't ask Justin, especially since I'm planning on telling him that I can't go to the concert and why. Before my big confession I need to get to the bottom of this Cecilia situation.

I head to the lobby to talk to Amanda. She's the front desk receptionist and she knows Cecilia better than I do. "Amanda, do you have a second?" In her twenties, with glossy chestnut brown hair and big doe eyes, she slightly resembles a Disney princess character, complete with the Barbie doll sized waist. Every time I talk to her, I imagine little birds and woodland creatures appearing and singing with her.

She puts up one finger to indicate she will be off the phone soon. "I'm transferring you now. Have a great day!" And the birds chirp and the squirrels sing. Perky Amanda smiles and says, "Hi, Claire. What can I do for you?"

"Actually, I wanted to ask you something about Cecilia."

Amanda visibly winces. "What did she do? I mean,

what's up with her?" She forces a fake smile, but I have a sneaking suspicion Amanda is frightened of Cecilia.

"She just seems to know a lot about my behavior, and she's been giving me a lot of grief over my friendship with Justin."

"She can be super jealous." She whispers, "I dated Justin for a little while last year. Cecilia was so mad because apparently she liked him, but he wasn't interested." She looks around the empty lobby. "I shouldn't tell you this but she did a lot of crazy, unprofessional stuff."

I raise an eyebrow. "Like what?" Hopefully not boiling pet rabbits. Or wiener dogs.

"She left things in his office."

"Things?"

"Like her bras and panties. One time he was hosting an IT Review in his office with Tim and all the execs, and Pam almost sat right on her thong."

I laugh and reply, "What? How did he recover from that?"

Amanda bites her lip to stop the giggles. "I think he just swiped it up before anyone saw it and stuffed it in his pocket." She puts her hand to her mouth to stifle her laugh.

"What? We can't have employees doing things like that. What if we had a new author visiting or a client? I guess he kept it quiet so he wouldn't draw attention to his office romances."

Amanda puts her hand up to her mouth again and gasps. "Is that not allowed? Am I in trouble now?"

"No, don't worry. As long as the two people are not in any direct reporting relationship, it's okay." I pause and continue, "So Cecilia is a bit vindictive?"

"Yeah. She was mean to me too, even after Justin and I broke up. I was dating someone else and he used to come here to pick me up for lunch some times. At that time Cecilia was the one who covered for me on my breaks. She flirted with Brian relentlessly. It was embarrassing—he thought she was crazy."

"I am not dating Justin, and I guess I need to clear that up, but I still wonder where she's getting her information."

"E-mails?"

"She doesn't work in IT. She has no access to the server." Unless Justin…"Never mind, Amanda. Thanks for the info, and don't worry—I won't say anything to anyone."

"Whew, that's a relief. Good luck, Claire. Just try to stay out of her way."

I am already plotting my talk with Justin in my head and I absent-mindedly respond, "I will" as I wander back to my desk.

The new editor, Gina Rossetti, starts next Monday, and I need to ensure everything is ready for her onboarding. I send an e-mail to IT asking for her account to be set up, and a few minutes after Justin appears in my doorway.

"So you nabbed a new editor? Good work, Claire!" Word travels fast in this place.

"I sent that to Marcus. How did you know?"

"I know *everything*, Claire." He wiggles his fingers to indicate his mastery of spooky magic. He approaches me and leans forward, with his palms resting on my desk. "So are you ready for Shinedown?" He starts singing an off key rendition of "I Dare You," but very few men who haven't been castrated can sing that high.

"Actually I wanted to talk to you about that."

His face turns more serious. "You're not bailing on me, are you?"

"Justin, please sit down and close the door."

He sighs and follows directions.

"What's your excuse this time?" He folds his arms and reclines, as if this is going to be a long bullshit story.

"Justin, I can't see you anymore. I know we're not really dating, but—"

"I get it. It's the doctor guy. Things are getting hot and heavy pretty fast?" He's being a dick but I hear an underlying sadness in his tone.

"No. Maybe. That's not it." I breathe in and pause. Here goes. Maybe this will get easier the more times I share it with the men in my life. "Justin, I can't have children." I keep saying this with such dramatic flair, as if I am on a cheesy talk show and this is the point when the audience gasps.

He stares at me blankly. "What does that have to do with going to a concert?"

Everyone has a different reaction to this information, but strangely enough—no one ever gasps. "I know this is hard for someone like you to understand, but I can't date someone and risk getting close if I can't offer a family someday. I know that may sound ridiculous, and you aren't even thinking of that yet, but it's real for me. I need to date men who don't want children, who are past that point in life. And I don't even want to casually date—I want to get married again and have some security. No strings attached fun isn't an indulgence I can afford."

"But fun is important, Claire and I do want get married someday, too. I don't understand. You're right that I'm not thinking about kids at this point in my life. I just don't understand why you would want to sacrifice something good because of this." Justin is wringing his hands and puffing out his cheeks. A long exhale betrays his frustration.

"You *will* think of it someday, and then where would I fit in? It's the Demi Moore/Ashton Kutcher syndrome. I am going to get old a lot faster than you, and a lot sooner. The attraction will fade and you will begin looking at younger women and wanting a family. It isn't a criticism or bad judgment of you. It's just what happens. I can't set myself up for that, so I need to stop it before it starts, for both of our sakes."

Heavier sighing and more cheek puffing. "I'm sorry. You're right." He holds up his hand to halt my thought process, and quickly adds, "Not about the attraction part, but yes, someday I will want kids. I just feel like I have a lot of time, and I do. This sucks. I'm being a selfish dick yet again."

"No, you didn't know, but even if I could have children, I am a lot older than you and our timing wouldn't be right. I would want a baby now. Do you see?"

"Yeah, I do." He looks down at his hands resting in his lap. He raises his head up enough for me to see the shining emeralds staring at me with concern. "Claire, why can't you have children? Are you sure?" When I don't answer right away his face changes and he adds, "I am such an asshole. When I made that remark to you about how our children would be beautiful? I'm so sorry, Claire. I mean, I think they would be, but no wonder you got so upset."

"I should have been honest. I had several miscarriages when I was married, and then I had a hysterectomy. So, yes it's for sure."

"When?"

"Two years ago."

"Did your husband leave because of it?"

"No, that's another story." I shake my head and don't venture down that road. Ron and Natasha. *She's pregnant. I wanted you to find out from me and not some random person.* "Justin, you're a great guy, and I know that if I date you, even casually, I will fall for you, and no good can come from that. I have been through enough loss and disappointment. I hope you understand." My eyes are misty and I look away.

Justin gets up and walks around my desk to give me an awkward hug. He kisses my forehead, wipes away my stray tears and says, "I hope this guy deserves you, Claire. I'm here for you if you need anything."

As Justin stands up I think of something I need that will cut the tension in the room. "Actually, my laptop is totally screwed up. Can't get it to do anything, it's so slow. I want to throw it out the window."

"I'm your man. Bring it in—I'll take it home and work on it. It just needs to be cleaned up." He walks to the door. "Don't worry—I won't read all of the e-mails. Well, maybe just the juicy ones." He covers his face and ducks, expecting to get hit with something as he leaves.

"Go find a hot chick to go to the concert with—I hope you get lucky, but I know you don't need luck." I smile at him. I must be crazy to let a man like that go.

He smiles and gently closes my door.

No, I'm not crazy. I am finally becoming sane and I know what I have to do. Right now. *She's pregnant. I wanted you to find out from me and not some random person.*

I call Tim's direct line (I am not going over there to have another run-in with Cecilia), and tell him I'm not feeling well and I need to leave for the day. I get his voice mail. I shoot Rebecca a quick e-mail, telling her I'll catch up with her tomorrow.

I go home, and after greeting Dixie, walk upstairs to my

spare bedroom. The one where I keep all my wedding albums, old pictures and school memorabilia. I open the closet and pull down the contents of the top shelf, hidden behind dusty CDs and high school yearbooks.

I pack the contents in a box and include a brief note.

I carry the box to the car and place it in the backseat. On the drive to their house, I cry my eyes out. The little booties in unisex colors, scattered with bears and ducks. The pink baby book I bought when I was sure I was having a girl. A baby blanket one of Ron's co-workers knitted for us. I keep the sympathy cards, but I give away all the hopes and dreams. It's time.

As I place the box on their front porch, I say a silent prayer for the sweet souls I lost, and for new life. The little baby's and mine.

CHAPTER THIRTY-ONE

It's Friday, and I'm meeting Nathan at the new Asian bistro downtown. It's the same chain as the place Jackie and I went to in Tyson's Corner and they just opened in Richmond. The food is a little weird, but I don't even care. I would have liked to have done something other than go out to eat, and I had the idea to see a play at the Lonsdale Theater. They produce some original productions, and I've gone a few times with Audra. I checked online and there were tickets available for tomorrow night, but tonight they were sold out. I sent Nathan a text and he said he can't go tomorrow night.

I know doctors can work crazy hours, but it's becoming a little disappointing that we only see each other once a week. Hopefully when the renovations on his house are completed, I can start spending time there, but, how is Dixie going to factor into that plan? Maybe she does need obedience training.

As I pull into the restaurant parking lot I see a huge crowd of people heading for the doors. They are emerging from multiple cars, and there are diners of all ages, including quite a few children. Everyone is dressed up; it must be a dinner for some special occasion.

I have a hard time squeezing into the lobby area, and decide to wait for Nathan to claim our table. I don't see him yet and he hasn't sent a text. As I scan the room, I hear a little voice.

"Hi, I'm Abigail. But my friends call me Abby." A little girl, probably about four or five, is standing in front of me holding a panda and twirling in her lavender sequined skirt.

"I brought Mr. Panda because we are eating at the new fancy restaurant for Ryan's commuting." She points to an older boy wearing a polo shirt and black dress pants.

"Hello, Abby. Or should I call you Abigail, since we just

met? I like your panda."

"How about my skirt?" She twirls so fast she almost falls over, which reminds me of someone, except Abby is sober.

"Abby, what are you doing? Are you bothering this lady?" The tall young father turns to me and says, "I'm sorry. We're here to celebrate my son's Communion with the family. The *whole* family." He sighs and glances around at his group. "I am beginning to think descending upon this new, trendy place on a Friday night wasn't a good idea, but their mother insisted."

I quickly glance at his ring finger and notice it's empty. Self-consciously I avert my eyes and reply, "Oh no, I think it's nice. Communion. I see. Abby said he was commuting, and I didn't think he looked old enough to drive or have a job." Abby is out of ear shot or I would not have said anything—she is so cute, now holding hands and twirling with a little girl in a yellow polka dot dress. Probably a cousin.

"That's funny. Yeah, she knows some big words but gets them wrong." He extends his hand. "I'm Rick."

I look around to see if Nathan is watching this exchange but I don't see him anywhere. My phone is buzzing—that could be him. "Hi, Rick. Claire." I shake his hand and it feels warm and slightly rough, like Brandon's did that day on his front porch. What do Nathan's hands feel like and why don't I know? "So you're here with the whole family?"

"Yes, my ex demanded a full family dinner with both sides. She keeps saying that we need to present a united front for the kids. I guess she's right." His soft brown eyes look a bit sad, and I can see some strain on his face.

"I think it's great that you're doing that. It'll be good for the kids. Do you just have the two?"

"Yes, do you have any?"

Just as I am about to answer, I hear a commotion at the front door. Nathan is here and he is yelling at someone. Now I hear crying. Abby comes running to Rick. "Daddy that man yelled at me." She is clutching her panda and holding onto Rick's leg.

I just met these nice people and now Nathan is yelling at the little girl. He must have had a bad day. I wish we had arranged to meet somewhere quieter, less popular. He isn't used to kids, but I didn't think this restaurant was going to look like Chuck E. Cheese tonight.

Rick starts consoling Abby as Nathan spots me.

"There you are. It's a damn madhouse in here. Why are all these *children* in here? You should have mentioned that it was a family restaurant. That's the last thing I need after a day at the hospital."

"Did you yell at this little girl?"

He looks confused, as if he has already forgotten anything happened. "What? She was jumping around by the front door and ran right into me. People should watch their kids, Claire."

Rick glares at Nathan and then looks back at me. "I'm sorry, she's a little excited to be out for the night with all of her cousins, and she loves getting dressed up. Say you're sorry, Abby."

Abby's face is going to make *me* cry. I want to hug her.

"No, really the nice man should say he's sorry for losing his temper." I stare at Nathan. He doesn't look happy about being called out in front of a stranger.

"Do you two know each other?" He points from me to Rick.

"We just met. I was talking to Abby about Mr. Panda and her father came over to see who she was talking to."

Rick extends his hand to Nathan. "Rick Forrester."

Nathan returns the handshake. "Dr. Nathan Kleinman."

Abby stops sucking her thumb and says, "Do you give lollipops?"

"Is she talking to me? Why would I give lollipops?"

"Nathan, pediatricians give their patients lollipops." How could he not know this?

"Um, no I don't. All my patients are grown-ups." He stoops over and pats Abby on the head. "I'm sorry I yelled at you, but you should be more careful. I'm sure your father would agree." He looks at Rick.

Rick is being gracious, but I get the feeling he's looking at me with pity. I get that a lot. I make a mental note to steer Nathan away from kids as best I can in the future. Maybe I can get him to talk about what's bothering him. I know he isn't a kid friendly person, but his rudeness indicates a bigger problem. He is too kind and giving to act this way.

"Yes, Abby please be more careful, Sweetie. Now why don't we go find Mommy?"

"Yay!" She smiles, presumably at the thought of Mommy.

A lump is forming in my throat. "I do love your dress, Abby. Purple is my favorite color."

She starts twirling again to show off her dress, and runs off through the mob of her relatives.

I am left standing with Rick and Nathan.

"I'm going to see if I can get us a table. I am assuming you haven't been to the hostess stand yet?" Nathan looks annoyed.

"No, I was talking. I'm sorry, I—"

He disappears in the throng of Rick's family.

"I should go with him. I'm sorry. He is usually not like this. He's had some very sick patients lately and it seems to be affecting him."

"Hey, I understand. It was nice meeting you. Enjoy your dinner." He starts to say something else and then stops.

"What was that?"

"Nothing. It's just that until he came in I thought I was doing well with you. I was going to ask for your number. I didn't know you were attached. No ring." He points to my left hand.

"Right. No, we're not married, but we probably will be some day. I'm flattered." I pause and see Abby smiling at me, making Mr. Panda dance.

"It's just hard to find someone who likes kids. I have taken enough of your time. Have a good night, Claire."

"You too, Rick." I turn towards the hostess stand and Nathan reappears in time to hear me say, "And God bless Ryan on his Communion."

"Our table is ready, Claire." Nathan appears even more perturbed.

I follow him to the back of the restaurant. He probably demanded to sit as far away from other people as possible, especially twirling little revelers.

"That was a nightmare. I don't understand why people

would bring young children to a place like this." He pulls on his tie and rips it off, throwing it on the seat beside him. Why is he wearing a suit? I decide not to ask him.

"They're celebrating the little boy's Communion. I think it's nice." I start drinking the wine Nathan took the liberty of ordering. He must have done that before we sat down.

He takes a huge swig and already refills his glass. "Communion? What's that, some kind of Catholic thing?"

I decide to change the subject instead of telling him how I enjoyed my First Holy Communion day. We had a big party at my grandmother's house and my mother made special cupcakes with little crosses on them. I twirl the little gold cross ring I received that day. I wear it on my pinky now.

"So did you have a stressful day at the office again?"

"Claire, you have no idea! Those nurses are total morons sometimes, and the patients' families are so clueless." He is still chugging the wine.

I was alluding to the patients' health and the stress of saving lives, but I don't mention this. Why is he in such a bad mood? Just the other day he was practically in tears telling me about almost losing a patient.

Before I get a chance to reply he continues. "Let's not talk about my work, Claire. How was your day? I did some research on that company of yours. I saw an interesting press release about the new line of books you're carrying."

"Yeah, I'm not too happy about that, but our sales are down and we need to produce something highly marketable." I feel my cheeks flush.

He motions to the waiter. The bottle of wine is already gone and we haven't ordered any food yet. Fortunately, I am stone cold sober. "Nathan, should you be drinking so much wine? Didn't you say you have an early tee time tomorrow and then rounds and—?"

"Sweetie, don't worry about me." Nathan reaches for my leg, misses and almost slides off his chair. It was a far reach though, since I am sitting across from him at this booth in the corner. Did he start drinking before he got here? Luckily, we are as far away from the other diners as we could be. Rick and his family must be in the other room. Little Abby is probably drinking a Shirley Temple with an umbrella.

Nathan breaks into my day dream. "Sweetie, I just remembered. I need you to come with me to a medical conference in June. It's being held in Phoenix. You'll love it." The waiter has brought another bottle of wine. I interject and suggest that we order food, which of course Nathan does without any input from me.

Wait, Phoenix in June? It must be 110 degrees there by that time of year. "Is it a weekend thing?"

"No, it's a week-long professional conference. Spouses and significant others are invited, though. There are lots of social opportunities and you can get to know the other women during the day. Do you have any formal wear?"

Aren't there any women doctors attending the conference? I guess they don't bring their husbands? As for formal wear, I don't want to remind him that I didn't have many formal UPS events to attend with Ron, and my evening wear consists of the dress I wore to Rachel's wedding, more than five years ago. "I have a few things."

"We'll set up a date to shop for you. I want you looking amazing. Not that you don't every day, Sweetie."

"I'll ask for the time off at work." I was planning on a beach vacation with Rebecca this summer, but I have enough time left to do both. Unless Nathan wants to take me somewhere else.

Finally, the food has arrived. The egg rolls *are* amazing. No, all Asian food does not taste the same.

"I forgot to tell you that I'm working on getting you set up with a golf pro at Windy Hill to give you lessons. They have a nice women's league you could join." He smiles and pats my leg, steadily this time.

"I thought we could play together and you would teach me. I guess it makes sense to learn from someone else, though. Ron tried to teach me to ski when we were young, and I almost stabbed him with the poles." I laugh as the waitress presents us with our main dish. It looks hot and delicious, and I am famished.

Nathan gasps and I jump in. "I wouldn't have actually *hit* him. I'm just saying that it's hard to learn a skill from a man. I mean a husband." I add quickly, "Or boyfriend." Especially if he's an asshole, like Ron.

"I see. Yes, I think Daniel will be an excellent teacher for you."

My heart drops into my stomach. Daniel? No, Daniel, the bug killer can't possibly be a golf pro at Windy Hill. He just plays there and it's a common name.

"What's the matter, Sweetie?"

"Nothing. That sounds great."

We continue to talk about the conference and all the things I can do there, like look at cacti and scorch my skin. There isn't enough sunscreen in the world to protect this blond girl from the Arizona sun in June! I want to ask about volunteering, but I don't think Nathan has time to help me with that. Plus I can just go to the hospital's website and find the name of the contact person myself. No need to pressure him about it. It's not like I need a doctor's endorsement to be accepted as a volunteer.

Nathan looks drained as we get ready to leave. He pays the check and we start walking to the car. I catch Rick's eye as I see him corralling his brood to leave as well. He smiles and gives me a half wave, which I return as Nathan is distracted by the mints at the front door. Rick was a nice guy. I hope he meets a good woman to help him with those kids.

As we leave the restaurant, I begin, "Nathan, I hope we can start to spend more time together. Is there anything I can do to help you free up more time? Maybe I could help with the renovation, like call people or supervise, or something that would—?"

We are walking to our cars and he wraps me up in a big hug. "Little Claire, I'm sorry. I know we need to make more time for each other. Hopefully the renovations on my house will be done soon and we can spend more time there. I enjoy relaxing at home too, especially with you."

I open my mouth to say that my home is five minutes away, but I don't. I have already made myself look pathetic enough, and Dixie is still a problem we haven't dealt with. I can see he is in no mood to be jumped on by a frantic dog. Maybe an out of town trip is precisely what we need. Screw the burned skin, I wish the conference was next week.

He kisses me good night, and again I feel ready to go

further, but I'm the woman, and I don't want to be the aggressor. I know that sounds like antiquated thinking, but I believe the man should lead the relationship. I've never had to do it and I don't know how. Nathan has a plan and I need to trust that. I have never been treated like a lady and it's foreign to me. This is probably how my father courted my mother in the seventies. On second thought, more like my grandparents in the forties, but it's sweet and charming. And exasperating.

Just before he gets to his car on the other side of the lot, he yells out. "Sweetie, I will call you tomorrow if I can get away from my work dinner. It should be an early night. Maybe we can get together then. Drive safely and sleep well." He disappears into his car.

I wish I knew a doctor's wife or girlfriend to compare notes. Perhaps this is just the life they lead. Obviously, if we lived together I would see him more. I need my own hobbies and interests. The volunteering would be good. I have always been one of those women who has no hobbies. When I was married to Ron, I just did his stuff with him, like tagging along on fishing trips and watching sports. We did go to quite a few games, which was fun. Maybe Nathan would like to go to a baseball game, and have a *Nathan's* hot dog. Haha... That really doesn't qualify as a hobby for me, though. A hobby. For me. I need to ponder that.

I wish I could short circuit the electric currents I feel in my body—damn it. You would think baseball and fishing would be enough of a turn off to extinguish the flames, or any thought of Ron. I didn't think I would become sexually frustrated in a relationship, but it's so new! Patience is a virtue I don't have. I hate patience and virtue—they both suck! The sucking twins of celibacy. What the hell do nuns do?

As I pull into my cul-de-sac, I'm tired. Worn down from thinking and over analyzing. Brandon's front porch is lit up and he is perched on one of his rockers. He is playing the guitar, and what is that around his shoulders? I can't quite make it out. I squint and realize it's the afghan he offered me after the party. *My mother sent this for my birthday. It's good for a cold little chick.*

I smile and get out of the car. Walking slowly to the mailbox, I strain to make out the song Brandon is playing.

CHAPTER THIRTY-TWO

I should just march right through my front door and pretend I don't notice anything, but I'm drawn to the quiet strumming and the soft vocals. It can't hurt to go over and say hi. It isn't too late and I have nowhere to be tomorrow morning. Brandon knows I'm dating someone and we're just friends—it isn't like I'm flirting or doing anything wrong.

As I walk across the cul-de-sac I see him look up and smile at me. He stops singing and puts down the guitar.

"No, don't stop. I was enjoying the free concert." I walk up the steps and plop down on the other porch rocker. It feels good to relax—this was a weird night.

"Were you out on a date with the doctor?" he says playfully.

"Yes, I was out with *Nathan*. He had an early tee time so he had to get home, and the golf course is all the way on the other side of town."

"Yeah, I tried golfing once. With my dad and my uncle. By the end of the day I was throwing the ball towards the green. I don't have the patience and I guess that isn't where my physical abilities lie."

He stares at me and I can feel myself blushing.

"I mean the guitar playing, of course. I can also play the piano, fool around on the drums a bit. What did you *think* I meant, Claire?" He smirks and continues. "So what would you like to hear, since I know you came over for my musical abilities and not the comedy?" He picks up the guitar and peers at me.

"You pick. I don't know what you know."

He twists his mouth in a puzzled expression. After a moment he nods his head and says, "I know just the thing to get you ready for bed." He laughs again. "I mean sleep."

I only allow myself to display a mildly amused grin, and settle back in the chair. That stubble on his face isn't the least bit distracting—I think he's growing a beard now. Wordlessly, he hands me the afghan and I pull it over me as if I am a little girl getting ready for her lullaby.

"This is an old one. Before our time, but I think it's fitting."

As I close my eyes I hear the first few bars of "Wonderful Tonight" by Eric Clapton. It is before our time. Even mine. I would say this came out around the time I was born. When Jackie and I were little, my parents used to play music after we went to bed. A few times I caught them dancing in the living room when they thought the kids were safely tucked away. They liked this song. My mother has blond hair, too.

Brandon is telling the story of a woman getting ready for a night out, just as I did earlier this evening. Only I didn't have anyone there to tell me I looked wonderful. Rick from the restaurant might have told me, if I had been alone. Did Nathan say I looked nice? I can't recall that detail, but I could describe Abby's skirt and panda perfectly.

When Brandon reaches the part about her long blond hair, he looks up at me and fixes me with a soft gaze. His voice makes me shudder. Do I have goose bumps? This lullaby is not having a sleepy affect at all. When he gets to the line where Eric Clapton says he loves her I shut my eyes tight. Maybe I should have followed my first instinct and gone home. It's just a song. Just a song some guy wrote for a woman long ago when I was a fetus. Nothing to do with the people on this porch.

Brandon finishes and I open my eyes. I'm glad it's dark. I turn and wipe my eyes quickly, and put on a forced smile. "That was beautiful. That's the first time I've heard you do something that quiet."

"Yeah, the head banging stuff gets us the gigs and the fans, and pumps my adrenaline, but I do like the classics. Plus, I had some inspiration tonight." I ignore that comment as he puts down the guitar and gestures towards his beer. "Want one?"

"No, thanks. I had wine. I'll get a headache, and I don't drink beer. Actually, do you have any hard ciders left?" What the hell. My nerves are shot. *Plus, I had some inspiration tonight.*

"I might. Let me check." He carries a couple of empty beer bottles in the house and comes back a few seconds later with two hard ciders. He pops off the cap and hands one to me.

"It's a little cold out to be drinking this, but you *do* have Mom's afghan." He smiles and leans back, gently rocking. "So how did you get into the heavier music? Did you always like it?"

"Not really. I was the typical pop music girl in my youth. My sister had a boyfriend a few years back who had played in a metal band, and he introduced us to all the newer stuff. I love it, but I can't ever find anyone else who does. I missed seeing Shinedown the other day." That sounded like whining and I hope he doesn't think I was baiting him. "I was really impressed at your party that you can do some of their stuff. That guy is a phenomenal singer."

"Thanks, but I can barely touch his vocals—they were great the other day, by the way. I wish I had known you wanted to go. I know what you're saying, though. A lot of people our age are already giving up on the heavy stuff." He swigs his cider.

"We aren't the same age." I am not telling him about Justin asking me to go because that will lead to another line of questioning about Nathan and why *he* didn't want to go, and how many guys I'm dating.

He rolls his eyes. "That's right. You're so *old*. I should get a shawl for you to wear over your arthritic shoulders. Would you like to hear some Frank Sinatra? How about Elvis?" He studies my mock grimace and adds, "They are both actually cool, by the way." He pauses and adds, "Right, Granny Claire?"

I shake my head and sigh. "I actually wanted to go to the theater tonight but it was sold out. There's a new play at the Lonsdale downtown I wanted to see. Have you been there?"

"Yeah, Bianca's friend Katie works in stage production there. It's a cool place. I've been a few times. Is it sold out tomorrow? I could see if Katie could get you guys some tickets."

"No, Nathan can't go tomorrow. He has a dinner with some colleagues."

"That sucks. He's a busy guy, huh?" An awkward silence follows that question. Brandon clears his throat. "The band has a gig tomorrow at O'Malley's. You could dance with the girls on stage and make me look popular." He flashes me his best sparkling smile.

"I don't know, Brandon. I won't know anyone."

"You do know people. From the party. You can hang out with the other wives and girlfriends." He catches himself and says, "I mean *you're not* a wife or girlfriend, but you seemed to get along with the other women at the party." He fiddles with the cap from his cider and takes another drink.

"I did like Bianca and her friends, and I would like to meet Katie." I exhale deeply. "I think I'll go." I stand up and put down my empty bottle. "That was good, thanks." I jokingly lay the afghan across Brandon's legs. "All tucked in—sorry I can't sing any lullabies."

"Good night, Claire." I feel his eyes on my back as I descend the porch steps.

I swing around and point my finger at him. "But I am *not* dancing on any stages."

As I turn around and start walking back to my house Brandon yells out, "Yeah, we'll see. They have a *lot* of hard cider on hand there."

I glance back one last time, shaking my head and grinning, before closing my door.

CHAPTER THIRTY-THREE

Friday Night Claire has really gotten Saturday Night Claire into a pickle. Why do I do these things? I can say no. That's allowed. Jeez. I thought about calling Rebecca or Jane to talk me off the ledge but I don't need to hear any judgments or advice. I need to have some damn fun, and I'll be hanging out with the girls. Brandon will be on stage, and we're just friends. He just likes to tease and flirt.

Besides, Nathan texted this morning and I told him I might go see my friend's band. He told me to have a great time, but he may get done with his dinner early, and maybe he can meet me at the show or he'll come to my house. I'm still going to go, but I'm excited that he's making more time for us.

After many stressful hours of changing outfits and agonizing over shoe choice, I arrive at O'Malley's. It's an upscale Irish pub with lots of wood and fun Irish posters and sayings all over the walls. The food is good, too, and they have a nice outdoor patio and courtyard area in the back. The bar area is set up for the band, with some of the high top tables removed to create a pseudo dance floor. I know there isn't going to be any actual "dancing" with this type of music, but I still need to be prepared to stand all night, unless I can prop myself up against a bar stool during the band breaks.

Speaking of standing all night, I have yet again sacrificed comfort for fashion. This is going to be a young crowd, and I am not going to be seen in even semi-frumpy footwear. My sequined spike slides are not the least bit comfortable, but they are sparkly and they match my gold halter top perfectly. The light sweater material has metallic beading weaved through it and my jeans have just a touch of bling on the pockets. My huge gold hoop earrings round out the outfit. I just hope my toes can handle the workout of trying to keep these shoes attached to my feet all night.

Max and Bianca spot me right away and come over to say hello. Max buys me a drink (something fruity and blue), and I scan the room for anyone else I may know. We're having a great conversation about the band, and I love watching Max and Bianca tease each other. They introduce me to Katie, who is busy waiting on tables, but we exchange numbers to chat more about the Lonsdale Theater. Max hangs around and buys me another drink until he needs to join the band, and before I know it I am standing there with Bianca on drink number three. I don't know what's in this stuff, but it's potent.

"He really is a nice guy. What happened with you two?" I sip my drink and twirl my straw in the blue liquid. It's close to the color of Brandon's eyes. I don't see him anywhere.

"We break up and get back together all the time. We're back on right now. He can be a moody asshole, but that's all musicians. Don't you find Brandon to be that way?" Bianca is slurping down her hard cider.

"No, I think Brandon is pretty nice all the time, but we're not dating. He's cute, but he's not in my league. I'm too old for him." She's had more to drink than me, but somehow she is steadier on her feet. I look down and see she is wearing flat biker boots. No wonder she seems so tiny tonight.

"No way! He's obviously crazy about you. Is he not your type or something?" She looks past me but then regains her focus. Her eyes are rolling around a bit.

"Really, he isn't. I prefer brown eyes, and really a *much* bigger man." I break out in a fit of giggles.

Bianca almost snorts her drink through her nose when I do my imitation of a *big* man by pulling back my shoulders, sticking out my chest and pretending to flex the non-existent muscles in my spindly little arms.

"You kill me. So, as big as *Max*? He has a brother, you know." She can't stop laughing.

I am doubled over and squeezing my legs together so I don't pee in my pants.

"No, Max would crush the life out of me. You must spend more time riding him than you do his motorcycle." Now we're screaming in hysteria. Everything is hilarious.

Bianca is wiping away some of her smeared black eyeliner. "Yeah, one time he was drunk and tried to get on top of me. That was touch and go. If he passes out, you need a crane to haul him off." More cracking up, then she pauses and takes a deep breath. "You are too funny. So seriously, why not Brandon?"

I stop laughing and reply, "Actually, I met someone else. A tall, handsome doctor, and besides—who wants a man you can beat up?" I don't really think I can beat Brandon up, but it sounds so funny right now.

We both start laughing again and Katie comes by to ask us if we want more drinks, and of course we accept in our idiotic state. Just as Katie walks away and I finally compose myself, I turn around and see Brandon sitting on the bar stool behind me. He's talking to another girl. How long he has been there? Did he hear me? It's loud in here—he couldn't have...Bianca would have said something if he was *right behind me*. Wouldn't she?

"Can you hold my drink, Claire? I have to pee so badly!" I take Bianca's bottle and she staggers off to the ladies' room, which some genius put downstairs. In an Irish pub? Stairs to the bathroom? They must have at least one head injury per night with that set up.

I feel conspicuous standing here alone with two drinks in my hand. Brandon's conversation partner walks away and he turns to me.

"So you made it? Having a couple of drinks?" He gestures to my hands.

"This one is Bianca's." I hiccup and sway a little.

Brandon looks down at my feet. "Yeah, I saw you talking to her. Where's the big doctor?"

"Nathan couldn't come. I'm excited to see you guys play, though." I put a huge smile on my face, and toss my head slightly from side to side, to push the hair out of my face. I wish Bianca would come back for her drink and free up a hand.

"We're on in a few minutes. Be careful with those drinks, Claire. You can't hold your alcohol like Bianca." He throws some cash down on the bar and smirks at me.

"I know I'm out of control when I drink too much, but so

is she!" I laugh and hiccup again. "Hey Brandon, have fun, good luck...or..." I have no idea what I'm saying.

He shakes his head slightly, and opens his mouth to respond, when a guy appears to grab him for a sound check.

Did he hear us? Why do people buy me drinks? I need to duct tape my mouth shut. He probably just referred to Nathan as big because I told him that he was, and maybe he has a short man complex. Shit, where's Bianca. I need to ask her if she saw him, and how long he was sitting there.

She returns from the bathroom and grabs her drink. I lean in to ask her and she shouts that she can't hear me. Unfortunately, the band has now started playing and she grabs my hand, pulling me up to the front of the stage. I'll have to remember to ask her later.

The band is awesome, the sound is phenomenal, and Brandon's voice is pitch perfect on every song. The group is screaming and singing along, and I am caught up in the music and the emotion of the crowd. It's only at the first band break that I remember what happened earlier.

I try to get Bianca alone, but now she's doing shots at the bar, and Max is laughing like crazy watching her get more and more wasted. Before I know it, I'm doing shots and I can barely stand up. I hope I don't have to throw up because there is no way I am getting down those stairs in one piece. As I teeter back to the floor Bianca screams that I should take my shoes off. I look to the side of the stage and see a pile of poor footwear choices. Screw it, I'm doing it. I wander in that direction, holding my shoes. I hope no one steals them, but right now I don't care.

As I approach the side of the stage, I hear two voices. They can't see me because there is a curtain hung up to create a makeshift stage. Even though the crowd is loud, I'm close enough to hear them because they are shouting to hear each other.

"Wow man, that's awesome! Congratulations! Why didn't you tell me sooner?" I peek through the slit in the curtain and see Brandon shaking hands and hugging his bass player, Jon.

"I know how you are with the whole baby thing and I didn't know if you'd be into hearing about it, but Cassie and I are pretty stoked. A little baby rock star."

Jon punches Brandon's arm. What does he mean—*I know how you are with the whole baby thing?*

"No—don't ever feel like that. I have my own opinions, but you and Cassie should do things your way. I'm really happy for you guys."

Jon picks up his bass and says, "Thanks. Pregnant women are totally nuts. The crying, the food cravings, and it's only been two months."

"Yeah, but you'll get a great kid out of it. Who doesn't want to be a dad, right? But you know I just..."

I drop my shoes in the pile and take a deep breath before taking off to rejoin Bianca and her friends in front of the stage. I don't care anymore if he overheard me. *Who doesn't want to be a dad, right?* Lots of men, Brandon. Men who do *important* work. How does he think he could support a child anyway?

I return to the jumping and gyrating carousers, and now that I can move around unencumbered by stilts, I shake my ass off. A good time is had by all, and as the night draws to a close, I realize that I have had a wee bit too much to drink. Again. And I even ate before coming here. Why was the room not spinning when the band was playing? It's like Brandon's voice saying "You guys want one more?" triggered a case of severe dizzies and a realization of how many *I've* had—drinks, not songs. Now in the hustle and bustle of the aftermath, everyone looks as horrible as I feel. Smeared makeup, disheveled clothing, discarded shoes—shit, I hope I can find mine.

I don't see Bianca, but I have no idea why I want to talk to her anymore. Right now I just want to get home and go to bed. Two problems with that. Really three. I need my shoes. I can't possibly drive like this, AND Nathan is supposed to come over. It's almost two o'clock, though. He can't be planning on coming over now. Shit again. I think my phone was vibrating and I mistook it for the buzz of blasting speakers and blue drinks.

I stumble over to the shoe pile, which is like a mass grave of bad decisions, and start sifting through all the stilettos and platforms. I think I see mine. Yep, that's one.

Damn it, it's a little smashed. I think I can fix that. Where the hell is the other one now? I think I've spotted it. I can't reach it so I lean forward and end up laying on the pile. I did not fall! I simply placed myself in the cradle of leather and bling, which is not entirely uncomfortable. Maybe I could climb inside the pile and sleep awhile before the bouncers see me.

"Jesus, Claire. What the hell are you doing?"

Why does this man keep catching me doing stupid things?

I turn over and realize that my halter top has shifted and it is *possible* a boob has escaped. Not that it would be any great big flopping display, but there's enough to identify it as an actual boob. As I try to adjust myself, Brandon looks away, shaking his head and offering me his hand.

"I can't find my other shoe." I stumble forward, unable to articulate any more words, like "I'm sorry" or "the show was great" or "your beard looks really good." It's probably a good thing the stupid thoughts in my alcohol soaked brain can't find their way out of my dry, disgusting mouth.

Brandon grabs a chair, seemingly from thin air, and pushes me down into it. He asks one of the guys to stop breaking down the equipment and watch me for a second. "Hey, man, could you just hold her in place for a second. I need to find her goddamned shoe." The guy mumbles something I can't make out. "No, she's not my girlfriend. I'm not her *type*." More mumbling. "Right, I know man...a handful...just want to get her home...thanks."

I accept my indirect scolding and try hard to stay put in the chair. I want to check my phone but it's in my pocket. My jeans are so tight, and my movements so unsteady, I'm afraid I'll fall on the ground if I try to retrieve it, and Brandon *will* leave me here in a footwear tomb.

"I got it. Thanks, man." The guy stops holding me and I immediately slump in the chair. I try to right myself and Brandon takes the other shoe out of my hand. He motions to put them on my feet, but examines them more closely and decides not to bother.

"Claire, I'm going to take you home now." He holds my face in his hands. "You should have some water and aspirin. I'm going to take care of you, but I need you to walk to the car with me. I could carry you—I'm a little stronger than you think I am, but I think if you just lean on me I can manage."

Even in my drunken stupor I am catching on to the subtle hints here. He heard me. Now I have to trust him to take me home. Hopefully he won't dump me on my front porch or in the bushes.

Brandon pulls me up to standing and leads me out of the bar. He's fully supporting my weight, and I'm choking him with a death grip around his neck. He places me in the car and buckles my seatbelt.

"Fuck, now I need gas!" He bangs the steering wheel and this causes me to jump.

"I'm sorry, Claire. We aren't that far from home and there's a gas station right across the street. Maybe I can get you some water and those little aspirin packets they have. That's what we'll do. Just lay back and relax." He reaches across my body to fiddle with the seat back adjustment, and his stubbly face lightly grazes my cheek. I hold my breath so he can't smell my undoubtedly rancid breath.

At the gas station, he reminds me that he'll be back in a minute, starts pumping the gas, and disappears into the convenience store to get my water and aspirin. I make the mistake of turning towards the passenger side window and catch a fuzzy glimpse of myself. Holy crap—I look *scary*! What if Nathan *is* coming over? I have to get to my phone, but first I need to fix my eye makeup. I look like a crack whore coming home from a bad night on the job.

He must have some tissues or napkins in the glove compartment. I fumble with the latch and the door pops open. There's a lot of crap in here. I see some napkins buried under all these papers. Is that a lipstick? Maybe it's just Chap Stick. Why do I care? Damn it, now my leg is vibrating. That's my phone. I lean back and dig into my pocket for the phone, but now my legs are hitting the open glove box. Jeez, there isn't much room in this car. I don't care what he says, but a *big* man could not own this *tiny* car. I guess they needed his truck for the band equipment.

I manage to grab the phone, but it slips out of my hand onto the floor, of course all the way in the corner. This is ridiculous. I still need the napkins, so I lean in to swipe a few, slam the glove box shut, stretching forward to grab my stupid phone, which is vibrating again. As I do this I hear Brandon returning to the car. Shit, I wanted to answer that.

I start to sit up and realize my halter top is not only untied, but one strap is caught in the glove box! I drop my phone in my lap and begin to wrestle the strap, which promptly rips off. I can hear Brandon replace the gas nozzle and shut the gas cap. As I peek back and see him collecting his receipt, I attempt to tie my top, but now one string is longer than the other and my motor skills are significantly challenged. Dizziness has turned to double vision, and as two Brandons open the car door and begin to present me with my bag of drunk girl remedies, I jump up holding each string straight up in air, as if I am surrendering to the authorities or creating a goal post with my arms.

He throws the bag in the cup holder and jumps in the car, slamming the door.

"What the hell happened now?" His angry eyes look dark blue, reflecting the gas station's illumination and the moonlight. He sighs deeply and takes the straps from my hands, attempting to tie them. Of course he sees the problem right away, opens his mouth, presumably to ask how this happened, and gives up. He drags the one string far enough around to the side, so that he can make a tiny bow resting on my shoulder.

"That's all I can do for now. At least you're covered up. Jesus. It's a good thing I noticed you before we packed the truck. Are you going to answer that phone?" He points to my pulsating lap.

I somehow find the silencer and press it, and scroll through my texts. I have received about twenty messages from Nathan.

"I hope you're having fun. Can I stop over?"

"Sweetie, I would like to see you."

"A patient of mine died tonight. I'd like to see you and talk about it."

"Claire, where are you? You're worrying me."

"Where the hell are you? I am calling the police if you don't respond soon!"

The messages are increasingly emotional, becoming

angry. His patient died? Which patient? Maybe that's what he was so grumpy about at dinner. Why are men so close mouthed about their problems?

"Is the doctor worried, Claire? Frankly, he should be because I think you may have alcohol poisoning. Is he coming over?"

I nod my head yes. He opens the bag and pulls out the water and aspirin, opening the cap and popping out the pills. I dutifully follow his instructions, gulping down half the bottle of water.

"...and when you get home you should not go to bed right away. Drink more water. That poor bastard, you are going to be useless for a booty call tonight." Brandon smiles.

"Hey, it's not a booty call! He isn't that type of man!" My voice sounds strange and hoarse, even to me. Brandon flinches and blinks.

"*Now* she can talk. You're right. Most nice guys come over to see their girlfriends at this hour, after refusing to accompany them to a social event. That is completely normal and—"

"SHUT UP!" My head bobs and weaves from the force of my words.

Brandon glares at me, and backs the car out, heading towards home. We sit in silence the whole way. I want to tell him that I enjoyed the show and I'm sorry for my behavior, but now I'm too pissed off. This is *not* a booty call! Men like Nathan have probably never even *heard* that term, and he *will* take care of me. I don't need Brandon's medical advice.

I am still seeing two of everything as we pull up in front of my house. I guess he isn't planning on walking me to the door. He hands me what appears to be four shoes, and I slip them on my corresponding feet. I start to say something and he points towards the house. Nathan is on my front porch and walking down to greet me.

"Thanks, Brandon. The show was great," I whisper and get out of the car. Nathan waves to Brandon and starts walking towards the car, but Brandon pulls up his own driveway and into his garage, closing the automatic door.

CHAPTER THIRTY-FOUR

Here we go with the damn lawnmowers again. I know people have to mow, but why do they all have to do it at once? As I shift to an awakened state, my head screams in throbbing agony, and a deluge of last night's events saturate my hung over brain. I gasp and flop my arm over to the other side of the bed. Empty. My front door slams and I hear footsteps on the front porch. Nathan? I fling my debilitated body out of bed, and peek out the blinds in the guest room across the hall, just in time to spot Nathan speeding away to the end of the cul-de-sac.

I crumble into the chaise lounge next to the window and curl up in a ball. The house is chilly this morning, and I just want to grab a fuzzy blanket and stay here forever. I need Brandon's afghan. Brandon. He was so mad at me and I don't blame him. My behavior was disgraceful, and I wasn't even nice to him while he was trying to help me. And poor Nathan. What a night. I don't think we fell asleep until after six. I prop my head up and squint to see the clock on the end table. Eight forty-five. No wonder I feel like death.

Just trying to sit up is agonizing. I need to take Dixie out but she hasn't stirred. I stagger downstairs holding on to the railing. I need water desperately—my mouth is dryer than cotton. Cotton would be like a moist towelette compared to the barren desert wasteland that is the hole in my face. I must look like a puckered prune. I vow to avoid any mirrors for the rest of the day. Maybe the week, considering the severity of the situation.

I locate a bottle of water in the fridge, which isn't hard, given the sparse contents. It looks like a teenaged boy is in charge of my shopping. Only one with no money, car or knowledge of where to find a grocery store.

Nathan practically carried me in the house last night. He asked a lot of questions about where I'd been and what I'd been doing. Obviously, he could see I was completely wasted. Like Brandon, he thought I might have alcohol poisoning and he wouldn't let me sleep until I had consumed gallons of water. Miraculously, I have not thrown up once.

We finally retired to my bedroom, where he tucked me in and laid down next to me. He even took care of Dixie. She had pooped on the floor because I was gone so long, but he didn't even yell at her. He took her outside on her leash, brought her in and gave her a treat, and put her in her crate for the night. He kept telling her how silly and irresponsible Mommy was; his indirect way of sending me that message. That was all he said, though. I certainly deserved a bigger lecture.

He began to tell me about his patient who died. Apparently she had heart disease and wouldn't stop smoking. He had been treating her for the past year, and had grown fond of her. This lady, Nora, reminded him of his favorite aunt.

"My Aunt Dolores lived with us. She was the only bright spot in my family. My mother was—I should say *is*—cold, and my father was controlling and demanding. Dolores believed in me. She took me to the playground, and she encouraged me to have fun and enjoy life. She was my only cheerleader and positive adult role model."

"What happened to her?" My words were faint and weak, muddled with sleepiness and intoxication.

"She had a bad heart. Smoked. Ate bad food. Didn't exercise. The usual." He paused and wiped a tear from his eye and started rubbing my back. It took tremendous willpower to stay awake at that point, but I didn't want to drift off when he needed to talk.

He went on to explain how she died when he was fourteen and he was never the same after that. He didn't feel like he had an ally in the family. His sister Barbara was his closest family member, but she was four years older and not the best influence.

"Barbara was a nice girl at heart, but she was a wild one. She was promiscuous and a drug user—some of it was rebellion against our parents. They were so conservative, and Barbara drove them crazy."

I turned over slightly to see an amused grin forming on his face, and then quickly fade.

"I started spending a lot of time with her friends, and they all thought I was cute. There was one friend, Janice, who was especially interested in me, if you understand my meaning."

I did, but I didn't want to hear about this.

"I wasn't ready for that level of intimacy, not like that." He shudders and continues. "She was an odd girl, but I craved the attention. It wasn't a healthy relationship, but looking back, I don't know if I would have avoided her. In the end she helped shape me, and got me through a bad period. When I went away to college I lost touch with her. She was older then and out on her own. I think the novelty of our game wore off at that point." He sat up and rubbed my back more firmly. "And the rest you know."

I wanted to say that isn't true at all. I know almost nothing about his adult life, but I'm grateful for what he has shared about his youth. It explains why he was so upset at dinner, and why he's been agitated since right after we met. *She was my only cheerleader and positive adult role model.* Nora was dying and he couldn't save her, and that triggered his feelings about his beloved aunt *and* his difficult childhood.

Maybe our relationship has him thinking about his early relationship with Janice too. *There was one friend, Janice, who was especially interested in me, if you understand my meaning.* I wonder what she did that made him shudder at the memory. Maybe she was just an older girl pushing a shy, inexperienced boy out of his comfort zone. She was obviously much too old for him—actually that was illegal, come to think of it. *I think the novelty of our game wore off at that point.*

I continued to enjoy the massage and drifted off. The next thing I remember is waking up to the grass cutting concerto.

I know he left so I could get some rest and he'll check on me later. Even though I feel like total shit, I am so happy that he opened up to me. I can't let him find out that I have high cholesterol. That will trigger more bad memories and fears. Enough with the psychoanalysis—I need more sleep and aspirin. I pluck Dixie from her crate, take her out (in the backyard!), and curl up with her on the couch for a long slumber.

I wake up in the late afternoon, shower, eat a light meal of soup and some crackers, and pass out again until morning.

I look and feel a little rough at work on Monday, but I'm holding it together.

"You look like shit! What the hell happened to you?" Rebecca grabs me by the arm and drags me out of the lunch room into her office.

"I need to get to work, Rebecca, and I need coffee!"

"You don't drink coffee!"

I throw myself in her guest chair and wish we had elected to order the more comfortable ones for the HR offices. I proceed to give Rebecca a censored version of the weekend's events, leaving out the parts about arguing with Brandon about the supposed booty call, and Nathan's deep confessions.

"Claire, you absolutely have to stop drinking like this. You were better for a while, I don't understand." She sighs and offers me a bottle of water. "Maybe you should go home sick."

I accept it and take a big swallow. "No, I have stuff to do."

"This weekend you need to come out with me. The Meetup group is doing a wine tasting on Friday night—just a tasting, not a swigging, and then there's a disco bowling thing on Saturday."

"I am not going to any more singles Meetups." I rub my temples and fidget in my chair.

"What? Why? I know. You think Nathan is the one already, right? Just like that and he's the guy!" She snaps her fingers.

"I think he is."

"What happened to fun and meeting new people? Claire, you barely know this guy."

"This weekend he really opened up and I found out a lot about his childhood—"

"So, he comes over and tells you about his childhood and you think you know him? You need to know about his *adulthood*, his life now. You still haven't been to his house, right?"

I shake my head no.

"That's not normal, Claire, and you haven't even had sex with him. You can wait, but you can't go around planning a future with a man you have only known a couple of weeks, especially when you aren't even intimately involved." She exhales and purses her lips. "You don't see any of this?"

"He's busy and—"

"He can't possibly be too busy to take you to a play or to accompany you to a show. He wasn't even concerned about who you were with or how you would get home?"

"He was worried, but he trusts me."

"I would like to believe all of this, but I'm not buying it. Tell me why you can't go to his house again?"

"It's being renovated."

"Right. So is it like the movie where the kid is lost in New York running from the bad guys, and he finds his uncle's house and there's that huge hole in the floor, and the bad guy steps on glass and gets chicken feathers stuck to him? That kind of renovation?" She is so damn sarcastic sometimes.

"The chicken feathers and the glass are in the first movie. The one where he's left 'Home Alone.' You're getting them confused."

"That's not the point! Do you just fall for any guy who wants you?" I think of Ron and how I settled at sixteen. "Wait, no you don't—because Justin and Brandon are both obviously crazy about you, but you have blown them off for the smoke and mirrors guy."

"They are *boys*. Nathan is a man. An important man."

Rebecca sinks back in her chair and lowers her voice. "I think you've forgotten what that word means?"

"Which word—important or man?"

"Both."

I blink back tears and stand up, placing the water bottle on the desk. "I really have to get to work. Pam wants to meet Brandon and talk to him about a contract. I need to set up a

lunch
    meeting." I lower my head and walk towards the door.

    "Wait. I'm sorry, Claire. Your behavior is just reckless lately, and I worry about you." Rebecca pouts and smiles weakly.

    "This is precisely the reason I haven't told my *real* mother any of this, and I definitely don't need a second one. Really." I muster up a little grin and walk out the door.

CHAPTER THIRTY-FIVE

"Let's just stop in my office—we left the paper work in here and—" Tim is interrupted by giggling.

We all stop in the doorway of Tim's office—me, Tim, Pam, Frank and Brandon. Cecilia is sitting behind Tim's desk and the back of a familiar head is peeking over the top of Tim's guest chair.

"Nathan?"

He sits up straight and turns around abruptly.

"What are you doing here?" I smile to hide my annoyance and confusion. My heart rate quickens.

"Hello, Sweetie. I was looking all over for you and Cecilia was kind enough to entertain me until you came back from lunch. I was going to surprise you and take you out." He is beaming back and forth between Cecilia and the rest of us.

Cecilia jumps in and breaks the silence. "Yes, Claire your office door was locked, but I told him you would be back soon." She smiles, but I'm probably the only one who sees the contempt behind all those perfect white teeth.

"How nice. Thank you, Cecilia." I stare at Nathan. "We were just taking Brandon out to lunch to discuss acquiring his book." I gesture towards Brandon, who peeks his head around the corner. The doorway was jam packed, but Pam and Frank have receded back into the hallway, deep in conversation and oblivious to the show going on in here.

Tim interjects, "Cecilia, did I miss anything while I was gone?" He raises his eyebrows and she jumps up from his desk.

"No, I was just making our guest comfortable and having a quick coffee break." She grabs her empty coffee cup and heads for the door. "Nathan, it was so nice to meet you." We step out of the way so she can make her escape. She has some nerve! I would never sit behind Tim's desk.

Cecilia pauses when she passes Brandon. "Hi, I'm Cecilia." She offers her hand and he shakes it while looking over at me. "I'm a budding writer, too! I hope your book will be successful." She glares back at me over her shoulder. Tim doesn't notice, but I think Brandon does.

She's a budding writer? What? Now that she's gone, I can introduce Brandon to Nathan, and get that whole ordeal over with. Brandon is acting like the other night never happened, thank God.

I walk over to Nathan, who is now standing, give him a quick peck on the cheek, and introduce him to Brandon. The two men shake hands, and the differences in their ages and statures is pronounced.

"Pleased to meet you, Brandon. You're the neighbor who's in the band, right? I was going to say hello the other night, but I understand you must have been tired and eager to get home. Thank you for bringing Claire home safely—I had a pressing matter at the hospital." He clears his throat and smiles at me.

"Nice to meet you, too. No problem—she wasn't in any shape to drive."

I sneak a glimpse out in the hall to see if everyone else is still occupied. I don't want them hearing about my weekend escapades. I hear a new, but familiar, voice in the group.

"How was lunch?" Rebecca barrels her way into Tim's office, which we have now completely hijacked.

I introduce her to Nathan and Brandon, and I'm not sure which one she is more impressed with.

"I am so glad I stopped by. It's great to meet both of you. So where did you guys go for lunch?"

"The steakhouse on the other side of the plaza," I reply.

"Shame on you, Claire." She wags her finger at me. "You shouldn't be eating steak. Didn't Dr. Mason say—"

Mercifully, Tim interrupts. "Hey folks, sorry to barge in to my office, but I need to get this young man's contract signed, sealed and delivered." His tone is light, but I know he wants us to get moving. Not a moment too soon. I don't want Nathan to know about my high cholesterol, and how does the human resources expert think my medical problems are appropriate office discussion? I'm going to kill her later.

We all laugh and head back out to the hall, apologizing to the big boss for commandeering his office. Nathan shakes Brandon's hand again. "A pleasure, Brandon. We'll have to come see one of your shows some time."

Brandon smiles and catches my eye before Tim shuts the door.

"I'll leave you two alone. Nice to meet you, Nathan." Rebecca excuses herself and walks away, as I scowl at her disappearing frame.

"How long have you been here?" We start walking towards the elevator and my office.

"Not too long. That Brandon is a nice young man. I pictured a rougher character—because of the music and late night partying."

I push the button for the elevator, which arrives immediately. We step inside.

"And what was Rebecca saying? Why can't you eat steak?"

"What? She's crazy. We were just doing this diet and cutting out fat and—"

Nathan is not smiling. "Seriously, Claire? You were on a diet? Do you have high cholesterol?"

"No! Maybe a *little* high." Nathan's eyes widen and I continue. "But my overall risk is low. I'm thin and there is no history of heart disease in my family."

"I can't believe you kept this from me, Claire. This is distressing. You should be on a strict diet and exercise program. I saw *donuts* in your kitchen!" He raises his voice and the people in open cubicles are staring. I pull him by the arm closer to my office door and put the key in the lock.

"I'm sorry. It's just not a big deal and I didn't know—"

"Not a big deal? That is an irresponsible attitude. I will not allow the woman I love to have heart disease. Haven't I suffered enough?"

Woman he loves? I start to respond and he holds up his hand. "I will put together a program for you, and we will recheck you in three months, and every three months after that, until your numbers are in normal range."

I sigh and look down at my feet. "You're right, Nathan. I

need to take better care of myself."

"Good girl." He comes closer and kisses me on the forehead. "I'll call you later."

He walks towards the door and I stop him. "Nathan, did you mean it that we can go see Brandon's band?" I wince and await his response. "They're playing again this Saturday."

He grins and says, "Of course, Sweetie. Whatever makes you happy. I will bring earplugs, just in case." He sees my dejected expression and says, "I'm kidding, Claire. It will be fun. Now eat a salad tonight and go for a walk with Dixie. Doctor's orders."

As soon as he leaves I collapse in my chair. Boy, did this day take a turn for the worse quickly. Cecilia is a crazy bitch, and I could strangle Rebecca. I know I shouldn't be hiding things from Nathan, but we've only been together a short time. I was going to tell him, but after everything he told me the other night I didn't want to spring this on him, and I know I can get it under control.

Lunch was great. Brandon is impressive with his writer's hat on! I know what Nathan means—I know him pretty well and even I wondered what he would be like in this professional setting. Tim offered him a nice advance on his next book and a tidy sum for the rights to his submitted manuscript. I'm happy for him. He seemed like he wanted to say more when I was leaving Tim's office, but I will see him at home. I mean if he's outside. Speaking of outside, I need to take Dixie for that walk. Maybe we can go to the park for a change of scenery.

I arrive at home a few hours later, and decide to tie Dixie outside. It's the first of May and a beautiful day. The tie-out stake is secure now, thanks to Brandon, and I just need a quick change of clothes and we can be off to the park.

I am only inside a few minutes, grab a water bottle and my keys, and I hear a voice on my porch. I swing open the door and Brandon is standing there holding a wiggly and excited Dixie.

"Why are you holding her? Come on, don't tell me she got loose again?" Brandon hands Dixie to me before she jumps out of his arms. I attach her leash to her harness and put her down. Now that she has Mommy back, she is jumping on Brandon's leg. She's a confused little chick— must be catching.

"I was sitting on the porch reading over my contract again and she came running over. I *know* that tie-out stake was secure. But it's loose again. Has your lawn guy been here? Maybe he hit it with the mower, or the weed whacker?" Brandon bends down to pet Dixie, who has flipped over for a belly rub and gotten tangled in her leash.

"That's possible, I guess. Damn it, she's such a little whack-job. I wish I could leave her out here once in a while. I guess I need a fenced yard." My stomach hurts thinking of her running across the street, even though it's only a cul-de-sac.

"No, that thing should be secure. You just need to check it before you tie her up. I fixed it again." He stands up. "Where are you off to?"

"Thanks, and we're just going to the park. Me and little Miss Houdini." We both smile and shake our heads at Dixie's antics.

He continues to stand there a moment longer than necessary. I begin, "Did you want to come with us?"

"I could do that. It'd be good to get some exercise in the fresh air." He picks up Dixie and we walk to my car, which is filthy as ever.

"Sorry about my car. Do you want to put her in the carrier?"

"No, she's fine on my lap." Dixie licks Brandon's nose and we're off.

The whole way there he holds onto her as she frantically peers out the window, taking in all the excitement. She doesn't get out much, and she clearly loves it.

We go on a nice long walk, and before getting in the car to go home I spot the swings.

Brandon notices and gestures to them. "Did you want to play on the swings, Claire?"

"Actually, I kind of do. Does that make me a whack-job now?"

"A little bit, but it's cute."

I try to punch him in the arm, but of course he is way too fast for me, and easily dodges my blows.

He picks Dixie up and carries her. Before I can protest, he ties her leash around the picnic table leg, right next to the swings. "She's not going anywhere now." She flips and hops but finally settles down. That was a long walk for her miniscule legs.

We sit on side by side swings, and start to leisurely pump our legs.

"You wanna hear something funny? When I first saw you across the street I thought you were a young father, and I imagined you putting together your swing set for your little family." When I first saw him. Hopefully he won't want to reminisce about any other aspect of that encounter.

"That is funny. I would love to be that guy someday, but I need the right woman, you know?" His blue eyes are gleaming in the late day sun.

I attempt to swallow the lump in my throat. "So are you excited about your contract?" I lean my face up towards the waning sunlight and close my eyes.

"I am—it's nice to have my work recognized. I sold a good number of my self-published books, but it feels good to have publisher backing. The advance doesn't hurt either."

I catch his smile as I open my eyes and see him pumping higher in the air.

"So, what did you think of Cecilia? She's the office hottie."

"Really? Hmm..."

"Come on, you thought she was attractive." I smile and glance over at him. He is swinging higher than me.

"Yeah, she is, but she's kind of prickly. Like a porcupine."

I burst into a fit of giggles. "A porcupine?"

"Yeah, both her looks and personality scream 'prickly little creature.' She was enjoying making you squirm— getting caught talking to your boyfriend, sitting at the boss' desk. And with that spiky hair and all those skinny sharp angles, she could be dangerous."

"She would want to kill you if she heard that." I don't care if she talks to Nathan. He is so much older than her—

she would never be interested in him. Now Brandon, yes. I wouldn't be surprised if he just got himself a new stalker. Justin will be relieved. "You've got her pegged. She isn't the sweetest woman in the office. Too bad you missed Amanda, the front desk receptionist. She's out sick today."

Brandon stops swinging and looks at me intently. I slow down. "I doubt she's prettier than you."

There goes my heart rate again. Maybe I do have a serious cardiac condition, but more likely it's the excessive competitive swinging. "That's ridiculous, Brandon. She's more than ten years younger than me."

"It's too bad you can't get over this age thing. Younger does not always mean prettier."

"I think you need to see an eye doctor. You know, you don't need to butter me up anymore. You have your signed contract." I grin at him.

"I didn't see anyone in the office prettier than you."

I glance over at little Dixie lying next to the picnic table just to have somewhere else to look. "Push me," I announce.

"What? You mean on the swing? You were doin' pretty well by yourself. Almost as high as me." He smiles and stands up.

"Don't gloat, I've always needed help to get as high as I wanted to go."

"I think maybe you still do."

"What does that mean?"

He starts pushing me. "Nothing, I just meant on the swings."

After I am so high that I am in danger of flipping over the top, I scream for him to stop. I slow down and come to a rather abrupt standstill using my feet. "Whew, that was fun. Your turn now."

"*You're* going to push *me*?" He points from me to him. "I don't think you'll be able to do that—you're just a little chicken."

I put my hands on my hips. "Really? I am mightier than I look."

He laughs and sits down on the swing.

"Prepare to fly!" I can barely make him budge. "Come on, you're not helping."

He smiles and starts doing a bit of the work, but not so much that he is going to knock me over on the backwards motion. As I gently push him I look at the back of his neck. It looks soft and sweet, like a little boy's neck or like Dixie's velvet ears. Stray little fuzzy hairs rest gently on his skin. I get the sudden urge to kiss it, and not really in a sexual way, but sort of. It's a confusing sensation. Maternal and sexual at once. I'm glad he can't see my face.

As he slows down and turns to me, I grasp for something to say. "So, why did you buy that big house? Did you just want the basement for the band? You have a lot of room."

He gets up from the swing, and walks over to Dixie and sits on the picnic table bench. *Who doesn't want to be a dad, right?*

"Yeah, for the band, but I also do want to have a family someday, so I thought it was a good idea to get a big place."

Maybe I misunderstood him. Why would he disapprove of his friend's wife's pregnancy if he wants a family? *I have my own opinions, but you and Cassie should do things your way.* I'm beginning to think Brandon is a big bullshitter. *I didn't see anyone in the office prettier than you.*

"So how are things going with Nathan? Are you sure he doesn't want kids? You know, you guys could adopt—I mean if it works out between you two." Brandon has untied Dixie and is holding her on his lap. She is gazing at me while enjoying her massage.

"He doesn't want to be a father and I'm fine with that."

"I'm confused. Didn't you really want to be a mother? Why would you give that up so easily?"

My heart is racing and my cheeks are burning. "I didn't *give it up.* It was taken from me."

"But you could adopt. There are so many children who need—"

"No, I don't want that. And besides, if a man wants kids, he wants his own. Unless *he* can't have any. So even if I did want to adopt, I don't have time to launch a worldwide search to find hot, successful infertile men who are longing for a family. That isn't something I can *advertise* for, and I can't quit my job to go on a yearlong journey around the world, even if I got to eat delicious food, meditate in the jungle and meet foreign lovers."

He gives me a perplexed look.

"You don't even know that reference, do you?"

"As a matter of fact I do. Authors know the work of *other* successful authors. Besides, my sister dragged me to see the movie."

"Your sister, huh?"

"Yes, Claire, my sister." He stands up, still holding Dixie. "You do have options, but you think you have it all figured out, so I guess the doctor solves all your problems."

I avert his gaze, and he continues. "The sun is going down, we should go." His voice has dropped to just above a whisper.

We ride the short distance home in silence. When I drop him off I tell him that Nathan and I are coming to his show this Saturday. He doesn't look as excited as I had hoped.

CHAPTER THIRTY-SIX

It's Saturday, and Rebecca and I are going to the hairdresser's together, and of course, out to lunch and shopping. Rebecca colors her hair to hide the grey. I like to tease her about the way she looks with all the goop piled on her head, but she doesn't share my amusement.

"Someday, you'll have to color your hair too, Goldilocks."

Sitting in our respective side-by-side salon chairs, I begin to tell Rebecca (and the hairdressers and others in earshot by default) what's going on with both Brandon and Nathan.

"I thought he seemed pleasant enough when I met him at the office the other day, but seriously—you *still* haven't been to his house?"

"Rebecca, I am not rehashing all of that again. He was coming to see me to take me out to lunch. I think surprise visits are romantic. You're just used to dating gropers and creepers." I smile and stick my tongue out at her.

She thinks I can't see her, but I catch her rolling her eyes in the mirror, as Tina spins her chair in my direction to cover the other side of her head with dark auburn goop.

"Actually, you have no idea who I date because I don't talk about it."

"And why is that? I *know*, because it is *so* exhausting talking about my dating woes we run out of time." Jennifer trims and shapes my wet hair, repeatedly pulling my chin up and repositioning my head. It's her way of telling me to stop talking unless I want my hair to look like it was caught in a blender.

"Yep, that's why. Seriously, Claire, I know he's a doctor and all, but that Brandon is so cute." Tina piles the red sticky mess on top of Rebecca's head and sets a timer.

The lady next to me must be at least eighty years old,

but she seems intent on listening to our conversation. She just shushed her hairdresser when she tried to make small talk about the weather.

"Brandon is a pain in the ass. He was questioning me about why Nathan doesn't want kids, and how we could adopt. It's none of his business, and I do have it all figured out now. Nathan is perfect for me and I'm not interested in adoption. I'm trying to simplify my life, and maybe Jackie will have a baby someday and I can be an aunt." I wince at this thought.

"You don't think, do you? Maybe Brandon is interested in you and he's trying to see where you stand on certain issues. Maybe *he* would want to adopt a baby with you. *He's* adopted, right?"

"Why would a healthy twenty-eight year old guy want to adopt?"

"Maybe his guys can't swim. You never know. He could have been kicked in the balls as a toddler or something."

I really hope the old lady's hearing aid is on the fritz. I glance over and she's quietly attentive, and I see her attempting to suppress a grin. I guess this replaces her weekday soap opera viewing. Something catches my eye—is that a copy of our first new book release sticking out of her tote bag? Is that hers? Maybe it's the hairdresser's. If that's her reading material, an innocent groin injury comment shouldn't shock her.

I sigh and say, "No, he feels sorry for me, I think. I shouldn't get so mad at him. He is a nice guy and he's so good with Dixie. He'll find a nice girl, settle down and fill that house with babies. He has so much time." I shift in my seat, toss my hair and nod approval of a job well done to Jennifer. "Besides, things are going well with Nathan. I'll probably have a ring by Christmas."

"What? I better not see a ring on that finger for at *least* a year. A full *calendar* year! How can you marry a man when you don't know how he celebrates Groundhog Day?"

"I think there's a different February holiday that would be more pertinent to this conversation, but that isn't the point. Nathan is the one. When you know, you know."

"You are impossible. Is he at least making more time for

you?"

"Yeah, he's doing better with his schedule. I saw him last night. He came over and we watched movies. Dixie is starting to warm up to him, too. After all, he's a cardiologist, Rebecca. He's an import—"

"I *know*, he's an *important* man. He's *saving* lives."

I could do without the sarcasm and air quotation marks. Jennifer asks me to take a seat in the waiting area so she can do her next haircut. I happily oblige, grateful to end this conversation. Hopefully, by the time the goop is washed out of her hair, Rebecca will think of something else to talk about. Maybe I will ask her about her love life for a change.

I pick up a trashy magazine. I haven't indulged in celebrity gossip since my visit to Dr. Mason's office, when I was interrupted by Roberta. I'm just getting into an interesting article about movie star weight loss plans, when I hear, "Excuse me, Dear." I look up and it's my elderly salon seat neighbor.

"Yes, hello." I put down my magazine and sit up straighter.

She comes walking over very slowly and asks, "Do you mind if I sit down?"

"No, of course not." I hastily move my purse out of the way and shift over. That was her tote bag.

"I know I should mind my own business, but I'm a nosy old lady." She giggles and pats my leg. "My dear girl, it sounds like you have gotten yourself into a love triangle."

I open my mouth to protest, but she forges on. "I don't know anyone named Brandon, except my grandson in Arizona, but Nathan is a familiar name. You said he's a doctor?"

"Yes, a cardiologist. Why?" I search for Rebecca to see if she's getting shampooed yet, but she's still sitting where I left her, reading that stupid new book of ours.

She leans in and whispers, "His last name isn't Kleinman by any chance, is it?" She raises her eyebrows.

My breath catches in my throat. "Yes, it is. Why, do you know him?"

"Yes, he's my doctor." She pats her heart and says, "My old ticker is giving me some grief lately." If so, she better stay out of the erotica section of the bookstore. I wonder if Tim has given any thought to lawsuits involving horny little old ladies and heart attacks.

"I'm sorry to hear that. But he's a good doctor, right? He just recently lost a patient and he was broken up about it." Probably not an appropriate thing to share.

"Yes, I think he's a good doctor—I'm still here." She laughs but quickly turns serious again, leaning in even closer. I recline a little so the other customers don't think I'm about to make out with my grandmother on the couch.

"My dear, there is something you need to know about him. Others might mind their own business, but I am eighty-seven years old and I believe in speaking my mind. I would like to save you some heartache." She smiles and pats my leg again. "You're such a pretty young girl. My granddaughter has hair like yours."

"Mrs., what did you say your name was?"

"Call me Betty, Dear."

"Betty, what do you know about Nathan?" It's probably nothing, but she has piqued my curiosity, and I also want her to spit it out before Rebecca sticks her nose in this conversation.

She folds her hands in her lap. The soft, wrinkled flesh stays put when she releases her grip. She grasps her tote bag handle and continues, "Dr. Kleinman used to be a gynecologist."

What is she babbling about? Did he work with Dr. Mason? Maybe they were partners?

Betty studies my puzzled expression and says, "He was accused of misconduct. Now there were never any charges, just rumors. But I think that's why he switched."

I shake my head and furrow my brow. "What? He switched? What was he accused of?"

Betty raises her eyebrows and widens her eyes, stretching the paper thin skin of her creased lids. She mouths the words almost inaudibly, "Sexual misconduct." She puts her hand over her mouth as if she can't believe she has said this out loud. However, since I have seen her reading choices, she's not fooling me.

"But he wasn't charged? There were just rumors?"

"Yes, but I think he decided to take some time off and retrain or whatever doctors do. He came back to Richmond a while later and joined a cardiology practice."

"But wouldn't they be reluctant to let him join?"

"I'm sure he had lots of doctor friends and they helped him out. It wasn't a public scandal—I just know from the girls in my bridge group. One of their daughters was involved. Apparently he was making suggestive comments and behaving unprofessionally. As I said nothing was ever proven, but I think he became a cardiologist because most of his patients would be older and not all of them female. Maybe less *temptation*." She leans in again and I catch a whiff of permanent wave solution and throat lozenges.

My heart is pounding and I want to ask her more questions, but I don't even know if she's a reliable source of information. Plus, Rebecca is in the shampoo chair now, and I want Betty out of here before she comes waltzing over.

"Thank you, Betty. I appreciate you clueing me in to this...information."

"I did hear you talking about marriage, and I just thought you should know. As I said, as far as I know it wasn't public, but if there was anything documented you may be able to find it on the computer. You could look it up on Gaggle or Giggle, or whatever that thing is the young people use nowadays."

What the hell does she mean? "Oh, you mean *Google*? Yes, I'll look it up. Thanks again."

Betty holds on to the side of the couch and slowly raises herself up to standing. She leans forward and grabs her tote bag. She spots me eyeing her literary selection and says, "I was at the bookstore and I picked this up for my granddaughter. She's about your age, do you think she'll like it? It was in the 'new and hot' section. Sounded like it would be a nice book for a young girl."

I clear my throat and reply, "I bet she'll love it." I suppress a grin and she is on her way.

I sigh and slump down into the nest of pillows. How do I know if there's any truth to this story? She can't use the Internet and doesn't even recognize porn when she sees it! I mean the people on the front cover are half naked! But who cares about that—I need to get home and Google Nathan and see what comes up.

Do I know anyone I could question about this? Melanie? She's the one who set me up with him. No, that would be so awkward. I bet doctors get accused all the time, especially gynecologists. He probably had some crazy religious fanatic for a patient and she misread his normal charm for something more.

Rebecca is headed my way. I take a deep breath and vow to keep this to myself, at least until I can do further research. Even though I feel sick from this news, I can't help but laugh to myself thinking of Betty's granddaughter's expression when she gets her gift from her old Nana.

CHAPTER THIRTY-SEVEN

"**A** doctor—how cool!" Bianca is less steady on her feet tonight, teetering on spike heeled red leather boots. She grabs onto Nathan's arm to steady herself so she doesn't end up on the floor. What time did they start drinking?

Nathan looks at me and discretely removes Bianca's hand. I really wish he had dressed more hip and casual. His tweed sport coat and pink polo shirt stick out in O'Malley's like a—like an old guy at a hard rock show. Thank God they're not playing at the Shark Tank tonight. He would have looked even more like a dweeb there.

"So when are they starting? It's after nine." I look at my wrist, as if there's a watch there, even though I haven't worn one since the nineties.

"Pretty soon—look there's Katie and Lacey!" She teeters off in pursuit of her friends.

"Do all your friends drink this much?" Nathan holds his wine glass and makes a sour face. "The wine here is atrocious." He swirls the red liquid in his glass and places it back on the bar.

"It's an Irish pub. They are more likely to have better beers, but the wine isn't—"

"You don't really know wine, Sweetie, do you? Your ex-husband wasn't exactly a man of great taste and refinement, right?" He smiles and continues to swirl.

Ron would punch Nathan for that remark, as would my father, who has a well-stocked wine cellar. I begin to respond and see that Brandon is standing there observing this exchange.

"Hey, guys. Thanks for coming." Brandon takes in Nathan's ensemble and shakes his hand. "Sorry, the wine sucks here, man. This is probably not your crowd, but Claire has a good time." He starts laughing when he sees my expression, and glances down at my shoes.

"Are you starting this show soon, Brandon? Us old people need to get home and get in bed." I glare at him, pleading with him to behave. I am second guessing my decision to bring Nathan.

"We go on in about ten minutes. I just wanted to say hello. Enjoy the show." He leaves his empty beer glass on the bar and heads to the stage area.

"He's a bit obnoxious, Claire, and I am not old. This is just nonsense, but I know it makes you happy." He squeezes me and I feel better.

When I got home today I was rattled by what Betty had told me. I wanted to Google Nathan, but I couldn't bring myself to do it.

He came to my house to pick me up, and while I was putting together some salad for dinner, he started humming the song "Cecilia," by Simon and Garfunkel.

"That song is always in my head when I talk to Cecilia, too. Isn't that funny?"

"What, Sweetie? It's catchy." He was busy scrolling through his e-mails on his laptop, which he has started bringing with him when he comes to my house. I wished he would get pulled away on a call from the hospital so I could sneak a look at Google. "She's a nice girl. Spoke highly of you."

I almost spit my wine and turned back to my salad preparation. She actually reminds me of some violent death metal lyrics more than a cute pop tune from the sixties, but I bit my tongue and kept quiet. I didn't want Nathan to think I'm jealous, or get into the whole Justin situation.

While we were eating, Nathan was still a bit distracted by his computer. He was looking away from me when I blurted out, "Were you always a cardiologist?"

He stopped and looked up at me, putting down his fork. "What?"

"I met a lady at the hairdresser's today, an older lady, who said you used to be a gynecologist." I took a big gulp of wine.

He sighed and replied, "Yes, Claire, I did switch specialties a few years back. I presume she also told you about some nasty rumors." He sat up straighter and his lips were pressed in a straight line.

"She did say you had some problems and decided to switch and—"

"Claire, listening to rumors is not a good idea, but I'm so glad you're bringing this to my attention." He smiled warmly and relaxed his posture. "There is no basis for any of those rumors. Being a gynecologist is difficult, Claire. You never know what kind of women you're treating, and what kind of mental problems they may have, hidden agendas." He was talking with his hands and shaking his head. "I didn't like it— delivering all those babies, all those women coming for their appointments with screaming little kids. Plus, I decided that I would honor my aunt's memory by helping people with heart disease."

"I just felt like I had to say something or else it was going to continue to bother me."

He stood up and took me by the hand and looked into my eyes. "Claire, you have made me so happy. I was so shut off from my feelings in the past, but you have awakened my senses. You're an extraordinary woman."

He kissed me like he never has before and I was almost certain he was going to lead me upstairs. The spell was broken by a phone call from the hospital, but I decided not to touch his computer or my phone. I believed him and I was excited about coming back to my house after the show. Maybe we wouldn't stay the whole time, and we could come home and pick up where we left off.

I am jolted back to reality by the opening note of the band's first song. They aren't starting off quietly and Nathan already looks perturbed. I grab his hand and drag him over to the front of the stage. Maybe if he gets the full experience he will be able to loosen up and have some fun.

As the show continues, and the mass of people flood the stage and girls are screaming for Brandon, I can see that Nathan is losing it. His face is flushed and he must be dying of heat exhaustion in that jacket. What was he thinking wearing that? Surely he has been to a show like this at some point in his life.

He stoops over and yells in my ear, "Claire, I have never experienced such a deafening spectacle. I know you like this music, but I have to go."

I take his hand and lead him downstairs, near the restrooms, so I can hear him. Just as I start to speak the music stops and Brandon says they'll be back in a few. The DJ starts playing the usual hip hop band break music, and I know that is not going to help Nathan's mood.

"I'm sorry, I should have known you would hate this." I fold my arms and look at my feet.

"That's not even the point. How could *you* like this? Don't you see you are standing in the midst of juvenile, uneducated twits? They're pushing and shoving, and some moron spilled beer on my shoes. Beer, Claire! As if it isn't bad enough, I had to throw away a *perfectly* good pair of expensive shoes because of *dog shit!*"

The hordes of people on the way to the restroom are beginning to stare and my face is on fire, both from the heat in the bar and the humiliation.

"We can go if you want. I just thought—"

"You didn't think. But I blame myself—I should have realized what a den of debauchery we were entering, and what low class people this horrible music would attract."

I'm not sure which part of that they heard, but the band has just filed by on their way to the restroom. Great. Brandon looks at Nathan and back at me, and disappears into the mens' room.

"It isn't the music, it's just a young crowd and—"

"And why is *that*, Claire? Because all of these young idiots have no taste in music or anything else. They drink cheap crap beer and gyrate all over the place to blaring noise and their clothes are hideous! Your friend was wearing *red* boots. She looks like a hooker!"

Brandon appears at the door of the mens' room and suppresses a smile. I know he's laughing at Nathan's clothes, and the irony of his tirade. Brandon looks anything but hideous in his black jeans, biker boots and Chain t-shirt. Standing behind Nathan, his expression softens when he sees the tears forming in my eyes.

Before I get a chance to respond, Nathan says, "I'm leaving, Claire. Obviously you enjoy this nonsense and you won't have a problem getting *this guy* or any one of these other idiots to drive you home!" He storms out the back door and leaves me standing here with Brandon, who was obviously unsuccessful in concealing his presence, based on that remark.

"Are you okay?" Brandon tries to grab my arms to pull me into a hug, but I resist.

"He's just cranky because he's been working so much, and one of his patients died this week. I shouldn't have brought him here." I wipe my eyes with the back of my hands. Brandon goes back into the mens' room to retrieve a wad of toilet paper for my tear stained face and runny nose.

"Do you want someone to bring you home? I can't do it right now, but I'm sure someone would be willing." When I don't respond he lowers his voice, "Hey, Claire." He touches my chin like he did that night at Jane and Mike's house, and the tears start flowing harder. "He was out of line. Look at me. That guy is a jerk, Claire. I don't care if he's a doctor or the President. He has no right to talk to you like that, or to insult everyone in this bar."

I let him hug me now and it feels good to get some comfort. I excuse myself to the ladies' room so I can fix my makeup. There's no point in trying to defend Nathan any further. "Thanks, Brandon." I turn around at the door and add, "You guys sound great, by the way." I manage a slight smile.

"Thanks. I'll drive you home later. Just lay off the booze—we don't need a repeat performance of last week." He looks at my feet, presumably to see if my shoes are still firmly attached to them.

I find Bianca and the girls so I can immerse myself in mindless chatter, and shake off thoughts of that humiliating episode. I am not going to drink, and Brandon and I will have an uneventful ride home. I don't like the things he said about Nathan, but his behavior *was* inexcusable. I expect an apology tomorrow.

The band returns to the stage for two more sets, with another break in between, before we can leave. I was being sarcastic when I said us old people need to get home, but I feel that way now. My head hurts and my feet are aching— there's definitely a blister forming. Nathan was right in some ways—this is juvenile behavior.

Brandon says good night to the band while I wait for him at the door. I stare out into the parking lot at the few remaining cars. Tears prick the corners of my eyes again, and I swiftly wipe them away before Brandon appears. If it wasn't for waterproof eye makeup I would look like an extra in a Zombie movie. Except none of my flesh is chewed off, but I still look pretty bad. I catch my reflection in the glass doors, and the distorted appearance makes me look ridiculous in my glittery tight shirt and jeans—like a caricature of a young blonde band groupie, but with an old, puffy face.

"You ready?" Brandon has his bag slung over this shoulder. He is wearing different clothes and his hair looks wet. I guess he did get pretty sweaty up on stage.

"Yep, let's go." He tries to catch my eye, but I look away.

We get in the car and Brandon sighs. "Claire, I'm sorry I got so angry before but I just hate to see you treated that way."

"Your concern is touching, but I really don't need it. I told you—it was my fault for asking him to come. He isn't in the right frame of mind."

"I know, his patient died. I just don't see that as an excuse to act that way. He's a heart doctor. Lots of his patients will die over the years. Is that the kind of man you want around in a crisis? Bad things happen sometimes, and you need a guy who can weather them, and not take his frustrations out on you." He is staring straight into my eyes.

I sigh and lay my head back against the seat. Quietly, tears start rolling down my cheeks. My hands are resting on my lap, and before I can react, Brandon puts his hand over mine, and starts rubbing it. The touch is breathtaking, and for a second I forget where I am and what's happening. In that second Brandon leans across the seat. He raises my chin again and gives me the softest kiss. I feel the warm, wet inner flesh of his mouth, in contrast with his lips, slightly chapped from hours of singing in the steamy bar. The stubble on his face grazes my skin. I return his kiss and let my body take over from my weary brain.

As his hand moves a bit further up my leg, I snap out of

my trance. I pull back. "Brandon, stop."

He recoils, looking bewildered and wounded. "Why? Claire, you know this is right."

I turn so my back is facing the door, as far away from him as possible, without getting out and facing a deserted parking lot at two in the morning.

"I'm in a relationship and I have not given you any indication that I wanted that!" My eyes are wide and darting all over the car.

Brandon slams the steering wheel. "That is complete *bullshit* and you know it! We have had an undeniable chemistry between us since day one. What is your problem? I am not that arrogant to think every woman wants me, but I am not some stupid kid, contrary to what you and your *boyfriend* seem to think."

"Nathan is a good man and...damn it, I can't be with someone like you!" I pound my fists on my thighs and curse myself for getting stuck in this confrontational situation.

He glares at me and says, "Claire, are you or are you not attracted to me? And I don't just mean do you like the way I look. Do you feel what I feel?"

"I told you it doesn't matter! You are too young for me, and before you dispute that again—I am not ending up with a man who wants children and I can't have them, and then he leaves me for a younger woman. And I am not adopting any babies and letting their real mothers see them—that's all insane! I have been through enough pain and disappointment, and I am not fucking doing that!" I am bawling again, and bury my head in my hands.

"Claire, you don't know anything about what I want or don't want. You don't even ask me. You just jump to the worst possible conclusion. You think you know everything and I am some young guy who just wants to use the older woman. You're reading way too many Hollywood gossip magazines."

"Look what happened to Demi Moore once Ashton grew up!"

He turns to face me again and gets closer to my face. His hand moves towards my chin but my flinching stops him from touching me. "Claire, you are beautiful and sexy and funny and smart and I—"

"It doesn't matter! It can never be! You should not be toying with me like this. You need to find a young girl who can give you a family, on *your* timetable. I overheard you the other night—I know that's what you want." *Who doesn't want to be a dad, right?*

He retreats back to his corner. He starts the car and backs out of the parking spot, headed for the exit. I buckle my seatbelt and take a few deep breaths. The silence is worse than the yelling.

As we pull into our neighborhood, he finally speaks. "I give up. I am not going to beg you to be with me, to trust me. I just hope you dump this guy because he is *not* a good person." I look up and he quietly adds, "And you are, Claire."

He stops the car and this time he is the one who looks away. I touch his arm and he shakes off my hand. "Just go."

I grab my purse, jump out of the car and slam the door. I am hysterical by the time I get inside and grab Dixie for comfort. She licks my face, but wiggles too much for me to hold her.

As I pull myself together to take her out for her late night potty run, I see Nathan's computer on my kitchen table. Of course he couldn't retrieve it—he doesn't have a key to my house and he obviously headed straight home. I could Google him—maybe I could erase the search and he wouldn't know I did it, but I don't remember how to do that. I could use my phone, but do I really want to know anymore? What a mess I have gotten myself into.

Back in the kitchen a few minutes later I open up the laptop and see that he is still signed in. That's odd—doesn't he have a login password? *He is not a good person. And you are, Claire.* I start typing and right before I hit search my phone scares the crap out of me. The shrill beeping is magnified in the tranquil, silent house. My heart is pounding. I abandon my search and reach for my phone to see who is texting me. I am not talking to Brandon anymore tonight. He has some nerve.

In my haste, I knock the phone off the table, onto the floor. I walk over to the corner it sailed into, and sit down on the cold tile. Dixie runs to me and I finally check the message. My stomach drops and I exhale the breath I didn't realize I was holding, lowering my head and hugging Dixie. It isn't Brandon. *I am not going to beg you to be with me.* He's given up.

CHAPTER THIRTY-EIGHT

It rains for the next three days, which matches my mood. Nathan's heartfelt apology interrupted my act of espionage, and diverted my attention. He drove all the way back to my house, full of apologies and self-recriminations. He even brought flowers. Where the hell do you get flowers in the middle of the night?

He told me that he knows I'm the one and he's so afraid that he's blowing it. He said he wants us to go on a trip before the work convention, just the two of us. He kept talking about our future and how he knows we belong together—he even hinted at marriage again. He said his house is almost ready, and soon I can just come live with him. A promising prospect since I would never have to face Brandon again.

It should have made me feel better, but I just wanted to fall asleep and wake up in high school the day I met Ron, before everything went wrong and things got so messed up. I would have picked a different seat in English class. I've felt this way before, but who knows if my alternate reality would have been any better. Maybe I would have met a worse guy on the way home from school or at a party that weekend, or many years later. Maybe I would still be single, but with my fertility untested, and I might not know I could never be a mother. I would still have a shred of hope.

We slept in the same bed for a couple of hours again, but once again he was gone in the morning. He left a sweet note, but I don't understand how golf is more important than spending the day with me. Maybe he was still embarrassed by his behavior.

On Wednesday, Pam lets me know that they have signed another promising young author and they want to have a party to celebrate the launch of a new line of literary fiction. Her team is going to handle the details but she wanted to thank me again for finding Brandon and operating outside of my job description.

"This was good work, Claire. You should consider getting out of HR and coming over to our side. Talk to Tim." I hung up feeling good about myself for five seconds before it hit me. A fucking party where I will have to bring Nathan as my date and Brandon will be one of the guests of honor. Pam will probably even publicly acknowledge me for finding him. Where's a good case of strep throat now? Actually I need something stronger than that, like malaria or ebola.

"Hey, did you hear about this big party we're having? All the industry hot shots will be there. Do you want to come dress shopping with me?" Rebecca stands in my door way, tilting her head to the side as she studies my blank expression. "What?"

"Close the door."

"What now?" She heaves herself onto my guest chair and slowly lets out her breath in preparation for the latest bombshell.

I proceed to tell her what Betty shared with me.

"What? Sexual misconduct? Holy shit, Claire! And you bought his excuse? What am I going to do with you?" She rubs her face with her hands so firmly her eyeballs almost pop out.

"If he was guilty surely he would have been *charged*. Or at least lost his medical license, if not arrested. What do you think—he paid off his victims?"

Rebecca purses her lips and looks away.

"Rebecca?"

"I'm sorry, but the crap you told me the night before was bad enough—acting like an asshole and leaving you at the bar. I don't get it. Are you really in love with this guy?"

"I think so. I don't know. I don't even know if I believe in love." I collapse back in my chair.

"That's a cop out, Claire."

"I mean it. Love is a big asshole! I just want to find some peace and security."

"Even if you are willing to *settle* for that, I still don't think he can deliver. Since you met him you are sleeping less, drinking more again, and you are completely distracted at work. These are not signs of peace and security. And he may actually be a sexual predator! This is serious shit!"

"I just wanted someone safe who won't abandon me." My voice is barely a whisper.

Rebecca folds her arms across her chest and frowns. "Nothing about this guy seems safe."

I study my fingernails. The polish is chipping. "I need to think. I know you mean well, Rebecca, but this is complicated."

She offers me a forlorn smile and sighs. "Okay, lecture over. Let's talk about what you're wearing to the party."

"The fucking party—like *that's* a better topic. I can't believe I have to face Brandon with Nathan. I could go alone, but that'll leave me even more exposed and vulnerable."

"I don't think you need protection from Brandon." She raises her eyebrows. "Or do you need protection from yourself when he's around?"

My nostrils flare and I breathe in, trying to fill my lungs with patience. "I saw a girl at Brandon's yesterday. The car has been there a lot. He probably decided to start dating one of his groupies, and that's fine by me. He's nothing but trouble." Rebecca's eyes widen and I quickly add, "It's a different kind of trouble, but trouble nonetheless."

Rebecca stands up and straightens her skirt. "I have to run, I have a meeting in five minutes. I'll be there if you need someone to help you hide from the asshole men. Speaking of men, I met a new guy and I'm bringing him to the party."

I finally have a reason to smile. "That's awesome. Did you meet him in the singles group?"

"Yep. At the wine tasting last week. He was funny. He kept imitating the serious wine connoisseurs and making me laugh. He's a college professor. Lost his wife about a year ago."

I wince. "Lost, as in she *died*? You don't normally date widowers. Do you really want to go down that path?"

"I would usually run, just like you would from a guy with dreams of spreading his seed, but Steve is different. I have to see where this goes."

I narrow my eyes at the seed comment, but say, "I can't wait to meet him."

Rebecca gives me a few more gossipy details about her new love interest and heads off to her meeting. What am I going to do about this party? And everything else? Love really is an asshole, but I hope for Rebecca's sake it doesn't have to be that way. One of us needs to end up with our Prince Charming. Or at least avoid the slimiest toads.

CHAPTER THIRTY-NINE

The following Friday comes way too soon. I have spent the week largely hiding in my house—I wish I had trained Dixie to use puppy pads, but at least I have a backyard.

That girl's car has been in Brandon's driveway most of the week—it looks like she's moved in. So much for all of his *feelings* for me. She looks young, definitely younger than Brandon. She has a ballerina's body—I saw her jogging the other day. Jogging! That made me want to throw up, as if her flowing chestnut brown hair and long legs weren't enough to make me lose my lunch. She *jogs*! Lately I can barely muster up the energy to get the mail or bring up the trash can.

Nathan has been sheepish and apologetic, which is a big switch from his usual persona. Supposedly, he wants me to come to his house to see the renovations, which are almost done, but we're doing that tomorrow night. Tonight he is coming to my house to get ready for the party, since he's working at St. Vincent's.

It's Friday night, and I'm all dressed and ready to go (I am always early when I'm anxious), and Nathan arrives from the hospital in a harried state.

"I shouldn't have even agreed to do this with you—I'm going to make you late." He rushes in and drops his bags on the kitchen floor. "You look beautiful, Claire." He takes in my satin, emerald green halter dress and kisses me on the forehead. He grabs his suitcase and heads up the stairs. "I'm just going to take a quick shower and change, and then we're off. They have food at this thing, right?" His voice disappears up the stairs with the rest of him before I can answer.

At least he's in a good mood, even though he is his usual stressed out self. I will have to get used to that, though. A doctor's life is not an easy, carefree one. I decide to ignore the bigger potential problems, at least for tonight.

I take another look at myself in the mirror. This dress is pretty, and my hair looks soft and feminine pulled up into a loose bun, with a few curled tendrils hanging out on both sides. Oops, I forgot my earrings! They complete the outfit. My father gave them to me for Christmas the year I got divorced—dangling emeralds with diamond clusters.

I climb the stairs in my bare feet—I'm waiting to put on my black satin sling backs with the gold and rhinestone accents—and slowly open the door to my bedroom. How ridiculous that I'm afraid I might see Nathan undressed. It's about time we get that over with.

I hear the water running in the shower and the door is slightly ajar. My earrings are in my jewelry armoire, and once I can grab them I will give him his privacy. Besides, the last thing I need is an unplanned seduction scene. He might think I'm throwing myself at him, and besides—I'll never be able to get my hair to look like this again in time for the party.

As I tip-toe over to the corner of my room, I am startled by Nathan's booming voice. "Claire, Sweetie? Are you up here?"

Does he have bionic ears? If I was in the shower someone could come in with a full marching band and I wouldn't hear it.

"Yes, I'm just getting my earrings," I call out.

"Can you do me a favor and get my shaving cream out of my bag?"

"Sure!" Can't he use mine? It isn't like the scent lingers and he will go around all night smelling like rose petals.

His suitcase is unzipped, but closed on my bed, and I lift the top and start sifting through his stuff. He has a lot of clothes in here for one night. Maybe he keeps it packed all the time because he could get stuck at the hospital? I'm rooting around for a toiletry bag when I pull out a bag from an expensive lingerie store downtown. My heartbeat quickens as I peek inside and pull out a sexy black lace teddy. And what is that? It looks like a feather duster, and *what the hell is that*? I immediately drop the bag on the bed.

"Claire, did you find it?"

Nathan's voice assaults my train of thought, and now my hands are shaking and a fine sheen of sweat is forming on my face. "No, I don't see any. I have some in there!" I shove the bag back under his clothes. Why is it peeking out now? I don't want to rearrange things too much or he will know I was snooping. Wait—he knows I was looking for the shaving cream. Now I see the side pocket, which is where he probably keeps that stuff, but how would I know that? But if I say I didn't see the shaving cream in the main area, then maybe he'll know I found his surprise gift. I toss the clothes around and close the lid.

"I'll just use yours. I could have sworn I had some in there. Did you look in the side pocket—"

My best bet is just to get the hell out of here and pretend I didn't hear him. As I fly down the stairs, I fumble with the clasp on my earring. My hands are trembling. I get to the kitchen and grab a bottle of wine I opened last night, drinking a few swigs right out of the bottle. Now my lips will be stained red. I rush to my purse to get out my bright coral lipstick and smear it on, careful to keep it off my teeth and gums.

"What do you think, Sweetie?" I look up and see him looking handsome in his tux. I smile and fan myself with a piece of mail sitting on the counter.

"You look very handsome. I need to grab my evening purse. Can you start the car?" I run back upstairs to find my sparkly black bag.

The suitcase is sitting there on the bed, zipped shut now. It's taunting me with the memory of its contents. I guess I know the agenda for tonight now. Isn't this what I want? But I am not sure what he has in mind based on the contents of that bag, and should I be having sex with an alleged sex offender. *He was accused of misconduct.* Why can't anything go smoothly?

My stomach churns, I decide not to snoop anymore, and run for the car. In these heels running isn't advisable, and I twist my ankle on the steps. Oww! My eyes dart to the car, but luckily Nathan is occupied with his phone.

What a night this is shaping up to be.

CHAPTER FORTY

Damn trash cans rattling! It sounds like the drumming of those kids who bang on the lids after all the events at the Coliseum. Putting my pillow on top of my head to drown out the noise, I get a weird feeling. My sheets feel so soft—I didn't think I used the better ones the last time I made up the bed.

I am *not* opening my eyes because once I do I won't be able to get back to sleep. The trash can show has stopped, but now I hear a scary sounding dog barking, and what is that loud, rumbling vehicle going by my house? It sounds *huge*—someone must be getting a furniture delivery. My head is killing me, and I'll probably have to get up and take something to be able to fall back to sleep. Damn it—why can't people be more considerate on weekend mornings? Speaking of which, where are the lawnmowers?

I can't believe I drank too much again, but with the free open bar and all that anxiety about Brandon and Nathan I was out of control, and then I almost fell in the fountain...I bolt up in bed with my eyes wide open. It's all coming back now—where the hell am I? What kind of a drunken whore wakes up in a strange bed? Obviously I'm not at home—there are no metal trash cans or guard dogs in my cul-de-sac. That sounded like a city bus!

Panicking, I scan the room and see a tuxedo thrown over a chair, and a cluttered desk. There is some kind of diploma on the wall in that corner, but I can't make out what it says from here. I spot my dress lying on a chair in the other corner, neatly folded. I know I'm not at the Madison Hotel, where the party was held. This is someone's bedroom.

My concentration is broken by a piercing ambulance siren, and I leap out of bed to look out the window, wobbling on my injured ankle. How did I make it through the night in those shoes? Suddenly I am flooded with relief—I'm so stupid! Of course I know where I am. Nathan brought me home after I got so drunk and tried to get in the fountain. I kept yelling, "I want to swim!" I don't think anyone from work heard me. They were all inside enjoying the elaborate spread of food. After all, the Madison is Richmond's only five star hotel and restaurant. It's a gorgeous spectacle with a big sweeping double staircase in the lobby, like something out of the pre-Civil War south.

I'm *sure* Nathan followed me out and took me to his house, which was the original plan this weekend. That's why I'm sleeping in this monstrous t-shirt. What does this say on it? Something about an IT conference? That's weird, but men always seem to have stupid t-shirts. He probably didn't want to put me in anything too good since I could throw up again. Did he undress me?

My mouth is dry and disgusting, as usual, after a bad night of foolish choices. I drag myself out of bed in search of the bathroom. Does he have any little Dixie cups for water? Oh no, poor little Dixie! She's been alone all night. I need to get home.

I open up the cabinet under the sink and spot some cups. That's a big box of condoms, and they're *Magnum* size! Shit—most women would be happy to see that, but I'm not up for that today. Uh oh, did we have sex? I guess I would still be feeling it if we did, especially with the drought I have endured, and he wouldn't want me to be nearly unconscious for our first time. He's too good for that. He was probably disappointed that I was too drunk to try on my gift.

That's why I am waking up with this uneasy feeling. He didn't give it to me, and I was feeling anxious about it. By the time we arrived at the party, I was off in conversation and business networking. Pam did publicly congratulate me for finding Brandon. Brandon. That was hard. He looked so handsome in his tuxedo—even clean shaven he made my heart skip a beat. Or three.

Nathan was charming—he talked to a lot of people. Of course Cecilia was chewing off his ear, but I didn't give her the satisfaction of thinking I was jealous. She looked as prickly as ever. I guess she was trying to dress like one of the characters in our new books with her leather dress and scary pointy boots. Her black hair was extra spiky, and her lips were a deep blood red. So *appropriate* for a formal work event at a beautiful southern landmark. I don't think she got the memo explaining *which* new books we were celebrating.

I mingled early in the evening, and Tim even said he would like to talk to me about a new role in the company. Now that's exciting! Rebecca was there with her new guy. He was so nice and a lot of fun. I need to call her and tell her how happy I am for her.

I drink my third mini cup of water and wish I could conjure up a toothbrush. Maybe he keeps a spare—heaven knows with that many condoms he must bring home unexpected guests at times. That's not good. None of this is good. Betty's words are in my head. *He was accused of misconduct. Now there were never any charges, just rumors. Maybe less temptation.*

What am I doing? The details from last night are so sketchy—I *must* stop drinking. I *do* remember Brandon was with that ballerina girl—I think she has even less on top than I do. She's so young and pretty though, but what did I expect? He did not say one word to me—barely looked at me. When Pam congratulated him on his success and welcomed him to the Bella Donna family, he caught my eye for a split second, but quickly looked away and started whispering to his date again. They were doing that all night, with their heads together, conspiring. *They* probably got a room at the Madison, even though they looked completely sober.

If only I hadn't consumed those last couple of shots with Justin. He stopped me when I was coming out of the ladies' room later in the evening, and I tried to pretend I was fine. My academy award winning performance wasn't working on him. He brought me back out to the bar and I started to tell him something. Shit, I think I told him about the gift in Nathan's suitcase and maybe even what Betty told me. He was trying to tell me something about Cecilia and the computers? Did he say he *found* something? Now I remember—that's why I ran outside. Something he said upset me. *Justin* followed me out there and dragged me away from the fountain. Where the hell was Nathan? *That's right*—when I said I wanted to swim I didn't mean it in a happy, drunk girl way. Hopefully I wasn't planning on drowning myself—how did I get here if Justin was the one who—GODDAMMIT!! My heart is thumping, and I'm suddenly drenched with sweat. "Justin!"

"I see you're up, do you need something?" I stare at Justin in horror and he bursts out laughing. "I'm sorry. You remember what happened, don't you?" He walks towards me and I step back. He sighs and shakes his head. "Here, put this on." He reaches into the bathroom and pulls out a gigantic blue bathrobe.

Feeling less exposed, as I can almost wrap it around my body twice, I delve into the mess that got me here. "It's starting to come back to me. I remember sitting at the bar with you and drinking shots. I think I was upset about Nathan."

"Yeah, I would like to murder that asshole." He sees my shocked look and adds, "Sorry Claire, but who accompanies his girlfriend to a party and then disappears when she gets drunk?"

"That's why I'm here?"

He narrows his eyes and frowns. "Claire, do you seriously think I would take advantage of a semi-conscious woman? I rescued you from jumping into a fountain, fully clothed, at a work function. Your decision making abilities were not exactly sharp."

"No, I don't think you would do that. I'm sorry." I rub my face with both hands. "So he disappeared? I'm sure he had a good reason. Where's my phone?"

"It's over there in your bag, I guess." He motions towards the chair with my dress. I see my lacy panties on top of my evening bag.

"So how did I…?"

"You were pretty out of it, but don't worry—I didn't look and it was dark." He starts laughing again.

"This is not funny!"

"I'm sorry." He reaches for my arm. "Let's go in the living room and sit down. Do you feel like eating something? Toast maybe?"

"Fine, but I need to piece this night back together and you need to be serious."

"Uh oh, I'm slipping back into dick mode again. It's so natural how that happens."

I punch Justin in the arm, which clearly hurts my hand more than it hurts him. "That felt like a hamster punch, didn't it?"

He laughs, and I follow him into his living room, letting the black leather sofa swallow me up.

Justin retreats to the kitchen. He calls out, "You were wasted and I shouldn't have let you keep drinking, but you were a mess emotionally." He comes back with some juice and a couple of pieces of buttered toast. "When it was time to go your boyfriend couldn't be found. Claire, I hate to say this but he was spending a lot of time talking to other women."

"I was talking to other men. I even went home with one."

I pick up a piece of toast and take a small nibble.

"You're missing the point. I think this guy is trouble. I have a bad feeling. And Brandon—he's no better. I know you live across the street from him and he wouldn't take you home, either."

I wince at this news, but why *would* he? I don't think his new girlfriend would be too happy to have me along for the ride. "He said no?" My voice is soft and hopeless.

"Yeah, he seemed pissed that you were in this state, especially when I told him the doctor was missing in action. But he was staring at you all night, Claire. I'm guessing you broke his heart, too?"

"Come on, I didn't break your heart."

He ignores my protest. "So I brought you here. I was going to drive all the way to your house, but I didn't think you would be capable of telling me where you lived." In response to my raised eyebrows he continues. "Seriously—you were so out of it. I could have looked in your wallet for your address, but I figured this was smarter. I didn't want you to be alone."

Alone. That word reaches directly into my tear ducts and releases all my frustration and fear.

Justin jumps up and sits next to me on the couch. I melt

into his embrace and rest my head on his shoulder. We sit like that for a while—me crying and him squeezing me and rubbing my arm. Maybe I made a mistake. I have made too many to count.

I sit up and wipe my eyes. "Jewish men are supposed to be good to their women. This is unprecedented in my experience. What am I going to do? I have to get home to Dixie. She's been alone all night, and I need to check my phone." I get up but Justin gently pushes me back down, and goes to retrieve my purse from the bedroom.

He hands me my phone and says, "Asshole men come from all backgrounds, and a guy can usually tell when another guy is an asshole. This guy is a classic case."

I tuck my feet under my body and try to adjust the yards of extra fabric this bathrobe provides. If I had this one I never would have flashed Brandon in the yard. Brandon. He must really hate me now.

I have about ten messages from Nathan, again each one angrier than the last. "He says he looked for me and he couldn't find me. He had a medical emergency."

Justin twists his mouth in disbelief and leans back into the couch, holding his head. "Do you honestly believe that? I think he had an emergency, but it wasn't medical."

"I don't want to hear it!"

"You need to hear it."

"Did you see him leave with another woman?"

"No, but he was talking to—"

I cover my ears and yell, "I said I don't want to hear it." I ball my hands up into fists. "I can't deal with this right now. I need my car and I need to get home. I don't want to hear any more opinions or gossip."

Justin's expression softens. "Why don't you get dressed and I'll drive you to your car. I would lend you some clothes but I don't have any rope to tie around you to keep them from falling off." He smiles as he looks at me standing there, trying to keep the robe from dragging on the floor, like I'm wearing Cinderella's ball gown. Too bad I didn't turn into a pumpkin at midnight.

CHAPTER FORTY-ONE

Justin drove me to my car and I quickly ducked inside before anyone could see me in my dress from last night, *especially* with Justin. The last thing I need is to be the subject of *that* kind of office gossip. If Cecilia got wind of that she would probably send out an all employee e-mail complete with pictures of my walk of shame. Some of my co-workers *did* spend the night here, and I'm guessing Brandon and Twinkle Toes are among them.

I called Nathan from the car once I was alone. He was apologetic and sounded genuinely concerned. He wasn't crazy about the fact that Justin brought me home, but he didn't have much room to argue.

"Claire, you must stop this excessive alcohol consumption. I couldn't even find you. I'm going to continue to get called away at odd hours; it's just the nature of my profession. Thank goodness Justin was there and he's trustworthy. So many men aren't these days."

I wanted to yell at him for not being there for me, but I realized he's right. My behavior is disgraceful and all I am doing is avoiding my problems. I promised to call him back after I got home and tended to Dixie. We made plans to see each other tonight, and I will confront him about the mystery gift and all of my other concerns.

Now as I pull into my driveway, I see Brandon's car. I guess they went home last night or maybe they checked out of the hotel early. Once I take care of Dixie I'm going over there to talk to him. I need to get all of these problems addressed today. No more hiding. I owe him an apology and I'm not going to weasel out of it again.

Poor little Dixie is beside herself with joy at seeing her mommy. After several minutes I still can't get her to calm down. I'm not in the mood to search the house for evidence of her extended indoor stay, so I grab her and the harness and bring her out to the tie-down stake. I don't have time to walk her all over the yard right now—this will have to do and I'll get back to her as soon as I talk to Brandon. I run back inside and look at myself in the mirror. I wash my face and slap on some quick eye makeup, while brushing my teeth. My hair goes up in a sloppy pony tail, and I pull on yoga pants and a t-shirt. I still look like hell, but I'm not going over there to do anything but apologize.

Dixie is sitting in the sun, but starts jumping again when she sees me.

"Be good, Dixie. Mommy will be right back." I sprint across the street, now noticing the girl's car is not in the driveway. Hmm…they could be out in her car.

I ring the bell and wait several minutes before I hear footsteps. Brandon opens the door and immediately looks annoyed. He runs his fingers through his hair and sighs.

"Hi, Claire. What's up?"

Now I'm mad again. He didn't even care how I got home or what happened to me.

"Hi. I'm sorry about my behavior last night. I'm happy for your success, I just…I have some other stuff going on and I know I drank too much again, and you were with your new girlfriend and I didn't want to bother you. You didn't seem like you wanted—"

Brandon's eyes dart behind me as he pushes past me and flies down his porch steps.

"What are you doing? I am trying to tell you—" I turn to see Dixie running down the road out of the cul-de-sac, with Brandon chasing her!

My heart rate has jumped to the level of sprinters at the Olympic finish line. I start running after them, but become winded and weak before I get to the end of the street. Hangovers are not good for physical endurance. Fully expecting that Brandon has caught her and is on his way back, I sit on the curb and attempt to catch my breath.

What seems like an eternity later Brandon jogs back to me, but without my baby.

"Holy shit, that dog is fast. I'm so sorry, Claire. I tried to grab her but she went through a few backyards and I couldn't catch her. I think she was chasing an animal, probably a squirrel. I'm going to get in the car and drive around to where I last saw her. You should go inside and send out an e-mail to the neighborhood mailing list. If someone spots her they can grab her before she gets too far." Brandon is also out of breath and panting on the way to his car.

I don't know what to do first. Tears immediately form and I am frantic. She's so little—she could get hit by a car so easily. She doesn't even have an ID tag and her microchip monitoring expired! If I wasn't so caught up in all this stupid men shit I would take better care of her.

I want to go with Brandon, but he has already taken off. I run back to my house and remember I don't have my computer. I didn't even think to ask Justin if he was done with it. Nathan's computer is still here. Nathan. I must tell him what's going on. As I get onto his computer and sign into my own e-mail, I call him.

"Yes, Claire, what's going on? I'm with a patient."

"Nathan, my baby ran off and I don't know what to do!" Now I'm hysterical.

"What do you mean? You don't let her outside off leash."

I explain what happened, leaving out the part about going to Brandon's to apologize.

"Brandon is riding around looking for her and I'm going to send an e-mail to the neighborhood, but she's so little and she has no idea how to get home!" More hysterical bawling.

"Claire, try to calm down. If Brandon is looking for her, he'll find her. I'll be over as soon as I can, but you have to be more responsible."

I don't have the energy to defend myself, and really there is no defense, except he is the one who got me all screwed up in the first place.

I send out a blast e-mail to the neighborhood and include a picture of Dixie. Since this is not my computer, I find one I had sent to my mother in another e-mail. Now I need to update her microchip monitoring. I keep glancing at my phone, praying that Brandon will call any second and say he has found her.

I go back to Google and begin to type in the name of the

microchip company. It starts with an S and as I start to type the name I see previous searches for all kinds of other sites. Sex and sadomasochism both start with an S, as do suck and slut and other words that lead me into Nathan's porn fetish. Son of a bitch! I can deal with him looking at a little porn—that's normal, but some of this stuff seems a little disturbing. I am beginning to think that the feather duster is just the tip of the iceberg, and he isn't using it to clean his knick knack shelves.

I need to find out more about Nathan, but I don't know a *single* person who knows him. It hits me that he has never introduced me to anyone. I wonder if there's someone at the golf club I could talk to, since he's there so much. Uh oh, I just thought of someone.

I can't believe I'm doing this after calling him a bug killing freak the last time I saw him, but I'm desperate. I hope I still have his number. I *do*, and dial it while updating the microchip information.

"Hi, Daniel. It's Claire. Do you remember me?" I wince in anticipation of an angry response.

"Oh yeah, of course. We didn't have a good night, did we? I'm glad you called. I've been thinking about what happened during my meditation sessions, and I do owe you an apology. You were not sober, and tantric sex requires two willing and centered people."

"I understand. You just made an error in judgment. I'm sorry, too. I know you weren't expecting to hear from me, but I need some information and I'm wondering if you can help me."

I tell him about Nathan, leaving out my specific concerns. "I just don't think he's being completely honest with me, but I can't put my finger on it."

"Dr. Nathan. Yep, I know him. I'm sorry, Claire, but he hasn't been here in months. He was caught with the owner's wife in the back room of the pro shop. Some nasty stuff too. I had to smudge the place with sage."

I swallow hard and reply, "Are you positive?"

"Yes, I'm afraid so. I think he was also rumored to have had some kind of improper conduct with patients at some point in the past. I wouldn't recommend him as a doctor, let alone a boyfriend. Sorry to be the bearer of bad news."

I thank him with promises to get together for coffee one day. Turning back to the computer, which is now like a blinking light of evidence, I freeze up. I bet there is a ton of incriminating information in here. Why does he even want to be with me? My thoughts switch back to Dixie. Where is my baby? If lose her I don't know what I'll do. I can't even breathe...

"Claire!"

I run to the doorway and Brandon is standing there, shoulders hunched.

"I spotted her but she ran once I tried to grab her. I need more help with this. I can't cover enough ground. I called Max and Bianca. They're on their way."

"I'm coming with you!"

He pushes against my shoulders, holding me in place. I try to punch him and he grabs my wrists.

"Oww, you're hurting me!"

"Claire, get it together. I know you're upset, but you need to stay here. Check your e-mail and phone. Wait to see if she comes back here, if someone brings her back here." He relaxes his grip on my wrists and looks me in the eye. "I promise I will do my best to find her and bring her home safely." I drop my head in defeat, and he lifts up my chin. "Claire, I *will* find her."

He runs out as I see Max and Bianca pull up in front of his house. I close the door. As much as I appreciate them helping, I can't talk to anyone right now. I sit down and stare into space. My baby is missing. She could go in a storm drain! I should have reminded Brandon of that. But if that happens he will never find her. She'll be gone forever. I put my head down on the kitchen table and bawl my eyes out.

"Claire, are you here? I just got your e-mail. What happened?" Jane charges into my kitchen, frantic and wild-eyed. She hugs me and I proceed to tell her the whole sordid tale, from the events of last night to the discoveries of today.

She leads me to the couch and starts making tea. I don't want any, but I let her perform her motherly ritual.

"They'll find her. She won't go far. She's probably scared—she could be hiding somewhere. The neighbors will be on the lookout. It's Saturday and a beautiful day. People are outside."

She comes over to sit beside me and hugs me again. "I know what she means to you, Claire."

"She's all I have. I'll never be a mother and it looks like I'll never find a man, either." Fresh tears explode out of my eyes like a garden hose.

"Claire, I think maybe you should have gone to see a therapist after your divorce. You've tried to handle too much on your own and—"

"And I'm fucking it all up. I know."

I sit with Jane for several hours, and it seems like days. Brandon checks in periodically, but he hasn't seen Dixie. I ask if I can come back out with him and try to find her, and he agrees if Jane stays at my house. He comes back for me and we park in an area in the next neighborhood, closer to the highway.

"Do you really think she went this far?"

Brandon takes my hand to help me out of the car. "We've searched our neighborhood to death, and Max and Bianca are still over there. A few of our other neighbors are looking, too. Let's just walk around here a bit."

I see storm drains everywhere and I feel sick. I walk over to one of them and yell. "Dixie!" I look up at the grass and through my tears I see two little poops. They look recent. Never in my life did I think I would be excited to see shit, but just as I open my mouth to yell for Brandon, my heart sinks again. The storm drain. She loves disgusting smells and dark underground places. Dachshunds are a burrowing breed, bred to root out creatures who live in dark holes. She sleeps under blanket and pillows, she digs, and she hides under the couch. Wait, she hides under...

"Brandon! I have an idea!"

I look up and I see Brandon walking towards me, clutching a wiggly wiener tightly to his chest.

My heart races and I run across the lawn to meet him.

"Where did you find her?" She leaps out of his arms into mine and whimpers. I cover her little face in kisses and squeeze her so tight she could pop.

"She was hiding under the back porch of this house. I

was calling her name and I guess she recognized me and came running out." Brandon pats Dixie's head and she licks his hands.

"Of course she did—she loves you!" I look at his eyes and the joy from a moment ago is gone. I turn back to my little runaway. "Dixie, you little whack-job. You made Mommy sick with worry, but I love you so much!" I bury my face in her fur.

Brandon looks away and says, "Let's get home."

I follow him to the car, gripping Dixie to my chest.

"Brandon, thank you so much!" I reach out to hug him, which is awkward with a wiener in the way.

He accepts the embrace, but barely returns it. "You're welcome. I didn't want anything to happen to her."

I continue to pet and cuddle Dixie on the way back to our street. Brandon calls Max and tells him we found her. I grab the phone and thank him and Bianca.

Brandon parks the car and starts getting out.

"Hey, wait a minute. You don't have anything else to say?"

He sighs and looks like he's gritting his teeth. "Claire, what more do you want me to say?"

"Is your girlfriend due to come back tonight and you need to ditch me quick? Is that why you're in a rush?" I regret blurting that out.

He pounds the steering wheel, which startles Dixie. And me.

"Claire, if you must know, and I don't know why you would care, that was my sister, Colleen."

"Oh." His sister. "But wait, didn't she have blond hair?"

"This is ridiculous. You know some people's hair gets darker as they get older. Some women color their hair. I think I know my own sister and why would I lie to you? Wait, I know—you think all men lie. How much lying is the doctor doing?"

"What makes you think he's lying?"

He looks down at his hands and licks his lips. "Claire, I wasn't the one almost passed out drunk last night." He looks up and turns to face me. "Why don't you ask him what he was up to?"

He gets out of the car, and since it's his car, I have no choice but to follow.

"Brandon, come back!"

He is up his porch steps. "I am done with this bullshit. I am not arguing with you. You think you have it all worked out. Just keep Dixie in the house until your latest man crisis blows over." He walks inside and slams the door.

Dixie and I are left alone at the end of his driveway. I hastily walk back to the safety of my house. I have no more tears left. I sit with Dixie on the couch, who seems to have recovered from her ordeal and wants to play. If only I could be as resilient and forgetful as a wiener dog.

CHAPTER FORTY-TWO

Brandon is right. Nathan is trouble, but I don't know how to just break it off with all these unanswered questions. He said he loved me—doesn't that mean something?

Going back to the dreaded computer, I send out an e-mail letting everyone know Dixie is at home, safe and sound. Jane wasn't here when I got back. She left a note on the kitchen counter. She had to leave to take the kids to soccer practice, so I text her to let her know we found Dixie. I have several other texts, but none from Nathan. Here's one from an unrecognized number. Probably one of the neighbors about Dixie.

"Hey, did you find your dog?"

"She was found. Who is this?"

"Cecilia."

I have lost count of how many times my heart has dropped into my stomach today.

"How did you know my dog was missing?"

I wait a minute or so for a response, tapping the table with my fingernails.

"Justin told me."

What the hell is she talking about? Justin doesn't know.

I stop responding and go straight to the source for an answer.

"Hey, what's up? How're you feeling?" Justin sounds concerned.

"Justin, did you talk to Cecilia today?"

"No, why would I talk to that crazy bitch?"

I explain the events of the day, including Dixie's disappearance and all the work Brandon did to find her.

"Claire, she's baiting you. Don't you see that?"

"What do you mean?"

"Who else did you tell that Dixie was missing?"

"Just my friend Jane and Nath... shit."

"I tried to tell you this morning, but you wouldn't let me. Remember how we were wondering how Cecilia knew about our relationship, and I said I was going to figure it out?"

"Yes, but what does that have to do with Nathan?"

"Turns out she is screwing one of my guys and getting access to company e-mail."

"Justin, I don't see where you're going with this."

"I'm getting there. Keep your panties on. In the process of discovering this I read all of her company e-mails. And...there was some correspondence between her and Nathan."

I inhale sharply and grasp the phone tighter. "What did they say?"

"She's tricky. None of them came right out and said anything really incriminating, but there was a lot of flirting and ego stroking. My guess is that Nathan knows enough to be more discreet, but Cecilia isn't stupid. She wants you to find out."

Discreet. Yeah, that's probably how he avoided losing his medical license and going to jail. She wants me to find out?

"Claire, I think he left with her last night, and used your drinking as an excuse for not being able to find you. He was watching you closely and he slowly distanced himself. He saw me take you to the bar. I ask you—what kind of a man sees a good looking young guy feeding his woman alcohol and runs the other way?"

"I feel like such a fool."

"Claire, you didn't know. You trusted him."

"I think he just wants a socially suitable wife to legitimize himself so he can continue to screw around and live a double life. I can't believe I didn't see that. I was so blinded by his charm and he's the right age and—"

"I know, you thought he was safe and he wouldn't want children. Don't beat yourself up. But I will say it again— Brandon was watching you all night. He was with that hot girl, but he couldn't take his eyes off of you. I don't think he's into her."

"She's his sister."

"That makes sense. He was probably telling her all night

how he feels about you."

"And I thought he was telling her what a freak show I am and how I was a total bitch to him."

"He was probably saying that too, in between the other stuff."

"You're lucky this is a phone call because I would—"

"I know, you would throw heavy objects at me. You're a tough little chick, Claire."

As I smile at Justin's comment, I am scrolling through Nathan's computer. I know I probably have enough evidence to be sure I'm not being hasty, but I want more. I want the smoking gun, as they say in the detective shows. I gasp audibly. Here it is.

"What's the matter? Are you there?" Justin's voice has turned to one of worry.

"I just watched the beginning of a video on Nathan's computer."

"Uh oh, I'm guessing it isn't from a birthday party or a trip to the beach."

"It starts out with him singing the song, "Cecilia," and let's just say that Nathan and Cecilia are wearing what looks like Halloween costumes. Only they would get arrested if they wore them trick or treating."

"I'm sorry, Claire. If it wasn't for the fact this is a devastating blow to you, I wouldn't mind seeing that video. I can give you my personal e-mail address."

At first I am angry at him for making light of this serious situation, but then I burst out laughing.

"I'm sorry. Wait, you're not really upset?" He sounds confused.

"I am, but maybe also relieved. I just couldn't shake the hope that he could be the one, but I have no real feelings for him."

"I know I'm just a young guy who doesn't know anything, but I think you should talk to Brandon. If he really cares about you, you can fix it."

"No, I can't. He's still too young for me and I still can't have children. Nathan being a lying slime ball doesn't change any of that."

"I know you would punch me for saying this, but being a

317

mother isn't the only reason for a woman to live, Claire. You're a woman first. And you assumed the best about Nathan and got the worst, right?"

"Yes, but what does that have to do with anything?"

"Maybe you expect the worst from Brandon and you'll end up getting the best."

"I don't know why I haven't come to you for advice sooner. You're like a wise old sage."

"Nobody sees my sensitive side." I can envision his beautiful smirking face through the phone. "And maybe while you're over there you can get me a date with his sister, but right now I have to run. I need to figure out how to handle the Bella Donna sex scandal. Peter can't get away with allowing Cecilia access to employee e-mails. But I guess a sex scandal goes along with our new company image, now that our first erotica release is in bookstores."

"Justin, you're impossible. Our image is changing all the time. Brandon is starting a new book. Maybe I should suggest he write about a misguided thirty-something, divorced woman who falls for the cute guy across the street, but is crippled by fear and doubt. Hey, that sounds pretty good."

Justin laughs and starts to say goodbye.

"Hey, Justin?"

"Yeah."

"Stop reading everyone's e-mail. I am going to have to report you to HR."

"Claire, there's no—"

"Expectation of privacy on the company network. Got it. Bye."

I hang up and lay down on the couch, holding my head. Cecilia and Nathan. I never saw that coming. He's so *old* for her. *I need you to come with me to a medical conference in June. She's a nice girl. Spoke highly of you. My parents will love you. What do you think about going to Miami in the fall? My Aunt Dolores lived with us. She was the only bright spot in my family. There was one friend, Janice, who was very interested in me, if you understand my meaning.* Obviously some bad things happened to Nathan, and he's unstable, but that doesn't excuse his behavior.

Now I hear another voice in my head. Handsome, smart Justin. *Being a mother isn't the only reason for a woman to live, Claire. You're a woman first. Maybe... you will end up getting the best.* I jump up and run upstairs to shower, since I look and feel disgusting. I dry my hair and throw on some minimal makeup in record time, and find a pair of clean pink shorts and a cute tank top. I want to look pretty, but not like I'm trying too hard. This is going to be the last time I go over to apologize to Brandon, no matter what the outcome.

CHAPTER FORTY-THREE

It's too bad stress raises, rather than lowers, cholesterol. It seems like this much cardiac activity would have to be a good workout. I am standing on Brandon's porch, waiting to see his face, and hoping I will get the best.

"What's wrong now?" Brandon leans in the door frame and swigs a beer, narrowing his eyes.

I'm about to say something about him drinking this early in the evening, but then I realize it's dinner time and who am I to talk?

"Nothing is wrong, Brandon. Listen, I know I come over here to apologize all the time, and then we fight, but I don't want to fight. You were right about everything—Nathan is an asshole and I'm a fool and—"

Brandon takes a step forward and pulls me into the house, resting his beer on the hall table, kicking the door shut. He holds my hands up over my head and kisses me like I don't ever remember being kissed before.

"But wait—" I break our embrace and try to say more.

"No more talking." He goes back to kissing me.

"But really Brandon, nothing has changed. I still can't—"

"I love you." He holds my chin and stares directly into my eyes until I don't see anything but two brilliant blue orbs. "Does that change anything?"

"Yes, but—"

"Claire, I do want children. I want to adopt a family. Not every woman will accept that, and if she can have her own kids, I would understand why. But you want to be a mother so badly, and I know you can be. You're just afraid."

"So that's why you said...never mind." It's all clear now. *I have my own opinions but you and Cassie should do things your way. Who doesn't want to be a dad, right?*

"Why I said what?" He tilts his head and gazes down at me suspiciously.

"I sort of overheard you talking to Jon about his wife's pregnancy, but I guess I didn't hear all of it. I was so confused. And drunk. It seemed like you wanted kids, but then you didn't want to get anyone pregnant, which made no sense. I figured you were just pro-adoption because you're adopted. It never dawned on me that you would want to adopt. I thought you were just saying I should do it out of pity."

"Claire," he wraps me up in his strong arms and says, "You know—I've overheard some things, too. Would you like to take your best shot?" He pulls up his shirt, displaying a perfect stomach and chest, and for a second I'm distracted from his meaning.

"I didn't mean that—I was drunk and Bianca was—"

He can't stop laughing. "Claire, you're the little whack-job. Dixie only takes after her mother." I give him a mock look of anger and he continues, "Adoption works for many couples. It could work for us, if we end up together. All I'm asking is to give me a chance and throw all of your fears and assumptions out the window. What have they ever done for you?"

"Not one damn thing." A mischievous grin forms on my face. "And you are a sexy hunk of man—I was just trying to pretend otherwise."

"Yeah, I'll show you how strong I am." He scoops me up and tosses me over his shoulder. I start beating him with my pathetic little fists.

"Hey, before I carry you upstairs in caveman-like fashion, maybe you should go get that blue bathrobe." I turn to face him with a quizzical expression. "I have a little fantasy to finish."

I start punching him again and he puts me down delicately.

"I love you too, Brandon." I look down and once again he lifts up my chin.

"Let's go upstairs, my little whack-job."

He carries me upstairs to begin a new chapter. No matter what the future holds for us, I am fairly certain I will not have to worry about meeting any more old men in worse hats.

THE END

ACKNOWLEDGEMENTS

Sending this book out into the world is the culmination of a lifelong dream. It has been a long journey from my childhood 'scribblings' to my name in print, and there are many people who have helped me on this road. I hope I am thorough in remembering all of them. My gratitude is vast and deep.

Where to start... my amazing writer friends! When I decided to pick up the pen, I reached out into the world of aspiring writers and found the most supportive group. The Featherstone Writers welcomed me from day one and made me feel that my voice was relevant and inspired me to do my best work. Thanks and love to Ruth Perkinson, Julie Harthill Clayton, Diane Rhone, Beth Brown and Margaret Duke for their kindness and encouragement. You are all wonderful writers and amazing women.

Special thanks to Elle Lothlorien and Isobel Irons of the Book Escorts. Elle's guidance and experience, coupled with Isobel's marketing genius, have brought my brand, "Rom-Com on the Edge", to fruition. Both Elle and Isobel are tireless in answering e-mail after e-mail with all sorts of neurotic and often silly questions. They are also funny chicks with razor sharp wit, and I love that.

Through Elle I met my editor, Garrett Cook. As an aspiring romantic comedy writer, I was a bit concerned that a Bizarro fiction expert may not be the ideal editor for my first novel. Boy, was I wrong! Garrett's open minded nature and varied experiences made him my perfect partner. His editing clearly brought my story to the next level and inspired me to keep going. Plus, he is hilarious and a very cool dude.

The beta readers! What a group of smart, savvy women – Betsy Flynn, Victoria Ficco, Sara Moody, Katrina Lakey, Lin Rasmussen, Jessica Hughes, Katrina Danon, and CJ Jackson. I can't thank you all enough. When I asked people to read my story and give me feedback I never expected pages of detailed notes and suggestions that would make the book even stronger and sharper. Your dedication to my work is touching and I will never forget how good it felt to receive all of your praise as well as your knocks upside the head when something didn't make sense. Well done, ladies. Well done.

Special thanks to all of my social media friends! Without all the Facebook likes and blog followers I would never be able to spread the word so fast! I truly appreciate each and every one of you. For me, my characters are as alive as all of you in my head. It is my sincere hope that they will jump off the page and come alive for you too, as you connect with their stories.

Just when I thought everything was perfect my expert proofreader, Julie Harthill Clayton, took out her red pen. Her final editing job caught all the pesky style and grammar details that I despise, and sprinkled even more goodness into my manuscript. The perfect ending to an amazing process.

There are others who inspired and helped me, including writer/motivational speaker Maryann Makekau. Like me, she started her writing career a little later in life, but she does so with tenacity and grace. I appreciate her sharing her story of success with me, and offering support and encouragement.

Of course my true inspiration is at home. The character of Dixie is based on my sweet little Daisy. Without her antics and never ending puppy love and devotion I never could have dreamed up such a sweet and funny companion for Claire. There has not been one day in the past five years that Daisy has not made me smile and thank God for the unconditional love of animals.

Humor was always important in my family and I come from a long line of funny people. My parents, Ed and Carol Maloney, and my sister, Jennifer Maloney, know what I'm talking about. They have instilled in me a love of laughter and life, and have supported me in all of my endeavors. They are also master storytellers, and our family 'performances' of things that have happened to us will continue to find their way into my writing.

Speaking of performances, no one makes me laugh

harder than my son, Nick Rissmeyer. He is most often recognized for his artistic talent, and he is the creator of the fabulous cover design for "There Are No Men." But anyone who knows Nick well knows that his talent for storytelling and observing the world around him is unbelievable. He makes me laugh so much that I routinely spit food and drink, and I have almost choked to death on more than one occasion. He has been a constant source of pride as well as support. I love you, Nick!

I have always wanted a little girl to complete the perfect family. My step-daughter to be, Jaime Scott, has been an unexpected blessing and addition to my life. She has been interested in my writing, and I have enjoyed sharing it with her. She's a smart girl with a very bright future, and I am proud to be a part of her life.

Jim Scott came into my life when I was almost ready to give up on love. Not a good thing for an aspiring romance writer. With his gentle encouragement and strong belief in me, he formed a stable base from which to launch my dream. He makes me laugh, and he has renewed my faith in love and second chances. His endless patience with my frequent anxiety over this very big project has been the rock upon which my work rests. I know that with him by my side for the rest of my life I will always have the strength and confidence to push forward. There are as many books in me as there will be years with Jim.

Here's to many, many of both.

ABOUT THE AUTHOR

My name is Carol, and I'm addicted to Romance.

I grew up in the Hudson Valley area of New York, surrounded by "city folk," like my Manhattanite mom and Bronx-native Dad, who taught me to be sweet on the outside, yet tough on the inside.

As a result, I'm often gifted sassy labels like "firecracker" or "feisty," which I choose to take as a compliment, due to my Irish/Eastern European heritage.

My romantic history is as real (and complicated) as that of the heroines in my novels. I've been divorced, relocated, plunged fearlessly into the turbulent waters of online dating—only to retreat, yelping, at the occasionally shocking climate before bravely renewing my efforts—until finally, I grabbed hold of happiness and refused to let go.

While I did eventually find my "HEA" in the form of a real life relationship, I also fell in love with writing, and it's a romance I can't get enough of.

That's why I can't help chasing after that thrill of first love, of never-ending passion, of self-discovery, of romance—even if that chase leads me to (and sometimes over) the edge.

WALK THE EDGE OF ROM-COM...*ONLINE*

Website:
http://carolmaloneyscott.com/

Goodreads:
https://www.goodreads.com/user/show/31420814-carol-maloney-scott

Facebook:
https://www.facebook.com/carolmaloneyscottauthor

Twitter:
https://twitter.com/CMScottAuthor

Pinterest:
http://www.pinterest.com/carolmaloneyris/

JOIN ME ON THE EDGE

Go to this link (http://carolmaloneyscott.com/become-a-fan/) to become an Edgy Chick (or Dude), and receive my new author newsletter,
Scoop From The Edge!

What to expect, you ask?

News on upcoming releases! Contests and giveaways exclusive to "Edgy Chicks" or "Edgy Dudes" – we are equal opportunity at Rom-Com on the Edge! Cover reveals! Updates on projects and new series in the works! Polls asking for your opinion! Blurbs! Excerpts! Members-only sneak previews and exclusive content!

I can't wait for you to join the party!

Book Club Questions – THERE ARE NO MEN

SPOILER ALERT!

Please use these questions as a guide to lead a lively and thought provoking, as well as hilarious, conversation with your groups. I wish I could be there for every meeting!

1. Claire is struggling in an unfamiliar world. Can you think of a time when you were thrust into a new life situation? How did you cope?
2. Claire tries online dating, then meetup, to try to find a man. However, she ends up with the proverbial "boy next door". In this world of online dating, singles groups and social media is it still possible to meet someone in the "real" world? Has technology made it harder or easier?
3. Discuss the symbolism of Claire's dog, Dixie? What is her purpose in the story? If you have pets, what is their deeper meaning in your life?
4. What is the funniest scene/line in the book? Why?
5. Which guy were you rooting for? Was there anyone you thought might be "the one" or play a bigger role?
6. How would you have handled Nathan? Before you answer, think about a time when you were as confused and fearful as Claire. What part does fear play in our dating lives?
7. Motherhood is a big issue for many women. Has your fertility/infertility or biological clock played a role in your relationships with men? How has that positively or negatively affected your search for love?
8. Which character/situation do you think contributed the most to Claire's growth?

9. Everyone loves a happy ending. Can you see any potential pitfalls down the road for Claire and Brandon?
10. Let's all share one dating disaster story. Has anyone had an old man's hair fall off, a chanting guy in a leather thong? Ever throw up in your date's shoe?
11. I think most would agree that Nathan is somewhere between a jerk and an evil sicko. Do you see any redeeming qualities? Any understanding for how he came to be the way he is? How might he change through his experiences?
12. Alcohol can be used to mask pain or cope with life, in a very unhealthy way. Have you ever resorted to self-medication? Do you think Claire has a drinking problem?
13. Claire has a tense relationship with her mother and seemingly nice one with her sister. How could Claire better manage these relationships? Is she missing out on the support of family? Do you lean on your female family members or your girlfriends more?
14. Is Ron really a bad guy? Have you ever judged an ex very harshly, only to realize that your behavior played a larger role in the demise of the relationship?
15. Who is your favorite character?
16. Who is your least favorite character? Besides Nathan?
17. How about the minor characters? Anyone stand out?
18. Would you like to see a sequel? If so, another Claire & Brandon story? A tale featuring another character?
19. Claire is very naïve when it comes to sex. How does that affect her choices? As you have matured, how has your own sexual experience level changed your dating choices?
20. Did you like the ending? Imagine an alternate ending that also would have satisfied you.

SNEAK PREVIEW - COMING JULY 2015!

Read Chapter One of the heart-warming and hilarious new novel by Carol Maloney Scott. Available July 2015!

Forty something, self-proclaimed cougar, Rebecca is committed only to her cats and her career. Her veteran single girl lifestyle has been peaceful and happy – that is until she started dating age-appropriate Steve, an entomology professor with a sweet smile and demeanor to match. Who knew an insect scientist could be so appealing?

The problem? Steve is a widower with baggage to spare. Memories of his late wife fill his home. Smiling photos and jars of bugs serve as constant reminders of Steve's continued attachment to his dearly departed wife, Noreen, who shared his passion for creepy crawlies!

Now that Rebecca is facing her commitment phobia by moving in with Steve, she is becoming more unhinged. Behaving more like her zany friends than her level-headed self, she burns her butt at the tanning salon, crashes on energy drinks, and even loses a hamster. Throw into the mix a few delusional relatives, a sarcastic teenager, and a fluffy dog who sheds a new dog every day, and Rebecca doesn't recognize her old self.

And if that isn't enough to push her over the edge, her smokin' hot ex returns, reminding her of a simpler time with a man who carries no more baggage than a wallet.

AFRAID OF HER SHADOW

CHAPTER ONE

"...and if someone doesn't do something about the toilet paper in the ladies' room, I'm writing to my Congressman!"

Harriet's face is sweaty. It's red as a tomato, as if she ran a marathon instead of shouting at me about the state of her private parts due to the company's poor restroom maintenance. I sigh and shift in my seat. This has been a long day, and it isn't even noon.

"Well, what are you going to do about it?" She fixes me with a glare through narrowed eyes.

I resist the urge to tell her that she *should* write to her Congressman about the toilet paper, because after all—politicians are full of crap.

"Harriet, I'll call Maintenance and see what I can do to improve the quality of your...experience." No one ever told me that being the head of human resources for a growing publishing company would be like this.

"Well then...that's better." Harriet pulls herself up to her feet, wipes her forehead (did she just rub her sweat on my guest chair?), and starts breathing heavy on her way to the door. I pray for no heart attacks on my watch today.

She shouldn't be sweating—it is *plenty* cold in here. They've already started putting the air conditioning on in the office (it's only May, but Richmond is a hot city), and working in a meat locker would be an improvement. Maybe if I threw them a t-bone or a couple of sausage links, these people would ease up some. And I certainly wouldn't mind if a young Stallone came by to practice his right cross on a side of beef.

Harriet slams the door behind her and I consider hiding under my desk until lunch time. It's eleven-thirty and I am hoping to get a little bit of work done before the next looney comes knocking. Last week someone was mad because the smokers get more breaks than the nonsmokers. Apparently, one extra ten minute break a day is a good tradeoff for cancer. Then it was the tuna in the cafeteria. They don't put enough mayonnaise in it. It was always *somewhat* like this, but in the past year Bella Donna has grown rapidly, and we have hired anything with a pulse to fill the new positions. Hence, Harriet and the toilet paper fiasco. These things all involve humans or resources but never human resources.

I wish Claire was still in charge of recruiting, but right after we launched the hot, new erotica line, she discovered a new novelist—and love. Brandon's quality work attracted more of the same, jump starting our success as a publisher of serious fiction (in addition to our new status as quality smut peddler), which meant Claire got an editor position. I am left to deal with the crazies all by myself.

Actually, that's not even true. I have my own *special* crazy person. Some rocket scientist decided to put Cecelia in charge of hiring. She used to be our CEO's "administrative assistant," but that challenging position is now filled by Amanda, who was formerly the front desk receptionist. (Though not literally. Amanda is a nice girl.) Cecelia is a nut and doesn't know the first thing about recruiting, and Amanda is too timid and naïve to keep Tim in line. With the exception of Claire's promotion, it's been a game of musical chairs that everyone loses.

On a brighter note, this time last year I met a wonderful man and we've been dating for a year. Today is our anniversary and I'm meeting him downtown at our favorite restaurant, The Crab Cracker. Steve is a widower. His wife died at thirty-seven in a cycling accident.

I shudder at the thought, but the real challenge is that I dwell on this event almost constantly. I didn't know Noreen, yet her death causes me tremendous anguish and confusion. There's the guilt over my desire to pretend she didn't exist, coupled with the jealousy and insecurity that rear their ugly twin heads when confronted with her memory.

I may be handling this poorly, but I am terrified of death. I can't even say the word out loud. I can't make sense of it, and how it fits into my life. Our relationship. Life in general. Now it's here. In my face. The longer Steve and I are together, the more I feel the creeping shadow of his loss bearing down on...

My thoughts are interrupted by a knock on my door, followed by a little blond entering with a purse three times the size of her head.

"Are you ready for lunch? I need to show you some wedding stuff." Claire is all smiles, but anxiety is emanating from her diminutive frame the same way Harriet's sweat oozed onto my furniture.

"After the morning I've had, I would love to talk about flowers and seating charts—"

"Okay, let's go then." She heaves the tremendous satchel over her shoulder and almost collapses from the weight. I look down at her feet.

"If you're going to continue to schlep around a wedding planning suitcase, you better start lifting weights or wearing stable shoes."

She glances at her stilettos and barely regains her balance. "If I just lean the right way, I'm fine."

I shake my head and search around my desk for my purse. Where did I put it? It was right here this morning...

Never missing an opportunity to return my sarcasm, Claire's eyes brighten as she spots my stockpile of office comfort items in the corner, behind my desk. "Is that your stash of bedding over there? Near the massive mound of cookies? In case you have to pull an all-nighter or get snowed in?"

"Ha-ha...very funny. The air conditioning is frigid in this place and a girl needs her treats and blankets to stay warm." I mock shiver and hug myself. Maybe my purse is under that afghan...

Claire does not comprehend sacrificing organization for preparation. I may be messy, but I am ready for all eventualities. "You'll be sorry when the zombie apocalypse comes and you have nothing but eyeliner and party shoes in your arsenal," I warn.

Claire rolls her chocolate colored eyes. I'm so hungry they look like my favorite Godiva truffles.

"Where do you want to eat lunch? Is Gina coming?" she asks.

I open my mouth to respond and then see a new face at the door. "Speak of the devil. I mean our brilliant erotica editor."

Gina maneuvers her way in, and throws Claire off balance again. She grabs the bride-to-be and steadies her. "Are we going to talk about the wedding *again*?" She shakes her long auburn hair and places her hands on her curvy hips. "Before you say anything, it's fine. I understand." She puts up her hand in defense. "I'm just sayin'...I am *not* a big fan of marriage, but you and Brandon are so adorable."

Claire rolls her eyes again—they are beginning to resemble a slot machine. Gina sighs and continues, "Besides, any distraction is better than work. Our recruiting slogan could be, "Join us on the barge to hell—when a hand basket just won't do."

I rise from my desk to halt Gina's forthcoming rant, and grab my purse, which I have located, right next to my feet. "Hey, at least we all get to take turns being the captain. Let's get out of here before someone comes in to report a stolen stapler."

If only this place were as stable as "Office Space."

We arrive at our favorite Italian restaurant, just minutes from the office. The waitress spots us and plasters a big smile on her face. I am never sure if she likes us or if she is *trying hard* to like us. I know it's very shocking, but we can get a little loud, especially Gina. Even little Bridezilla has her moments.

"So what's new in wedding planning hell...I mean heaven?" Gina begins with a smile, but Claire is not amused.

"I'm just *so* glad I hired you." Claire playfully sticks out her tongue.

"Okay, ladies let's behave in public." I am the peacekeeper in every area of work. Like Gandhi. I should be wearing flowing robes and chanting mantras.

At least work is the only place full of conflict. At home with Steve, everything is blissful. He is the easiest guy to get along with. So even keeled and level-headed. When I say "home," I am referring to *my* home. He spends a lot of time at my place. It's convenient to work for both of us, and I have cats, so I don't spend much time at his place. Actually, very little.

"...we want something casual because of the pool party reception, so I think this church will work." Claire is showing Gina her proposed wedding site on her iPad. No wonder she needs such a big purse.

"Oh yeah, those nondenominational churches are great. NOT that I am saying I would get married again, but if I *did* I would have to go that route, too. We divorced Catholic girls have no other choice." Gina purses her lips and takes a sip of her diet Coke.

Claire starts waving her hands around. "Yes, they are SO accepting! They would marry two gay Satanist dogs."

I spit my iced tea all over my bread plate, and they both turn to look at me, bursting into a fit of giggles. I catch the waitress' eye across the room and she shakes her head, as if we are a bunch of silly teenagers instead of professional middle-aged women.

Claire wipes her eyes and sighs. "So Rebecca, what's new with you? Tonight is the big one year for you and Steve, right?"

She turns to Gina and says, "Yesterday was one year for Brandon and me. We got together right after the big launch party last year, and Rebecca and Steve the day after, right?" She looks at me and adds, "He was your date and you had just met him."

Before I can respond, Gina jumps in. "By 'got together' you mean it's the anniversary of the first time you slept with these guys. Am I right?"

"Wow, yes. It's funny that's how we mark anniversaries these days. My mother would pull her hair out if she heard this conversation," Claire replies. Her mother is conservative, whereas mine is a lot older, but was a wild woman in her day. Or so I hear. Yuck.

"Yep, that party was a launching pad for more than one thing." I propose a toast, and we all raise our glasses to our sexy anniversaries.

We order lunch, and when our food finally arrives, Gina starts picking at her salad. I think I am the only woman I know who actually eats. And forget pintsized Claire—hopefully Justice or Gap Kids sells wedding dresses. My pasta is steaming, and the sauce is rosy and mouthwatering.

Gina begins, "So, Rebecca, how did you and Steve meet?"

I recount the story of meeting Steve in the singles Meetup group at a wine tasting event. It was the weekend before the launch party that celebrated signing Brandon and another new author to our lit fic imprint. Steve was cute and funny, and kept mocking the pretentious wine people by swirling the liquid in his glass extra deliberately, and peering at it closely over the rim of his glasses. He whispered obnoxious responses to the wine guy's comments in my ear, and I was hooked. Plus he's cute (did I mention that?) with his thick light brown hair and strong, but not monstrous, build. Then there's the hair on his chest...

"He sounds great. I love a man who can make me laugh. I should probably join this singles group of yours." Gina has been avoiding my attempts to drag her to events, but she would love it. She's been at Bella Donna for a year now, and only divorced for two. Recently, she's gotten friendlier with me and Claire, and has begun talking about meeting someone new.

Claire pipes in. "You should do it, Gina. I joined before Brandon and I got togeth...met. There were a lot of nice people, but some odd ones, too. Remember Chris, Rebecca? I actually *did* help her with a makeover. I can't let a woman run around town without some makeup on her face and a proper hairstyle." Claire's perfectly adorned appearance and golden locks confirm her interest in this community service.

"Yep, I see her all the time." I turn to Gina and explain, "She was dying to date Steve. I just laid low and ignored her. Luckily I was able to get to know him as a friend, while continuing to date a few 'weirdoes from the Internet,' as Claire likes to call them."

We take a break from my story to reminisce about the weirdoes. Claire has an especially impressive list, including the "old man with the hat" and the "new age leather thong guy." Even Gina can't top Claire's tales of dating woe, and she's twice divorced, with a twelve-year-old son.

We're getting ready to pay the check and leave, but

Gina's curiosity steers her back to my story. "So do you guys split your time going back and forth between houses? I had to do that when I was dating my second husband because of little Vinnie. I went to Andrew's house when Vinnie was with his father. What a pain in the ass that was, carting all my crap back and forth."

I dig in my purse for my credit card, as I sense two sets of pretty brown eyes upon me.

Claire clears her throat. "Should I say it for you?"

I roll my eyes and scowl. "Whatever."

Gina may blow up from anticipation. "Oh, this sounds juicy."

I nod at Claire and she continues. "Rebecca has only been to Steve's house the first night they slept together a year ago, and one time after that. They spend all their time at Rebecca's place. Right?"

"*Why?*" Gina leans forward as if she expects me to tell her that Steve lives in a trash can or a tent under a highway overpass. "I guess your house must be cleaner than your office." She smiles at me, but then frowns when I don't return her gesture.

"Rebecca is uncomfortable in Steve's house. Steve's a widower."

"Sorry to hear that. Is that hard for you?"

"Rebecca?" I guess Claire doesn't want to share the whole story, but neither do I.

"We really need to get back to the office." I take a deep breath. "She was killed in a cycling accident. Let's just say the house hasn't been cleaned out yet, and it isn't very healthy for me to be there."

"Cleaned out? Do you mean...?" Gina's eyes widen.

I lose my composure and blurt out, "Her stuff is all over the goddamned house! Pictures of them, smiling on the walls. In the *bedroom*. I found her *deodorant* in the bathroom. It's been *two* years." I'm almost shrieking now, and the waitress is coming over to collect her money and get us out of here before I scare the other diners.

Gina clicks her tongue and sighs. "Oh, Sweetie. I don't know if this guy is ready for a relationship. In my experience—"

The waitress interrupts by swiftly grabbing our credit cards and the check from the table.

I watch her walk away, and lean back in the booth. "Gina, I know you mean well, but Steve is a wonderful man and I adore him. He treats me well and he *is* willing to come to my place. I *know* I'm avoiding the issue, but for now this is the perfect set-up. I'm in no rush to settle down."

Claire starts packing up her iPad and wedding magazines, raising an eyebrow at Gina. "Let's get back to the office. Gina, I need to show you a new manuscript I received yesterday. It looks promising and I want your opinion."

Gina relents and lets the conversation shift away from me and my seemingly dysfunctional situation.

On the short ride back to the office, I stare out the window of Gina's Mini-Cooper and daydream. Steve will mess up my hair tonight, and tell me I look beautiful. I'll tell him about Harriet, the crazy toilet paper lady. He'll laugh and his eyes will sparkle with the little crinkles at the edges. As long as we stay away from that house, he is who I need him to be.

Manufactured by Amazon.ca
Bolton, ON